Saskia
A Story of Survival

Carly McIntyre was born in London in 1946. She travelled widely in her childhood while her father was in the British army, living for several years in Egypt, the Sudan and Paris. She was educated at the SHAPE School, Paris and St Mary's, Calne. After ten years working in the film industry she became a publishing editor specializing in popular fiction. As a journalist, writing under her real name, Caroline Upcher, she has contributed to numerous publications including *GO*, the *Oldie*, the *Mail on Sunday* and the *Daily Telegraph*. *Saskia* is her second novel. Her first, *Next of Kin*, was published in 1989.

By the same author

Next of Kin

SASKIA
A Story of Survival

Carly McIntyre

ARROW

First published by Arrow in 1994

1 3 5 7 9 10 8 6 4 2

Carly McIntyre 1993

First published in the United Kingdom in 1993
by Century
Random House, 20 Vauxhall Bridge Road, London SW1V 2SA

Random House Australia (Pty) Limited
20 Alfred Street, Milsons Point, Sydney,
New South Wales, 2061, Australia

Random House New Zealand Limited
18 Poland Road, Glenfield
Auckland 10, New Zealand

Random House South Africa (Pty) Limited
PO Box 337, Bergvlei, South Africa

Random House UK Limited Reg. No. 954009

ISBN 0 09 996650 6

Typeset by Deltatype Ltd, Ellesmere Port, South Wirral
Printed and bound in Great Britain by
Cox & Wyman Ltd, Reading, Berkshire

My thanks go to the following:

LillianWickens
David Tatton
Stephen Bayley
Terence Conran
Emily Nott
Ziva Kwitney
Kari Allen and all those who helped her including
Stephen Bartley, George Hulme and John Norton

Saskia's story is one of survival. I too left home when I was sixteen in order to survive – but in a very different way. My mother relinquished me reluctantly into the world because she did not have a strong enough voice to stop me going.

I dedicate this book to her, to Alexandra Shulman, whose looks first inspired the character of Saskia, and to Matthias Mahrenholtz, wherever he is.

When we were still quite young, my sister and I used to play a game created by our mother called the Hunted and the Dispossessed. One of us would be the Hunted, the other the Dispossessed. We didn't really understand what it was all about, but we were aware that our mother was trying desperately to teach us something about values, about our futures.

Once a month we would each amass our favourite toys in a bundle and deposit them in the kitchen. Then we each drew a piece of paper out of a hat to decide who would be the Dispossessed and who the Hunted. The Dispossessed had to leave her toys in their bundle and not go near them for a week. She would be, quite literally, dispossessed of the things she loved. She who became the Hunted, on the other hand, was allowed to play with both bundles but at the same time she had to be prepared to carry out onerous tasks for our mother – tidying up our bedrooms, washing the dishes, polishing the piano.

I must have been somewhat in awe of my mother for I never complained about the game nor did I ever question its rationale. Sometimes she would try to explain: it was so that we would realize that we should expect nothing in our lives to be easy; that while one of us might appear to have the advantage over the other, this would not necessarily be so.

We were children, sibling rivals but innocent all the same. But our mother was someone who worried constantly about our destiny. I know she favoured me because I had a serious introverted side with which she could identify, yet she always deferred to my sister's more frivolous, whimsical nature and this irked me. I noticed that I drew the piece of paper with *Dispossessed* written on it more often than my sister and I began to wonder if this was as accidental as it was made to appear. I pictured my sister, allegedly the Hunted, playing with my toys and being tracked down by our mother throughout the week, not to be asked to peel the potatoes or lay the table but to share secret treats in the sanctity of the kitchen.

I harboured this resentment long after we had ceased to play the stupid game. Yet as I look back I realize that I became not only the Dispossessed but also the Hunted and whatever it was my mother had been trying to teach us, there was no way she could have prepared me for the horror that was to come.

But then neither did she prepare us for the joy we would encounter in our lives, which in my case arrived in the form of Barney Lambert . . .

One

Most people liked Barney Lambert. It probably had something to do with the fact that he liked himself. Ever since he could remember he had enjoyed his own company as well as other people's.

He was born in May 1925 to Northern working class parents and although his childhood coincided with the Depression years of the thirties, he never felt that he suffered in any way. 'Not the suffering type,' he would say of himself when calamity struck him later in his life. And he was right.

Joe and Vera Lambert decided their only child was born optimistic. Not that they themselves were pessimists. They were content with their lot and rarely dreamed of a better life. Joe ran a corner shop handed down to him by his father and he ran it with pride. The only building to break the monotony of rows and rows of rain-soaked terraced houses, it was the neighbourhood general store of a kind that would one day begin to die out with the advent of the supermarket and the new shopping centres. Electricity was not widespread but Joe's shop had it and the light shone out like a beacon on the corner of the street.

Joe sold everything, or at least everything everybody in the neighbouring streets required. There were never any new arrivals asking for unfamiliar wares. If you needed something, no need to go into town, Joe on the corner would have it. Everything was jumbled up together: the bottles of HP Sauce and the baked beans beside the packets of Lux and Robin starch, bottles of pop – Vimto and lemonade – alongside Woodbines and Colman's mustard. Horlicks and Bovril were stacked on top of blocks of Basildon Bond – for which there was little demand – and sweets were sold in paper cones. The cheese stood in a large triangular lump beside the till and if people found it unhygienic that Joe would garotte a quarter of Cheddar with the wire slicer without first wiping his hands clean of dirty change, they never mentioned it.

The sound of the bell that pinged each time a customer entered the shop echoed through the family home above. When Joe started selling the *Northern Echo* (and no one said anything about newsprint on the cheese either) he had to open up an hour earlier in the morning, and Barney didn't need Vera or an alarm clock to wake him for school as the bell pinged continuously below his bedroom.

Apart from the fact that it had electricity, the Lambert house was like any other on the street once you went through the curtain that divided it from the shop. Two up, two down – except one of those rooms on the ground floor, which would have been the parlour, was taken up with the shop, which left only the kitchen and the pantry downstairs. Outside in the yard was the coalhouse and the 'outside lav' as the privy was called, implying there was an inside one as well, which was definitely a figment of someone's imagination. The shabby green lino on the floor of the shop stretched through to the simple kitchen where Joe's hard Windsor chair by the hearth reigned supreme.

They lived in Liverpool, not right in the heart of the city but close enough to the Mersey that Barney could hear the booming sound of the huge liners as they navigated their way into the docks. Many of the fathers of the families living on the neighbouring streets worked at the docks and Barney would watch them coming home, often black with the oil and grease from the shipyards.

From an early age Barney was aware that they were what was called 'working class' and proud of it, but a more accurate description would have been that they were

4

content with near poverty. 'Working class' was synonymous in people's minds with manual as opposed to mental labour, but as Barney grew up, he began to question this assumption and his parents' futile pride.

Every evening on the dot of six Joe closed the shop and came through for his tea. He ate the same thing virtually every day: cold meat and salad. Before the meal he always mixed his mustard, pouring a little of the Colman's powder into a bowl, adding drops of water till it reached the right consistency when he would put it down in front of Barney and say, 'There, lad. There's mustard for you.' He was also partial to a quart bottle of ale with his meal. Occasionally Vera would make a meat pudding but it was never really appreciated and back would come the cold ham or pork pie – from the shop, of course – and the lettuce, tomato, cucumber and salad cream. On Sundays they always had a roast – which Joe had again cold on Mondays – and on Saturday nights they went down the road to the fish and chip shop, bringing home their supper wrapped in newspaper.

Spontaneity was out of the question. An impromptu suggestion that they might go to the pictures, take a walk along the canal, or eat in a restaurant would be met with sheer horror on the faces of Joe and Vera. Going to the pictures – and Vera liked them, make no mistake – was a birthday or an anniversary celebration, carefully planned way in advance. And as for restaurants, they weren't 'for the likes of us'.

Joe Lambert was not a particularly political man. Massive unemployment surrounded him but he'd always had his shop, and although they made sure never to say so in front of Vera, some of the neighbours felt he turned a bit too much of a blind eye to what was going on around him. Oh, he listened to the anguish as he stood safe behind his counter every day, and he was sympathetic, but you'd never see Joe Lambert in a dole queue and somehow that set him apart from the rest of the community.

Individualism, as Barney was to realize, was akin to

degeneracy in Joe and Vera's eyes. Joe was no entrepreneur. The idea that he might one day own a string of corner shops was totally alien to him. Change was a dirty word to him yet he laughed like a drain when a local wag told him, in Barney's hearing, 'If things don't change, they'll stay as they are.'

Right from the start Barney knew he was different. His parents' cocoon was stifling. He felt anger at it rising up time and time again until he was ready to burst but he was not combative by nature. His teacher at school made a joke of it: 'I know one lad who's not looking for a barney in the playground.' But no matter how different he might feel there was one thing Barney did have in common with his parents and that was their innate good nature. Joe and Vera were, quite simply, genuinely nice people. They were cheerful, they laughed a good deal of the time and they enjoyed themselves, perhaps not by doing anything Barney might find remotely entertaining but in their routine way they had their own version of a good time. They were as pleasant to each other as they were to the neighbours. In short, they had impeccable manners, and these they passed on to Barney. It was perhaps their most important legacy to their only child for manners were manners whatever your station in life and the difference between good manners and bad would always stand out.

'How you treat others, Barney lad, will show them how to treat you,' Joe told his son, 'Well, sometimes anyroad,' he added sadly.

Barney wanted to break loose but he was not a cruel rebel out to hurt Joe and Vera just for the sake of it. Indeed, it was the puzzled expression on his parents' faces, which greeted so much of what he tried patiently to suggest to them, that hurt him rather than the other way round. He loved his parents, but the time was fast approaching when he was going to have to find a world beyond their confines.

The last thing he expected to change his life was the arrival in the family of a dog.

★

Although he was regarded by his parents as having strange, individual tendencies Barney was popular at school. His teacher constantly reassured Joe and Vera that they had a remarkable boy.

'Of course, he'll be a killer when he's older,' she whispered to Vera, 'a real ladykiller with those looks, fancy!'

Vera looked at her twelve-year-old son in amazement. She'd never considered her son's physical attraction before. It was enough for her that Barney's clothes were clean and she saw to it that he had at least one session a week in the tin bath in the kitchen. But she realized that the teacher was right. Barney had her own fair hair but while hers was fine and straggly, forever escaping from the bun at the nape of her neck, Barney's was thick and abundant, crowning his head like a golden thatch. He had Joe's brown eyes set wide apart in his square face. She couldn't place his mouth which had a tendency to break into a grin. The boy's lips were much fuller than either hers or Joe's.

'Such a sensuous mouth!' murmured the teacher as if she'd been reading Vera's mind.

Vera was shocked. 'You're talking about our Barney,' she said rather tartly.

'He's going to bring you to the school fête then Saturday, is he?' the teacher asked.

'Well, I don't know about that.' School fêtes were not part of Joe and Vera's routine. 'Our Barney works in the shop Saturdays. He wouldn't want to miss that, would he?'

'Wouldn't he?'

Barney went to the school fête and came home with a puppy wriggling in his arms. There had been a competition to guess its name. Barney, who was in the middle of reading *Great Expectations*, had suggested Estella. The puppy's name was in fact Stella, but Estella was deemed to be close enough for Barney to win the competition.

Stella's arrival at the Lamberts caused the first hint of a rift between Joe and Vera.

'We're not having a dog in the shop, Barney lad. It's unhygienic. The customers'll complain. You'd best take it back.'

'Unhygienic!' Vera was bright red in the face. 'I'll tell you what's unhygienic, Joe Lambert, and I blame myself for never having told you before. It's your cheese standing right next to your till, that's what I call unhygienic. How many customers have complained about the taste of silver in their cheese butties? Well, none, but they've every right, I'm telling you. I've got to speak up now. Anyroad, the pup'll not go in the shop. I'll keep her out the back with me when the lad's at school.

Vera had taken one look at the pitiful little black creature in Barney's arms and known that she hadn't the heart to turn her away. She could see that she was barely weaned, her eyes only just open and she was still making sucking gestures with her tiny pink tongue, searching for the mother's teat. Unlike Joe, Vera had not always lived in the city. By birth she was a Lancashire country lass and she knew enough to go into Joe's shop and root around till she found a baby's bottle.

'Watch me, now, Barney. Stella's too small to eat proper food yet. We'll have to feed her with this bottle just like we did with you when you were a baby. You know what she is, do you? What breed, like?'

Barney shook his head, intrigued that his mother was suddenly so knowledgeable.

'She's a baby Labrador by the looks of things. They had them on the estate where my father worked when I was a lass. Used them as gun dogs when they went out shooting.'

'Well, we don't want gun dogs here. Sounds much too violent for the lad, Vera. Whatever are you doing, filling his head with all this nonsense?'

'It's you that's talking nonsense, Joe Lambert. Labradors are soft, kind dogs. Their mouths are so gentle they can pick up a bird without hurting it if they have to. With Stella you want to take that advice your father's always giving you about people, Barney. How you treat

8

Stella will show her how to treat you. The only thing that does worry me is that she's going to need a lot of exercise. She's a country dog, she's born to live in wide open spaces . . .'

'There you are then,' said Joe triumphantly. 'You'll have to take her back.'

'Well, if Stella goes, Joe, I go with her. Now what do you say to that?' And Vera winked at her son.

Stella never went near the shop. As she began to lope around the kitchen, unsteady on her young legs, she was much more interested in the back yard.

'Good job she's black anyway,' said Barney when he went to rescue her from her first exploration of the coalhouse.

He lived for Stella. He made her a bed out of newspapers and an old blanket in front of the hearth but she soon learned to crawl up the stairs to his room, lifting both front paws at once up to the next step and bringing her hind legs up behind. She scrabbled at Barney's door till he let her in and made her a nest in his eiderdown. Then when the bell pinged in the morning with the arrival of the first customer she awoke and barked fiercely before padding up the bed to snuffle her way onto Barney's pillow and lick him on the nose.

As Vera had predicted, she grew fast and had boundless energy. She ran around the yard most of the day, barking at any sound coming from the alley at the back.

'Barney lad, you must never ever leave the door to the alley unlocked,' said Vera. 'She's waiting for someone to open that gate and then she'll be out of there like a shot. Then where would we be?'

'Rid of her,' said Joe hopefully.

'Oh, Joe, give over.'

Barney made her a makeshift lead out of a piece of rope and took her for walks, proudly parading her along the street so the neighbours could see.

'Dead soft,' muttered Barney's schoolfriend Eammon

every time he saw them, but his father, Sean, who worked on the dock, made Stella a leather collar with a little disc attached on which he had engraved the words *Joe's Shop, Liverpool*.

'I'll not put her name on it 'cause then if someone wants to nab her they'll know what to call her. Teach her only to answer to her name and then she'll only come running to folks who know.'

When Barney got back from school each afternoon Stella went mad, rushing round and round the kitchen in frantic excitement, jumping on and off Joe's Windsor chair, trying to lick Barney's face. 'I've only got to say your name and her ears prick up,' Vera told her son as Stella lay by his feet, panting heavily, worn out, but still able to wag her tail, making it thump on the floor. Soon she came to understand that Barney always came home through the gate leading to the alley and she would lie waiting for him. He locked it behind him each time until one morning he was late, hurrying, flustered. He rushed out, slamming the gate and running for the bus.

No one would ever know who it was who opened the gate at some point during the day but Stella was out like a flash, and when Barney came home from school that afternoon there was no thunderous welcome for him.

They told the neighbours. They told the police. But after a week there was still no trace. And it nearly broke Vera's heart to know that while they were searching for Stella she was undoubtedly wandering further and further away, somewhere in the city, looking for her master on whose face Vera saw for the first time a look of sheer desperation.

Two

'Saskia, sit still. How will we ever get a good picture of you if you keep moving? You want to look nice for Mrs Atwell in London, don't you?'

Saskia scowled at her father. He knew perfectly well she didn't want to have anything to do with Mrs Atwell, whoever she was. She wanted to stay right here at home with her family.

She was born Saskia Kessler in Berlin on 24 June 1922, only a few hours after the Jewish Foreign Minister, Walter Rathenau, was assassinated. Anti-semitic nationalists threw a hand grenade into his limousine as he was riding down the Königsallee.

Her father, Hermann Kessler, who like Hitler had won an Iron Cross in the last war (if one believed Hitler's self-propaganda), owned a shop that sold musical instruments. Her mother, Klara, played the violin. They were prosperous and lived in an apartment in the Zehlendorf, one of the very first garden suburbs in Berlin on the edge of the Grunewald. Hermann and Klara doted on her and she rewarded them by growing into a delightful little girl, secure in her parents' love.

Four years later Christiane was born. She grew fast; before long she was taller than the elfin Saskia. Her Jewish blood was mysteriously invisible. Where Saskia was raven haired and sallow skinned, Christiane was a German through and through with golden hair and fair skin. She exuded good health while Saskia appeared fragile.

11

Hermann and Klara could hardly believe Christiane was theirs. She was perfect. Saskia was just *there*.

'*Die kleine Kessler, sie ist aber schön.*' Everybody thought the little Kessler girl was beautiful. No one noticed the other one any more. Christiane was the one who was taken to the top of the Funkturm to see the view of Berlin while Saskia stayed behind, ensconced in her room drawing her 'stupid pictures', as Christiane called them. Christiane was taught to ride in the Tiergarten but Saskia was frightened of horses and so once again she was left behind.

In Saskia's eyes it was Christiane who was responsible for her parents' decision to send them away. Every Saturday night Hermann and Klara took their daughters out to eat dinner in their favourite restaurant. Recently a sign had been placed on the door saying *No Entry For Jews* but Hermann ignored it.

Then, one Saturday when they were there, an SS officer in black uniform entered the restaurant and marched up to a table where a family of Jews were sitting. Three words – 'Your papers, please' – and out came the papers stamped with a big red J for *Juden* – Jews. The Jewish family was escorted out of the restaurant.

Next the SS man approached the Kesslers. Hermann's papers had the same red J and he knew it was only a matter of time before he had to show them. But twelve-year-old Christiane was at her most captivating, smiling at the SS officer and his cohorts and looking so undeniably non-Jewish that they passed on. Christiane had saved them with her Aryan looks. But as he left the restaurant the SS officer looked back at Christiane.

'Next time don't bring your little Jewish friend in here,' he said but it was the words he didn't say that hung heavily in the air: *Get rid of your little Jewish friend altogether*.

'But I'm her sister,' Saskia wanted to cry out after him, 'and she's Jewish too.'

When he learned that the other family who had been escorted out of the restaurant had been arrested, Hermann knew the time for action had arrived. He contacted the

12

Jewish *Hilfsverein* who gave him the name of a Mrs Maud Atwell in London to whom Hermann sent Saskia's photograph and particulars, taking care to point out that his daughter already spoke near-perfect English. When Mrs Atwell replied saying she would be delighted to be Saskia's guarantor and was looking forward to meeting her 'little traveller', Hermann frantically set about obtaining a passport. Now, with her *Reisepass* stamped with the ubiquitous red J, Saskia was all ready to go.

'Sit still, Maud.'

'Oh, Selwyn, *please*.'

'No, seriously, you must sit absolutely still till I've finished my sketch.'

'Well, do you imagine you might be finished by noon? I rather thought we might go out for a spot of lunch.'

'We might indeed. If you're very good and sit quite still I might even take you to the Café Royal – if I've finished that is.'

'And if you haven't?'

'I'll take you there for dinner.'

Maud groaned. For the first time in her life she was beginning to wish she had a well-covered rear end. She was stick thin, always had been, although as a girl her lanky frame had been a blessing when it came to wearing twenties fashions. But now sitting for hours on end in the same position, she acknowledged a little more cushioning would be a distinct advantage. Yet she couldn't let Selwyn down. Such a brilliant designer, everyone said so. She didn't quite see what his endless sketches of her had to do with design, but what did she know about it? At least she could dream while she sat for him, think about poor dear Freddy, yearn for a cigarette.

At thirty-two Maud Atwell was a widow. Poor dear Freddy had fallen off his polo pony, caught his foot in the stirrup and been dragged the length of the field. Maud had watched the whole thing with her hands held frozen in midair, in front of her face as, somewhere along the way, Freddy's head had been struck a glancing blow by one of the other ponies' hooves. And that was the end. He never regained consciousness and died two days later.

That had been five years ago. Now Maud was beginning to entertain foolish thoughts of marrying again .

Selwyn Reilly had one aim in life and that was to design a perfect chair. Not *the* perfect chair but one which he would deem to be perfect, both structurally and aesthetically, despite what anyone else thought.

He was born at the beginning of the twentieth century. Within a few years the search for a totally new style of architecture and design would take a radical turn. Selwyn was a Northerner, raised in the shadow of his father's Lancashire cotton mill, but he was educated at a public school in the south of England and obtained an English degree at Cambridge before moving on to study drawing at the Royal College of Art where he found the emphasis to be on fine art and there was no one to nurture his growing interest in design. His father had been unable to understand this passion of Selwyn's. The old boy had misconstrued it as a desire to become an artist and had boasted to his friends about 'my son, the painter'. At least Selwyn hadn't turned out to be an Oscar Wilde, as old Ben Reilly was apt to call homosexuals: 'judging by the number of young girls he's squiring round London.'

Selwyn, whose first love was furniture design, might have embraced the Arts and Crafts Movement with open arms and rushed to join their activities in the Cotswolds, safely removed from the industrialization they condemned. But he didn't. He thought it was all a load of bunkum. He had grown up with the cotton industry and it was part of him. It was all very well to produce beautiful handmade craftsmanship but the fact that it was economically impossible for the craftsman to make a living from what he had made, and all too easy for similar products to be mass-produced by machine, which paid a higher wage – or could be made to do so – made Selwyn think that perhaps man

14

might be made happier by a slightly more progressive outlook.

He also found the sheer wholesomeness of the movement deeply suspect. At Laurel Bank, his father's mill, he had known real working men, not these affected middle-class craftsmen with their bogus high-minded values.

Once he had left the Royal College, Selwyn travelled round Europe and became aware, particularly in Germany, of Modernism – an uncluttered style geared more towards industrial production. Inspired by the simple elegant designs, Selwyn knew he'd found his vocation. Poor Maud Atwell, introduced to him at the Chelsea Arts Ball by a well-meaning matchmaker, never realized that he took one look at her angular frame and saw it as the inspiration for his new chair.

'Selwyn, darling, do look, here's her photograph. Isn't she a poppet? Such gorgeous dark eyes.'

Selwyn glanced at the photograph, agreed that the girl's face was indeed an arresting one and proceeded to guide Maud gently back to the stool on which he liked her to sit while she posed for him. He almost flinched as he found his fingers able to encircle the upper part of her arm with such ease. He hadn't realized she was losing weight so rapidly.

He knew she was expecting some kind of commitment from him before she died but he did not think he could go as far as marrying her. Her doctor had told her she had a couple of years left at the most, probably much less. Meanwhile the cancer was eating away at her throat.

Selwyn was the only person in Maud's life who knew about her illness. She felt people were only just beginning to treat her like a normal person instead of poor dear Freddy's grieving widow. To have to cope with the fact that she herself was now dying was more than she felt she could ask of her friends.

Somehow with Selwyn it was different, probably because deep down she knew he was unable to commit himself to anyone, would only ever be someone passing through her life. She had been able to confide in him and now it had become something of a game they played. One day they would marry. One day she would die. Maybe both events would take place soon. Maybe neither.

Meanwhile Maud had embarked on some frenetic journey of her own. She was unable to have children – she had discovered this while Freddy had still been alive – but recently she had unearthed within herself a social conscience: she had become interested in the World Movement for the Care of Refugee Children from Germany, the British people's response to *Kristallnacht*.

Maud was not Jewish but for some time now she had been more aware than most people in England of Herr Hitler's campaign to make the Third Reich *Judenfrei* and it appalled her. When, on 8 November 1938, a Polish Jew, Herschel Grynszpan, walked into the German Embassy in Paris, demanded to see a senior official and was sent to Ernst von Roth, the third secretary, whom he proceeded to shoot five times, it was used as an excuse for a monstrous pogrom against the Jews in Germany two days later which became known as *Kristallnacht*.

Maud discussed it endlessly with Selwyn who tried hard not to become involved. Maud knew what she was doing and it would be totally unfair of him to encourage any notion of the two of them sponsoring a refugee together. She was on her own in this one – as indeed she was in every other area of what remained of her life. But she was allowing him to use her as the model for his chair and in return he was prepared to give her companionship and support. It even crossed his mind that once the child arrived she might not have so much need of him.

By the time Maud contacted her own local Committee for the Care of Refugee Children from Germany it was almost too late. The Children's Movement could not take any more refugees but, because she specified that she wanted a Jewish child, they contacted on her behalf the Jewish *Hilfsverein* in Berlin and in due course Maud found herself in correspondence with Hermann Kessler. Secretly she had hoped for a younger child to sponsor but she knew she had to be content with Saskia Kessler. It would never do for the child to feel she was not wanted.

Maud began to plan for Saskia's arrival. If only she did not always feel so tired . . .

'What's the name of this woman you're going to in London, Saskia?'

'Mrs Atwell. I told you, Christl. Go to sleep. We'll need a good night's rest. We've both got long journeys tomorrow.'

'Yours is longer than mine. You're going all the way to London.'

'Yes, but you're going to be with Tante Luise. You'll be closer to the family.'

'Of course I will, Saskia. Mutti and Vati would never let me be far away from them.'

She's only twelve years old, thought Saskia, her face buried in her pillow, *yet already she makes me feel inferior. I ought to be crowing with excitement about going to London. I ought to be making her jealous but oh, no, Christiane always has to have the last word. Is she right? Doesn't it matter to Mutti that I am going so far away?*

'Saskia, are you still awake?'

'You know I am. What do you want?'

'Saskia, may I take your pink blouse? May I borrow it while we're away?'

'But Onkel Wolfie gave it to me, it's special.'

'I know but it looks so much better on me with my fair hair, you know it does. You won't need it in London.'

'How do you know? Anyway you're too young for it.'

'No, I'm not! Everyone always says I look as old as you do. Everyone thinks you look much younger than sixteen and I look much older than twelve. Oh, see if I care. I expect Tante Luise will buy me lovely clothes. Will your Frau whats-her-name buy you lovely clothes in London, Saskia? Do you think she will?'

17

I don't know, whispered Saskia into her pillow, *I don't know anything about her.*

Klara Kessler lay awake every night wracked with worry about Saskia while her husband, Hermann, fell asleep beside her. She understood why Hermann was sending the children away. She had come to accept it almost. But secretly she wished it was just Christiane who was going, that she could keep Saskia with her. She had a favourite. Now that her daughter was being taken away from her, Klara admitted it for the first time. Hermann didn't know it but she knew instinctively he preferred Christiane. She was sunny, outgoing, without a care in the world, too young to realize the danger they were in. The only thing she seemed to have grasped was that her role in life was to charm people, whoever they were, Nazis included. Klara knew it was wrong to hold against Christiane the fact that she never suffered, but she couldn't help it. Saskia had suffered dreadfully during her awkward teen years. She was so sensitive. She had always been an exceedingly vulnerable child, young for her age, whereas Christiane was precocious beyond belief. Saskia spent most of her time locked in her room, lost in a world of her own, conjuring it up in a series of drawings of strange, exaggerated creatures.

Saskia's other obsession was clothes and to this end Klara had enlisted the help of her brother, Wolf, who was a tailor. Onkel Wolfie taught his niece about cut and cloth and reported back to Klara that Saskia had talent. She should be sent to art school to study dress design. Only Wolfie had been taken away by the Nazis for questioning. Klara knew there was something Hermann was not telling her about Wolfie, that it was more than just questioning, that he might not be coming back . . .

His wife, Luise, Klara's neurotic sister-in-law, was not Jewish. Wolfie had caused quite a scandal in the family by marrying out. And now Luise had announced she was going

18

to Switzerland, and at Hermann's request she was to take Christiane with her.

'But why only Christiane? Why can't she take Saskia too? Hermann, answer me. Why does Saskia have to go all the way to England? Why can't she just go across the border to Switzerland too?'

'Klara, I've told you. Luise can only manage one child. She's not used to children, you know that. Christiane is too young to be the one to go to London on her own. It has to be Saskia. We're lucky enough as it is to have found this Mrs Atwell at such a late stage.'

'But when we leave – if we leave – where will *we* go? To Switzerland or to London?'

'Don't fret about that now. Just pray that all this will blow over and we'll have the children back; we won't be going anywhere.'

But Klara did fret. Saskia was like her, overimaginative, easily frightened. Hermann had spoken to her about going to London as if it were some big adventure but Klara had watched Saskia's dark eyes grow larger and larger and she knew that her elder daughter was apprehensive. Yet Klara was also aware that she was merely procrastinating the moment when she must face up to the hideous truth: once Saskia left there was a possibility that Klara might never see her again.

Saskia and Christiane were due to leave the same day, Saskia in the morning, Christiane in the evening.

Then, at the last moment, Tante Luise changed her mind. She arrived at the Zehlendorf apartment at seven in the morning and proceeded to throw one of her hysterical fits just as Saskia was sitting down to her farewell breakfast.

'I can't go to Switzerland. I can't leave Berlin. What if my Wolfie comes back? How will he find me? I'm not going, Hermann, I'm not!'

Klara kept silent, studying her husband closely. Would he voice his fears in front of the girls – in front of her – that

Wolfie had been taken to one of the camps they had been hearing about?

'So, Luise, you'll go later on. You'll wait for Wolfie to come back and then you'll go for a nice holiday and take Christiane with you. Sit down, have a cup of coffee. Relax!'

'*Unsinn!*' muttered Klara. Nonsense! She was furious with Hermann for maintaining this charade. Didn't he realize what it was doing to her? Her brother was gone and now she was about to lose her daughter.

'See,' said Christiane slyly as they were about to leave for the *Hauptbahnhof*, 'I knew Mutti and Vati wouldn't let me go away in the end.'

Klara saw the tears begin to well up in Saskia's eyes and ushered her quickly out of the room.

'Mutti?'

'*Liebes Kind, was ist's?*'

'When we go to the station . . . could . . . could Christiane stay behind? You always take her everywhere and I always stay behind in my room. This time couldn't she . . .?'

'But you've never said . . . Do you mean to tell me you always wanted to come with us? We thought you liked being on your own. We didn't think you wanted to come. Oh, how could I have been so stupid . . .?'

'Klara, come on. We'll miss the train. Saskia, are you ready? Got your passport? Come on, hurry, Christiane's already in the car.'

'Hermann, Christl's staying behind. I don't want her coming to the station. We must say goodbye to Saskia on our own.'

'Oh, don't be so stupid. We must all go. The whole family.'

'Hermann, I mean it. Christiane stays behind or I won't let Saskia out of this house until the train's left.'

Hermann stared at his wife. She hardly ever argued with him but he knew when she did he had to give way.

Saskia was so happy to be the centre of attention for once that she embraced Christiane fondly.

'Goodbye, little sister. Take care of Mutti for me.'

And Klara watched in agony as Christiane merely shrugged and said: 'Fine, fine, whatever you say – and by the way I took your pink blouse out of your suitcase. You don't mind really, do you?' and ran back into the house waving behind her as if Saskia would just be gone for the night.

At the station Saskia was ushered into an enormous waiting room packed with children and their parents. The noise was horrendous, everyone was weeping or shouting. Saskia looked around her and suddenly realized she was not alone in her sadness. Here were hundreds of people, nearly all of them Jewish, sharing it with her. She was about to become one of them – a refugee.

'Mrs Atwell will meet you at Liverpool Street Station in London,' said Klara, raising her voice.

'How will I know her?'

'She will know you. She has your photograph, remember. And so do we.'

The last image Saskia had of her parents was of Hermann holding up a print of the photograph he had taken of her, waving it at her, while with his other hand he stroked her mother's back. Klara had broken down at the last moment and was sobbing uncontrollably into her husband's shoulder.

The train windows were hermetically sealed and could not be opened. Saskia hunched herself as far back as she could into her corner and pressed her face to the glass. Despite the swaying mass of waving hands she kept her eyes resolutely on the shrinking figures of Hermann and Klara. Long after they had disappeared altogether she continued to peer into the distance.

When they arrived at the German–Dutch border the Nazis boarded the train for a last inspection. They seemed to swarm all over the place, one Nazi per compartment. Saskia had with her one small suitcase, which she was made

21

to take down from the overhead rack and open. The Nazi threw out clothes and the small knick-knacks she had packed for sentimental reasons. Then he asked her if she had any money or food. She didn't answer. He grabbed her by the shoulder and shook her till he could hear the change jangling in her pockets. He made her empty them and took the money at which point Saskia lost control. Reaching under her coat, she withdrew the *Wurst* sandwich Klara had made for her journey and threw it at him.

'You want my food? Then take it. I don't need it any more. I'm leaving. I'm going to England where you can't touch me. Go on, take it.'

All around her the other children froze. What would the Nazi do now? Saskia stood, shaking, with her eyes closed, waiting for the blow she was sure would come. Her eyes were still closed when she heard the whistle and felt the train move out of the station. She had not even realized he had gone.

It wasn't until she turned to reassemble her suitcase that she knew how lucky she had been. If the Nazi had removed just one more item of clothing he would have seen her cartoons, about twenty of them, wickedly depicting Nazi soldiers. Each one was more deformed than the last: humped backs, clawed hands, dripping noses, squinting eyes. She held them up to show the other children in her compartment and immediately the tension was gone. Grouped together they made faces at the Nazis on the platform from behind the safety of their sealed windows as the train drew away. They were leaving the Fatherland, they were leaving their homes, but they were also, as Saskia fully understood for the first time, leaving behind the Nazi regime.

Entering Holland was like coming out of a dark tunnel. Waiting for them on the platform were big trolleys filled with jugs of steaming hot chocolate and sandwiches, and at each subsequent station the Dutch people crowded forward to wave at them and cheer. Saskia saw that they too had food and thinking quickly she rushed along the carriage every time the train stopped to open the doors as they could not open the windows. Food was literally thrown in.

The train went as far as the Hook of Holland and from there Saskia made the journey by boat across the North Sea to Harwich. She arrived early in the morning when a customs officer asked her if she had any valuable jewellery or money. She laughed at the absurd notion that anybody might think she had any valuable jewellery but then she remembered that the Nazi had taken all her money. Her ticket only went as far as Harwich. How was she going to get to London?

In the end it was quite simple. There was nothing else for her to do but tell the truth.

'Well, we'll just have to let you travel for free, won't we, ducky?' said the porter to whom she poured out her tale of woe. He had a strange accent and Saskia couldn't quite follow his words but she understood 'free' and smiled. "'Ere, Charlie, bleedin' Nazis took 'er money. Put 'er on the train for Liverpool Street –and do us all a favour, keep quiet about it, eh?'

Saskia was fascinated by English trains. German trains had wooden seats but these seats were upholstered. As the train trundled through the Essex countryside towards London she began to grow excited and not a little apprehensive. When they reached Liverpool Street they were shown into a vast hall with high electric lights and told to wait. Saskia watched as almost immediately children began to be claimed by relatives or sponsors. Slowly but surely the hall began to empty until there was only a single line of children left.

The unclaimed. Saskia was the eldest and she knew it was up to her to comfort and reassure the younger children. She herself was achingly tired and suddenly quite terrified. Some of her fellow travellers had told her how the English only wanted girls her age as servants. The smaller children were beginning to cry for their mothers.

'*Mutti, Mutti, wo bist du?*' echoed plaintively round the hall.

By midnight Saskia was the only one left. She began to panic. Were they going to leave her here all night? She had Mrs Atwell's address but she did not know how far away it was. Could she walk it? She began to gather together her belongings but stopped when a station attendant came running across the hall towards her.

'Your name Kessler?'

'Yes. Saskia Kessler.'

'Someone telephoned. Said to hang on a bit, they'll be here for you soon.'

'Mrs Atwell?'

'Sounded like a bloke to me. Didn't give his name.'

It was a bloke. A tall one who came striding over to her in a long coat flapping about his ankles. He might have appeared menacing had his face not been such a kindly one, wrinkled and smiling despite the worried expression.

'Dreadfully sorry I'm late, I've been at the hospital.'

Saskia looked at him suspiciously.

'Ah, of course, hang on a mo. Where is it? Here we are. That's you, isn't it?' He waved Hermann's photograph of her.

She nodded. 'Where's Mrs Atwell?'

'Ah, well, yes, you see that's why I've been at the hospital. Mrs Atwell's dead.'

Three

In Maud's bijou little house in Chelsea, Selwyn put Saskia in Maud's bedroom and, instead of spending the night at the Chelsea Arts Club as he usually did, he crept up the narrow stairs to the empty maid's room in order not to leave Saskia alone in the house.

Saskia was too tired to unpack. Without thinking she had reached under the pillow, pulled out Maud's silk nightgown and put it on. The next morning she opened her eyes to a large photograph of poor dear Freddy in a silver frame standing on the bedside table. Waves of shock as she realized where she was were followed by an intense curiosity to know more about the woman who had lived in this house.

Saskia reclined against the mound of pillows and stroked the smooth silk of the nightgown against her skin. The dusky pink of the walls and the elaborately-swathed curtains, far too heavy and overpowering for such a small room; the delicate ornamental kidney-shaped dressing table with its triptych mirror and glass-topped surface covered with boxes of loose powder, a silver-backed set of hairbrushes and mirror, an open jewellery box, overflowing ashtrays, uncovered lipsticks; a little circular stool covered in pink velvet – the sensuality of all these things closing in on her were in such stark contrast to the spartan asceticism of Mutti's bedroom in the Zehlendorf apartment that for a few moments Saskia could only stare around her, breathing in an unfamiliar smell of stale scent and cigarette smoke.

When she finally got out of bed another shock awaited her. She had started her period and she hadn't packed any sanitary towels. Opening a door she found an adjoining bathroom and sat down gloomily on the lavatory, taking in the tiny cramped bath and the ludicrous basin standing incongruously large beside it on a wide porcelain pedestal.

Hearing Selwyn's footsteps on the stairs she stuffed some lavatory paper between her legs, pulled down the night-gown and hobbled, pigeon-toed to keep the paper in place, back to the bedroom.

'I have my days . . .' she called out, catching Selwyn on the landing. His face was a complete blank as she poked her head round the door. Clearly the literal translation from the German wasn't right. She searched around and came up with half a word: 'Menstru . . . where do I find some things?'

She tried hard not to notice the look of sheer horror that came over his face. Mutti had always told her not to be embarrassed about such things. It was only nature after all.

'Good heavens, child. Maud was a woman. She must have . . .' He pushed past her into the room while she reflected on the fact that he had called her a child when she had just given him ample proof that she was already a woman. He started flinging open cupboards and pulling out drawers.

'Do you know exactly what it is you're looking for?' he asked her suddenly, 'because I'm not sure I do. Here, keep searching. You're bound to find what you're after.'

'But the clothes . . .?'

'Oh Lord, take them as well if you want,' he said, misunderstanding her, 'It's not as if Maud will be needing them any more.'

Without realizing it, he had made one of Saskia's wildest dreams come true: to own a wardrobe full of expensive clothes. Maud Atwell had been five feet nine to Saskia's five two but that didn't deter Saskia for a second. As she pulled out dresses, jackets, coats and skirts and blouses by the dozen she began to plan in her head the alterations she would make to them.

A sudden warm trickle down the inside of her leg reminded her what she was supposed to be looking for. She found them in a drawer of Maud's dressing table. The belt was much too large and even when adjusted, slipped down over her hips. She found some safety pins in Klara Kessler's sewing kit which her mother had slipped into her case as a memento and she used these to attach the towel to her underpants.

Then she selected one of Maud's more simple afternoon frocks and neatly turned up the hem by several inches, blessing Mutti's sewing kit with each stitch. She found a belt with which to gather it in at the waist and finally she rolled up the sleeves to her elbows. She surveyed her reflection in the row of mirrored doors on Maud's cupboards. She looked odd but in her opinion it was a vast improvement on the girlish dirndl skirts and blouses with Peter Pan collars and little puff sleeves Mutti had dressed her in for so long.

Feeling almost elegant she went downstairs and confidently presented herself to Selwyn. Who ignored her.

'Breakfast?' she asked tentatively.

Again Selwyn looked blank. She might as well have asked for half a dozen oysters. 'Help yourself,' he mumbled finally, nodding in the direction of the kitchen, and very soon Saskia would come to recognize these two words as the code by which she now had to live her life.

Selwyn spent the morning on the telephone in Maud's tiny sitting room letting people know of her death. He didn't even want to stay in town for her funeral so as soon as he had contacted her sister and she had volunteered to come and take over from him, he called up to Saskia that they were off.

Saskia barely knew who he was but there was a spirit of adventure about the notion of going 'off' with a near-stranger that appealed to her sense of romance. What she didn't know was that one of the first things Maud would have done would have been to take her to register with the police.

Selwyn never even thought of it. As far as he was concerned she was a refugee not an alien, and in Maud's absence it was his duty to take care of her. And so with the back of his car strewn with Maud Atwell's clothes, Selwyn drove Saskia up to Lancashire and installed her at Laurel Bank. On the way up he even attempted conversation.

'Rum do, these concentration camps. Heard about them from Maud. Amazing the amount of stuff she found out. Didn't believe her at first but then I met a chap from Germany who made it out before you did and he confirmed it. Any news about your uncle?'

'My uncle?'

'Yes, the one they arrested. He's probably in one of those camps Maud told me. She was quite upset when she got your father's letter about it. I'm so sorry, my dear Saskia. Rotten for your family. I say, hold on . . .'

Saskia burst into tears. That was what had happened to Onkel Wolfie. No wonder she hadn't been able to say goodbye to him.

'Here, take this,' Selwyn handed her an enormous silk bandana handkerchief. 'Blow your nose, don't be a goose.'

Saskia took it and Selwyn drove on in silence. He was terrified of women's tears. After a while she sniffed loudly and turned to him.

'Perhaps you could tell me a little more . . . I mean, about Germany, what's happening . . .?'

'Didn't your parents tell you anything? About *Kristallnacht*? No? Extraordinary thing to do – send you over here and you not understand the reason why. Well, I'll do my best.'

He told her gently just how grave the situation was in Germany and why.

When he had finished she said simply: 'Thank you.'

'What on earth for?'

'For treating me like an adult. My parents only told me things they thought a child should know, yet they sent me away as if I were an adult.'

'Well, I sincerely hope you are. I don't keep a nursemaid at Laurel Bank, you know?' And at that she smiled for the first time since arriving in England.

Selwyn loved showing Saskia round Laurel Bank, was thrilled by her childish excitement at everything she saw. He was even more delighted to learn that she could cook a little, was not above doing some housework and had no apparent interest in going anywhere.

At Laurel Bank Selwyn lived a secluded life in the Bell House of the mill and spent most of his time in the studio he had converted from one of the old weaving rooms. Saskia, he was pleased to note, spent time in her little room at the top of the Bell House which could be reached by a narrow staircase leading from the kitchen. His own quarters on the first floor could only be reached by the main staircase leading from the hall. Sometimes he did not see her all day until they met for supper in the kitchen at half-past seven.

Selwyn was used to dining alone but his good manners decreed that he must share at least one meal with his guest. For that was how he thought of her – as a guest. Someone who was staying for a while and would be gone soon.

The trouble with Selwyn, as his beloved mother had always told him, was that he never thought things through properly. If he had only paused to consider the responsibility he was undertaking by bringing a sixteen-year-old German refugee into his home, he would have remained in London until other lodgings had been found for her. But his biggest mistake was in omitting to contact her parents straightaway and inform them of Maud Atwell's death. As it was he waited until Saskia had been at Laurel Bank for nearly ten days before telephoning Hermann Kessler's number only to discover it had been disconnected.

'We'll have to try my Tante Luise,' Saskia told him, but they could not get through there either. Saskia's letters to her parents addressed to the Zehlendorf apartment were not answered and there was silence too from Tante Luise.

It was then that it began to dawn on Selwyn that he might have his guest for rather longer than he thought. He made a few calls to London and learned from friends just how bad things were reported to be in Germany but he kept his growing fears from Saskia. Yet what on earth was he going to do with her? Her English was good but it was pointless to try to send her to school. Suddenly he had an unexpected and constant companion on his hands.

To his horror Selwyn found that he missed Maud Atwell considerably more than he had anticipated. He missed the visits to her little house in Chelsea, her idle chatter, her surreptitious smoking when she thought there was no one else in the house, even her futile planning of their wedding. He had been furious with the doctor for having miscalculated how seriously ill she was. He had tried to continue with the design of 'the Maud', an angular wooden chair with a high, narrow ladder back, but found that he could not –although this might well have been due to the fact that it had begun to look far too artsy-craftsy for his liking. They had never indulged in any sexual activity, she out of some prevailing loyalty to poor dear Freddy, he out of respect for what he assumed to be her frail condition as the cancer continued to eat away at her. Sex had always been alluded to coyly as something that would happen after the wedding. Ridiculous at their age but there it was. Or wasn't.

Selwyn was encouraged to see that Saskia liked drawing and it was while she was showing him some of her sketches that he thought of a way to keep them both occupied.

'How'd you like to pose for me?'

They were in the middle of supper – roast chicken hot from the Aga and *Bratkartoffeln*, Saskia's own recipe – but Selwyn pushed his plate aside and, taking her by the hand, he pulled her away from the table and into his studio. He led her over to the window and pushed her gently onto a stool.

'No, turn around, sideways, that's it . . . so I can see your profile. Now, here's the chair I'm working on. See? I'll make it like your shape. We'll call it "the Saskia". Only one problem . . .' Saskia was looking at him as if he was quite mad. '. . . I can't really see your shape at the moment. You'll have to take your clothes off.'

It was typical of Selwyn that he never once considered the enormity of his request. He did not take into account that she was a mere girl who might not have even had a friendship with someone of the opposite sex yet, let alone exhibited her naked body. Yet it was because he appeared to think it was such a natural thing to ask that Saskia jumped up from the stool and began to unbutton her blouse.

'What about supper?' she asked, ever practical.

'Oh, stick it in the Aga. It'll keep warm.'

When she returned from the kitchen she found that he had positioned a tall Chinese screen at one end of his studio.

'There! You can get undressed behind that.'

It was as ludicrous as a doctor's consulting room where it was all right to be examined naked but you were not to be observed taking off your clothes.

When she emerged Selwyn gulped. He hadn't bargained for his own reaction to the sight of her perfectly formed naked body. Yet he couldn't quite reconcile himself to the fact that Saskia was almost a woman and no longer a child.

Saskia sat quietly while he sketched her. She trusted this gruff, bearlike man. It was just as well. She had to. Some day – maybe sooner, maybe later – her parents would summon her back home to Berlin but in the meantime, to her utmost surprise, she found she was secretly beginning to enjoy being away from them, being able to do exactly as she pleased all day, not having to compete with Christiane for anyone's attention.

As for Selwyn, it was as if his dream had come true. A beautiful model who wasn't going to make any demands on him. For if there was one thing that terrified Selwyn it was commitment. He knew his mother had died an unhappy woman knowing that her favourite son had still not found someone to marry but there it was. He liked his freedom.

But a few weeks later, when there was still no word from Berlin and he felt duty-bound to explain to Saskia how grave the situation was, she burst into such a torrent of weeping that Selwyn instinctively drew her into his arms to comfort her. As he held her, rocking her gently from side to side, patting her on the back in a fatherly manner, he found himself becoming a little confused in his own feelings towards her.

Oh Maud, you poor old booby, he thought for the umpteenth time, *why did you have to go and die on me?*

Barney never even noticed the long grey object gliding down the street and easing to a halt outside Joe's shop. He was so wrapped up worrying about Stella he could barely wait to get home from school to find out if there had been any news.

'It's a Brough Superior,' declared a man who had worked in a garage, proud of his knowledge, but no one took any notice of him. Half the street were outside staring in amazement. It wasn't often they saw a car of any kind let alone one as grand as this.

The man who got out was tall, with something of a bearlike appearance, probably due to the huge coat he had wrapped around him. It reached almost to his ankles and hampered his progress to Joe's. If wearing such a heavy winter coat in September was one sign of the stranger's eccentricity then his prematurely grey hair was certainly another. Like his coat this too was long, brushed back away from his forehead and falling over his collar. There was not a man in the street who did not have a close-cropped head of hair flattened down with Brilliantine unless they were bald, and the sight of this flowing mane was grounds for further speculation. Yet there was no doubt that here was a distinguished person, someone who commanded authority with or without the Brough Superior, a patrician gentleman with an aquiline nose and a ruddy colour to his cheeks. Someone who lived well.

The bell pinged as he entered Joe's shop and Joe looked up with a smile, expecting one of his locals. When he saw the man his mouth fell open in shock.

'Name's Reilly,' said the stranger, 'Selwyn Reilly. D'you have a dog by any chance?'

'Close your mouth, Joe,' hissed Vera, who had raced into the shop at the sound of a stranger's voice and found Joe speechless, gaping in astonishment, 'Give the gentleman an answer.'

'No, no, we haven't,' Joe stammered.

'What's the matter with you, Joe Lambert? Of course we've got a dog. What do you think Stella is?'

'But we haven't got her any more,' Joe pointed out. 'She ran off.'

'About a week ago?' enquired Mr Reilly.

'Aye,' said Vera.

'Black Labrador, was she?' Selwyn Reilly looked at Joe who nodded. He would have nodded if he'd been asked if Stella were a Tibetan spaniel. 'Well, I've got her then. Excellent.'

'She may not be our black Labrador,' Vera began hesitantly.

'But you're Joe's shop, aren't you?' asked the man impatiently, 'The dog I've found has a tag on her collar which says *Joe's Shop, Liverpool*. Can't be many black Labradors with that on their collars, now can there? I've been driving all over Liverpool looking for you.'

'Why didn't you go to the police?' asked Joe suspiciously, 'we reported her missing.'

'Oh, I know, I should have, shouldn't I? But that would have been too simple. I wanted to treat it as a kind of quest, discover the owners for myself.'

'Well, the real owner's right behind you,' Vera told him beckoning to her son who had just entered the shop. 'Barney lad, this is Mr Reilly. He's found our Stella. There now, aren't you made up?'

'Have you really, mister? When?'

'Week ago.'

'But why did you wait so long to tell us? Why haven't you brought her with you? Why didn't . . .?'

'Hush now, Barney, give the gentleman a minute's

33

peace. So what kept you then, eh?' Joe glared at Selwyn Reilly. Not their kind. Not their kind at all. He didn't want people like this in his shop. All that hair . . .

'I'm sorry, Barney.' Suddenly the man was less formidable, had become kind and gentle. 'Stella, d'you call her? Lovely name. You see Stella was wounded when I found her . . .'

'*No!*' cried Barney.

''Fraid so. She'd been run over. I nearly ran over her myself lying there in the middle of the road on the way out to where I live in the country.'

'But she's not . . .?' Barney couldn't quite get the word out.

'No, she's not dead. She's absolutely fine, you'll see. She's a lady of leisure but I can't move her yet, you understand? That's why I couldn't bring her with me. You'll have to come and visit her till she's ready to come home.' Selwyn turned towards the door. 'Shall we go now? Car's right outside.'

Barney ran towards the door.

'Barney!' Vera reached out. 'Joe, stop him. He can't go on his own. One of us'll have to go with him.'

'Well, it'd best be me,' Joe said gravely. He didn't hold with this peculiar man appearing out of nowhere and waltzing off with their Barney. No knowing what he might do to the lad. 'You mind the shop, Vera. We'll not be long.' Then it struck him he did not even know how far they were going. He looked at Selwyn.

'Oh, it'll take about an hour from here.'

'An hour! Joe, you'll not be back for your tea, nor will Barney.' Vera was mortified.

'Maybe you'd like to come too, Mrs . . .'

'Lambert,' intercepted Joe. 'No, someone's got to stay behind to mind the shop. I'll not be shutting the shop for some dog,'

'She's not some dog. She's our Stella and Mr Reilly's found her.' Barney's vehemence surprised everyone, including himself.

34

'Well, how'll you get back?' Ever-practical Vera.

'Now do stop fretting, my dear Mrs Lambert. I'll get them back to you safe and sound, never fear. I only wish you could come with us. Still, another time perhaps . . .'

Joe didn't like the 'my dear Mrs Lambert' at all. She wasn't anybody else's dear anything. She belonged to him, Joe.

'Will you be wanting anything?' he asked gruffly. Chap looked like he had a bob or two, might as well get him to spend it in the shop while he was there.

'What did you say? Oh, well maybe a box of matches,' Selwyn pointed to the Swan Vestas. *Mean bugger,* thought Joe, *going for just about the cheapest thing in the shop.* '. . . and a packet of corn flakes, some lavatory paper, a sliced loaf if you've got it, a jar of Marmite, oh, and a pound of that Cheddar on the counter. Looks awfully good.' Vera shuddered. 'I'll do the cheese, Joe,' she said quickly, 'You fetch the rest. Will that be all, Mr Reilly?'

But Selwyn Reilly had only just begun and twenty minutes later Vera and Barney were still loading boxes with provisions for him. She wondered who he had keeping house for him. Whoever it was obviously didn't do a very good job with the shopping. He appeared to have run out of everything.

'Mr Reilly's waiting,' said Barney.

'Well, your mother's on the till and I'm busy as you can see. You'd best go on with Mr Reilly if you're in such a hurry.'

'But Joe –' protested Vera but stopped when Joe cast a wary eye at the listening neighbours. It wouldn't do to have them think he and Vera didn't trust Mr Reilly. Not now. Things had gone too far.

'I'll be back with him around seven o'clock,' said Selwyn.

The neighbours watched dumbfounded as young Barney Lambert walked out of the shop with the stranger and drove away in his fancy car cool as you please.

*

Barney was beginning to feel distinctly uncomfortable. He couldn't figure out for the life of him where they were going. They'd been driving for more than an hour, past St Helens and on up the big wide roads towards Blackburn. They were right in the middle of cotton country now. Through the torrential rain Barney could make out cotton mills looming here and there. They seemed to be on the edge of the moorland. Barney shivered. He'd barely ever left the city in his life. He began to think about the warnings Vera had given him in the past about not talking to strange men. He'd never bothered to ask her why and now he wished he had. Still, he was fourteen now, his voice had broken and while he didn't really feel like a man he was old enough to be accompanying someone who claimed to have found his dog and not worrying himself sick about it. He found his tongue at last, asking a question if only to take his mind off his discomfort.

'You're not from these parts then, are you, Mr Reilly?'

'Now, why ever should you think that? Of course I am.' Selwyn Reilly sounded astonished. 'My family were in cotton, what else? Mill's been in the family since the eighteenth century.'

Laurel Bank had been built by his great-great-grandfather as a simple water-powered mill to spin cotton. Since the beginning of the century there had been little economic justification for its continued operation, yet if Selwyn's father had closed it, it would have meant unemployment for an entire community who worked there. Instead, he employed a pretty good cost accountant who guided the mill through the 1920s – even modified the looms that were used for calico weaving so that he could produce laundry bags – but finally the old man had to concede defeat. He tried to sell it, put it up for auction, but while a building like that would have fetched £100,000 twenty years earlier, no one bid. It destroyed him. Reillys had been cotton kings for a hundred and fifty years and had installed some of the finest machinery in Lancashire.

'Well, it's all over now. My father died sixteen years ago

and my mother before him. I've got sisters and brothers, but they're all down south, married with responsibilities. I'm the black sheep. Reillys were rich, I'm not saying they weren't. Rich enough to live the life of Riley, they used to tease me at school. So, where was I?'

'Your father died,' prompted Barney.

'That's right and I came north from London for the funeral. That's when I saw the mill again. Nostalgia. Pure sentimental nostalgia. Can't call it anything else. I knew I just had to find a way of hanging on to the mill somehow. So I sold a house my mother had left to me – great big pile up near Preston, felt like a mausoleum, been in her family for years – my brothers and sisters weren't too pleased even though the old girl did leave it to me to do what I wanted with it. Well, what I got for it I spent converting father's mill, or part of it anyway. See these little houses, these were where our weavers lived. Still do on their pensions, wouldn't want to turn them out. Now, here we are, here's my mill.'

It was as far removed from the image of an industrial cotton mill as anyone could have imagined. Driving slowly down into the unspoilt river valley, past the weir and a large mill pool, they came upon what seemed at first glance to be an elegant Georgian building topped by a bell tower and flanked by a tall square chimney rising high into the clear blue sky. They were in the heart of the countryside surrounded by woodland and, as they approached the mill via the road which followed the curve of the river, rhododendron bushes began to arch on either side of the drive forming a tunnel until suddenly they emerged in front of a large plain-faced stone building, five storeys high, the walls pierced with row after row of small-paned windows. Here the rhododendrons had been replaced by the laurels which gave the mill its name: Laurel Bank.

Barney glanced up at the round blue-faced clock set in the stonework just below the bell tower on the roof and a movement at a tiny window under the eaves just to the right of the clock caught his attention.

When Barney saw Saskia for the first time it was a fleeting glimpse of her face high above, looking down at him, but it would remain with him for the rest of his life.

Four

Saskia turned away from the window. Who was the boy with Selwyn? Was he bringing another child to live at Laurel Bank just as she had begun to bask in his undivided attention? He was her Selwyn. She did not want to share him with anyone.

He wasn't handsome, at least not if she contrasted his looks with those describing the heroes in the romantic novels she had read in the sanctuary of her room in Berlin. But she liked to look at his face, especially when he laughed, and to this end she remembered the things that made him laugh. When she screwed up her face in a certain way he said it made her look like a little mouse and it made him laugh. When she said she was going to 'have a swim' when she meant she was going to have a bath, it made him laugh. When she sang 'Gott Save De Qveen' in her German accent it made him laugh.

But he spent all day in his studio and he had temporarily abandoned work on 'the Saskia' in order to complete a design for a new table that had been commissioned. He didn't need her to pose for the time being. Her time was her own once again.

The summer had been unbearably hot. She had discovered a stream at the end of the fields behind the mill and had gone there every day to take a dip. Indeed, now when she said she was going to have a swim she quite often meant just that. And on her return to the Bell House she rarely put on her clothes again. She loved to wander through the cavernous weaving rooms with the sun shining through the tall windows onto her bare skin.

She wondered why he was not married. One evening she had plucked up enough courage to ask him and found that that too had made him laugh. Yet he didn't even seem to have any friends. Ah, he had told her, that was her fault. Up until the day she had come to live with him his life had been divided between London and Laurel Bank. In London he had friends; at Laurel Bank he had his work. He knew them all in the village – after all they had worked for his father, even his grandfather – but he was different, and when he was up at the mill they knew they should leave him alone.

'But what about me?' Saskia had protested. 'Why don't you go to London any more? If you went you could take me with you.'

'I suppose you've got a point, my little Sassy,' He said, using his new pet name for her, 'I'm going to have to think about introducing you to people if you're to stay here much longer . . .'

She'd been with him several months and there was still no word from Berlin, yet today on the wireless, while he had been away in Liverpool, she had heard the news. Without even bothering to dress she rushed downstairs as she heard his voice below.

'Come in, Barney. We're in what used to be the Counting House where the head bookkeeper and his clerks did all the paperwork. It's known as the Bell House because of the bell tower on the roof which you no doubt noticed. My great-great-grandfather rang that bell to summon everyone in the village to work. We live mostly in the Bell House but the actual mill's just through that door. Come on, I'll show you . . .'

But they stopped right there.

'Selwyn! Where have you been? All day I have been waiting. The news. You have heard the news? WE ARE AT WAR!'

It was the first time Barney had seen a naked female

body. She was like a little fawn skittering down the stairs on slender legs towards them and hurling herself into Selwyn's arms.

For a second Barney's mind flashed back to the time his class had been taken to the Walker Art Gallery in Liverpool and he had managed to escape and spend four glorious minutes gazing at Hacker's *Pelagia and Philammon* before anyone came looking for him. But nothing had prepared him for the disturbing difference between a nude in a painting and a real life flesh and blood girl. Barney had felt no compunction whatsoever to touch the nude in the Hacker but it was all he could do to stop himself reaching out and running his hands down this girl's smooth body.

Barney guessed she was about his own age, maybe a little older but not much. She was slight, not much more than five feet, but beautifully in proportion except for her bosoms. They, by contrast, were large and round with spreading pink nipples. Below them her waist appeared minuscule before her hips curved down to tapering thighs, knees, calves, perfect ankles, trim little bare feet. And despite Selwyn's persistent murmurings in her ear, she had no intention of 'running to put something on'.

'War, Selwyn. Don't you understand. It's happened. Hitler invaded Poland two days ago and your silly Mr Chamberlain has to go and stand by what he promised Poland. He's declared war against Germany. We're at war. I'm at war with you. Oh, Selwyn, it's so awful.'

'Ah, my poor Sassy,' he said, stroking her tangled black hair, trying to calm her. 'I knew it was only a matter of time. Saskia's German,' Selwyn told Barney by way of explanation, 'Go through, won't you please.' Selwyn motioned towards a door. 'Stella's in there. I must just take Sassy upstairs.'

But Barney stood rooted to the spot, awkwardly turning his school cap round and round in his hands as Selwyn took off his coat and wrapped it round the girl's pale body.

'Go on,' Selwyn nodded again towards a door down the corridor, 'please, we'll be down in a minute.'

41

Barney stepped through the door into another world – a vast space, and to one side rows of wonderful painted cast-iron pillars supporting a long gallery. As many as eight or nine of the smallpaned windows along each wall accounted for the light airy feel of the room. Barney couldn't begin to fathom its dimensions – eighty feet by thirty possibly? – but then it began to dawn on him that this must once have been one of the spinning or weaving rooms with probably fifteen to twenty rows of mill workers crammed into it. Now it was virtually empty with the exception of a small island of furniture marooned in the middle. A large easy chair with a sheet thrown over it and two elegant little tables either side. On one stood a bottle of whisky, a tumbler and a soda siphon and on the other a table lamp balanced precariously beside a wireless. A chintz-covered sofa faced them with a standard lamp behind it. A large faded Persian rug lay diagonally across the bare floorboards of this bizarre room within a room. Beyond it, incongruously, stood a carpenter's workbench and it was what lay under this workbench that caught Barney's attention.

Stella was reclining in a dog basket filled with old clothes. Barney crouched beside her and her great pleading eyes, fixed on her young master. She was trying to thump her tail but could only manage a feeble wag. She whimpered a little as Selwyn reappeared.

'Hear that, Barney? She's still in pain. Not much, mind you, not nearly as much as she was when I first found her but the vet said she mustn't be moved for a few weeks yet.

'Who was that?' asked Barney, getting to his feet.

'Who was who? . . . Oh, Sassy. My heavens, I should have introduced you properly, shouldn't I? Do forgive me. It was just that perhaps it wasn't quite the right moment for formal introductions. Sassy models for me, you see. Only thing is, she's quite taken to wandering around in her birthday suit and we're so out of the way here, we hardly ever get any unexpected visitors so I've never bothered to stop her. Not exactly cause for complaint, Sassy's body . . .'

Barney stared at the ground hoping his flush would die down. 'Sassy . . .?'

'Short for Saskia. Saskia Kessler.'

'Why doesn't she live with her parents?'

'They're in Berlin.'

'So why doesn't she live with them there?'

'Because they sent me away.' Saskia had returned clad in a flowing silk robe several sizes too big for her.

'Why?' persisted Barney.

'Because she's Jewish and it's not safe,' explained Selwyn but Barney still looked bewildered.

'Aren't your parents Jewish too? Why would they send you away? What's happened to them?'

'Exactly!' cried Saskia, 'I don't know. Now it's war. I must go back and find them. I have to, can't you see?'

'No, Sassy darling, I can't see at all.' said Selwyn. 'You're safe with me. Your parents sent you to England on purpose. They knew what was going to happen, they wanted you to be safe at least. Think how upset they'd be if you went running back to Germany straight into Hitler's arms. Stay with me. I need you. You know that. You're my muse. It's true,' he said, turning to Barney, 'she inspires me more than you would believe possible.'

'You an artist then, Mr Reilly?'

'No, I'm a designer but that doesn't stop me from drawing Sassy here. She has the most beautiful form, such perfect shape, don't you agree? When she sits in front of a window I look at her profile, her body, and it gives me inspiration for designing a chair. She's my muse in every way. And I've been doing some drawings of Stella,' Selwyn told Barney, 'so that's another reason I want to keep her here a bit longer. I'm not quite sure what I can use them for but maybe by the time she leaves I'll have had a few ideas about designing the perfect dog basket.'

As Barney continued to cast surreptitious glances at Saskia, trying to remember what lay underneath the voluminous silk robe, he suddenly realized that more than anything else he too wanted to capture those images of

Saskia's body. At school they had tried to encourage him in his art classes, told him he had potential, but he had never seen the point. Now he did.

'Oh, can I see them please, the drawings I mean?' Barney was excited.

'You can even pick one to take home and put on your wall. Come along, I'll show you my studio.'

'I'll stay with Stella,' Saskia reassured Barney. 'See, she likes me.' As Stella licked her hand she began to tickle her under her jaw. 'She likes this, all dogs like this. It's the secret trick with them. You can try scratching the top of their head or stroking their ears but if that doesn't work you know they will always like this.'

'Do you have a dog then?' asked Barney eagerly.

'I did. Back in Germany.' She pronounced it *Chermany*. 'He was a Weimaraner. One of the finest German shooting dogs, established over a hundred years ago at the Court of Weimar, beautiful animals.'

'Was he a Jewish dog?' asked Barney before Selwyn hustled him out of the room.

'He lives in a what?' Vera was incredulous. Selwyn Reilly had deposited her son back on her doorstep well past midnight and instead of offering an explanation all the boy could talk about was how Mr Reilly lived.

'In a cotton mill and he . . . and he gave me this drawing he did of our Stella, look, Mam . . .' Barney held out the pencil sketch to her.

'Well, you'll not be going back there, Barney lad.'

'But what about our Stella?'

'Mr Reilly'll bring her back when she's well enough but I repeat you'll not be going back there.'

But Vera was wrong.

'Joe Lambert, whatever are you doing on the floor?'

44

Vera towered over her husband who glared up at her. She couldn't seem to leave him alone these days, nag, nag, nag, always edgy. He couldn't work out what had got into her. But he knew one thing: it'd only make her worse if he rose to her provocation. If he remained calm and gentle with her maybe she'd follow his example.

'Barney's got my chair,' he explained patiently.

'Well, fetch another.'

'Not the same.'

'Give over, Joe. Why's he got it anyway?'

'He's drawing it, I believe, upstairs in his room.'

'Well, I'll put a stop to that right now.'

Vera had made up her mind not to mention it to Joe but while she had been giving the house the weekly top-to-toe last Friday she had come across a bundle of drawings stuffed under Barney's mattress. Drawings of a naked girl. Filthy drawings in her house! Where they came from didn't bear thinking about. At the back of her mind she had to admit to herself that she harboured a faint suspicion Barney himself might have had something to do with their execution and she had to accept the fact that he was nearly a man and, well, men were men. But she also realized that if she showed them to Joe he might remember he was one too and start going on about his marital rights. She'd managed to keep him at bay for eight years now, save for the odd lapse at Christmas or on his birthday when he'd had a few too many. It wouldn't do to break the routine.

'Vera, leave off. He's happy and it's not many a lad as would be with just a piece of paper and a pencil. I reckon we've got a lot to thank Mr Reilly for.'

That did the trick. Mentioning Selwyn Reilly's name always worked miracles with Vera. Although she'd laid down the law very firmly about Barney not going back to Laurel Bank she'd succumbed to ten minutes of Selwyn's undiluted charm and his generous bouquet of late summer roses and readily agreed to Barney going over there once a week for drawing lessons.

But the war was beginning to make its presence felt.

German U-boats lurked in Liverpool Bay waiting to attack ships going in and out of the docks and before long the booming sound of the freighters was drowned by the petrifying whistling of the air raids for which the docks were a prime target. Vera was severely rattled. Joe's contrasting calm only exacerbated her frayed nerves.

And she wanted Barney out, evacuated, safe in the country like many other children from the area who had already left. But Joe would have none of it. He wanted his lad close to him, could see no reason to break up the family. In the same way that he had for years remained impervious to the unemployment all around him, Joe Lambert refused to acknowledge the war. And all the time Vera was driven closer to distraction.

Saskia sat, ramrod straight, on a stool in front of the window. Her left side was presented in silhouette to Selwyn and he was sketching her. As usual he was using her as the model for his chair design. The line of the chair followed Sassy's curvaceous form so that its curved back appeared to narrow to a tiny waist before filling out to a rounded rump for the seat, the whole thing balanced on elegant legs.

Selwyn was aware that Sassy had begun to cry but he said nothing. She was heaving, silently, her tears welling up. She often wept these days. Sometimes she offered no explanation. Today it appeared she would.

'You're not my father!'

Selwyn was shaken by the ferocious tone of her voice.

'Of course not, Sassy,' he said warily.

'But you're old enough to be.'

'Well, yes . . .'

'My father could be dead. Are you trying to take his place?'

'Whatever made you think that?'

'What am I doing here? I think it's just for a while, holiday, but now you won't let me leave.'

'I feel responsible for you, Sassy.'

'But I'm not your daughter and you're not going to take my father's place.'

'You miss him dreadfully, don't you?'

'*Ach, nein*. He didn't want me! He sent me away.'

'Sassy,' said Selwyn, trying not to sound impatient, 'we've been through this. They sent you to London because they knew you would be in danger if you stayed in Berlin.'

'Because I'm Jewish.'

'Partly, yes.'

'But I'm German too. And now I have a feeling it's going to be a bigger problem being German in England than being Jewish.'

There was a ring of truth to that, thought Selwyn. 'The Germans', he told her, winking, 'make everything difficult both for themselves and for everyone else.'

'You know your Goethe.'

'So do you.'

'But my parents, why didn't they send my little sister with me? They kept her with them. They wanted her.'

Selwyn didn't answer. He knew to his cost that it was always best to let Saskia talk herself out when she got started on this particular subject.

'She is probably with my aunt. My uncle was arrested but my aunt is not Jewish. And I'm with you and you are not Jewish.' Selwyn tried not to feel guilty about this. 'So how should I think of you? As my uncle?'

Selwyn didn't answer. He might fool Sassy with his 'kind uncle' routine but he didn't fool himself for a second any more. He wanted to make love to this deliciously feminine creature before him. He wasn't sure when he'd first admitted to himself that this was so, but he knew that to make an advance at this stage would be madness. Sassy's insecurity was crippling her, and in any case as far as he was concerned the considerable difference in their ages made her out of bounds for the time being.

'He's really got it, you know,' he said in an attempt to change the subject.

'Who has? What?'

47

'Talent. Young Barney's talented. Today he brought me a drawing he'd done of his father's favourite chair but do you know what? He's adapted it to his own design, made it more streamlined, altogether more interesting. It was crude in its execution but there was something there. I could sense it. I haven't felt so excited about something for ages. Don't know where he gets it from, can't imagine those parents of his are blessed with much creativity. But I'm going to help Barney, I'm going to make him my protégé, just you wait and see!'

And without realizing it Selwyn had dealt a further blow to Sassy's confidence. A few days earlier she had shown him her latest sketches, a tentative venture into dress design. Selwyn had glanced at them, muttered something like 'How sweet' and dismissed them.

Now he was extolling the work of that boy.

In September 1940, a year after he had first set foot at Laurel Bank and a year into the war, Barney found himself in a state of utter confusion. He kept it to himself, voicing his fears and turmoil only to poor Stella whose life had been shattered by the arrival of the air raids. Barney and Vera had decided the only thing to do was to keep her down in the cellar, which they used as an air-raid shelter, as much as possible. They let her out once a day when the all-clear sounded to do her business in the back yard. Barney would creep down the cellar steps as often as he could to bury his head in the sleek black fur of Stella's neck and try not to look at the reproachful expression in her eyes. Her ears never pricked up any more, her tail had long since ceased to wag and she seemed to Barney to be perpetually cowering in fear. What made it worse was that he was at a loss to know how to explain to her about the war.

His father behaved as if nothing had changed. Joe Lambert continued to stand behind the counter in his shop despite his stock dwindling to practically nothing. The conscription age limit had been amended to include men from nineteen to forty-one but they didn't want Joe, who was thirty-four, because of the astigmatism in his right eye which sometimes caused him to see double.

'They're daft, that's what they are,' he told the neighbours. 'Don't they realize I'd probably kill two Germans instead of one?' And he'd roar with laughter at his own joke oblivious to the fact that once again people resented his attitude when all around him families were receiving news that their menfolk were dead.

On 11 September, when Buckingham Palace was bombed, Vera declared that if the King himself had been hit what hope did they have of survival and when was Joe going to come to his senses and allow Barney to be evacuated? But two days later a ship called *The City of Benares* slipped out of Liverpool in a convoy as part of the overseas evacuation programme. There were four hundred people on board, ninety of them children. Twenty minutes later it was torpedoed and sank. Only seven children survived and among the eighty-three dead were some of Barney's closest friends. Vera shut up about evacuation after that, overseas or otherwise.

Yet in a way Barney was being evacuated. He was spending so much time at Laurel Bank it might have been simpler to have him move there altogether but Vera could not bring herself to suggest it. No wonder he was confused. Once at Laurel Bank he found that Selwyn Reilly seemed even less interested in the war than his father was. And Barney was transported into another world, the world of design in which Selwyn was gradually beginning to immerse him.

'Design can brighten up the dullness of people's lives. It's exactly what we're all going to need once this blessed war is over. Think about it, Barney, make a product look better and you'll sell more of it. Simple, isn't it? What people in this country don't seem to realize is that appearance in a product is a saleable commodity.'

Selwyn would march up and down his studio talking almost to himself while Barney sat at his drawing board and

49

tried to recreate whatever it was that Selwyn had set him to draw. While Selwyn droned on about someone in America called Raymond Loewy and his design for a new Coldspot household refrigerator, Barney lived in hope that he would have another meeting with Saskia. She never seemed to be around when he came to Laurel Bank. He knew she was still living there as occasionally he caught a glimpse of her elfin face peeking through a curtain at one of the small-paned upper windows as Selwyn drove him up to the Bell House, but she always disappeared quickly and Barney wondered if she was avoiding him for some reason. Sometimes he tried to talk to Selwyn about her but all Selwyn wanted to talk to Barney about was design.

One day, on the drive back to Liverpool, he tried once again to ask Selwyn about her and this time would not be put off when Selwyn tried to change the subject. There had been a particularly heavy raid on Liverpool the night before and Selwyn had insisted Barney stay the night at Laurel Bank. Saskia had not even come downstairs to eat with them that evening.

'Quite frankly, Barney, I don't know what to do about her. The situation's pretty grim in Berlin. She can't possibly go back there. We don't even know if her aunt and sister are still alive. I've tried telephoning again but there's never any answer, and we've had no response to letters. Maybe they've moved. Who knows? But she doesn't understand. Thinks I'm trying to hold her prisoner instead of helping her. She insists on spending all her time in her room as if it really is a cell.'

'She's not made friends round here then?'

Barney had unwittingly put his finger on the problem. Selwyn, closeted in his studio, rarely ventured further afield than the village any more. The former millworkers and their families, still living in the weavers' cottages in the village, regarded Saskia with the utmost suspicion and were not above showing it. Word had got about that she was German and she had compounded the problem with her diffident behaviour on the rare occasions that she did go into the village. The plain truth was that she was terrified of these English people who looked upon her as the Enemy and that was why she hid from them within the confines of the mill.

As they arrived at the outskirts of the city, the lights of the Brough Superior heavily shaded, Selwyn and Barney were appalled at the fresh devastation, the flattened buildings and the constant ringing bells of the ambulances and fire engines. ARP messenger boys raced along on their bicycles, hurrying to deliver their messages to hospitals, fire stations and rescue squads. Barney watched them with envy. He could be doing something like that if only Vera would let him. Suddenly he began to think about what Vera would have to say when he got home. The Lamberts weren't on the phone so Selwyn hadn't been able to let her know that he was keeping Barney for the night. She'd be frantic by now and Barney knew his mother well enough to realize that she wouldn't waste time before having a go at him in spite of her relief when she saw him safe and sound.

But Vera would never 'have a go' at him again.

As the Brough Superior crawled down his street Barney immediately sensed something was wrong. Long before they got to the corner he knew what it was and began to scream and cling to Selwyn, forcing him to stop driving.

Where Joe's shop had stood there was now a huge bomb crater.

Barney rushed to try and climb down into it but Selwyn and a neighbour held him back.

'Your dad ignored the blackout,' the neighbour told Barney. 'I was visiting your mother. She went straight down to the cellar when we heard the air-raid siren but your dad wouldn't move. Sitting there in his Windsor, he was. Stubborn to the end. They're both gone now. Your mother was fussing about you, Barney, wondering where you were. She probably died worrying about you but all I can say is it's a blessing you weren't with them. At least you're still alive even if you are all alone now . . .'

But he wasn't alone. He had Selwyn who steered him

51

gently away from the hole in the ground that had been his home. Just as they were about to climb into the car Barney stopped. He sensed something, heard something. He looked back.

Climbing out of the rubble, shaking the dust from her black coat, Stella bounded towards him, ecstatic to have escaped at last. Selwyn opened the car door and she jumped in.

All the way back to Laurel Bank she licked Barney's tears from his face. Although he never once looked back, Barney knew that as well as saying goodbye to Joe and Vera he was leaving behind him the upbringing they had given him.

Five

The boy was good-looking, she had to admit that. A perfect blond little Aryan. Pity he wasn't German. He'd be just what they wanted in the *Hitler Jugend* in a few years' time.

She knew she ought to feel sorry for him. After all, he knew his parents were dead. There was just a chance hers might still be alive. She had hope. He had nothing.

Sometimes she could hear him crying way into the night and she knew she should go to comfort him. Maybe one day she would, but for the moment it was too soon. She was still far too resentful of his presence at Laurel Bank. The stupid drawing lessons had been bad enough; all that attention Selwyn had showered on him. Why hadn't Selwyn noticed her? He never even asked what she did all day, he was so wrapped up in the boy.

The Boy. She would not call him Barney. She would not call him anything. She would try to pretend he didn't exist. She would go into her dream world and he would be outside, unable to get in. She'd done it before.

With her sister. With Christiane.

Now as she sat immersed in her dream world at Laurel Bank, Sassy opened a drawer and reached inside it for her precious *Reisepass*. Sometimes it felt like the only proof she had left that she was both Jewish and German. She opened it and read: *Permitted to land at Harwich on 4 May 1939 on condition that the holder registers at once with the police and that she does not remain in the United Kingdom for longer than twelve months.*

53

Twelve months! Sassy had already been in England for sixteen. And she had never been near the police.

'It's too frightful. We've been forced out of our home.'

'My dear Lady Sarah, whatever do you mean? Surely you're not walking the streets?' The vicar clasped his hands to his face in an expression of mock horror.

'On the streets? Really, Vicar! No, it's the Air Force. Doing our bit and all that. They want The Hall for an officers' mess or something equally ridiculous. Can you imagine? They'll probably turn the library into a bar.'

'But surely there's still room for you? I mean, I know The Hall isn't Blenheim Palace but it's not exactly a cubbyhole.'

'Well, quite, but there's to be hundreds of them apparently, swarming all over the place. We have to sacrifice our home. There is a war on, you know.'

The Reverend David Appleby ignored this. 'Well, Lady Sarah, there's only one thing for it.'

'What's that?'

'You must move into the Vicarage with myself and Mrs Appleby.'

Lady Sarah Sanders opened her mouth to protest, then shut it again. It had always been a source of amusement to her that the Vicarage was only fractionally smaller than The Hall. Her husband, Geoffrey Sanders, had always thought he had the largest pile for miles around, never realizing that it was a perfectly ordinary Georgian family residence, with a rather grand name, on the edge of the village. The really palatial houses stood in their surrounding parks right out in the country. Sarah could have told him that but he had never asked. Nor, she reflected, had she been invited to any of the grander houses since her marriage to Geoffrey.

'Vicar, you know, that really might not be a bad idea. There'd only be the three of us – myself and the girls. Geoffrey's taken it into his head to rent a flat in London. Now, of all times. Sheer lunacy but there you are. God knows what he's up to. Now, I've a group captain or some such person coming for a glass of sherry before luncheon. Let me try and get a moving date out of him and then I'll be in touch with Mrs Appleby if I may. Hadn't you better have a word first?'

'Consider it done. She'll be delighted to have the company.'

'Well, in that case, Vicar, one last thing,'

'Of course.'

'I've been meaning to ask you; who is that enchanting dark-haired creature with Selwyn Reilly? Oh, do look, she's giving a little bob to Mrs Appleby. Now I know about the boy, so sad about his parents. Marvellous of dear Selwyn to take him in. His father would have been proud of him. But the girl . . .?'

'Actually, Lady Sarah, she's been with him longer than the boy. She's a German refugee. Her family sent her to England just in time.'

'You mean she's . . .?'

'She's Jewish, yes.'

'And her people?'

'I understand she's had no word.'

'Poor child! Well done, Selwyn. I was going to suggest to the Air Force that they ought to try and billet themselves at Laurel Bank instead of turning us out, but it looks as if Selwyn is doing more than his bit already.'

'And he's begun coming to church again which is the best news.'

'Only as far as you're concerned, Vicar. Frankly I wonder why considering she's –'

'The Lord welcomes all his flock,' David Appleby reminded her firmly. Trust Lady Sarah to tackle head on the very thing he had been worrying about.

Selwyn had hit on the idea of taking Sassy and Barney to church on Sundays as a way of introducing them to people. He didn't take them to the village but to the parish of St Jude's about five miles away as more of his family's friends lived round there. It never occurred to him that, given their backgrounds, both Saskia and Barney might prefer the company of the children of his father's former employees than those of his own more exalted friends. In addition it was rather an extravagant use of his petrol ration but, as he never went anywhere else now, he had saved up plenty of coupons.

Initially he had broached the subject with Sassy with some trepidation, expecting her to offer resistance to the notion of attending a Christian service. But he had no way of knowing that the alternative – being left behind – was for her a far greater worry.

So she had come with them and had found the little Norman church with its low-walled churchyard oddly comforting. She felt safe sitting between Barney and Selwyn near the front of the nave, unaware of the rustling excitement her presence caused amongst the parishioners in the pews behind her. Selwyn gently nudged her when it was time to stand for a hymn or a psalm or to kneel on the embroidered hassock at her feet to pray. She didn't pray, of course. Not their prayers anyway. But she knelt and put her face in her hands and tried to summon up pictures in her mind of her mother playing the violin, of the excitement on her father's face when he sold a piano and came home to tell them about it. She even tried to remember Christiane, the early days when she had still been her little sister, smaller than Saskia, looking up to her, following her around, before it had all changed and her parents had begun to pay so much attention to their younger daughter.

Saskia hated the moment when the service ended and she had to follow Selwyn and Barney outside, be greeted by the vicar in the porch and linger in the churchyard while Selwyn chatted to people he knew. She was aware this was precisely the reason Selwyn brought her to church – to linger afterwards and be introduced to his friends. But she always hung back. She didn't want to meet these hostile people. Selwyn assured her they would welcome her into their homes but she didn't want to put this to the test. She couldn't help noticing they rarely looked her in the eye.

There was one family in particular with two daughters who stared at her so hard she thought she would evaporate under the intensity of their gaze. They were tall and long-limbed, at least the older one was. The younger girl, a sulky little thing, could still only be about ten years old. They both had fair hair. The little one had it braided into two long plaits hanging down her back and the older girl – by about five or six years – wore it loose in a neat pageboy to her shoulders. There was something faintly reminiscent of Christiane about them – that blonde, healthy glow they exuded. Of course, their hair was dead straight whereas Christiane's had been a mass of golden curls. Had been. Was she already assuming Christiane was dead?

The elder girl always had a following. Saskia had known the type in Berlin. They commanded an audience, it probably had something to do with their height. She was standing now in the midst of a group of girls her own age with the exception of her little sister whose hand she clutched fiercely in her own. Saskia had the feeling that the younger girl might have liked to have been elsewhere but there was clearly no escape. In order not to have to talk to anybody else, Saskia edged closer to the group. She was mildly curious to hear just what it was the tall blonde girl was saying that held them all so spellbound but as she approached one by one they turned to look at her and nudged each other. The blonde girl had her back to Saskia and continued speaking and Saskia froze as she picked out her words.

'Yes, I've been wondering about her too. She's German! I heard Mr Appleby telling Mummy. German! Think about it. We're fighting the Germans at war. That means she must be the enemy. I wonder why Selwyn Reilly has let her stay with him.'

'Probably because she's got nowhere else to go,' said the younger girl.

'That's not the point,' said her sister. 'The other thing is . . .' and the girl lowered her voice but Saskia could still make out what she said, 'she's Jewish.'

'What difference does that make?'

'Oh, honestly, haven't you heard Daddy talking about all the Jews pouring into the country and trying to take our jobs.'

'But, Nancy, you haven't got a job so what does it matter to you?'

'Oh, do be quiet. You're too young to know anything about it. I just know Selwyn shouldn't be taking Jews into his house, that's all.'

Saskia was numb with rage. She knew the type: silly, spoiled girls who repeated things they'd heard other people saying without knowing what they were talking about. She decided to put the girl in her place.

'Nancy?' Saskia held out her hand as the girl turned, 'I'm sorry but I couldn't help overhearing your sister call you Nancy. She is your sister, isn't she? I'm Saskia Kessler. I'm staying at Laurel Bank, as you probably know.'

Saskia was astounded at the girl's poise. She had the grace to flush slightly when she realized that Saskia had been listening, but that was all.

'So you speak English?' Nancy ignored Saskia's outstretched hand. The younger girl moved to take it but Nancy intercepted her, taking her sister's hand in her own and holding it down.

'Perfectly,' said Saskia.

Nothing more was said. Nancy made no effort to introduce her sister. She merely stood her ground, all the while looking Saskia straight in the eye.

Suddenly Saskia was aware of another presence. Barney had been listening quietly. In fact he had heard more of what Nancy had said than Saskia had. Nancy looked at him and this time her poise deserted her for a second. Her mouth dropped open slightly and Saskia saw Barney through the other girl's eyes: blond hair like Nancy's, tall for his age and, above all, that infinitely desirable object – a boy.

'Oh, I've been so wanting to meet you. You must come and visit us. What about playing tennis, you do play, don't you? I say . . . where are you going?'

For Barney was not listening to her. As she began to speak to him he turned abruptly on his heel and walked away, and as he did so he reached out and took hold of one of Saskia's hands, pulling her gently behind him. Saskia had begun to cry quietly. She had been shielded from blatant face-to-face anti-Semitism up to now. The *Sturmtruppen* had been a political rather than a personal issue. This was her first experience of someone she barely knew being nasty to her for no other reason than that she was Jewish.

'Oh, what's Nancy gone and done now?' Lady Sarah asked the vicar. 'I say, Selwyn, come over here, please.'

'Sarah! It's been ages.'

'Yes, yes, yes, simply ages. What do you expect with a war on? Now listen, I want you to take me over and introduce me to your charges. If I can ever teach Nancy any manners your girl might like to come over and spend the day with us.'

'Well, yes, she might, Sarah, and it's sweet of you to think of it. But she is quite a bit older than Nancy.'

'Really? She looks about twelve.'

'She's eighteen.'

'Is she?'

'And I'm thirty-nine so don't go getting any ideas, Sarah.'

'Dear boy!' Lady Sarah all but wagged a finger at him. 'Come along, you miserable creatures,' she called to her daughters and linking her arm in Selwyn's she strolled out of the churchyard to the Brough Superior parked at the end of the lane.

'I imagine that car must gobble up your petrol ration, Selwyn. Still, it's better than that ostentatious piece of rubbish Geoffrey drives about in. Good Lord, the girl's crying and Selwyn, do look, the boy's mopping up her tears with his handkerchief. What a wonderful pair you've landed yourself with.'

'I have, haven't I?' said Selwyn proudly.

'Never mind anything Nancy says to you, my dear,' said

Lady Sarah, poking her head through the open car window and dislodging her hat in the process. 'She's a silly girl and I'm most awfully sorry she's upset you. Please feel free to come and visit us whenever you like. Actually, hold on a moment. Selwyn, did I tell you? We're moving to the Applebys, the Air Force want The Hall, but I'm sure the Applebys won't mind. You come and see us, both of you. You're always welcome.'

'Mummy, how could you?' they all heard Nancy hiss at her mother as Selwyn climbed into the Brough Superior and drove them away.

'Well, now you've met Lady Sarah,' he said, 'a real Lady in every way, which is more than can be said of Nancy, stuck up little brat. Lady Sarah's the daughter of an earl but she married beneath her, as they say. It wouldn't matter a toss except that Geoff Sanders simply doesn't deserve her. He's jumped, of course. Nothing wrong with that except he's landed in all the wrong places. There's even a rumour that he's a Fascist, a Blackshirt, one of Mosley's lot, though we keep quiet about it for fear of upsetting Sarah. God only knows what ideas he's putting into Nancy's head. She's grown into a perfect monster and it can't be Sarah's doing. The little one's all right though. So far, anyway.'

Barney couldn't remember even noticing a 'little one' but Saskia recalled the tentative hand held out to shake her own.

'Well, we'll have to go over and see them, you two. Nancy's the nearest in age to you around here, Sassy, even though she is a bit younger. Might be worth getting to know her.'

'Never,' said Sassy firmly and explained why.

'Saskia, I hate to say this but you are going to come across this sort of thing now and then. We British are a funny lot. We distrust anything that is unfamiliar to us and let's face it, Saskia, you're an exotic . . . in more ways than one.'

'Nancy and Sassy are enemies for life,' said Barney,

It sounds melodramatic, thought Sassy, *but I wonder how he knows that's exactly what I was thinking*. Maybe she ought to revise her view of this strange boy beside her.

'Where does Geoffrey Sanders get his money?' asked Barney.

'You won't believe this,' said Selwyn, 'but he's made a fortune out of manufacturing jam pot lids,' and at this even Sassy roared with laughter.

'Of course,' said Barney, 'Sanders jam. My dad used to stock it in the shop. Very popular it was.'

'I don't know what he'll do now the war's on but I've no doubt whatever it is it will be lucrative. I only hope he takes good care of Sarah. She's a thoroughly nice old bag. A real gent!' Selwyn tooted his horn as if in celebration of Lady Sarah as they sped along the empty country lanes towards Laurel Bank.

But he stopped abruptly when Sassy asked him shrewdly: 'And what are you going to do during the war, Selwyn?'

Early in the New Year of 1941 everything came to a head at Laurel Bank when Selwyn was called up.

He tried to make arrangements for Sassy and Barney to join the Sanderses at the Vicarage but Sassy wouldn't hear of it.

'I won't go, Selwyn. I won't go and live under the same roof as that Nancy. Did you see her in church on Christmas morning? She all but spat at me.'

'Well, what else do you suggest?' Selwyn was becoming increasingly exasperated by Sassy, who would no longer sit for him and appeared to spend her days flitting about the mill like a ghost.

'I suggest we stay right here. I am not a child, Selwyn, in spite of what you might think, and nor is Barney. We can look after ourselves perfectly well. As well as you can anyway. Maybe even better. Who does the cooking and washing around here these days? Who planted seeds in the vegetable garden so we would be able to eat last year? Hmmmm?'

Selwyn shrugged. It was true. She had proved herself to

be quite a little hausfrau over the past year. As for Barney, he had become her shadow. He followed Saskia everywhere and Stella followed him. Selwyn was forever encountering the three of them traipsing about the place in a ridiculous Indian file.

'Well, then, we'd better get your identity card sorted out so you can get a ration book.'

'Oh, no, I'll just go on using yours,' protested Saskia. If Selwyn contacted the authorities about something like an identity card he'd open up a real can of worms. She was an illegal immigrant; her time in England had run out long ago and, if she only believed a quarter of what Nancy Sanders reported hearing from her father, Sassy could soon be just another Jew not wanted in England. Worse, she might even be sent to one of those detention centres she'd heard about.

'What do you mean, using mine?'

'How do you think we've been getting any food at all over the past few months? I haven't noticed you doing any shopping. I just go down to the village and hand over your ration book and say it's for Mr Reilly.'

'What about the chicken we had on Christmas Day?'

'Black market. George Thompson. The only sadness was that we couldn't give the bones to Stella. They'd have splintered in her throat.'

'George Thompson? But he's a poacher.'

'Of course he is, but his father worked in your mill and for some reason they think they owe it to you.'

'Reg Thompson, so he did. Well I never.'

'Exactly! Well you never would if I wasn't around to see that it happened. All that time you spend with that stupid chair. You're going to have to leave it behind, you do realize that, don't you, Selwyn? The Army won't want it.'

'Barney's going to finish it for me. I take it you'll sit for him even though you won't come near me any more? He'll need you.'

'He'll be at school.'

'He's not learning much there. It's just the village school and he's far too bright for that but I have to send him somewhere. No, seriously, Sassy, he must keep on with his design work. I've set him several projects and when I'm home on leave I'll –'

'You will take care of yourself, won't you, Selwyn?' Nearly two years of gentle rural life at Laurel Bank had lulled her into a feeling of security. With Selwyn gone she intended to keep a very low profile indeed. Mercifully Selwyn had not insisted that she visit any of the locals and only the Applebys paid what were obviously duty calls to see how they were. Saskia knew that these would no doubt increase once Selwyn left and she could handle the vicar and his well-meaning, bovine wife. But if Lady Sarah and her snooty daughters came poking their noses in, it would be disastrous for her.

Little did she realize on that cold February morning in 1941 when Selwyn embraced them both and waved goodbye how differently things would turn out. All she could think of was that she was trapped in a foreign land while Christiane was safe at home in Berlin.

Six

It was different without Saskia. Christiane had to admit to herself that despite their differences in the past, she wished her older sister had not left. Worse, she was beginning to think it might be more fun to get away from her family, to join Saskia in London. With all her parents' attention focused on her, Christiane felt stifled. When Saskia had been there Christiane had basked in her parents' love, enjoying the fact that they spent more time with her than they did with Saskia. But had that in fact been the case? Now Christiane was starting to reassess things. Was she imagining it or was her mother just the slightest bit reserved towards her? Christiane could sense Klara's disapproval and she didn't like it.

The problem was that she had never really understood Saskia. She had never understood why Saskia liked to be alone for long periods of time, how she could spend hours with just a book or her sketch pad for company. Christiane needed people. In the past she had always been able to go looking for Saskia. Now she just had her parents and they were beginning to bore her. Life was no fun in Berlin any more. Maybe she could get them to send her to London too. She would take it up with them just as soon as her party was over.

Klara slipped into the dining room, grateful for a moment's peace as she laid the table for dinner. The noise in the living room next door had reached the level where Klara was worried that the neighbours might complain. She knew she should have prepared the table earlier but there had not been time and besides, she had not known how many people would be able to come. As it was, only a diminished group of relatives and friends had gathered to celebrate Christiane's fifteenth birthday. Hermann had produced a couple of bottles of French champagne which, although hard to find in France, seemed curiously available in wartime Berlin. The champagne had now been followed by schnapps which Hermann had offered his brother, Otto, even though they hadn't yet eaten, and now Otto was trying to get Christiane to drink some. Klara could hear her younger daughter's high-pitched laugh as she laid the table including a place for Saskia as she always did even though it had remained empty for over two years. It was Klara's way of keeping her memory alive.

It was the end of September 1941. A Monday. Ordinarily Klara and Hermann would be listening to the weekly broadcast on the radio of a concert played by the Berlin Philharmonic.

They no longer lived in the Zehlendorf apartment. They had long since been relocated in an apartment in Wilmersdorf, overcrowded quarters, several Jewish families packed together in one house. Jews were required to sell their businesses at a fraction of their real worth and Hermann had been forced to relinquish his shop. Klara yearned to return to the Zehlendorf district if only to visit, but Jews were forbidden to leave their districts without permission or to be outdoors after the evening curfew. He and Klara had been commanded to register their valuables – gold, silver, jewellery – and finally to give them up. All Klara had left was her violin and every night after their meagre supper she played to Hermann before they went to bed.

A few weeks earlier the Nazis had ordered all Jews over the age of six to wear a Star of David over their hearts, a yellow star outlined in black and embroidered with the word *Jude*. Jews who walked the streets without their Star of David would be arrested by the Nazis.

What her parents had not told Christiane was that they had received instructions to remain at home for the whole of her birthday. Such orders from the Nazis had come to mean only one thing: deportation. But Hermann and Klara did not want to ruin Christiane's birthday. They had planned the celebration gathering in the afternoon so that the guests could be gone and safely home by curfew. It was nearly time for that now and people were beginning to talk about leaving as soon as they had had a little food.

Klara came back into the room and watched Christiane. Who would have imagined that she would bear such a tall, big-boned Aryan-looking girl. How proud Hermann had been of their enchanting little blonde daughter, so much more biddable than Saskia, so much more outgoing.

Klara felt the stab of pain that always came when she thought about Saskia. Over two years now and still no news of her. Of course they, like Luise, had moved only days after she had left for London but none of the letters Klara had written to her daughter, care of Mrs Atwell in Chelsea, giving their new address, had been answered. If only she could get to the Zehlendorf apartment. Saskia must have gone on writing there unaware they had moved, although the new occupants had no doubt long since thrown out her letters.

So what had happened to Saskia? To her baby? For Klara still thought of Saskia as her baby despite the fact that she was four years older than Christiane. Klara knew that Saskia still had to be small and fragile, that if she were to appear there and then and stand next to her sister, Christiane would tower above her. But Saskia, her beloved, sensitive daughter would not miraculously appear.

And Wolfie, Klara's brother, had never been heard of again after he had been 'resettled'. Nobody ever mentioned his likely fate but Klara had watched Luise, who would now never go to Switzerland, deteriorate. If she and Hermann were also 'resettled', then Christiane would have to go and live with Luise in the apartment she had moved to after deciding to stay in Berlin. The only other alternative was Otto, Hermann's brother, but Klara did not want her child going anywhere near Otto. So she had put it to Luise: would she, in the event that anything happened to Klara and Hermann, take care of Christiane?

'Of course,' Luise had replied.

She knew she should be thankful that she still had Christiane, but looking at the girl, already slightly tipsy, Klara was only aware of a feeling of weariness.

'She's drunk. Hermann, do something.' But Hermann ignored her. Christiane had never been able to do any wrong in his eyes. He worshipped his True German daughter, as he called her. Did that mean he had been ashamed of Saskia for looking so undeniably Jewish? Klara watched Otto. She saw the way he was ogling Christiane. She had never liked him. She hated herself for thinking it but he epitomized the worst of their race. He was everything the Nazis claimed all Jews were: oily, grasping vermin. Otto still had his business, though. She wondered why. It didn't add up.

Christiane was smiling now at her Onkel Otto and suddenly Klara was struck by something that had never occurred to her before. It was an uncomfortable thought but it might just be the truth: she was jealous of Christiane. She was envious of her daughter's ease in life, her natural grace with other people, her complete lack of self-consciousness. At fifteen, Christiane was everything she, Klara, had always wanted to be, and with a jolt she realized that she loved Saskia because Saskia was just like her. All these years, had Saskia felt the same as she did now? Had Saskia been jealous of Christiane? Klara shook herself, lifted her head and noticed Luise watching Christiane who was swaying unsteadily around the room.

'Don't say a word,' implored Klara, 'It's her birthday, after all.'

'Of course it is,' Luise slipped her hand through the crook of Klara's arm, comfortingly. 'But even so, I don't like it. She looks so, I don't know – wanton is hardly the word to describe a fifteen-year-old but it's the only one I can think of when I look at her in this state. Hermann's useless, I take it?'

'Quite useless. How are the headaches, Luise?'

Ever since her husband had been taken Luise had suffered from fearful migraines which kept her awake for most of the night. She twitched at the slightest movement, uttered sudden little cries for no reason. Klara suspected her sister-in-law was on the verge of a major crackup but Hermann refused to listen, dismissing poor Luise as a hopeless neurotic.

'I must be on my way, Klara dear. I won't stay for supper. Shall I see if I can persuade Otto to accompany me, pretend I need him to help me home?' She winked. Luise might be shaky but she hadn't lost her sense of humour.

'He's the very last person you need but, yes, I would be grateful. We must do something about Christiane, she's wobbling about like jelly, and with Otto out of the way it might makes things easier.'

Klara went into the bedroom to fetch Luise's coat, noticing immediately the absence of the Star. Luise did not need one. Hermann's coat was lying on the floor where he had flung it earlier in the afternoon. Klara picked it up intending to hang it in the closet.

It did not have a Star either.

'Hermann, where is it? Where is your Star?' Klara thrust the coat at her husband in her anxiety.

'Oh, it's there, it's in the pocket somewhere.'

'But I sewed it on for you very tightly. It could never have come off so soon . . .'

'No, I took it off.' The room had gone very quiet. 'I'm not going to wear it, ever.' Hermann looked round the room defiantly. 'That's why we've been told to stay home today, Klara. They picked me up yesterday on the Kurfürstendamm without it . . .'

The guests left quickly after that. Christiane flung her long arms around everyone's neck and planted drunken kisses on everyone's cheeks. Klara couldn't help noticing that Otto's landed on his mouth.

'Come,' she told Hermann and Christiane, not wanting to end the day on a sour note, 'I'll play for you.'

Christiane leaned heavily against her father, drowsy with drink, as Klara raised her violin to her chin and lifted her bow. As she struck the first note the sound of heavy boots on stone steps could be heard outside.

Klara acted fast. She had lost one daughter. She would not lose another. Clasping Christiane by the wrist she hauled her to her feet but the second she let go, Christiane slumped back down again.

Klara screamed: 'Hermann, for God's sake do something!'

Hermann helped her raise Christiane to her feet once more.

'Come on, help me take her out to the balcony.'

Hermann shook his head but obeyed.

The apartment next door to theirs had a similar balcony at the back.

'Frau Brandt,' called Klara to their neighbour, and then she turned to Christiane.

'You are going to climb up here on these railings and when Frau Brandt comes out, you are going to jump across to her balcony. She will catch you and hide you. She knows what to expect. We've discussed this very moment so many times . . .'

'Klara, you're as drunk as she is,' said Hermann.

In fact Klara was quite sober but she was lying about Frau Brandt. She had barely spoken to the woman but she wanted Christiane to accept what she was being asked to do.

'But why, Mutti . . . I don't see why . . .'

'Just do as you're told for once,' said Klara in uncharacteristically strong tones. 'Do what I want instead of what your father wants for a change, please, Christiane, I beg of you . . .'

Klara knew they always took the whole family. They hadn't come for just her and Hermann. A young girl, almost a young woman, Christiane would be helpless in their hands.

Frau Brandt came out onto her balcony.

'Jump, Christiane, go on JUMP!'

'*Halt!*' cried Frau Brandt, flinging out her arms towards Christiane who mistook them for arms of welcome, the arms that would catch her. '*Wir sind keine Judenknechte.*'

Judenknechte – lackeys of the Jews – was what Nazis called Gentiles who helped Jews.

Too late the words penetrated Christiane's befuddled brain as she threw herself off her parents' balcony. In her confusion she tried to turn back in midair.

She missed Frau Brandt's railings and fell, plummeting heavily to the ground as the Gestapo burst into the apartment and onto the balcony.

As he looked down at Christiane's body spreadeagled on the ground below, one of the men told Klara: 'Take one last look at her. She's saved us a lot of trouble, that one.'

It took Hermann twenty minutes to stop Klara screaming before they could take her away to the Gestapo headquarters on the Burgstrasse.

Seven

Saskia hated going to the village but she had to face doing the shopping there once or twice a week. There was no active hostility but she could sense the villagers' reserve towards her. Small children would run out of the cottages to stand in the road and stare at her until their mothers came out to shepherd them inside again. Saskia would smile at the women but they never smiled back. No one ever said good morning or good afternoon. In the shop they fetched her provisions and took her coupons with barely a word exchanged between them.

It was small compensation that this had nothing to do with her being Jewish. It had everything to do with her being German. She had heard the whispers the first time she had gone: 'She's German . . . German . . . German . . . German' all around her. She trudged slowly home from the village, her string bag with a few ounces of sugar and a quarter of a pound of margarine slung over her shoulder. As she walked, she studied a new recipe for a cake from the Ministry of Food that Mrs Appleby had given her. Mrs Appleby had said it was quite delicious but then she probably knew how to get hold of some real eggs. What Sassy herself missed most was coffee. *Richtig Kaffee*. It had been part of Berlin life and the eternal British panacea, a nice cup of tea, was utterly wasted on her.

The real problem when it came to food was Stella. George Thompson provided the odd bone and some scrag ends of meat, sometimes he even took her with him on his poaching

71

expeditions – if she caught the odd rabbit before he got to it he turned a blind eye. But it was the soulful expression in her eyes when they sat down to a rare treat of corned beef and cabbage from the garden that melted Saskia's heart. Yet she had to be firm. If she didn't stop him Barney would give her half his plateful and a growing lad like him needed all he could get.

Was he still growing? At sixteen he was already almost six foot. She wondered what kind of mood she would find him in once she was back at the mill. She knew he resented her position, that he felt he ought to be in charge of her rather than the other way round. He hated it when she called him *Barneychen* – Little Barney – even though she had tried to explain it was a term of affection. It wasn't that she looked upon him as a child. It was more that she felt responsible for him. She was the elder and she had sensed that Selwyn had left Barney in her charge. She had to admit they were an odd couple yet somehow they were well-matched. Both misfits: he a working-class boy catapulted up the social ladder with no real training for it. He was still going to the village school when he probably should have left: there was no evidence he was actually learning anything there. He spouted the odd bit of history or geography from time to time but he seemed oblivious to the fact that elsewhere in the world history was there in the making. Saskia couldn't help thinking of the boys in her class in Berlin when she left and how they, younger than Barney was now, had already been involved in political discussion, however basic. She'd taken it upon herself to teach him French along with German and he had a natural ear. His written work was still very shaky but he was beginning to hold conversations with her in German. She realized he had picked up her Berlin accent along with some of her dialect, but what the hell?

As for English, she was no help there. Indeed, he gave her lessons, not that she needed much tuition any more. She was fluent but like he was with German she found it harder to read and write. Every night, once he'd finished his homework, she watched him sit down and read. He didn't seem to have any special friends at school, no one he'd asked to bring home. All he wanted to do in his spare time was read or draw. The walls were plastered with pencil or charcoal sketches of her. She noticed he had long since abandoned his design work and she knew Selwyn would be disappointed. At first he'd been incredibly gauche about asking her to sit for him but now he seemed totally at ease with her nakedness. She wondered if he talked about her at school. How many of the other boys his age had seen a naked woman? How many of them knew about the woman's time of the month? She'd had to explain to him gently one day when he'd asked her to strip. She'd even gone further and told him that Jewish women didn't like to be with men during that time. That had made him feel proud, she could tell. She had treated him as a man, not a boy.

But she was the true misfit. Even if she wanted to, how could she fit in with people like Nancy Sanders? These fair-skinned well brought up English girls, war or no war, all they expected of life was to marry a suitable man and produce an endless stream of equally fair-skinned children. Well, there was no chance that she would find a suitable husband stuck out here in the country. She had heard there were many Jewish refugees in Liverpool itself but it was unlikely that one would stray in the direction of Laurel Bank. Not that she wanted a husband in any case. She wanted to work. But what could she do to help during the war? She felt so inadequate yet if she did do good work she'd be helping her own country's enemy. It was all so confusing.

Then she found the sewing machine.

On the days she spent wandering round the vast expanse of disused mill it unnerved her to see so much space going to waste. Selwyn had only renovated the Bell House, leaving the actual mill to stand gutted and empty. It looked magnificent and imposing from the grounds but inside the cavernous weaving rooms exuded a sense of desolation. The four floors above Selwyn's ground-floor studio cum sitting room were bare.

Yet it was here that Sassy found the peace and solitude she sought. She would sit for hours on the floorboards, glad of the light streaming in from the rows of windows on both sides, and try to imagine the activity in the weaving room when it had been in use. Sometimes she took her sketch pad and tentatively outlined some ideas for dresses even though she knew it was something of a futile exercise. For where would she find the material to make them?

One day, in exasperation, she had flung the pad against the wall only to see it suddenly appear to move. The force of the sketch pad had dislodged the door of a cupboard in the wood panelling that Sassy had never noticed before. And it was in that cupboard that she had found the sewing machine.

It was a Singer and it had to be at least fifty years old but it was a beauty. The mechanism was covered in a black japanned metal casing, exquisitely decorated with stencilled floral patterns, and the stand and foot-treadle were also patterned with scrolls and latticework. She had hauled it out of the cupboard and had barely been able to believe her good luck when she found a box of different coloured threads as well.

Later she found an old trestle table and with Barney's help she established her own sewing corner at the far end of the weaving room on the fourth floor where she would disappear each day to spend a few precious hours bringing her dream that one day she would become a dress designer closer to reality.

Her beloved Onkel Wolfie had been a tailor and he had taught her to sew when she was only nine years old. She could still hear the phrase he repeated over and over again as she struggled to master the shuttle and the treadle:

'*Du brauchst die Engelsgeduld Erfolg zu haben, Schatzi, nicht so schnell, nicht so schnell!*' Not so fast, little darling, to be successful you must have the patience of Job . . .

What would Onkel Wolfie think of her now in her baggy slacks, drab woollen jersey and mud-coloured turban covering her dark curls? She hated the depressing look of austerity in wartime clothing, the prevailing attitude to 'Make do and mend'. She longed for billowing skirts, dangling fur stoles, décolletages and silk stockings instead of the blue, green and khaki uniforms of women in the auxiliary forces, which she saw every time she ventured into the village.

But in June 1941 clothes rationing had come in with a vengeance and while George Thompson might still come up trumps with regular black market meat for them when it came to black market clothes he was useless. What irked Sassy more than anything was that she had the sewing machine, she had the patterns designed and ready to be cut out, all she lacked was the material.

'Why don't you use some of Selwyn's clothes?' Barney asked her. 'He's got masses and you could make them into all sorts of things, make some for me as well,' he added wistfully.

'How on earth do you know he's got masses of clothes?'

'I've seen them, of course, in his dressing room.'

'Barney, you've no right to go poking around. You shouldn't even be going near Selwyn's rooms while he's away.'

'Well, I got bored and he never said I shouldn't. Haven't you even seen his bedroom?'

'No,' said Sassy, not without some curiosity.

'Well, come and see it then, and you must see his bathroom. It's stupendous compared to ours.'

Selwyn's charges now shared the top floor of the Bell House where they had a room each and a rather primitive bathroom between them. The main staircase from the hall led only to Selwyn's suite of rooms on the first floor. Saskia had never asked Selwyn if he had redesigned the Bell House deliberately in such a way that he was cut off from the rest of the house nor had she ever dared to venture into his private sanctuary. Barney had clearly felt no compunction about having a thoroughly good snoop. Feeling distinctly guilty she followed him up the main staircase and into a large sitting room lined with books from floor to ceiling.

'I love this room,' said Barney hurling himself into one of the two leather armchairs in front of the fireplace. 'It smells so wonderful.'

Sassy sniffed the air. Cigars. Funny how the smell should still linger on so long after Selwyn had gone. She sneezed. There was dust everywhere. It was an untidy room filled with objects, lamps, decanters of whisky and brandy left lying around. To Sassy it seemed somehow oppressive, unwelcoming, but clearly Barney felt quite at home. After a while she realized why: it was a man's room. Selwyn's private domain. She wondered if any woman had ever been here before her.

'Now through here's his bedroom.'

She followed Barney into an almost monastic bedroom in complete contrast to the room they had just left. Just a large French wooden bed and a chair and a locker on one side of the bed with a flask still filled with water covered by an upturned glass. Barney pounced on a round silver tin and opened it. He withdrew a biscuit and nibbled it tentatively.

'Gingernuts. Selwyn's favourite. Only two left but they're awfully stale by now.'

Saskia stared at the spartan room, the neatly made bed. Barney followed her gaze.

'A double bed,' he said meaningfully. 'Listen, Sassy, I think you ought to come and see what he's got in his dressing room.'

There was a wall of cupboards, obviously specially designed, broken in the middle by an inset glass-topped dressing table on which were laid out ready for use ivory-backed hairbrushes, a tortoiseshell comb, a glass jar with a silver monogrammed top, filled with cotton wool, nail scissors and file, tweezers, a shoe horn, a clothes brush, boxes of cuff links and a small carriage clock.

But underneath the glass were sketches, Selwyn's sketches of her, naked. The ones he had used for his blessed chair. Then, as she turned and looked around the room, she screamed. They were everywhere, framed, pinned to the wall, propped up against the windowsill. He had kept every single one and brought them up here to his inner sanctum where he could savour them in privacy.

'Bit of a dirty old man, isn't he?' said Barney, not noticing how Saskia winced. 'Don't worry, I haven't touched them. He won't know we've been up here. But do look at all his clothes.' Barney started opening up the cupboards. 'I'm sure he won't notice if we take just a few of these.' Sassy stared at the rows and rows of coats, suits, jackets, evening clothes. It wasn't as if there was just one of everything. She counted at least four velvet smoking jackets, five or six grey flannel suits and several silk dressing gowns. Would it be stealing to take just one of each? Yes, of course it would. How could she even think of it?

'Now for the best part,' Barney called to her. 'Come and look at this.'

The huge white enamelled bath with claw feet stood majestically in the middle of Selwyn's bathroom.

'It has to be the biggest bathtub I've ever seen – not that I've ever seen very many,' said Barney. Dusty towels were still hanging over the wooden towel rail. A bar of Pears soap lay in a china dish on the rack across the bath beside a large Greek sponge and a long-handled brush for back scrubbing.

'Think about it, *Barneychen*, he'd need a big bath, wouldn't he? He was a big man.'

'Don't keep calling me that and why do you say "was"? He's still alive so he still is a big man.' Saskia smiled at his eternal optimism, his refusal to believe that anything bad could happen to Selwyn.

'Of course he is. Now come along, we shouldn't really be here at all.'

Barney grinned mischievously. 'I've had an idea. Just let me tell you about it, wait one second before you drag me away. I thought we could have a bath. Just one. He'll never know.'

Saskia could understand the temptation. The bathroom she shared with Barney was never exactly enticing. It was so small there was only room for a hip bath and given the five inch wartime water restriction it invariably became a footbath.

'Since when have you been so keen to have a bath?'

'Oh, come on, Sassy. You know what I mean. In this it'll be more like having a swim.'

'And how do you suggest we swim in five inches of water?'

'I've got it all worked out. We can share the water and that will make ten inches altogether.'

They ran the allowed five inches into the bathtub, then five inches more, and Saskia got in. It wasn't as if he'd never seen her naked. Then Barney began to take off his clothes. Before Saskia could stop him he had climbed into the bath with her. She stiffened as his naked body slithered down alongside hers.

'Here, I'll scrub your back,' Barney had grabbed the long-handled brush. They were sitting facing each other and he had to lean forward and across her to reach over her shoulder to her back. He steadied himself by putting his other hand on her shoulder. Out of the corner of her eye she could see him glancing down at her breasts every so often.

After a while she decided to challenge him: 'Why do you keep looking at them, Barney? It's not as if you haven't seen them before.'

'Sorry. I . . . before they were . . . I could never really see them properly. I don't know why but being so close I want to touch them. May I, Sassy?'

He doesn't really know what he's asking, she thought. *He genuinely wants to touch them out of curiosity. What can it hurt?*

'Go ahead,' she told him, 'but be gentle. They're quite tender, you know.'

Immediately his hand slipped off her shoulder and onto her breast. He stroked it clumsily for a while, then, as his touch grew more confident, he began to pull gently at the nipple, making it grow hard.

'May I try the other one?' he asked as if he thought it might be different. She nodded. But he didn't let go of the first one. He dropped the back brush, leaving him free to caress her breasts with both hands.

She loved it. Without thinking she glanced between his legs and saw his penis stirring. Did he know what was meant to happen? She didn't even really know herself. She might be older than he was but she had had no more experience.

He smiled at her happily. 'It's nice, isn't it? You feel lovely, Sassy.'

'Dearest *Barneychen*,' she whispered and drew him gently against her. They sat in the bath for a moment, their arms about each other, his blond head resting on the breasts he had just been stroking while she planted kisses in his hair. He was so right. It had been a wonderful thing to do to have a bath together. Somehow he always managed to find happiness on the greyest of days. She was really very lucky to have him. His parents were dead and he must miss them, but he never complained. Suddenly she felt a surge of pleasure rush through her, she wanted to hug him tight, bury her face in his smooth young neck.

'All right, now let's wash each other. Here, Barney, you take Selwyn's sponge. No, don't put soap on it, we'll never get it out, just sponge me down all over and I'll work up a lather and wash you with my hands.' After a moment she asked him softly: 'Barney, there, between your legs, do you know what's happened?'

He looked at her proudly.

'Of course I do. I've got a hard on, haven't I? So would any bloke lucky enough to be sitting in the bath with you, Sassy.'

'So you know all about it? Do they teach you at school . . . you know, about . . .'

'Heavens no! Look, Sassy, I'm sixteen. Some of the boys at school have actually done it. They've told me all about it.'

For a second Saskia was horrified. He seemed to know more than she did. Did that mean he had actually . . .

'Don't worry, Sassy, I haven't done anything yet, though one or two girls in my class let me feel their breasts. They weren't nearly as nice as yours though,' he added hurriedly.

She ran her soap-filled hands all over his back and down

over his buttocks. Tentatively she began to bring them round to his thighs. She allowed her nails to run up and down the inside of his thighs and he leaned back in the bath and groaned.

'Sassy,' he said, his eyes closed, 'wash me there.'

She dropped the soap in her surprise. Barney sat up and took both her hands in his. He placed her cupped palms around his erect penis and, clasping her wrists, moved her hands very slowly up and down.

'It's okay,' she whispered, 'you can let go. I think I know what to do but wait, I want you to do it to me too.'

She twisted herself around so she was lying beside him in Selwyn's big bathtub. She sank down into the warm water and reached for his hand, guiding it to her labia. She had accidentally discovered how to bring herself to orgasm a few years back but no one else had ever touched her there before. As he began to fumble inexpertly, she placed her hand on his penis and resumed the gentle rubbing motion. Within seconds they both climaxed, their bodies jerking in the water. Saskia held on to the side of the bath and cried out to Barney to keep on touching her and slowly he turned to face her and placed his lips on hers, but having never been kissed before, she did not know what to do and kept her mouth firmly shut.

Afterwards they dried each other tenderly with Selwyn's musky towels and after she had planted a quick kiss on his damp cheek and whispered, 'Thank you, *Barneychen*,' Saskia slipped away to her room leaving Barney alone in Selwyn's bathroom.

At supper that night they acted as if nothing had happened, discussing how many potatoes Barney would need to dig up in the morning, who would take Stella out for a run last thing and what was Saskia going to do about returning her overdue library book. After supper Barney disappeared to his room to do some homework. Later, when he got into bed, he lay there thinking about Saskia, the softness of her skin, her beautifully rounded breasts and how he had rested his head against them, her fingers stroking his hair. Then he began to go further, recalling what had happened next. He was so excited he came almost as soon as his fingers closed round his erection. He fell asleep, happy in the assumption that she was lying in the next room thinking about him too.

Saskia couldn't sleep. She knew that what she and Barney had experienced together was something unbelievably special. She wondered if he realized how much it had meant to her or had it just been a case of his boyhood dreams coming true? It was almost a question of the blind leading the blind. Should they do it again? Should they go further? She knew they should not. After all, he was only a . . . She stopped herself. She had been thinking he was only a boy but hadn't he proved to her that afternoon that he had become a young man capable of quite a powerful effect on her. Part of her was pleased, part was frightened. She knew the life she was leading was not normal, that she should be coming into contact with others of the opposite sex, people her own age. And in many ways Barney was still such a boy.

She thought about his suggestion that she use Selwyn's clothes as material to make others. Of course, it was out of the question, she couldn't possibly abuse Selwyn's kindness to her, although Barney was probably right when he said Selwyn wouldn't notice if she took a few things. But she'd know. It was bad enough she'd gone snooping around his rooms, taken a bath in his bathroom. She'd have to give the place a thoroughly good clean tomorrow, make sure they'd left no trace.

But what was she going to do about Barney?

She must stop worrying and turn her mind elsewhere – back to Selwyn's clothes. She wouldn't touch them but seeing them had reminded her that there was something she could do. She decided to abandon the idea of going to sleep altogether. She switched on the light and quickly put it off again. Yet again she'd forgotten the blackout. Standing on a chair she struggled to pin up a makeshift blackout curtain with the old blanket she used in her bedroom. She crept into Barney's room to see if he had remembered and saw that he had. She had imposed a curfew on going into the main part of the mill and turning on lights there after dusk. Imposing a blackout on all the windows of the weaving rooms would take them all evening. It was simpler never to go there at night.

Yet Sassy went there now, to her sewing room. She didn't turn on any lamps but fumbled around in the dark until she found an old trunk she'd installed there. In it she kept Maud Atwell's clothes. She had long since given up trying to alter them for herself. She was unable to make them look like anything other than what they were: clothes made for a tall woman cut down for someone considerably shorter. But what Barney had said about Selwyn's clothes could just as well apply to Maud's. She hated to do it to such beautifully made garments, but Maud would have no further need of them and there was no reason why she shouldn't use the wide lengths of material in the skirts and coats to make herself some new clothes.

She heard planes overhead and put her hands over her ears. They must be British planes and she knew she had nothing to fear from them, but she could not get it out of her head that they were probably on their way to drop bombs on Germany, maybe even on Berlin. She sat huddled in a corner for the rest of the night and as soon as dawn broke she grabbed her sketch pad and began looking for a design with which to begin.

Barney came looking for her at breakfast time. When he saw how engrossed she was he left and returned with a tray which he set down on the floor beside her. He'd made a pot of tea, toast and scrambled some dried egg.

'Last of the bread, this is,' he told her.

'Well, it has to be at least a week old. I'm surprised it

hasn't gone mouldy. Clever of you to toast it.' She joined him on the floor. 'Barney, what are you doing?'

He was spinning a knife. 'It's only a game we used to play at school in Liverpool. You ask the knife a question like which one of us will eat the last gingernut in Selwyn's biscuit tin and when the knife stops spinning, if it points to you, you do, and if it points to me . . . Oh, look, it's not pointing at either of us.'

'Quite right too,' said Sassy. 'Neither of us is going anywhere near that biscuit tin or Selwyn's rooms ever again, *verstehst du*, Barney? Yes? We had fun yesterday and that was fine but if we ever do it again we'd be doing something really wrong.' She tried not to notice his crestfallen expression, 'Now ask the knife another question.'

'I'm going to but I'm not going to tell you what it is, Sassy, otherwise it won't come true. You ask it one too but keep it to yourself.'

The knife seemed to take forever to stop spinning but when it finally came to a rest it was pointing at her almost accusingly.

'See?' Barney whooped with joy, 'What did I tell you? What did you ask it?'

'I thought you said it wouldn't come true if I told you?'

'And you want it to come true, Sassy, more than anything?'

'Oh yes,' she said, 'more than anything.'

But she did not see how it could possibly come true since she had asked which one of them would find someone to love by the end of the year.

Eight

Angela Appleby had been charged by her husband to summon his flock. Attendance at Matins was slipping. She had begun with an obvious target: the Air Force billeted at The Hall. An obliging wing commander had guaranteed to fill up a few pews.

'Thanks most awfully,' gushed Angela. 'It's only for an hour.' The Wing Commander couldn't help feeling that the vicar might not be tremendously impressed with his wife's recruiting style.

'Don't worry,' he beamed, 'we'll be there.'

It was Lady Sarah who reminded her about the twosome at Laurel Bank.

'They haven't been since Selwyn left eighteen months ago or more,' she pointed out. 'They've got no transport, poor things. I doubt Selwyn would entrust that girl with the Brough Superior. Anyway, when he went I imagine his petrol rationing went with him.'

'I'll collect them,' announced Angela, 'least I can do.'

'Well, for heaven's sake don't broadcast the fact, Angela my dear, otherwise you'll have half the countryside asking you for lifts and not necessarily to church.'

Angela could not have chosen a more opportune moment. Having worked frantically on the Singer to complete at least one outfit, Saskia was experiencing something of an anti-climax along the lines of being all dressed up and nowhere to go. Mrs Appleby's invitation to attend Matins would provide her with an audience who would appreciate her new clothes.

Angela Appleby's idea of dressing up was to exchange one Aertex shirt for another and her dungarees for a divided skirt. When she saw Saskia waiting outside the mill she nearly had a fit. Where on earth did the girl think she was going? Buckingham Palace?

Maud Atwell's pride and joy had been a voluminous scarlet cape that someone had brought her back from South America. Saskia had no way of knowing it had been a particular favourite of Maud's otherwise she would never have cut it up and used the material to make herself a very striking swagger coat. She had even added that something extra in the shape of a smart black velvet collar with enough stiffening in it for her to be able to turn it up to frame her neck. Her crowning glory was her hat – a jaunty little black felt box to which she had attached a veil covering her eyes and nose in an exceptionally alluring fashion. Barney couldn't stop staring at her. Suddenly she had been transformed from his Sassy into an elegant young woman.

'She looks a corker, Mrs A. Doesn't she look a corker?' he repeated over and over again.

Saskia had looked forward to the moment when she would enter the church but the wall of uniforms filling the pews at the back of the church took her by surprise. They all seemed to turn round at once and stare at her and one by one they started to smile and nudge each other. Barney swelled with pride at the attention she was getting as he accompanied her up the aisle and into Selwyn's old pew.

As Mrs Appleby began to pound the organ, Saskia stood up and glanced to her left. Their pew was directly opposite the Sanderses' and she knew she would never forget the delicious feeling of seeing the look of naked envy on Nancy's face across the aisle.

'Lovely to see you.' Lady Sarah's abrupt way of speaking was softened by the genuine smile on her face as she approached Barney and Saskia after the service. 'My word, you're looking awfully smart, my dear. Wherever did you find clothes like that with a war on?'

'She made them herself,' said Barney proudly.

'No! Really?' Lady Sarah peered a little closer. 'They don't look a bit home-made.'

'Well, they are. Aren't they, Sassy? Go on, tell her.'

'Tell Lady Sarah. Not *her*. Remember your manners, *Barneychen*. But, yes, he's right. I did make them.'

Barney scowled at the *Barneychen* and wandered off.

'And I designed them myself,' Saskia couldn't help adding.

'Admirable, simply admirable! Well done, Saskia. Jolly good show. Beautiful cloth too.' Lady Sarah felt the texture of the scarlet coat between her thumb and forefinger. 'I'd a coat of this colour when I was younger but the wool wasn't as good quality as this. Wherever did you find it?'

'Make do and mend, Lady Sarah. I cut up something belonging to a friend – a friend who died.' Saskia could tell Lady Sarah was dying to ask 'Which friend?' but her good breeding prevailed. Instead she said brightly: 'You haven't been over to see us, you and Barney. And you must. Now when shall it be?'

'It's just not fair! This bloody war, it's ruining everything.' Nancy's high-pitched voice cut through the babble of Sunday morning chatter. She had a group of airmen gathered round her. One of them stepped forward. 'What's not fair?' he asked.

'I can't come out. My season. I can't have one. The war's stopped it all. I can't be a deb.'

'Oh shame!' chorused the airmen and Nancy laughed prettily although Saskia could tell she was hoping to be taken more seriously.

She glanced slyly at her mother. 'Oh, do look. Mummy's talking to that German girl.' She lingered over the word German. 'And do you know what?' She had lowered her voice but she was perfectly aware everyone could still hear. 'She's Jewish.'

'So what? So am I.' One of the airmen had detached himself from the crowd and was challenging Nancy.

Nancy looked coolly at him. 'You don't look it,' she said, eyeing the airman's typically English features and fair hair.

86

'Well half, if you insist. Mother's not Jewish.'

'There you are then.' Nancy flashed him a brilliant smile.

'Oh, no I'm not. I'm half-Jewish and proud of it,' and with that he turned and sauntered casually over to Lady Sarah and Saskia.

'How do you do?' he held out his hand to Lady Sarah. 'I'm Flight Lieutenant Jonathan Rivers. No doubt you heard all that. Someone should teach that girl a few manners.' He smiled at Saskia.

'I quite agree and I'm the one who ought to do it. I'm her mother. Sarah Sanders. And this is Saskia Kessler, a visitor from Germany as my dear daughter has already told you.'

'I'm so sorry. I didn't –'

'My dear boy, of course you didn't.'

'Hello,' said Saskia shyly.

'I just wanted to say I'm sorry about what's happening in Germany. To us, I mean, to your . . . to Jews.'

'Thank you,' said Saskia.

'Goodbye, Mrs Sanders,' he held out his hand.

'Lady Sarah,' Saskia corrected him.

'Saskia, it's really not necessary.'

'Oh Lord, I've done it again, haven't I? We've taken over your house . . .'

'And I couldn't be more delighted,' Lady Sarah told him firmly.

He smiled quickly at Saskia, excused himself and fled.

'Well,' exclaimed Lady Sarah with satisfaction, 'that'll teach Nancy a lesson. What an exceedingly nice young man.'

'Yes,' said Saskia rather wistfully as he walked away from her, 'he is, isn't he?'

Over the next few months Saskia made herself four more outfits from material cut out of Maud Atwell's wardrobe. Since she didn't have anywhere else to show them off she wore them to church. Getting dressed on Sunday mornings became something of a ritual for her, followed by the lonely parade for Barney's benefit. He made her turn round and round in the hallway of the Bell House while he sat on the stairs and clapped and whistled. Then they huddled together listening for the sound of Angela Appleby's car coming up the drive. Often she forgot all about them and never turned up.

On the Sundays she did remember, Saskia found herself looking out for Flight Lieutenant Rivers in church. But she never saw him. Either he was away flying – did they fly on Sundays? – or he only went to church on the days Mrs Appleby forgot them. People had begun to notice her clothes and compliment her on them but somehow it wasn't quite the same. She knew deep down that while she had been sitting at her sewing machine she had been dreaming of wearing the finished outfit, sitting in a pew in front of him, turning every so often to meet his admiring gaze.

Then one Sunday Lady Sarah sailed up to her and announced she was going to give them a lift home to Laurel Bank. 'I've had an idea and I want to come and talk to you about it. Not perhaps the sort of thing one does on the Sabbath but never mind . . .'

'Could I offer you some lunch?' began Saskia tentatively, knowing it was a reckless offer. She hadn't a clue what there was to eat.

'No, my dear, I wouldn't dream of it. Nancy and I will come and take a glass of sherry off you if we may, and then we'll be off. It won't take long.'

Nancy! Saskia didn't want Nancy in her house. Correction: Selwyn's house. Nancy made to get into the front seat of her mother's shooting brake.

'No, Nancy. Let Saskia go in front. You can go in the back with Barney.'

'But, Mother . . .'

'Do as I say. Saskia's older than you are.'

Nancy glowered, climbed into the back and slammed the door. She sat as far away from Barney as she could as if she might catch something from him if she got too close.

Lady Sarah launched straight into her plan as she swung

the shooting brake at terrifying speed along the narrow lanes. 'We're having a dance for Nancy's birthday to make up for her not having a season. A small affair, of course, as there's not many young men around, but the Air Force has said we can use The Hall.'

'How exciting, Nancy.' Saskia turned to look at her. 'You must be thrilled.'

Nancy ignored her.

'Now here's where you come in, Saskia. I'd like to commission you to make a dress for Nancy specially for the party. And perhaps a few other items. As far away from utility as you can get. Just think what we can do to beat the coupons system. I'll give you plenty of old clothes of mine with yards of material so you can make Nancy something really beautiful. Now what do you say?'

'You want me to be your dressmaker?'

'Just for a while. I want to get in first. The word's going round, my dear. Those outfits you wear to church are causing a riot. Soon everyone's going to be coming to you. But just say you'll make a few things for Nancy first. You can be sure I'll make it worth your while.'

By the time they got back to Laurel Bank everything had been agreed. 'Would you still like to come in for a glass of sherry?' asked Saskia, knowing perfectly well they didn't have any. Mercifully Lady Sarah declined.

'Another day perhaps,' she said, strolling with Saskia to the door, 'now I'll drop Nancy off tomorrow morning at eleven for her first fitting. I'll go over to The Hall this afternoon and open up a few trunks, see what I can find that can be cut up.'

'But don't you want to discuss the design, see a few sketches?'

'My dear Saskia, I'm going to leave all that entirely to you. You can't imagine what a blessing it is to have found you. Of course,' she paused, 'you do have time, don't you?'

'Plenty,' Saskia reassured her. 'To tell you the truth, Lady Sarah, I've been wondering what I can do to help the war effort. I see everyone in the village working away and keeping cheerful but up here at the mill I feel as if the war is passing me by and there is nothing I can do to help anyone. I feel so guilty especially when my family must be suffering so much.'

'There, there, I know you do,' Lady Sarah put her arm round Saskia's shoulders. 'But look what you're doing for Barney. He's totally dependent on you. You're his mother to all intents and purposes. Mind you, I can see it's a strange set up and Lord knows what's going to happen to him after the war but for the time being you're all he's got. It's ludicrous for you to feel guilty about not being able to help. And now you're going to help me, in a perfectly frivolous cause I have to admit, but it will be such fun and heaven knows we all need some fun. There'll be those charming young airmen and the Air Force band has agreed to play although no one knows if they can play anything other than marches. We'll get out the gramophone, maybe Barney can be roped in to wind it up?'

'I'm going to start sketching now,' Saskia told her.

'That's the spirit. Expect Nancy tomorrow morning. Toodle-oo.'

Nancy's first fitting left Saskia tired and depressed. There was only one thing wrong with Lady Sarah's wonderful plan and that was Nancy herself.

Lady Sarah dropped her off the next morning and she strode into the hall and threw her coat at Saskia. Who promptly dropped it.

'Oh, you are clumsy, aren't you? You're supposed to take it and hang it up for me. Pick it up before it gets dirty. Now where do you want me?'

Out the door, thought Saskia, but said politely: 'If you will just follow me up the stairs I'll take you through to my sewing room.'

'I'm not going in there. It'll be freezing.' Nancy stood in horror in the doorway of the spartan weaving room.

'No, it won't. See, I've made a little fire in the grate. It's over there behind the screen. You can change there. Now if you'll just undress down to your slip I'll take your measurements.'

Nancy sniffed. 'I simply don't know what Mother's thinking of. Just because you've come to church ridiculously overdressed once or twice she's taken it into her head to hire you as my dressmaker. Normally I'd go down to London, of course, so you can count yourself extremely lucky.'

'Oh, I do.' Saskia had decided the only way she was going to get through this ordeal was to humour her client. 'Now,' she said, pulling her tape measure from around her neck, 'let's see . . . Stand up straight please.'

'Don't order me about!'

'I'm not ordering. I'm asking politely. Bust 34, waist 26, hips 32. Almost perfect proportions. You have a lovely figure, Nancy.'

'Miss Nancy to you,' snapped the girl.

Saskia took a step backwards and stared at Nancy in total disbelief at what she had heard. Then she recovered and continued: 'May I see the material your mother gave you? Thank you. Now what kind of dress did you have in mind? We have enough of this white lace here for me to cut a bodice with short sleeves and I could use this pink silk to cut a skirt on the bias. It would fall to your ankles.'

'Oh no, I want a skirt with yards and yards of tulle and a strapless bodice . . .'

'Nancy you cannot wear a dress like that in wartime even if I do have enough material to make it for you. What will people think?'

These appeared to be the magic words. Already it mattered a great deal to Nancy what people thought. She would not be able to bear it if anyone disapproved of her.

'Oh, all right,' she said sulkily, 'Do what you want. I don't suppose you've heard what people think about the clothes you wear to church?'

'Your mother tells me they're very well received. And they are made according to the regulations. It's just the materials that make them so special.'

91

'How long are you going to stay here?' Nancy changed the subject abruptly.

'Till Selwyn gets back to look after Barney. Till the war's over and I can go home to my family.'

'Where is your family?'

'Berlin.'

'You'll be lucky. We've been bombing it pretty hard, haven't we? Probably killed off all your family.'

Saskia shuddered. It was inconceivable that anyone could be so cruel. But she had to make some kind of reply. 'Probably,' was all she could manage.

'You shouldn't really be in this country at all, should you?'

Saskia looked up. 'Shouldn't I?'

'Well, you're the enemy, aren't you? You're German. Are you allowed to be here?'

'Of course.'

'What does it say in your passport?'

'Here, have a look at this sketch. It's only a rough design but I do think it would suit you.' Desperately Saskia tried to get her away from the subject of her passport. Nancy looked at it and shrugged. 'I suppose it will have to do. Not a patch on what I'm used to, of course, but if one can't get to London . . . When do I come for my fitting? The dance is in three weeks.'

Saskia seethed. She didn't want this obnoxious snob of a girl ever to come near her again but she reminded herself she was doing this for Lady Sarah and not for her daughter. Not for the first time she asked herself how such a 'perfect gent', as Selwyn had called Lady Sarah, could have produced such an unpleasant child. It must have something to do with the ever-absent father.

'If you come over in a week or so I expect I'll have something to pin on you.'

'If I must.' Nancy sounded bored. 'Now I'll get dressed and go to the lavatory. How do I get to it from here?'

'Oh, just go up the stairs till you reach the top of the house and turn left on the landing. It's right in front of you.

When you've finished perhaps you'd like to go down and wait in Selwyn's study. I've lit a fire there too. I'll make some cocoa and we can sit and drink it till your mother comes to pick you up.' And with that she walked out of the weaving room.

Five minutes later she carried a tray with two steaming mugs of cocoa into the study in time to see Nancy throwing something onto the fire.

'I don't drink cocoa,' she told Saskia sourly.

'Well, you could have told me earlier so I didn't waste it,' Saskia snapped, her patience beginning to wear very thin.

'You left the room so quickly I didn't have time to,' retorted Nancy, 'Ah, that sounds like Mother. Don't bother to see me out. You'd better get back upstairs to your work. I wonder what it's like to have to work for a living. I don't suppose I'll ever find out. Oh, and Saskia – that's your name, isn't it?'

Saskia just looked at her.

'You didn't answer my question about your passport. You're not in the country illegally by any chance, are you?'

She was gone before Saskia could reply. Shaking with rage, Saskia sat down on a footstool in front of the fire and pounded her temples with her knuckles. When the tension began to ease she looked up and sat staring into the grate.

A piece of white card was beginning to crinkle with the heat. Intrigued, Saskia reached out and flicked it away from the fire. It was already partially burned but once it had cooled down she was able to pick it up.

It was an invitation, hand printed – wartime economy – in a beautiful italic script:

> *Mr Geoffrey and Lady Sarah Sanders*
> *request the pleasure of your company*
> *at a party to celebrate the eighteenth birthday*
> *of their daughter Nancy*

followed by the date. Saskia saw her own name at the top. Instead of delivering it to her, Nancy had thrown it on the fire. If Saskia had not rescued it in time she would never have known that she too had been invited to the party.

'Just you wait, Nancy,' she whispered to herself as she stood up and placed her invitation on the mantelpiece above the fireplace, 'I'll make you the best dress you've ever had . . . but I'll make myself an even better one.'

Nine

Barney's mounting excitement as the day of the dance approached contrasted sharply with Saskia's apprehension.

Flight Lieutenant Jonathan Rivers was at the root of the problem. She had finally seen him again at church but the trouble was he hadn't seen her, or if he had he'd given no indication. And she had only herself to blame.

As well as Nancy's party dress Lady Sarah had commissioned Saskia to make her daughter a beautiful grey flannel coat and skirt with a smart piece of black velvet on the lapels. It was tight fitting with shoulder pads, showing off Nancy's tall slender figure to perfection. And it was the kind of outfit Saskia knew she herself could never wear. On top of this, making Nancy's clothes had taken up so much of her time that she had not been able to make anything new for herself.

Yet thanks to her, Nancy in her new suit made something of an impact on the Sunday morning before the dance and she had clearly decided to take advantage of this to move in on Jonathan Rivers. She invited him to sit with her and Lady Sarah in the Sanders family pew and on the way out of church she contrived to hook her arm slightly through his so they looked for all the world like an established couple. And what a splendid couple they made, thought Saskia, as she watched Nancy confidently throwing back her long blonde pageboy and laughing into Jonathan's face.

Saskia forced herself to sit in her pew till everyone had left. She couldn't very well run after the airman when

Nancy had him firmly marked out as her property. Besides, what could she say to him? I'm the girl you talked to for a second four months ago, you know, the Jewish one.

Now she was torn between very much wanting him to be there on Saturday night at the dance – when she would probably have to watch Nancy monopolize him – and the terrible disappointment she would feel if he were flying that night and could not be there.

'I'm going to dance every dance with you, Sassy, so don't worry, you won't be a wallflower,' Barney assured her sixteen times a day and she had to laugh.

She had been giving him very basic lessons in ballroom dancing every evening after supper. Round the kitchen table they went, one, two, three; one, two, three, while the wireless sputtered away in the background. It was the first time she had been close to Barney since the time in Selwyn's bath and she had to confess that it was not unpleasant despite his clumsy footwork. He was tall and blond and in the old dinner jacket of Selwyn's she had altered to fit him, she had to admit he cut quite a dash.

But Barney or no Barney, by Saturday her nerves were in shreds. Twenty years old and going to her first grown-up party. For all she knew, she might be thankful to Barney at the end of the evening if no one else came near her. On their first adult adventure she was glad of his presence, of the bond between them. Was this how it was to have a brother? She certainly felt a sense of sharing with Barney that she had never had with Christiane.

She was strangely reluctant to show off her dress to Barney, to go through the usual ritual of parading in front of him before they left. She flung a velvet evening cape of Maud Atwell's around her shoulders and hugged it to her so that nothing could be seen of the dress underneath.

At the last minute she did something she had never done before: she took the little key she had found in Maud's Chelsea dressing table and with it she opened Maud's jewellery box. Selwyn had had a letter from Maud's sister saying that in her will Maud had left her all her jewellery but until the war ended she would be grateful if Selwyn would keep it in his safe at Laurel Bank. Selwyn didn't have a safe at Laurel Bank so Saskia had kept the box at the back of her cupboard. She had been through its contents many times, and during the long bleak days before Barney had become her friend, she had amused herself for hours trying on this piece or that, imagining the fine clothes she would design to go with them. But she had never worn them outside Laurel Bank – until now.

She selected a pair of earrings and a necklace – rubies – and put them on. She had trouble with the diamond clasp of the necklace and pinned her hair up on top of her head to get it out of the way. Looking in the mirror she realized this was the only way to show off the jewellery to its best advantage and she swept her long dark hair up expertly into a chignon. In any case she knew it would have looked out of place for her to have her long hair down. Wartime hairstyles were short for practical purposes but Saskia had never been able to bring herself to cut her hair. Now in place the rubies stood out dramatically against her tiny earlobes and the pale skin of her long neck. Maud's cape had a hood with a red lining and when Saskia pulled this over her hair it added to the overall effect.

For a second she paused on the stairs and wished that Selwyn could see her – or her parents. But then she felt a familiar lump in her throat and lifting up her skirt she ran down to the hall and out to Angela's car calling to Barney that they would be late if they did not hurry.

She could not have been more wrong.

When they arrived at The Hall, Angela deposited them at the front steps and roared off down the drive to pick up other guests. Saskia and Barney walked nervously into the hall and were confronted with total silence.

'Doesn't sound like there's a party going on here. Do you suppose we could have got the date wrong?' asked Barney.

'Well, if we did why did Mrs Appleby pick us up tonight?' and then they both laughed remembering Angela Appleby's unreliable memory.

97

Just then a man in mess kit came running through the hall.

'Ah, now you must be . . .? We've already sat down, I'm afraid. Didn't realize there were any more to come. Actually, I'm just on my way to the . . . you know, so why don't you go on in. Dining room's down at the end of the corridor, last door on your right.'

'We've come for the dance,' Barney told him.

'Well, there'll be no dancing till we've had dinner. Probably won't get started till around ten, I'd say. Listen, hang on a tic, I'll be right back and then I can take you both in to dinner.'

He was back, literally, in a tic. 'I'm Smudger. Pilot Officer Gerald Smith but they call me Smudger. And you are . . .?'

'Saskia Kessler and Barney Lambert.'

He looked quizzically at Saskia for a moment and then stuck out both his elbows, inviting them to take one each.

Saskia would never forget the entrance they made when Smudger opened the double doors and propelled them into the dining room. A fifteen-foot mahogany dining table stretched before them, a sea of sparkling crystal, gleaming silver and soft candlelight emanating from a line of candelabra running down the centre of the table as far as Saskia could see. At least twenty-five people were seated round the table and they all stopped talking at once to turn round and stare at her.

'Found these two in the hall. Thought I'd better bring them along,' explained Smudger as Saskia suddenly realized there were no empty place settings for them to fill. Then to her intense horror a figure right in front of her rose from her chair and turned to face her.

Nancy Sanders, her fair hair newly marcelled and a pearl choker around her throat, confronted Saskia.

'Your dinner party must have finished terribly early. Who on earth were you dining with?'

'We didn't go to a dinner party,' said Barney before Saskia could stop him.

98

'No one asked you to dinner, did they? Well, this is my private dinner party. Did you bring your invitation to the dance, Saskia? You do have one, don't you?'

'Nancy, for heaven's sake shut up and find them places to sit. Poor things, they must be starving.' Lady Sarah came rushing down from the other end of the table. 'Lovely to see you, Saskia dear, and look at you, Barney, don't you look smart? Smudger, be a dear and take Saskia's cape.'

'Starving orphans,' murmured Nancy nastily and then gasped.

Everyone did.

As Smudger took her cape Saskia's dress was revealed for the first time. It made Nancy's white lace bodice and swirling pale pink silk skirt look like a child's party frock. Saskia had searched through Maud Atwell's clothes only to find that there was nothing suitable to make an evening gown. In desperation she had taken Barney up on his earlier suggestion that she raid Selwyn's dressing room and she had done so with a considerable amount of guilt. But she had found what she wanted: a wine-coloured silk dressing-gown. She had remodelled it to form the simplest evening gown imaginable and all the more effective.

Without the rubies it might have appeared that Saskia was dressed in a long dark red silk petticoat. Two slender straps held up the dress which, although respectably high in the front, plunged to a deep V down her back. The bodice clung to her exquisite elfin form and fell gracefully from her hips into a swirling skirt cut on the bias.

She looked, quite simply, breathtakingly beautiful and beside her Nancy was shown up to be exactly what she was: a young girl trying to look older.

But Nancy hadn't finished yet. Barney and Saskia found themselves at opposite ends of the table and Barney was clearly terrified. He was confused by the rows of silver on either side of his plate. He did not know which to use.

'What's the matter, Barney?' Nancy asked him sweetly. 'Don't know which one to pick up?' He nodded, not daring to look at her. 'It's quite simple. You just start with whatever's on the outside and work inwards.'

They had missed the soup and were now being served with chicken. Barney, remembering what she had told him, picked up his soup spoon. Nancy pounced.

'Oh, do look everyone, Barney's trying to eat his chicken with his soup spoon. Isn't he sweet?'

Barney flushed scarlet and picked up the knife and fork. Nancy watched him for a minute or two and then turning to the man on her right, said loudly: 'And he doesn't know how to hold his knife properly.'

'Nancy, that's enough,' snapped her mother. 'Barney, come and sit with us at this end of the table. Gerald, would you mind? Thanks awfully. Now, Barney, you take Gerald's chair. I remember my first grown-up dinner party, I was so frightened I knocked a glass of claret all over somebody's white dress. She was furious!'

As she prattled on, Barney caught Saskia's eye and she gave him a broad wink. Then she quietly cleared a space around her side plate and placed a knife in it.

'Let's ask it a question,' she mouthed at Barney. She never knew what Barney asked it but her own question was short and to the point: *Will anybody dance with me tonight?*

The knife seemed to go round and round forever but finally it came to rest and for a moment she thought it was pointing at Barney and she sighed, for hadn't Barney already predicted he would be there to stop her being a wallflower?

But then her gaze followed the point of the knife across the table and came to rest on a silk cummerbund and the studs on a starched white dress shirt. This couldn't possibly be Barney and when she looked up she found she was gazing straight into the openly admiring eyes of Flight Lieutenant Jonathan Rivers.

'I was wondering what had become of you,' was all he had time to say before a hand grasped his shoulder. Nancy, standing behind him, bent over to rest her cheek against his, pearl earrings to match her choker shimmering in the candlelight.

'Come along, Jonno, there's a spare seat beside me now. I've persuaded Gerald to move. Come down the other end of the table for pudding. It's much more fun,' and she looked pointedly across the table at Saskia.

'But your mother . . .' began Jonathan in protest.

'Oh heavens, Mummy won't mind a bit. Our dinner parties are always dreadfully informal. Everyone always gets up and down all the time. We love people to change places so no one gets stuck with an awful bore.' Again her gaze met Saskia's.

Saskia looked at Lady Sarah hoping she would do something to thwart Nancy's plan to spirit Jonathan away, but she was deep in conversation with the Wing Commander. Jonathan allowed himself to be dragged off by Nancy but not before he had given Saskia a surreptitious little wave.

Poor Smudger was wandering apprehensively round the table, clearly loath to sit down in case he was ousted yet again. Barney waved and patted the empty seat beside him. Smudger sat down with relief.

'I hope she knows what she's doing,' he told Saskia with a nod towards the departing Nancy.

'What do you mean?'

'Getting mixed up with Jonno . . .'

'You make it sound dangerous.'

'It could be. I wonder if she knows . . .' Whatever he'd been about to say, he changed his mind. 'It's just that he's fearless, is Jonno. He's our mascot. When you're flying with him you feel like you're on the Orient Express. He barely seems to notice Jerry, he's so busy talking about all the champagne he's going to drink at the Ritz next time he gets a weekend pass to London. Yet in our whole squadron he's Bomber Command's favourite. They're crazy about him.'

'Because he drops the most bombs on the Germans?'

'Yes, that's about it . . . Oh gosh, I'm most frightfully sorry. I didn't mean, I just never thought . . .'

'It's quite all right,' Saskia told him smiling. She couldn't help liking Smudger. It was perfectly clear he was entirely without malice and had not set out to upset her.

He turned to Barney. 'Now, young man, I hope you're going to help me serve the punch this evening.'

Saskia glanced down the other end of the table. Nancy had her arm draped around Jonathan Rivers' shoulders and was whispering something in his ear. Saskia turned away quickly so they would not catch her looking at them but even as she did so she could not help noticing that Jonathan was looking distinctly uncomfortable.

After dinner Nancy took her friends upstairs to powder their adolescent noses in her old bedroom only to find it had been requisitioned as an officer's sleeping quarters. Amidst much giggling they locked themselves in the adjoining bathroom. Saskia approached the closed door nervously and stopped dead when she heard snatches of the conversation from within.

'She's Selwyn Reilly's housekeeper, not his mistress, you silly.'

'Well, where did she get those jewels? Those aren't housekeeper's jewels unless she's a very special housekeeper . . .' Much laughter.

'And that awful dress. So common. How could anyone leave so much back exposed?'

'Better than the front.'

'She's a scarlet woman.'

'In more ways than one.' Hoots of laughter.

'And she's German.'

'And you know what?'

'What?'

Whispers.

'No! Seriously? However did she get in here tonight?'

'Mummy asked her. She's gone a bit over the top with her war effort.' Nancy's voice drawled above the others.

'Will Nancy ever learn?' A voice behind Saskia made her

102

jump. It was Lady Sarah. 'Come along, Saskia. We'll go and powder our noses in my room. They haven't dared put anyone in there. Now please don't go and take anything you heard Nancy or her silly friends say to heart. I have more to worry about than you do. She appals me, she really does. I've been thinking that nothing would give me more pleasure than to see her have a wonderful evening, to see her happy and dancing in the arms of a young man. I've been feeling quite romantic all week. But her behaviour so far tonight has made me wish I'd never bothered. Shall I tell you something, Saskia, you look so utterly adorable that I'm going to give this party tonight just for you. It'll be our secret but I want you to imagine that this is your coming out party, your début, the evening your own parents would have wanted you to have had they –' She stopped abruptly.

Without thinking Saskia flung her arms around the older woman. She knew exactly what Lady Sarah had been about to say: 'had they lived'. Why was it that the people who least wanted to hurt her always managed to put their foot in it, as the English said? She knew the answer. It was because they accepted her as if she were one of them and did not stop to remind themselves that she was German. Or Jewish. And she wouldn't have it any other way.

'Thank you, Lady Sarah. But tell me one thing: do you think my dress is common?'

'Not at all. But let me tell you why. Because you yourself are not common. You wear it like a lady. On another woman, someone who did not have your looks, your carriage, your sense of your own identity, I concede it might look cheap. But the simplicity of the cut is perfect for you, front and back. Now go and enjoy yourself. I said we should powder our noses, but of course the last thing you want is powder on that beautiful clear skin. But wait, there is one thing you do need, where is it? Here, give me your wrists . . .' and she sprayed Saskia with some scent. 'A little heavy for you perhaps but irresistible all the same. Guerlain's L'Heure Bleue. I've kept a little store in the cupboard of my bedside table. Don't tell Nancy. Now off you go, Saskia darling, have a perfectly blissful evening.'

And so Saskia floated down the main staircase of The Hall with a cloud of scent wafting after her. This was to be her evening.

An hour later she was sitting in deepest misery behind a pillar, watching the dancing in full swing before her.

Being an exotic had its disadvantages. The minute the guests started to arrive Saskia had known she would stand out all evening. Endless parties of fair-haired girls with healthy rosy complexions, broad shoulders and loud braying voices like Nancy's poured into the largest reception room at The Hall which the Air Force had gallantly converted into a ballroom for the night. They were accompanied by their escorts – gauche, well-bred youths, several sporting unsightly skin conditions, who were no match for their brash Air Force rivals. At first Saskia watched in amazement as the girls congregated at one end of the room to shriek and giggle together and the boys did the same at the other, trying to appear cool and nonchalant in front of the airmen.

True to their word the Air Force had indeed provided a dance band in the form of a bass, drums, a saxophone and a trumpet player. As they struck up the first number the boys began to shift about, shoot their cuffs, glance towards the girls, preparing themselves to dart across and lure their prey onto the dance floor. But the Air Force beat them to it. Between the county's own and the airmen, the girls were outnumbered two to one.

But no one asked Saskia to dance except Barney. He came padding across the dance floor towards her, attempted a formal bow and asked: 'May I have this dance, please?' He stood there, grinning expectantly, but she did not move. 'Sassy?'

She couldn't bear it. For nearly half an hour Jonathan Rivers had been dancing non stop with Nancy while Saskia sat there, the perfect example of that terrible thing, a wallflower. Yet she would make even more of a fool of herself if she danced with Barney who would probably push her round the floor whispering 'One, two, three; one, two, three,' and step on her feet. She looked at him and slowly shook her head, immediately deflating his puppy-dog excitement, and he stomped off to rejoin Smudger at the punch table. She saw Smudger ask him what had happened and watched as Barney proudly shook his head and refused to answer. When Smudger looked across at her she turned away but, when she looked back, he was having a word with the bandleader. Quite suddenly the music stopped and an announcement was made that the next dance would be a Paul Jones. Saskia couldn't follow the bandleader's words but then Smudger was standing before her, pulling her to her feet.

It was a strange dance. All the girls joined hands in an inner circle and danced round and round to the music facing outwards. The men formed a similar circle on the outside facing inwards, dancing in the opposite direction to the girls. When the music stopped each man had to dance with the girl facing him in the inner cirle.

Saskia's heart went out to Smudger. Suddenly she had a new partner for every dance. Airmen, boys, fathers, uncles – whomever she found before her when the music stopped promptly whisked her away.

But one person broke the rules. Saskia noticed that each time the music stopped Nancy picked up her skirt, raced around the circle till she found Jonathan Rivers and edged herself into position in front of him.

'One last time!' shouted the bandleader through his microphone and Saskia found herself opposite Barney. He began to back away before she reached out and gathered him to her.

'I'll explain later,' she whispered to him. 'I just couldn't dance with you then. I just couldn't, that's all. Now off we go, one, two, three . . .'

'I understand. It's just I couldn't bear to see you sitting

there all on your own. Smudger told me to do it. He wanted to come himself but he's in charge of the punch and couldn't leave it. Ripping chap, Smudger.'

'Oh, very ripping,' agreed Saskia, smiling. She hugged Barney to her, causing him, predictably, to tread on her toes. 'I do love you, *Barneychen*,' she whispered, 'I really do,' and was rewarded with a look of utter devotion on his face.

The bandleader was tapping the microphone again. 'Silence everyone, please. Can I have your attention, ladies and gentlemen. Tonight is Miss Nancy Sanders' eighteenth birthday. She's unlucky. She's turned eighteen while there's a war on but just for tonight let's forget about that, shall we?' This announcement was greeted by cheers round the room.

'Before we all sing "Happy Birthday" I have a surprise for you. In our midst we have a star. Besides Nancy, I mean.' Titters round the room. 'As you all know, many of our Polish allies have joined the RAF and we have one of them here with us tonight. His name is Ryszard Kosinski and I've been practising saying that for a week. He's going to play the violin for you tonight like you've never heard it played before. So top up your glasses and give a big warm hand for Ryszard Kosinski!'

The man who stepped out onto the makeshift stage was slight and not exactly charismatic. He looked down at the throng of young people scattered around the dance floor and blinked nervously. They stared back at him expectantly and one or two of the girls began to whisper rudely to each other.

Then he lifted his fiddle to his chin, picked up his bow and began to play. Very soon the whispering subsided. Ryszard Kosinski had everyone's attention. No one had a clue what it was he was playing – Polish folk songs, lively polkas and other more wistful melodies made all the more poignant by the plaintive strains of the violin.

Suddenly Saskia could stand it no longer. The sound of the violin brought back vivid memories of her mother playing to the family in the Zehlendorf apartment. She sensed Barney looking anxiously at her as the silent tears began to stream down her face.

'Why are you crying, Sassy?' he whispered, but she couldn't stop. She was out of control. Any minute now she would be unable to stop herself from breaking out into loud sobs.

She felt a hand in the small of her back propelling her forwards, pushing her towards the edge of the room. 'Keep going,' a voice murmured behind her, 'don't look round. I'll get you out of here.'

Ryszard Kosinski had now begun to play 'Happy Birthday to You' on his violin and Nancy's guests were singing along. She had been taken up onto the stage and the Wing Commander was poised to present her with a large bouquet.

'Now,' said Jonathan Rivers, moving in front of Sassy and taking her by the hand, 'while she's trapped up there and can't come running after me. I've been watching you. I don't know what's wrong but whatever it is I knew you couldn't hold out much longer.' They had reached the hall and the singing and laughter in the ballroom could only faintly be heard in the distance. They went out to the porch and stood at the top of the stone steps leading down to the drive. 'Now what would you like to do?'

She turned to him. 'Do you have a car?' He nodded. 'Then please would you take me home?'

'Home?'

'To Laurel Bank.'

He had a little two-seater sports car parked round the side of the house. He picked her up and lifted her into the passenger seat without even bothering to open the door.

As they sped past the front of the house and down the drive, two people were standing on the steps and the sight of them nearly made Saskia stop Jonathan Rivers from going any further.

As Nancy Sanders watched Saskia drive away with the very man she had earmarked for herself, Saskia knew from the look on her face that it would only be a matter of time before Nancy would seek her revenge.

But it was the total betrayal on Barney's face that stung her the most. She glanced at Jonathan. He reached out to take her hand and she knew that there was nothing she could do to stop herself going with him.

Saskia tried to pretend to herself that she was frightened because he was driving so terribly fast – and knew it was a lie. She was frightened, of that she was sure, but of what? When Selwyn had driven her up to Laurel Bank nearly four years before, she had been nervous but it had been a different kind of apprehension. She had been nervous of Selwyn and his gruff manner. And it had been her first week in England. Now she was an old hand, almost one of them – and yet she was still frightened. But it was a pleasant fear. She was excited. She knew something was going to happen and she could not stop it. She wanted it to happen but at the same time she was frightened because she did not know what to expect.

'Why do you keep darting those terrified looks at me?' asked Jonathan, releasing her hand to swing the wheel as they careered round a bend. 'I thought I was doing you a favour rescuing you from that ghastly party but now I'm not so sure. Do you want to go back?'

'No!' She grabbed his arm, almost causing an accident, then more quietly she repeated, 'No. It's just I don't know what you're going to do.'

'I'm going to take you home just like you asked me to. What else do you want me to do?' He grinned at her quickly before turning his eyes back to the road. She didn't answer. He gave her hand another squeeze.

'Well, come on, out with it. Are you afraid I might want to kiss you goodnight?'

'Will you?'

'Perfectly happy to. I've been thinking about it for quite some time. Long before tonight, in fact, but there was a rather large obstacle in the way in the form of Miss Nancy Sanders. Extraordinarily persistent, Nancy, and too young for my liking in any case.'

'You like older women?'

'Well, not much older than me but I like them to have a bit more experience than Nancy would have had.'

'Oh.'

'Anything wrong?'

'Everything.'

'How's that?'

'I have no experience at all, probably even less than Nancy.'

He stopped the car. 'You're joking?'

'I'm not. I've never even kissed a man.'

He turned around in his seat, leaned his head against the window behind him and stared at her. She looked back at him suddenly feeling totally relaxed. Now he knew her secret there was nothing else she could do but wait and see what he would do next. The more she looked at him the more she began to understand why people kissed each other. His fair hair seemed almost white in the moonlight and matched the silk scarf slung casually round his neck. He had donned his leather flying jacket over his evening clothes and the whole effect was one of studied nonchalance. He appeared to have all the time in the world, he wasn't going to hurry her, he was going to let her decide what she wanted to do.

She knew exactly what she wanted to do. She wanted to kiss him and she did not know of any rule that said she had to wait for him to kiss her first, so she moved her body awkwardly across the gearshift, put an arm around his neck to bring his face down towards hers and placed her lips on his cheek.

It felt all wrong. She moved her face away a fraction of an inch to gauge his reaction. Nothing. She tried again, this time moving her lips a little nearer his mouth.

'Was that supposed to be a kiss?' she heard him mutter in her ear. 'Come here, I'll show you what a kiss is.'

He moved quickly so that his lips were full on hers. His arms came around her and his fingers massaged the back of her neck and gripped the base of her skull, pressing her face forward into his. All the time his lips moved on hers, brushing them back and forth, sucking on them, gently probing them open. Then she could feel his fingers tracing the outline of her mouth, her jawline, her eyebrows and down to the inside of her ear. He tickled her there and she shuddered. It was delicious and she smiled in surprise. The moment her mouth opened his tongue was inside, licking, moving it round until she instinctively brought her own tongue to meet his.

She felt she could go on forever. Eventually she felt him slowly pull away and move her head to his shoulder. She buried her face in his neck as he unpinned her hair and pulled it down her back, running his fingers through it like a comb.

'Did you like that?' he whispered.

'You know I did.'

'Sit back now. I'll take you home.'

Disappointed she withdrew herself from his arms and sat rigid in the passenger seat.

'Don't sulk. Don't forget I still have to kiss you goodnight. Is there anyone else there tonight . . . where you live?'

She shook her head.

'What about that Selwyn chap who looks after you?'

'He doesn't look after me. I'm a grown woman.'

'A grown woman who's never been kissed. They ought to put you on show in a museum.'

'Well, anyway, he's away at war.'

'Ah! Away at war, is he? I do a bit of that myself.'

'Oh, of course you do, I didn't mean . . .'

'All right! All right! Keep your hair on. Now you'll have to direct me from here. I've never been to, what's it called? Laurel Bank?'

*

110

Saskia lost her virginity on the bare floorboards of her sewing room. The moonlight streaming in through the enormous windows bathed their bodies in an ethereal glow. She took Jonathan there without hesitation. It never occurred to her to invite him into Selwyn's study or even to her own bedroom. She did not turn on any lights, just led him up the dark staircase to the fourth-floor weaving room, *her* room.

They did not say a word to each other. She slipped out of her red dress and stood naked before him. He dropped to his knees and clasped her to him, pressing his head to her soft round belly. She stroked his fair hair and he lowered his face to slip his tongue between her legs. He was an expert and knew just when to withdraw it from her clitoris, when she was absolutely ready for him to enter her. She was not his first virgin and he knew it would hurt her so he was gentle. But he was not prepared for her uninhibited cries of passion after her first little yelp of pain.

And she wanted more. Time after time he made love to her until the hard floorboards began to abrade their naked limbs.

'Well, Barney, did you have a good time? Your first grown-up party, was it? I do believe I saw you on the dance floor . . .'

Angela Appleby prattled on as she drove past the weir and up the drive to Laurel Bank. Barney had not said a word the entire journey home. He was utterly miserable. Sassy had run off and left him. He had never felt such an idiot in all his life. All right, so he had calmed down after his initial euphoria following their bath together. He hadn't expected that to happen again but he had felt a closeness with Saskia. He wanted to kiss her again and had even dared to think that outside in the moonlight at some point during the party might turn out to be the perfect opportunity. And now she had gone off with someone else. An airman. Older than him. She probably thought he was still a boy in spite of what he had done to her in Selwyn's bath.

'I'll take a cup of cocoa off you if you've any milk, Barney,' Angela Appleby announced just as Barney thought he was rid of her. 'I'm so cold, I need warming up before I drive back.'

Barney put the milk in a saucepan to heat on the Aga. He could only find one mug. Damn Sassy! She had a terrible habit of taking her mugs of coffee up to her weaving room and leaving them there. Every so often he had to go and collect a row of dirty mugs and bring them down to the kitchen.

'Back in a mo,' he mumbled to Angela Appleby but she followed him, obviously keen to see how they were keeping house in Selwyn's absence.

Barney swore again under his breath and ran up the wide stone steps with Angela puffing behind him. As he reached the floor of Saskia's sewing room he stopped. He could hear something. He motioned behind to Angela to stop.

It was a cry. A moan. Saskia! Saskia was crying out for help. But then Barney heard a man's deep voice saying softly: 'You love it, you absolutely love it, don't you.'

Barney pushed open the door and almost cried out in misery.

There on the floor in front of him lay Saskia naked, and lying on top of her was Jonathan Rivers, moving himself up and down, in and out of her. Saskia was clutching him to her, shaking her head from side to side, biting his earlobe.

Angela Appleby reached the top of the stairs and before Barney could stop her she had come into the room behind him.

'Good heavens above, how perfectly disgusting! Barney, come away from there. You shouldn't see things like this. Perfectly disgusting!'

Saskia heard her. She looked over Jonathan's shoulder and saw the wretched look on Barney's face before Angela Appleby marched him away.

Ten

Angela Appleby was a born gossip. She thrived on it, much to the horror of her husband who implored her to be more discreet. Within two days everyone within a five-mile radius of Laurel Bank knew what Angela had seen there. Nancy was the third person to hear about it from Angela and she made sure the word spread fast from then on. That German girl was nothing but a trollop. A Jewish hussy.

Saskia, sitting happily at her Singer, was blissfully unaware of the gathering rage against her in the outside world. The only thing that was giving her cause for concern was the fact that Barney would not speak to her.

'Well, *Barneychen*, did you enjoy the party?' Sassy had come downstairs the next morning whistling, and had literally danced into the kitchen.

Silence.

Saskia ignored him. The only way to deal with the situation was to act as if nothing had happened last night. 'Feed Stella for me, will you, while I make us some breakfast. I'm absolutely starving.'

'Stella's not here,' he replied at last, 'You may remember I couldn't find her last night. I looked everywhere but then you called to say we had to hurry so I left for the party without finding her. She must have got out. She's probably been out all night.'

'Well, you know what that could mean, *Barneychen*?'

'Haven't a clue and don't you dare call me by that stupid name ever again.'

113

'It'll probably mean lots of little Stellas. What's that word you use? Ripping!'

For two whole weeks Saskia sat at her sewing machine by the window in her weaving room waiting for the sound of the telephone or Jonathan's sports car coming up the drive. On the Sunday of the first week she spent an hour getting ready for church, but it turned out to be one of the weeks when Angela Appleby forgot all about them. As she would on all subsequent Sundays.

In the middle of the third week Saskia heard a car coming up the drive and rushed to the window. To her amazement she saw that it was Lady Sarah's shooting brake. She ran downstairs and out into the driveway. As Lady Sarah stepped out Saskia flung her arms round her.

'You can't possibly know how glad I am to see you. I was beginning to wonder if I would ever see you again. Mrs Appleby hasn't been able to bring us to church these past two weeks.'

'No, I don't suppose she has,' said Lady Sarah drily, 'May we go inside, Saskia my dear? I need to have a talk with you.'

'Is it something serious? Has something happened to Selwyn?'

'Calm down. Nothing like that. Perhaps I might have a cup of tea?'

'But of course. Come into the kitchen while I make it.'

Lady Sarah noted with satisfaction the clean and ordered state of the kitchen. There was a pleasing smell of freshly laundered linen, and looking up she saw the sheets draped across the old wooden drying rack hanging from the ceiling. An ironing board stood to one side with some of Barney's clothes ready for pressing. At the kitchen table a place was already laid for his tea and she could smell a jacket potato cooking in the oven. Really, she thought to herself, Laurel Bank appeared to be considerably better run than the Vicarage.

'I must thank you for that wonderful party. Barney and I had such fun.'

'And I must thank you for Nancy's dress. I don't imagine she's had the grace to thank you herself.'

'How is Nancy?'

'Oh, my dear, you don't have to be polite with me. Why should you care? No, really, I know that sounds harsh but you have to admit she is going through a particularly bad stage at the moment. She can be quite unbearable at times.'

'You mean she isn't always like this?'

Lady Sarah pulled a face. 'Well, actually, now that you mention it, I have to confess she's always been a bit of a brat. Thank God I have another daughter on whom to pin my hopes. Nancy always was her father's favourite in any case. Now, Saskia, sit down here with me and listen. I've got something rather unpleasant to say to you and if I had the choice I wouldn't say it at all. But you're going to hear it sooner or later and I had the feeling you'd rather hear it from me.'

Saskia was beginning to look distinctly nervous.

'It's about that young man, Flight Lieutenant Rivers.'

Saskia said nothing.

'There's a rumour spreading like wildfire that he brought you home from the party and you let him spend the night here.' She paused to look enquiringly at Saskia. Saskia nodded. Lady Sarah sighed. 'I wish that was all there was to it but Angela Appleby's been saying she saw the two of you naked together and that Barney did too. Is that true? Angela's always been the most frightful tittle-tattle, it's sheer folly to believe everything she says.'

'No, it's quite true,' cried Saskia, 'but it's perfectly all right. Barney's fine. All he was concerned about was that I was all right and I couldn't have been more so.' Saskia was astonished that she could tell lies so easily. It had been days since Barney had come anywhere near her.

Lady Sarah smiled and patted her arm. 'I'm sure you were, dear Saskia. The way I look at it is that if it seems all right to you, never mind how it looks to anyone else, go right ahead.

115

The trouble is very few people think like that, especially in a small rural community like ours. It's not as if we're in a city like Liverpool or Manchester, or even London. Most people care desperately what other people think, they find it far more important than what they themselves believe. Ridiculous, isn't it? And in the country it's far harder to keep what you do to yourself. You see, making love with a man – you did make love with him, didn't you? I thought so – well, it's not considered the done thing before you're married. Perfectly all right by me, my dear. I always did as I liked and had tremendous fun twenty, thirty years ago, but that's another story. But you see there's talk about you all over the place at the moment and in Selwyn's absence I really do feel it's my duty to protect you.'

'Do you see Jonathan at all?' Saskia let it slip out as casually as she could and held her breath, waiting for Lady Sarah's answer. She would have to hold back a flood of questions if the answer were yes: Where was he? How was he? Why hadn't he been to see her? Had he been seeing Nancy?

'No, I haven't seen him. Saskia, do you really care for him?'

'Care for him?'

'Yes. Or was that night just a bit of fun?'

'It was my first time. The first time I had ever . . . you know . . .'

'Oh, my poor child.' Lady Sarah moved her chair closer and put her arm around Saskia's shoulders.

'Where is he? Why hasn't he been to see me? Has he been flying all this time? Do you know anything?'

'He has been flying rather a lot recently as it happens, but I'm afraid that's not the reason he hasn't been in touch. His Group Captain came to see me. Now, Saskia, you have to understand that these young airmen are most awfully brave. They could be killed each time they go up. Oh Lord, that was a stupid thing to say, wasn't it? But, you see, it means they feel they have to live life to the full when they're here. They're under the most terrible strain; you can't really hold them responsible for some of the things they do.'

Saskia looked at her. 'Like what? Making love to impressionable young virgins?'

'Worse than that,' said Lady Sarah. 'I don't think his Group knows about you. He came to see me because he thought that Nancy had fallen for Jonathan.'

'But why should he need to come to see you about it?'

'Brace yourself, my dear. He thought I ought to know that Flight Lieutenant Rivers is married with two young children.'

Barney was delighted by the news. He arrived home from school and heard Lady Sarah's voice in the kitchen but just as he was about to join them he heard her say, 'He came to see me because he thought Nancy had fallen for Jonathan.' Feeling rather guilty, he hovered outside the door until he heard that Jonathan was married. Then he slipped away. He stayed in his room long after he heard Lady Sarah's car racing down the drive. Let Saskia come to him if she needed consolation. And she would. He had no doubt of that.

Barney was not spiteful by nature but he had been badly hurt by Saskia's infatuation with Jonathan Rivers. Ever since the bathroom episode he had lived in hope of a relationship blossoming between him and Saskia. When nothing happened immediately he put it down to embarrassment on Saskia's part but he had pinned all his hopes on holding her in his arms all evening at the dance and leading her out into the moonlight at which point they would . . . There had been no part in his dreams for Jonathan Rivers.

Sure enough, after about an hour, there was a timid tap on his door.

'Okay, come in,' he said casually, keeping his back to her as she came into the room. When she didn't say anything he turned round and saw that the tears were streaming down her face and she was gesticulating helplessly at him, as if she was trying to tell him something. Suddenly he was stricken with remorse. This was his Sassy and she was suffering. Without

117

saying a word he stood up and she ran to him and clasped him round the waist, her face buried in his chest. He looked down on her raven curls. She was so tiny, so fragile. How dare that cad deceive her?

Slowly he brought his long arms out from behind his back, unclenched his fists and cradled her head against him.

'Don't fret, Sassy. I love you. You know I do.'

And Saskia cried all the more because while she knew Barney loved her she also knew that life was unfair because instead of loving him back, she loved Jonathan.

Saskia didn't know how she would have got through the next few weeks if it hadn't been for Barney. She was almost inconsolable. It was as if she had waited until now to give in to the anguish she had been feeling about the loss of her parents – for they were dead, she was convinced of it by now – the loss of her nationality, of her identity and now of trust in someone she had hoped would be there specifically for her.

Barney treated her rather like he treated Stella. He patted her, fondled her ears, tried to get her to go for walks, allowed her to curl up with him at night and cry herself to sleep. He placed bowls of food in front of her and sat beside her till she ate. Half the time she was barely aware of what she was eating. Mostly it tasted disgusting but what else could she expect from poor Barney who had never had to cook before. After a while she began to throw it up and tried not to see the hurt look in his eyes.

After about a month she was able to stagger up to her weaving room and sit staring at her Singer. She didn't even raise her head when Barney came running up the stairs one morning shouting in excitement: 'I've been watching Stella. She's getting fatter, Sassy. It's happened. She's going to have puppies. I say, Sassy . . .?' He blinked unhappily as she burst into loud sobs.

'The thing is, Barney,' she explained when she had calmed down, 'so am I.'

*

They had to tell someone so they told Lady Sarah on her next visit. She was not at all shocked, merely saddened by Saskia's circumstances.

'There is nothing we can do for the moment but nearer the time I shall be there to help you through it. Meanwhile, I shall take you to see my doctor upon whose discretion we can all count. I shall visit you every week and if there is anything wrong we must rely on Barney to get a message to me via the school. Whatever you do, don't telephone me at the Vicarage. Angela listens in. So does the party line for that matter and we don't want it all over the village. Of course my darling daughter Nancy must never, never know.'

'But who'll tell that bounder he's going to be a dad?' persisted Barney.

'If you mean Jonathan, I will,' said Lady Sarah, highly amused by the 'bounder'.

'No, I must,' protested Saskia.

'But how? My dear, you must accept that he won't be coming here any more. He's heard the gossip. I can't pretend to know anything about his character but even if he thought the world of you he'd know the best thing he could do for you would be to leave you alone.'

'Well, will you tell him for me? No, wait a minute, perhaps you could talk to him and ask him to come and see me. He'd do it if you asked. Tell him I have something very important to say to him but that I won't bother him after that, I only need to see him once.'

'I'm not sure it's going to solve anything if we tell him,' sighed Lady Sarah, 'but I suppose he has a right to know. I'll see what I can do. Now, first things first, Saskia, how are you in yourself? Any morning sickness? Yes? Well, I know it's rotten but it won't last forever. Try to keep walking regularly to the village to do your shopping until you begin to show – and even then you can wear a loose coat and no one will see. The exercise will be good for you and don't forget you'll be able to get extra coupons for pregnant women.'

119

'But if I'm to keep it a secret, how can I?'

'Oh, don't fuss, Saskia. I'll find a way. My doctor will help.'

There was something about Lady Sarah: both Saskia and Barney knew they could rely on her, that she would always 'find a way'.

True to her word she contacted Jonathan and the very next day he turned up to see Saskia.

Saskia ordered Barney to keep out of sight but she knew there was no way she could force him out of the room if he chose to stay. Thus she was immensely relieved when Jonathan suggested going 'for a spin in the motor' as if nothing had happened. Barney emerged into the hall.

'I hope you've got the hood up,' he said very seriously. 'Sassy mustn't catch cold.'

'Of course I have. Don't worry, Barney.' He turned to Saskia. 'Honestly, he's worse than a nanny.'

On impulse Saskia kissed Barney briefly on the cheek before she left. 'I'll be fine,' she whispered, 'I'll be back soon.'

As Jonathan drove off down the drive at top speed they passed the shooting brake coming up to Laurel Bank.

'Oh, there's Lady Sarah come to see us. Funny, she's not due until tomorrow. Shame to miss her. Well, no doubt Barney will make her some of his undrinkable tea.'

'That wasn't Lady Sarah,' Jonathan told her, 'it was her car but Mrs Appleby was at the wheel and Nancy Sanders was sitting beside her.'

'We've come to see Saskia but we've just missed her, haven't we?' said Nancy meaningfully as Barney let them in.

'Does she go out with Flight Lieutenant Rivers often?' enquired Angela conversationally.

'No,' said Barney. He knew he must not give anything away.

'Does he come here much then?'

'No. Not at all.'

'Not what we've heard. Aren't you going to offer us some tea?'

'No . . .' began Barney instinctively and then, 'Yes, yes, of course.'

'I'm going to wander up to Saskia's sewing room and have a look at her materials, see if she's got anything I can get Mother to commission to make for me.' Nancy was starting up the stairs.

'Oh, no, I don't think you'd better . . .' began Barney.

'Nonsense. I'll do what I want. It's not your place to tell me what to do in Selwyn's house, young man.' She was up the stairs before Barney could say anything.

'Tea?' prompted Angela, as Barney was about to go after her. 'In the kitchen maybe?' She wanted to take a good look at Saskia's housekeeping.

'China or Indian?' asked Barney.

'China,' snapped Angela, 'and put that dog out. It's made the most revolting smell.'

Barney ignored her. They had two cups of tea and there was still no sign of Nancy. Angela had had time to see that, much to her annoyance, everything was spic and span. She couldn't fault Saskia on her housework. Now she was getting bored.

'Go and find Nancy, there's a good lad, otherwise we'll be here all night.'

'I'm not really a lad any more, Mrs Appleby.'

'Well, you are to me. Go on, I'll come with you. We'll take her a cup of tea before it gets cold.'

'I've found it,' said Nancy triumphantly when they reached Saskia's sewing room.

'Found what?' asked Barney rushing into the room. 'What have you been doing? Why are Saskia's things all over the place? You have no right to go through her things.'

'Oh, do be quiet, Barney.' Angela pushed him aside. 'What have you found, dear?'

'Evidence. All the evidence we need.'

'Where?'

'There.' Nancy pointed to Saskia's passport lying on the trestle table beside the Singer. Angela picked it up, glanced quickly through it, smiled at Nancy and said, 'Clever girl!'

'You can't take that.' Barney snatched it out of her hand. 'Sassy might need it.'

'We wouldn't dream of taking it, would we, Mrs Appleby?' purred Nancy, 'and you've made me a cup of tea. How adorable you are. Now, I'll just take a few sips and then we must be off. Do give our love to dear Saskia and tell her I'll be by for a fitting soon. You won't forget, will you, Barney?'

When Barney had seen them safely out of the house and heard the shooting brake roar away down the drive he raced upstairs to look at Saskia's passport. He soon found the incriminating words: *Permitted to land at Harwich on 4 May 1939 on condition that the holder registers at once with the police and that she does not remain in the United Kingdom for longer than twelve months.*

It was now 1943. But, Barney reflected as he cleared up Saskia's things and tidied them away, they hadn't taken the passport away so there was no cause for alarm. Was there?

Eleven

'What's the matter, Saskia? We've been driving for ten minutes and you haven't said a word. I don't think you've been listening to anything I've said either. What's on your mind, for heaven's sake? It's not every girl gets taken out for a spin, you know? Petrol's hard to get hold of these days or maybe you hadn't heard? Look, I'm going to stop the car until you remember I'm here.' He slowed down and pulled over onto the verge in a quiet lane.

'It's Nancy.'

'What about her?'

'I should have made you take me back. She should never be allowed into Laurel Bank while I'm not there. Even while I am there . . .'

'Nancy Sanders? Why ever not? She's harmless enough.'

'How can you say that? Don't you remember what she was doing when we met? How you rescued me . . .?'

'. . . From a bit of perfectly harmless Jew baiting as far as I can remember. She's just a child, Saskia, she barely understood what she was doing. Anyway, I only got involved because I wanted an excuse to find out who you were. You made quite an impression on me. Don't pretend you don't know it.'

'But you told her you were Jewish too.'

'Did I really? How boring of me.'

'*Boring*? Is that all being Jewish means to you?'

'Steady on. Look, I'm genuinely sorry about what's happening to the Jews in Europe at the moment. Who

123

wouldn't be? It's grotesque. But I can't pretend to be one of that lot.'

'What "lot" are you then?'

'Well, *Anglo*-Jewish, I suppose.'

'And they're different?'

'Oh, hell, I don't know. I think they are, but what do I know? I feel different to European Jews, all those people who've been coming here over the last ten years. They seem more intellectual somehow. I mean I know my grandfather was very learned in the Talmud, or so I was always told on the odd occasions Father actually remembered he was Jewish, but it doesn't seem to have had much bearing on the rest of us. My family have been here for years, came over at the beginning of the century from the Ukraine. And that was only my father's family. Mother's not Jewish so I suppose I'm not really either. We're not orthodox, far from it. Father's family changed their name. It used to be Rifkin or something like that. Father let it slip once when he'd had a few too many. Made me promise not to tell Mother.'

'But Rifkin's a fine name. Why did they change it? What's wrong with it?'

'Nothing really, except it sounds too Jewish. Rivers is better. We're completely assimilated now, of course.'

'Assimilated?'

'Into English society. We're part of it now. We don't stand out at all and no one even knows we're Jews. My father married out deliberately. Mother was rather a good catch, actually, daughter of a baronet. He never suspected a thing. James Rivers. Who would have guessed with a name like that, and he certainly didn't look Jewish. Nor do I, for that matter.'

'And I suppose your children don't even know what the word means?'

'Who told you?'

'Lady Sarah.'

'I suppose she told you I was married too?'

'Married *out*?'

Jonathan laughed and to her surprise Saskia did too. He reached out and drew her into his arms.

'So that's what's been wrong with you? Finding out about my marriage?'

'Why didn't you tell me? Why haven't you been to see me?'

'Slow down. One thing at a time. I've thought about coming to see you but I heard all the talk that was going around and frankly I was a bit nervous. Rather a responsibility, taking a girl's virginity, you know? Anyway I've been flying. There's too much cloud today so I came straight over, didn't I?'

'Liar. Lady Sarah asked you to come and see me. Why have you lied to me, Jonathan?'

'I haven't lied to you. I never told you I wasn't married.' He stroked her hair and continued. 'She's very stuck up, my wife. Not much fun. We were sort of pushed together when we were very young. We've only been married five years but already I know it's never going to work. This war's been a bit of a blessing, tell you the truth. Given me a chance to get away from her. Why do you think I'm so popular with Bomber Command? It's obvious, isn't it? I haven't got anything left to lose. I don't care if I don't come back and that makes me take more risks than most chaps. I said my wife was stuck up – well let me tell you how bad she can be. Just before the war we had a telegram from Warsaw. It seems a few Rifkins strayed into Poland instead of coming to England. Of course, my wife couldn't make head or tail of the telegram and threw it away. Next thing we knew this couple turns up. Refugees, just like you, falling all over us, begging us to take them in. But my wife slammed the door in their faces and started making a terrible scene, upsetting the children. She wouldn't even unlock it when they were still there after dark, hammering at the window panes in the pouring rain. I'll never forget her words: "Be firm, Jonathan, we can't let people like that near the children. Bloody cheap trick, pretending to be relatives of ours." So you see why I feel I can't go back. On my leaves I stay here or go to London and paint the town.'

'Do you suppose that's why you were drawn to me?

Because I'm the real thing?' Saskia asked, not entirely joking.

'Who knows? But I certainly noticed you. I was nearly going crazy at that dance. I thought I was never going to be able to slip away from Nancy's clutches. She's not unlike my wife in many respects, you know.'

'What about your children? Don't you miss them?'

'I'll never let it get as far as that. Still always see them whenever I want. To be honest the more I think about it the more I doubt whether she'll give me a divorce. Think of the scandal! The old man, my father-in-law, he wouldn't like that. But one thing I do know, I won't be going back to live in the same house as her.'

'Maybe you'll meet someone else, have their children – Jewish children by a Jewish mother . . .' She should tell him. Now. Why was she hesitating?

'Maybe. Maybe not. It's not that important to me whether my children are Jewish or not. Try to understand, Saskia. I told you, I'm not orthodox, not remotely. I've never been inside a synagogue in my life. Don't look so shocked. You're bound to feel oversensitive. Think about it. You feel guilty. You've escaped. You got out and your parents . . . well, who knows?'

'Who knows?' she echoed quietly, clinging to him.

'Whichever way we look at it you and I – oh, yes, you too, Saskia – are very lucky Jews. We can choose whether or not we want to be Jewish, we're not ghetto Jews, herded together in one place . . .'

'Speak for yourself. I look so Jewish, I can't escape even if I wanted to.'

'So what are you going to do with yourself? You see, my little one, I think I care about you but you have to see that it's very early days. You must not depend on me. I can see how very easy it would be for you to do that. You're all alone in a way. Subconsciously you must be looking for someone to lean on. It can't be me, do you see? Later, maybe, when the war's over, but not now, it wouldn't be fair . . .'

'Wouldn't be fair? Fair to whom?' Saskia pulled away

from him and shouted in his face. 'You make me sound like some deserted orphan you've found wandering in the bombed out ruins. I'm a survivor with or without you.' As she spoke she realized the truth in what she was saying and it gave her strength. 'Maybe I would like someone to lean on but what I am aware of is that I already have someone who depends on me: Barney. And I feel responsible for him which is more than you seem to be prepared to be for your family, let alone me. You think you're so brave showing off in your Spitfire or whatever it's called, but all you're doing is killing my countrymen . . . and women . . . and children. Who knows, you probably killed my parents . . .'

'Stop getting hysterical. I've never bombed Berlin. And of course I realize how well you've coped with Barney. Quite the little Jewish mother!'

'Shut up!'

She couldn't tell him now. In a way she saw the sense in what he said. There was nothing he could do about accepting his responsibility as father of her child until after the war and who knew what would happen then?

'This blasted war. What *are* you going to do, Saskia? I genuinely want to know. You could have gone to university. They tell me there were double the number of Jewish entrants last year.'

'Oh, do stop making everything Jewish. I'm German too, remember?'

'It's not as if one could forget . . .'

'What do you mean?'

'Well, your voice . . .'

'I don't have an accent any more . . .'

'*I don't hef en eksent eny more* . . .' He was not a bad mimic.

'Do I really sound like that?'

'Fraid so.'

She was silent for a long time then she asked: 'Will I *ever* fit in?'

'Somewhere. Sometime. But don't be impatient. The English are notoriously xenophobic. It'd take years to get truly accepted here. I feel shut out from time to time and that's just because I know I'm not really one of them. They don't even know it but they can have that effect on me. America or Canada's probably the best place for refugees to go. But don't go rushing off there just yet . . .'

'Why not?'

'Because I want to spend a bit more time with you, that's why,' and he slipped one hand behind her neck, forcing her mouth to meet his. As they kissed, urgently, pulling on each other's lips, he placed his other hand under her open coat on her left breast and began to stroke gently. Without thinking what she was doing Saskia began to unbutton her cardigan and then her blouse beneath it. Within seconds she had exposed both breasts and Jonathan had bent his head to cover her nipple with his mouth. He reached out and guided her hand to his fly and when she held him he gasped: 'Quick!' and she moved across to sit in his lap facing him, drawing him inside her while he clasped her breasts hanging loose inside her coat. She felt his penis growing larger and larger inside her and she began to move herself up and down on him. She had no thought for him now, did not hear him cry out her name, she could only focus on the incredible surge of pleasure coming closer and closer . . .

'Aaaaaah!'

All at once she realized it was her own voice crying out and then, behind it, she could hear a long, deafening, monotonous sound. She was sitting on the horn. How long had she been signalling what they had been doing to the entire countryside?

'I tried to tell you,' laughed Jonathan, 'but you were somewhat preoccupied. You loved it, my little Jewish hussy, you really loved it and I'm going to give you lots more.'

Only so long as it does not hurt the baby, and suddenly Saskia remembered why she had wanted this meeting with him. Well, there would be many more and she would tell him when the time was right.

128

When they returned to Laurel Bank, Saskia made him park at the end of the drive.

'If Nancy's still there I don't want her to see you. Stay here till I come back and let you know if it's all right.'

As she approached the Bell House she could see no sign of the shooting brake. She ran back down the drive and waved to Jonathan, giving him the all-clear.

She heard the voice as she entered the hall. It was coming from the kitchen. An older, familiar voice. For a moment she had to stop and think who it was and it wasn't until she heard Barney's excited chatter in response that she knew for sure. There was only one person who would have that effect on Barney.

Selwyn. Selwyn was home.

He had his back to her as she came into the kitchen but even so she could tell immediately that he had aged, that he was cripplingly tired. Barney pointed towards her and he turned.

It didn't occur to her how she must look to him: radiant, glowing from the act of love. He just stood there, staring at her in disbelief. For a second she thought he was going to weep.

As she moved towards him, her hand outstretched, he said, 'Barney's told me. About the baby. You can't possibly know how pleased I am. You see, while I've been away I've seen so much death that to know there will be a birth at Laurel Bank has made my homecoming perfect. My dear, come here, come to me, congratulations . . .'

They embraced, Saskia weeping openly, Selwyn equally overcome with emotion. Only Barney caught a glimpse of Jonathan as he appeared fleetingly in the kitchen doorway, heard what Selwyn said about the baby and retreated. Only Barney heard the roar of the sports car's engine as Jonathan drove away from Laurel Bank as fast as it would carry him.

When the doorbell rang at six the next morning Barney went to the window to see who it was.

'Ripping!' he whispered to himself and hurried down to let Smudger in.

Smudger's news tore Saskia to shreds.

'I thought you'd want to know as soon as possible. It's Jonathan. He's bought it. There was a surprise mission last night. Dangerous. Of course, Jonno was the first to volunteer.' Smudger swallowed. 'He didn't come back. Missing, believed killed. I'm sorry, Saskia.'

Twelve

Tante Luise was crying again.

Christiane couldn't stand it a minute longer and stormed out of the house in exasperation. She knew it upset her aunt when she left without any explanation but each day it was getting worse. Luise's life was in ruins. Through her husband, Wolfie, she had been part of the Jewish community. Now she had seen many of her dearest friends driven out of Berlin, resettled, deported, never to be seen again. The rumours about the camps were terrifying. Many people she knew had gone into hiding. They were called U-boats – submarines – because they had gone underground.

Little by little her Jewish friends had abandoned her – in fact through necessity as they were not allowed to fraternize with non-Jews – but Luise had come to believe it was because they resented her. She felt unbearably guilty and terribly lonely. The fact that her Jewish niece, to whom she had given shelter, was sullen, rebellious and above all not in the least bit grateful for her aunt's kindness made Luise's life seem utterly pointless.

Being drunk the night of her fifteenth birthday two years ago had saved Christiane's life. Her young limbs had been in such an advanced state of relaxation when she hit the ground after falling from the balcony, that she had suffered only mild concussion and, amazingly, no broken bones. Word had quickly reached Luise of Klara and Hermann's arrest and she had hurried back to Wilmersdorf and taken Christiane home with her. The beauty of it all was that the

Gestapo, seeing the girl lying face down, immobile, had left her for dead. They had written her off. It was as if she no longer existed according to their records and thus she could roam the streets of Berlin safe in the knowledge that no one was looking for her. Furthermore, since she did not look remotely Jewish, she had no need to wear a star.

Two weeks after her fifteenth birthday, when she was fully recovered, Christiane had returned to the Wilmersdorf apartment only to find the house boarded up and the doors sealed. Later she was told what this meant: that the occupants had been deported to the East. It emerged that Hermann, and also Klara although she was innocent, had been charged with not wearing their Jewish stars, witnesses had come forward, people they had never seen before, and they had been sentenced. They had been among the first thousand Jews to be deported on 18 October 1941.

Christiane threw away her Jewish star. She ventured forth on her bicycle, travelling all over Berlin, wallowing in her new-found non-Jewish status. By early 1942 Jews were banned from the public streets on which government buildings were located as well as the shopping areas like the Kurfürstendamm. They could not ride on public transport nor could they use public telephones. They were restricted to yellow benches in the parks and finally banned from parks altogether. Little by little everything was taken away from them: milk, eggs, fish, cheese, cake, even white bread. But Christiane experienced none of this and, unlike her aunt, she delighted in her good fortune.

One single incident served to bring home to her just how precarious an existence others were leading. She had struck up a love affair with a boy called Kurt who still lived near her old home in the Wilmersdorf district. Her parents hadn't liked him. They had seen his eyes fastening on Christiane's large breasts and had known what it was he was after. When she went to live with Tante Luise the fact that he daringly tracked her down at night impressed her and she took to slipping out of the house and letting him press her up against a wall in a darkened alleyway. She let him slip his hand up her skirt and touch her until she was wet and she liked it. One hot August in 1943 they were daring in a foolhardy way. They met in broad daylight, barely realizing what they were doing, and strolled with their arms around each other down the Kurfürstendamm.

Suddenly Christiane felt Kurt being pulled away from her. Several Gestapo officers set upon him from behind, kicked him into the gutter and proceeded to beat him senseless.

'You're not allowed to touch a Gentile girl, you filthy Jewish swine! And you . . .' They turned to Christiane. 'If we catch you fraternizing with a Jew again, you'll be in real trouble!'

Christiane knew she would never forget the look of utter horror on Kurt's face as he looked at her and realized they didn't understand she was Jewish too and, furthermore, she was not about to enlighten them. Christiane fled before they could question her. Glancing over her shoulder she saw Kurt's limp body being thrown into a van. She didn't know if he was dead or alive.

That night leaflets were dropped on the streets of Berlin by the Allies warning all women and children to leave at once. Nine thousand tons of bombs had recently been dropped on Hamburg leaving over a million people homeless and killing over 40,000. The Americans had attacked by day and the British by night.

The British! Whenever anybody mentioned them Christiane was reminded of her saintly older sister probably living a life of luxury in the lap of the enemy. Her memories of Saskia were dim. She recalled a tiny, fragile creature whom the family had idolized in her absence. Tante Luise invoked her name at every given opportunity: 'Poor Saskia, sent away at such a tender age . . .' or 'Poor Saskia, separated from her parents. You don't know how lucky you've been, Christiane . . .' until the mere mention of her sister could be guaranteed to send Christiane into a rage.

Still shaking from the incident with Kurt and brooding

about Saskia, Christiane retrieved her bicycle and made her way back to Tante Luise's. As she approached the building the sight of a large crowd gathered outside made her stop. Several people, neighbours of her aunt, began to run towards her, motioning her to stay back.

'Brace yourself, Christl,' they told her. 'She's dead.'

Christiane smiled at them. Smiling at people always worked. It made them do what you wanted them to do. Now they would tell her they were only joking.

'She jumped, Christiane. She jumped from her balcony up there . . .' The man pointed up to the windows of Luise's apartment on the fifth floor. 'She hurled herself. We were down here in the street, we watched her. It was terrible . . . just before she hit the ground we could see she was smiling. She wanted to die.'

Christiane didn't answer them. It was as if her own accident of two years earlier had been re-enacted for her by her aunt. Suddenly she did not want to stay a second longer. As she ran away the neighbours shrugged and muttered amongst themselves: 'Let her go. She's a bit of trash. Let her go . . .'

For some reason she didn't quite understand, Christiane found herself making her way to Onkel Wolfie's old tailor's shop in what had once been the best shopping district of Berlin, a few blocks from Unter den Linden. It was almost as if she expected him to still be there so she could tell him what had happened to Tante Luise. As she entered the street she came to her senses, remembering he had been taken right at the beginning. She began to turn her bicycle around; it wouldn't even be worth visiting the shop. It could only be a neglected shell by now.

But it wasn't. She had visited it often when she was little and she remembered exactly where it lay in the street. There were lights shining. She leaned her bicycle against the wall and crept closer. As she reached the shop window she peeped in. There was a man behind the counter serving a customer, fawning over a rich woman, wringing his hands, smiling an oily, fawning smile. It wasn't Onkel Wolfie.

It was Onkel Otto. What was he doing there? How had he been allowed to take over Onkel Wolfie's shop? Christiane knew her mother would never have condoned it. She had hated Onkel Otto. How was it that such a blatantly Jewish person was being allowed by the Nazis to trade so openly? And why was there no Star of David above the shop any more?

Now, as she stood there pondering all these things, Christiane heard the steady drone of approaching aeroplanes. Without thinking she burst into the shop and flung herself against Onkel Otto.

'Your cellar. Let me go down to your cellar, Onkel Otto, please . . .'

If he was surprised to see her he made no sign, merely pointed to a door at the back of the shop. 'Down there. Now, *gnädige Frau*, the jacket will be ready for a fitting on . . .'

The bombing lasted for hours and Otto came down to join her in the cellar. She told him what had happened to her parents and asked why he had not been to see her. She told him about Tante Luise. And then she stiffened as, in the darkness, with the roar of crashing buildings overhead, she felt him pull her towards him and begin to unbutton her blouse. He squeezed her breasts and plunged his long tongue into her ear. Then he began to rub himself against her, trying to get her to take his long penis in her hand. His breath came in sharp pants in her ear until finally she panicked, pushed him away and rushed up the stairs and into the road.

She cycled furiously through the streets lit up by the flares of burning buildings. As the bombs hurtled down she swerved to and fro as if trying to dodge them but when she finally arrived home, where Tante Luise's building had been there was only a heap of rubble.

Now she had nowhere to go.

Thirteen

Within days of his return it became clear that there was something desperately wrong with Selwyn. To begin with his behaviour bordered on the euphoric, so happy was he to be back at Laurel Bank, but after a while little things began to displease him. There was no bacon for breakfast, no butter for his toast, only one egg the entire week. Gradually it dawned on Saskia what was happening: Selwyn was refusing to accept there was a war on in England. Something must have happened to him while he had been away and whatever it was he had chosen to deal with it by suppressing it deep inside himself. It was as if he had decided that once he returned to England everything would be normal.

Barney, however, was quite bewildered. For a multitude of reasons he had been greatly looking forward to Selwyn's eventual return, not least because he couldn't wait to show his mentor what he had been working on. Yet Selwyn was curiously uninterested. He merely glanced at his own design for 'the Saskia' which Barney had completed in his absence and murmured, 'Good, you finished it,' and that was that. He didn't want to see any of Barney's other sketches and when Barney persisted in trying to show him what else he had been doing Selwyn simply walked out of the studio without listening.

'Give him time,' Saskia tried to console the disappointed Barney, 'and in any case, *Barneychen*, you must continue for yourself, not for Selwyn. Don't give up now. You're too

136

good, you know you are. One day this war is going to be over and you'll be able to leave Laurel Bank and show your work to the world. Think about that. Don't you think I'm disappointed too? He hasn't said a word about how I've kept the house in order since he's been away, hasn't thanked me for anything, hasn't said anything about how I've looked after you and he was never interested in my dress designing in the first place. We've got to face it. He's just not talking to anyone.'

'Yes he is,' said Barney, 'he's talking to Vera.'

'What are you saying, Barney? Have you gone mad?'

'No, I haven't, but I think Selwyn might have. Next time I hear him I'm going to come and find you so you can listen. Then you'll believe me.'

Several weeks earlier Lady Sarah had delivered to Laurel Bank a tailor's dummy. She had found it in the attic of The Hall while she was searching for something and had known it would be of enormous help to Saskia. To Barney and Saskia the dummy had become a constant companion as it stood in the corner of the kitchen in the evenings when Saskia fetched it down from her weaving room so she could continue to work on her creations with Barney as he did his homework. It was Barney who gave it a name: Vera, in memory of his mother.

Two days later Barney came running to find Saskia in her sewing room. 'Quick!' he hissed. 'Selwyn's in the kitchen with Vera.'

They tiptoed downstairs and crept along the passage to listen at the kitchen door.

'I didn't betray her. You have to understand that.' Selwyn was half whispering and they had to press their ears to the door to make out what he was saying.

'Could I have betrayed her? Could I have done it without knowing?' Then louder: '*How am I ever going to find out?*'

'Find out what?' whispered Barney.

'Shhhh!' said Saskia. She knew it would be terrible if Selwyn discovered their presence.

'Oh, Vera, I didn't betray her,' Selwyn continued. 'You must understand.'

Barney giggled. 'I told you he talked to Vera. I wonder if he notices that she never answers back.'

'Barney, shut up.' Saskia took his arm and marched him firmly back upstairs. 'Can't you see it's *because* she never answers back that he talks to her? He's so frightened of something, he couldn't face it if someone gave him an answer. This is really serious, Barney. What on earth am I to do?'

In the end Saskia did what she had always done in an emergency: she summoned Lady Sarah.

Lady Sarah drove over to Laurel Bank rather slower than her usual breakneck pace. She was worried about her 'orphans', as she called the trio at Laurel Bank. Indeed, she was constantly much more concerned about them than she was about her own family. Nancy and Serena weren't orphans, she told herself, they had her and Geoffrey to look after them, though what use Geoffrey was to them, gadding about London as he did, she couldn't imagine.

Selwyn had been an orphan for some time now, yet in Lady Sarah's eyes he had become one when his mother had died and she had rather taken him under her wing. Lady Sarah knew that Selwyn would never marry unless he found someone to whom he could get as close as he had been to his mother. Selwyn had enormous charm but he was terrified of women. He had lived on his own for far too long, he was set in his ways like a neurotic old spinster, although for a moment everyone had thought that the Atwell woman might stand a chance. Pity she'd died. Now Lady Sarah knew she was the only person who would ever get him to open out. Saskia had been quite right to call her, Lady Sarah concluded. Whatever was the matter with Selwyn she would worm it out of him.

But what was she to do about Saskia? Lady Sarah knew she shouldn't but she already counted Saskia as an orphan, yet at the moment she was not dealing with the loss of her parents; indeed there was no proof that they were dead. She was facing instead the loss of Jonathan Rivers. After she had received the news about Jonathan, Saskia had gone into shock for twenty-four hours but then, she had emerged as cool as a cucumber.

She's still in shock in her own way, thought Lady Sarah. She's probably furious with him deep down inside but she can't bring herself to admit it. That young man targeted her for sex as clear-sightedly as he focused on the German cities he bombed. If she thought about it Saskia would probably realize that to him she was nothing more than a target for a specific mission and, once the mission had been accomplished, Saskia had been left devastated like Dresden or Cologne to rebuild herself in time. Lady Sarah wondered why Saskia had been drawn to him in the first place. Was it just because he was a dashing young airman or had it been more than that? Was it something to do with the fact that the young man had announced he was Jewish in front of Nancy that Sunday after church? Had Saskia told him about the baby?

Dinner was a nightmare.

'Perfectly disgusting meal!' complained Selwyn at frequent intervals. 'No meat – potato and onion pie, I ask you. Dreadfully sorry, Sarah, got you all the way over here for such a poor show. If I were still in France I'd have had –'

'Oh, do shut up, Selwyn. You're not in France – we didn't know that's where you were – and you should be ecstatic to be home. Even if the cuisine is a little inferior these days, Saskia's done her best . . .'

But Selwyn had stomped out of the kitchen.

'My dear, is it like this every night?' asked Lady Sarah.

'Worse sometimes,' said Barney gloomily.

'You go and join him in his study,' said Saskia. 'We'll go upstairs and leave you to it. I'll make a pot of coffee and knock on the door as I go up, leave it outside on a tray. Don't want to interrupt you. Besides, I'm so tired these days. Come on, Barney.'

'What's the matter with you, Selwyn?' Lady Sarah came straight to the point as she sat down on the sofa beside him. 'You're not yourself at all.'

'Nothing the matter with me, nothing at all. It's you I'm beginning to worry about. It's getting late, Sarah. Are we expected to put you up for the night?'

'Selwyn, I'm here to help if only you'd realize. You were in the SOE then, were you?'

'How on earth do you know that?'

'Well, you said France and you've obviously been through something harrowing. I guessed, that's all. Come on, Selwyn, tell me all about it. You must talk to someone.'

'Saint Sarah we used to call you as children. Did you know? Always rushing to the rescue, always barging in where you weren't wanted. You do so love to feel needed, don't you, Sarah? It's your *raison d'être*. Saskia and Barney must have been a godsend to you.'

'I've never *ever* seen you so bitter, Selwyn.'

'All right, I'm sorry. But you must understand, Sarah, that well-meaning kindness is not what I want right now. D'you know, it's odd, I was really quite looking forward to seeing you tonight. I thought you'd have a go at me. You always have. It's why I like you. I know where I am with you. I prefer people who can be guaranteed to keep their end up.'

Lady Sarah leaned over and gave his hand a gentle squeeze.

'Best to talk about it, Selwyn, and better to me than to most people.'

'It's complicated, Sarah, more complicated than you could ever imagine.' His voice was muffled. He had buried his head in his hands.

Here it comes, thought Lady Sarah, *here it comes*.

'There was a traitor in our cell and what I don't know, what I will *never* know, and I've been torturing myself ever since it happened, is whether or not that traitor was me.'

'Ever since what happened?' Lady Sarah prompted softly.

'Ever since Ginette was found.'

His hands had begun to shake; his whole body was trembling. She steeled herself as he broke out in loud convulsive sobs. It was several minutes before they subsided.

'She was our radio operator. Half-French, half-English. Perfect for our purposes. They caught her in the middle of her sked, broadcasting to London. They knew exactly where to look for her.'

'But why –'

'DON'T INTERRUPT, SARAH, FOR CHRIST'S SAKE . . . I was the only person, the *only* person in the entire cell who knew where she made her broadcasts. We arranged that right at the beginning. Only I should know. And I never told anyone. And yet I must have. I must have! My poor, poor Ginette.'

'*Your* Ginette?'

'All right, Sarah, all right. You want to know everything. Ginette was my lover in France. She was young and frightened and very brave and she trusted me. I felt responsible for her in the beginning, I watched out for her but she was determined to hold her own amongst us despite her fears. It's terrible to think of it now but I know our lovemaking gave her courage.'

'But, Selwyn, you didn't betray her, you know you didn't.'

'That's just it, Sarah. Of course I didn't – knowingly – but someone gave her away and I was the only one who . . .'

'You've been tortured in the worst possible way,' Lady Sarah told him. 'You've been torturing yourself. That poor girl's probably as free as you are by now. Who's to say she –'

'They killed her.'

'Oh, Selwyn . . .'

'They shaved her bald and shot her through the head. They left her body in the barn where she made her broadcasts for us to find. I collapsed. That's why I was sent home. I didn't come straight here. I . . . I've been in a clinic for a while. They've been trying to help me . . . well-meaning . . . like you. But it's not going to go away that easily.'

'It could take years . . .'

'What did you say?'

'It's ludicrous to think you're going to get over something like this in a matter of weeks. It could take months and months, maybe years. Selwyn, I cannot tell you how pleased I am that you have confided in me. You are to feel free to talk to me any time you want. I don't suppose I can be of much help other than as a sympathetic listener and I'll try not to ask too many idiotic questions. What you need is rest and lots of it. I'll speak to Saskia and Barney, particularly Barney as Saskia's going to need rest too once the baby gets under way.'

'Sarah, what is this nonsense? You're quite, quite wrong! The very last thing I need is to sit about brooding. I want to get back to work. Proper work. Design. I know I've been a perfect bore for the last few weeks but while I've been moping around I've been formulating a plan. A friend of mine, Dick Russell, came to see me in the hospital place I've been at, jolly decent of him. Anyway, the government have put his brother, Gordon, in charge of utility furniture. I mean, it's quite extraordinary but it's up to the government to decide what sort of design we can have if we want new furniture. Pity the poor war brides who have to start a brand new home. They've got to have Gordon's stuff or lump it. Dick suggested I go down and give him a hand and the more I think about it the more I like the idea . . . What are you staring at me like that for, Sarah?'

'You're not serious?'

'Not serious about what?'

'You can't be serious about leaving Laurel Bank?'

'I most certainly am.'

'But what about Barney and Saskia?'

'Oh, they'll manage. They seem to have managed perfectly well without me so far, they probably won't even notice if I disappear again.'

'Well, at least you've realized how well they've coped.

You might have said something to Saskia, Selwyn. She's been under the most terrible strain. I can see now you've had a dreadful experience but, please, can't you see that these two young people need you here, now more than ever? You can't go running off shirking your responsibilities.'

'Oh, you'd know about responsibilities, wouldn't you, Sarah? Married to a cad like Geoffrey, what can you expect? Rushes off to London and leaves you with the girls.'

'Geoffrey might appear to be a cad to you but I can assure you I didn't think so when I married him. Anyway, I don't want to bring Geoffrey into this now. Selwyn, you have to stay here.'

'That's just it, Sarah. I can't. Not a moment longer.'

'But why?'

'It's Ginette . . .'

'It'll take time, Selwyn. Much, much more time than you'll ever be able to appreciate now. And Barney and Saskia will help. They need you, they'll take you out of yourself. Saskia's been through a highly traumatic time herself recently. You could help each other, she'd listen to you, I know she would.'

'NO! No, I don't need her.'

Lady Sarah was shocked at the force of his denial. 'Selwyn, what is it?'

'Ginette. She's dead. Even if I didn't betray her to the Gestapo I betrayed her in other ways. I really love *her*. She was dark, Sarah, and she was beautiful. Like Saskia. She looked just like Saskia. That's why I became her lover. Each time I made love to Ginette I pretended she was Saskia. That's why I have to leave Laurel Bank. I have to get away from Saskia while she's in this condition. Don't you see, Sarah? Are you blind? The minute I saw her walk in the kitchen, so radiant, so changed, I knew there was nothing I could do. And every day it gets worse. I can't help it, Sarah. I'm in love with Saskia.'

143

Fourteen

Trouble always came in threes. Barney remembered Vera telling him this.

The first sign of trouble came when he invited a group of his friends to Laurel Bank for his eighteenth birthday in May 1943. Saskia had never been keen on the idea of strangers coming to the house. Despite the fact she had been in England for four years, she was still wary of native hostility towards German refugees. Unfortunately the villagers still kept their distance and she only had to think of Nancy Sanders to convince herself that it would be better for her if she kept herself to herself. But Barney managed to persuade her that he must do something to celebrate his eighteenth birthday.

In the event only half a dozen boys turned up; long, lanky youths, awkward in their dealings with Saskia. They were polite to her but Barney could tell they were not comfortable around her as she served them tea and birthday cake. Barney knew they were expecting beer and would have preferred girls to be present too but he knew the sight of young, lithe schoolgirls flirting with him and his friends would have made Saskia even more uncomfortable. If only Selwyn had stayed then everything would have been fine. His friends would have respected Selwyn, made an effort with Saskia out of deference to him.

After tea they went outside to kick a ball about leaving Saskia to rest in her room. One of Barney's friends produced the bottles of beer they had all been hoping for and he tossed them to the others. Soon they became reckless. When the ball landed in the middle of the river above the weir there was a race to see who could get to it first but when they arrived at the river bank they all stopped.

'It looks deep,' mumbled one.

'The ball's landed too far from the bank. We'd be daft to try and get it. Come on, Barney, let's go back.'

But Barney wouldn't be deterred. While the others watched from the safety of the wooden pedestrians' bridge to the side of the weir, he grabbed a long stick lying on the bank and leaned out from the weir's stone steps to guide the ball towards him. Almost immediately he slipped and fell, his body crashing down the slimy steps. At the bottom he hit his head on a rock and disappeared below the surface of the water. His friends did not panic. They ran across the bridge, down the bank and jumped in to haul him out. It took all of them to do so since Barney was unconscious.

It was a pretty serious case of concussion and Barney had to be kept in bed for a week. His skin was pale and clammy, his pupils frequently dilated and he vomited. For a while the doctor told Saskia he was worried but then Barney began to recover and the first thing he said was: 'What about my medical?'

They were due to have them that week, the lads in his class who had turned eighteen. The call-up papers were expected any minute. The irony was that it was not the bump on his head that caused Barney to fail his. It was the fracture to his left ankle that he had sustained while tumbling down the hard stone steps of the weir. As his head had hit the rock his ankle had cracked on the steps behind him. He hadn't noticed it when he regained consciousness but once he tried to stand on it, he collapsed immediately. The doctor explained it was out of the question for Barney to contemplate active service. It was a serious fracture in several places and there was a strong likelihood of Barney having a slight hobble even when he did fully recover.

'Besides,' asked the doctor, 'who would be here to look

after this young lady when her time comes if you went marching off to war?'

Barney's friends left two weeks later and he never went back to school. Saskia could see how depressed he was and she urged him to write to Selwyn and explain what had happened. For some reason when Selwyn telephoned he always asked to speak to Barney, never to her. Now that Barney was incapacitated and couldn't come to the telephone, Saskia would have brief informative conversations with Selwyn, sensing all the time that he was anxious to get off the line. Why was he so awkward with her?

It was while Barney was still confined to his room upstairs that the second 'trouble' arrived.

Stella died giving birth to her puppies.

The vet tried to explain about the complications that had set in during the birth but Saskia had not understood. They were a litter of seven but three died along with their mother. It seemed the father had been a springer spaniel since two of the puppies that lived had liver and white colouring. One even had long ears. The other two looked like black Labrador puppies. Lady Sarah removed the spaniels, promising to find homes for them, leaving the two Labradors – a bitch and a dog – at Laurel Bank.

The whole thing unnerved Saskia. While their eyes were still closed the vet found another bitch to wet nurse them and suddenly the kitchen seemed horribly empty. In the evenings Saskia sat and stared at Stella's empty basket, remembering the pain the poor dog had been in. Saskia had summoned the vet who had come as fast as he could but not before Saskia had witnessed Stella's agony. The question haunted her: would her own childbirth be like that? Would her baby survive?

When the puppies were returned she summoned up the energy to name them Schnutzi and Putzi after two favourite dolls she and Christiane had played with as tiny children. It was unclear which name was male and which was female. In any event, both dogs came running as soon as either name was called. Barney, up and about again, immersed himself in looking after them. He fed them with a baby's bottle as he recalled how Vera had fed Stella in the shop. At night he took them up to sleep in his room; by day he watched them stagger about the place and fall down suddenly looking very surprised. He laid down newspaper and tried to teach them to do their business but they didn't seem to understand what he meant. Lady Sarah told him he must wipe their noses in it when they made a mess to teach them a lesson but he couldn't bring himself to do that. And all the time Saskia watched his innate patience and gentleness and told herself how lucky she was to have him.

All the same her hormones got the better of her; she cried at the slightest thing. In June, when Leslie Howard was shot down and killed, she wept all night. Barney, by way of contrast, had become obsessed with the Dambusters.

'Pretty good, those bouncing bombs, don't you think, Sassy? Designed by a chap called Barnes Wallis. Oh, I wish Selwyn were here so I could discuss it all with him. Smudger's being pretty ripping about keeping me informed. He says they contain 6,600 pounds of under-water explosive and the planes have to be navigated so carefully so that the bombs are released and ricochet at exactly the right moment on the dams. Smudger says they use Lancasters and . . . Sassy, now what's the matter?'

'How can you talk about bombing Germany with me sitting here? How can you be so cruel?'

'Oh, Sassy, I'm sorry, I didn't think . . .'

'No,' said Saskia, smiling weakly, remembering how everyone who cared about her never 'thought', never remembered she was German, accepted her as one of them, 'you never do, do you?'

'It's miles away from Berlin anyway, isn't it, the Ruhr? Miles and miles away.'

'They're going to ruin Berlin one day though, aren't they?' said Saskia sadly. 'It's only a matter of time.'

The baby was early.

147

The waters broke as Saskia was clearing the table after supper.

'What do I do? What do I *do*?' Barney was totally panicked.

'Call Lady Sarah,' Saskia told him calmly, taking care to mask her own fear.

Lady Sarah arrived within half an hour bringing the midwife with her.

'Upstairs with you, Barney. Off you go now, out of the way.'

'Can't I do anything to help?'

'I don't think so,' said Lady Sarah firmly.

'That bed of hers is too small,' announced the midwife coming into the kitchen. 'Is there a big bed anywhere?'

'Selwyn's,' said Barney. 'I'll go and get it ready.'

'All right, take some sheets out of the airing cupboard and make up the bed and then make yourself scarce.' Lady Sarah was relieved to be able to give him something to do. 'She's going to have a bad time, isn't she?' Barney heard her say as he left the kitchen. 'Those tiny hips of hers, she's barely bigger than a child herself.'

Lady Sarah was right. Fourteen hours later Saskia was in screaming agony.

'*Mutti!*' she begged, '*Mutti, wo bist du? Soll ich dich wieder sehen? MUTTI!* Please come to me now.'

'She's crying for her mother,' explained Lady Sarah to the midwife, who had flinched slightly at the sudden torrent of German. 'Poor little thing. Saskia, darling, I'm here. Not much compensation, I know, but here, hold my hand, that's it, hold on tight and *push*! And again . . . no, don't talk, save your breath, you're going to need it.'

Saskia flailed with her arms. All reason had flown out the window. '*Scheisse!*' she yelled at the top of her voice.

'What's that mean?' asked the midwife.

'No idea. Probably better we don't know. Hold my hand, Saskia dear, and one, two, three, PUSH!'

'The head! Here's the head,' cried the midwife.

Saskia screamed again.

Upstairs in his room at the back of the house Barney pulled the pillow over his head. If he could hear her from so far away she must be . . . He dared not think what must be happening to her. Was it normal to make such a noise? Was she dying?

He must have fallen asleep because he was woken by Lady Sarah gently shaking his shoulder.

'Get up, Barney. Come with me, come and see her.'

He tiptoed into Selwyn's room and stopped in shock. Saskia was lying, exhausted, in the middle of Selwyn's bed. Her hair was spread out in damp strands on the pillow and her face was devoid of colour. In her arms lay a tiny bundle.

'There,' said Lady Sarah proudly as if the baby were her own, 'there she is, take a peek, quite adorable! Clever girl, Saskia, jolly well done.'

Barney glanced at the wrinkled little face, its skin a deep red contrasting vividly with Saskia's deathly pallor.

'What's the matter with Sassy?' he whispered to Lady Sarah. 'Didn't it go all right?'

'Shhh!' hissed Lady Sarah. She shepherded him outside. 'Don't say things like that in front of her. It went as well as could be expected. She has a tiny frame. She had a terrible time.'

'She didn't even say anything to me.'

'She will, Barney, she's very tired. She needs rest. Meanwhile we should all go downstairs and rejoice in the birth of her baby daughter. Only six pounds but quite, quite perfect. She'll talk to you tomorrow, Barney, you'll see.'

But Saskia didn't talk to anyone. She performed the necessary functions as if in a daze. All she said was 'Give me Klara, please,' from which everyone deduced that she wanted to call her baby Klara. 'After her mother, I expect,' Barney explained. She breast-fed Klara whenever the baby wanted it but apart from that she took no interest in her newborn daughter.

Lady Sarah was very worried but there was one compensation: Barney's disappointment at being declared unfit for active service was forgotten as he embarked upon his new role taking care of little Klara. When she cried in the night it was Barney who heard her and leapt out of bed to run to Selwyn's room, pick her up, rock her in his arms a little and then place her in Saskia's arms to be fed. It was Barney who sat and marvelled with Lady Sarah at Klara's tiny fingers and toes. And when Saskia gave up on breast-feeding altogether, Barney took the wooden cradle he had made for Klara into his room and kept her with him through some of the nights, getting up to warm bottles and sit rocking her till she went back to sleep.

The summer of 1944 brought dreadful weather: nothing but rain and cloud. Evacuees poured into Liverpool and Manchester to escape the Doodlebugs. Barney recalled how his mother had been so desperate to get him away from Liverpool.

'Still,' he told Saskia cheerfully, 'if Hitler thinks he can knock us for six with his silly secret weapon, he's got another thing coming, hasn't he, Sassy?' But Saskia didn't answer. She never did.

The only person to whom she appeared to respond was Smudger. Smudger came over as often as he could. At first Saskia treated him like the others, barely acknowledging his presence, allowing him to pick up Klara rather gingerly, but not engaging him in any form of conversation until one day he nearly dropped Klara when she said suddenly: 'Do you think she looks like him?'

'Like who? Oh, you mean like . . .'

'Yes, like Jonathan. Go on, say it, Smudger. Everyone around here never mentions his name. He was her father, you know. Everyone seems to have conveniently forgotten that she had a father. *Persona non grata* in this place is poor old Jonathan, dead or alive.'

She watched as Smudger brought Klara back to her, walking very carefully, holding her rigidly in his arms. He had always reminded her of Charlie Chaplin, a cheeky little man who walked with his feet turned out. She wondered if he had a girl somewhere.

'He was your best friend, wasn't he?'

Smudger nodded. 'I worshipped him, I have to confess. He was everything I'm not: tall, handsome, confident, reckless.'

'But did you like him, Smudger?'

'Of course. He was my friend, wasn't he?'

'I don't think Jonathan can have been an easy friend to have. He was quite selfish, I think. Is that why you come to see me and the baby so often, because he was your friend?'

Smudger flushed. 'Yes, well, sort of. Tell you the truth, Saskia,' he flushed even more, 'I like coming to see you. You're a good woman. I know you are. I think about you when I'm up there, you know, flying over your country. I think about what you've done for that kid.'

'What kid? Barney? He's hardly a kid any more.'

'Well, whatever he is. I'd like to find a girl like you. You know. One day.'

'I expect you will, Smudger.'

'Will you be going back when this wretched war's over, take little Klara back to Germany, will you?'

'I don't think I can, Smudger,' she said sadly. 'I don't think it will be possible,' and couldn't help noticing the look of pleasure that slipped across his face at this piece of information.

Smudger proposed to her six weeks later. He admitted he was doing it partly out of loyalty to Jonathan, taking care of his responsibilities, but mostly out of respect for Saskia herself. Saskia knew that love was not a word Smudger would be comfortable saying. She told him she would think about it and she did. It was not such a ridiculous proposition as far as she was concerned. She was in the country illegally; marrying Smudger would solve all her immediate problems and give Klara a father. No, it was not such a far-fetched idea after all . . .

★

151

'Selwyn? Is that you? It's Sarah. Sarah Sanders . . . Listen, for heaven's sake . . . Yes, they're fine . . . The baby's fine. I tell you, I'm still simply furious with you for not coming home to see her. Can you imagine how Saskia must feel? . . . What? . . . Well, if you'll listen for just one moment I'll tell you why I'm ringing. Saskia's thinking of getting married . . . Married! Yes, weddings, things like that . . . To Smudger . . . Oh Lord, I can't remember his real name, Gerald something. Nobody ever calls him by it . . . What? . . . I don't know when. Soon probably. I know Smudger was going to have a talk to David Appleby about whether he'd marry a Jewish bride in his church . . . You'll have to talk to her yourself . . . Oh, you will? When? . . . Shall I tell them? . . . No? You want to surprise them? . . . About time too . . . Come home as soon as you can, Selwyn. If you couldn't be bothered to come home for Klara's birth you might at least try and be here at the wedding . . .'

'Sassy, you're not really going to marry Smudger, are you?' Barney asked casually over supper.

'Why not?'

Barney's head shot up. 'You're not serious?'

'Barney, I ask you again, why not?'

'You don't love him.'

'Shhhh! And who are you to say whether I love someone or not?'

Barney flushed. She was absolutely right.

'Anyway, I thought you liked Smudger. Don't you think he'd make a ripping husband?'

'Yes, of course I do.'

'Well then?'

'But not for you.'

'Why ever not?'

Barney turned away. How could he tell Saskia he didn't want her to marry anyone? Not yet anyway. It was too soon. He couldn't bear the thought of her leaving Laurel Bank, starting a life of her own that didn't include him. Saskia saw

152

how miserable he looked. She carried the dishes to the sink and then brushed her hand across the back of his neck in a gesture of affection as she returned to the table.

'No, Barney, you're right. I don't love Smudger but if he's prepared to give me a home once the war's over, if he'll look after me, give me security, then I'd be lucky to have him.'

'But we'd give you a home. You could stay right here with Selwyn and me. We'd be your family if you didn't want to go back to Berlin.'

'Of course I want to go back to Berlin, but you know something, Barney? I'm terrified of what I might find there. In a way I know I'd be running away from everything if I stayed safely here with Smudger, but maybe it might be for the best. I just couldn't bear the thought of having to leave and start somewhere all over again. One day soon you'll be leaving Laurel Bank too and I couldn't stay here alone with Selwyn.'

'I don't see why not,' persisted Barney, 'and anyway I'm never going to leave. I suppose you want to marry Smudger because he reminds you of Jonathan.'

'Oh, don't be ridiculous! He's not a bit like Jonathan . . . but he would be a good father to Klara for Jonathan's sake.' She failed to see the look of unbearable hurt that passed across Barney's face. Surely if anyone would make a good father for Klara, *he* would. In that case maybe he ought to be the one to marry Saskia . . .

'Anyway there is one particular reason why I want to get married and if I tell you, Barney, I don't want you to tell a soul. Promise?' He nodded. 'I'm in the country illegally. When I arrived I never registered with the police and my passport ran out years ago. If I marry Smudger he'll make me legal. Do you see?'

'Yes, but how can that matter now? You've been here for ages, and you've kept your passport yourself, haven't you?'

'It makes no difference. If anyone found out I'd still be in trouble.'

Then Saskia listened, horrified, as Barney told her what

153

Nancy and Angela Appleby had done while she had been out with Jonathan.

'I'd better tell Smudger to get a move on.'

Barney silently kicked himself for having told her.

Klara's crying woke Barney at two in the morning. He lay and listened to the disturbing sound of her wails growing louder and louder. Why didn't Saskia do something? It was quite clear what had happened: Klara had woken early for her three o'clock feed. She was hungry. Why didn't Saskia get up and take her downstairs, give her her bottle? When he could stand it no longer, Barney hauled himself out of bed, pulled his dressing gown over his pyjamas, fished his slippers out from under the bed and shuffled next door. Maybe Saskia wasn't even there.

But she was. She was sitting up in bed crying her eyes out, silently heaving. Mother and daughter were in competition. Without saying a word Barney lifted Klara out of her cot and carried her downstairs. She recognized his embrace and quietened almost immediately. Rocking her gently in the crook of his elbow, he deftly heated a bottle.

He sprayed a little warm milk onto the back of the hand supporting Klara's head to test the temperature before plunging the teat into her greedy little mouth. She worked furiously on the bottle, her face going bright red and her miniature hands clasping either side, occasionally clawing the air.

'There, lass, get that down you.' He remembered his mother's words when she had been feeding Stella as a puppy with a bottle in the back of Joe's shop.

Barney gazed down at her, marvelling at her tiny, perfectly formed fingernails. When eventually she paused for breath he lifted her up to rest against his shoulder and patted her back until she brought up wind. Her head lolled and a ridiculous smile spread over her face. Lady Sarah had told him that this was not a real smile, just a reaction to release of wind, but he preferred to think that Klara was smiling at him, thanking him.

When she had finished the bottle he rocked her for a while and then carried her slowly upstairs. He laid her back in her cot and she went straight back to sleep. She always did. She was so good like that. He just couldn't understand why Saskia ignored her. He turned to Saskia, saw she was still weeping soundlessly. He crossed to the bed and sat down beside her pillow, putting his arm around her shoulders, drawing her to him.

'What is it, Sassy? Klara's fine now.'

'I know. I KNOW!' She screamed at him in sudden fury.

'Shhhh! You'll wake her up again.'

'So no one can disturb her, of course not. What about me? What about letting me have a good night's sleep for a change. I can't stand the sound of her crying any more. I don't want her anywhere near me.'

'Course you do,' said Barney soothingly. 'You're just tired out of your wits, that's all. You'll be ready to feed her again in the morning.'

'I won't, Barney! Can't you understand? There's something wrong with me. I don't want my baby. I'm a mother but I'm not fit to be one. Oh, Barney, I never should have had her . . .' And she began to sob again. Barney gathered her closer to him.

'There, there, lass . . .' he whispered for the second time that night. 'I understand. I really do.'

Saskia buried her face in his neck. 'I know you do. You're the only one I've got who does, Barney. I love you so much.'

Her voice was muffled but he had heard her. He didn't wait to ask her what she meant. He took her head in both hands and brought her face up to his. He placed his mouth on hers, parted his lips a little and began to give her little tugs. After what seemed like an eternity to him she responded. Her lips moved beneath his. Her arms came up around his neck and he could feel her full breasts straining through her nightgown against his chest. He longed to place his hands on them like he had done in the bath, but he knew

155

instinctively that he must go slowly otherwise she would pull away.

Saskia opened her mouth and allowed his tongue to meet hers. Then it was she who took control. She began to stroke his ears tenderly, occasionally slipping her finger inside to tickle him. He thought he would go mad. All the time her tongue probed the inside of his mouth, sucking on him, coaxing him. Before he even knew what was happening she had slipped her hand through the opening in his pyjama bottoms.

'Barney, you're hard as a rock. Do you think you can last much longer?'

'A bit', he said hoarsely, moving himself so that he lay across her and pushing up her nightdress at the same time. He fixed his mouth over her right nipple and bit gently. Her body jerked upwards in response and his erection slipped between her legs. She reached down and began to move her hand slowly along his penis, pushing the foreskin up and letting it slide down again.

'I'll come if you go on like that . . .' he told her and she realized he knew exactly what was going to happen. Then he placed himself inside her and began to move up and down, harder and harder, his long frame hovering above her, his blond forelock hanging down above her face. This was a Barney she had never seen before. There was no sign of the boy who had grown up alongside her. This was a man in full command of her and she gave herself up to him.

Suddenly he shuddered and slumped down heavily on top of her. His weight was crushing but she dared not move.

After a while she whispered: 'Barney, was that . . . was that your first . . .?'

'You know it was.'

'How could I know? Those girls at school . . .'

'I never wanted them. That was the problem – they were all after me but I only ever wanted you.'

'Sorry.'

Saskia held him in her arms and lay staring into the darkness. He wasn't circumcised, she mused to herself, just

156

like Jonathan (for all his claims for being half-Jewish).
Would she ever make love with a Jewish man?

Barney stirred and lifted himself onto his elbows. He
reached up and cupped her face in his hands and, looking
straight into her eyes, he said: 'You can't go and marry
Smudger now, can you?'

As Selwyn swung the Brough Superior over the bridge and
past the weir and the mill pool, he made up his mind.

Throughout the long, slow drive up to Lancashire he had
been turning the same question over and over in his head.
He loved Saskia although in many ways he felt he barely
knew her now. But he was not about to let her marry
Smithers or whatever his name was.

He would marry her himself.

If she'd have him.

He'd ask her straight away. If he waited even half an hour
he knew he'd lose his nerve. How many times had he been
here before – on the point of proposing marriage – only to
back off at the last minute? But Saskia and he had already
lived together. She knew his way of life, she accepted it. She
didn't have much choice. If he went on like this he'd talk
himself out of it before he arrived. But it was what he
wanted. He was sure of that now. He only hoped it would be
what Sassy wanted too . . .

Dawn had only just broken. The sun was coming up
slowly behind the mill. The sky was bathed in a red glow.

Red sky in the morning, shepherd's warning.

Selwyn turned the handle of the front door of the Bell
House and was relieved when the door swung open. He
wanted to surprise her rather than have to ring the doorbell
and wake her up.

He crept up the back stairs on tiptoe and pushed open the
door of her room.

There they lay in each other's arms. He would always think
of them as The Babes in the Bed: Saskia . . . and Barney.

★

The minute Klara let out her first cry of the morning, Barney was out of Saskia's bed in a flash. Saskia stirred, murmured something Barney could not hear before turning her face into her pillow and falling asleep again. Barney picked up Klara and carried her next door into the bathroom. He laid her down on a table by the window and set about changing her nappy. Every now and then he bent down and buried his face in her fine baby hair, loving the soft downy smell. She gurgled with pleasure.

'There,' he said, smiling down at her as he wiped in and out of the soft pink folds of skin around her bottom and dusted her with baby powder. 'Want your bottle now, I suppose. You're a bit early this morning, you know? Shall we go downstairs and see what we can find?' Klara brought her exquisite little hands together in the air as if she were applauding him.

He negotiated the back stairs gingerly with her in his arms. He was frightened of dropping her while he was still sleepy. When he reached the kitchen safely he put her down in the dog basket beside Schnutzi and Putzi who woke up and began to lick her face. Half-heartedly Barney told them it wasn't very hygienic.

He crossed to the stove to heat up her milk and noticed the cup of tea, half drunk, standing on the dresser. When he picked it up to put it in the sink he found it was still warm. When he turned and for the first time saw Selwyn sitting at the far end of the kitchen table, looking at him, it was such a shock he dropped the cup.

Selwyn's return brought everything to a halt. Saskia and Barney each knew they couldn't possibly share a bed with Selwyn in the house and because it wasn't possible it was what they wanted more than anything. They yearned for each other and made secret trysts, meeting fleetingly on the landing, clinging to each other, their mouths working furiously together.

Selwyn was curiously out of sorts. He glared at them

whenever they came into the room. He made no effort at conversation at mealtimes. It was almost as if he were angry with them about something. And a casual enquiry as to how long he would be staying this time only seemed to exacerbate his bad temper.

'It's my house, damn it, and I'll stay as long as I like.'

Lady Sarah came to see him but he was equally testy with her.

'Leave him be,' she advised. 'Something's upset him but he'll get over it. Give him time and he'll be his old self again, you'll see. Get him to bring you to church this Sunday and I'll make sure plenty of people make a fuss of him after the service, bring him out of himself . . . and don't go worrying about Nancy. We simply don't see her these days, spends most of her time down in London with her father as far as I can make out. No good will come of it, I'm sure. See you Sunday. Toodle-oo.'

It was while he was sitting in church on Sunday, listening to David Appleby read out the banns for a couple's wedding in the future, that Barney decided there was only one thing he could do. He'd marry Saskia himself. Then Selwyn would sanction them sharing a bedroom. Furthermore it would make him Klara's official father. It was ridiculously simple and obvious and the more he thought about it, the more it made sense. Throughout the sermon he began to plan where he would propose. The kitchen was not nearly romantic enough. Her sewing room, maybe? What about outside? If he could only get her to go for a walk then they could stop on the bridge and he could ask her as they looked down at the water rushing past the weir.

Yet Barney was woefully inexperienced in the art of courtship let alone proposing marriage. Saskia might kiss him passionately if they bumped into each other and Selwyn was not around and she might let him slip into her bed and hold her for a few minutes in the early morning before she rose to give Klara her feed, but she would also still chastise him for leaving his room untidy or for allowing Schnutzi and Putzi out of the kitchen.

159

'I've told you before, Barney, you must not let them upstairs. I want them to stay in the kitchen and please do stop this terrible habit of putting Klara in their basket. All those germs . . .'

She thinks I'm still a little boy, he thought miserably, and in a way he was right. Saskia didn't exactly think of him as a child but she had been looking out for him for over three years and it was hard for her to break her routine way of dealing with him. At the same time she craved his affection – it gave her a sense of security – especially now that Selwyn had become so withdrawn.

Finally Barney decided that the only way he was going to solve his dilemma was to spin the knife. Sitting late one night at the kitchen table he tore two strips of paper from Saskia's shopping list and wrote a large YES on one and NO on the other. Schnutzi, now fully grown and larger than Stella had ever been, clambered out of the basket to stand silently beside him, resting her black head in his lap and staring mournfully up at him.

'Hello, old girl,' he said. 'What do you think will happen? Will she say yes? Hmmmm? You think so? Wag your tail if you do.' There was a slight movement in Schnutzi's tail as if in answer. 'Okay. First we'll ask the knife: should I ask Saskia to marry me?'

The knife spun round and came to rest almost immediately, pointing straight at the piece of paper with YES written on it. Barney leapt in the air and hugged Schnutzi to him.

'One more question, Schnutzi: will she say yes?'

This time he gave the knife a spin with such force that it was several seconds before it finally stopped. Barney had closed his eyes. Would it be YES or NO?

The blade was pointing unerringly at one of the pieces of paper. The other one. The one on which he had written NO.

But what Barney could not know was that the reason Saskia would not say yes was because he would not have a chance to ask her.

Fifteen

'Quick, stop her! She's a thief.'

Christiane dropped the loaf of bread she had stolen in her panic to leave the bakery shop in the Fasanenstrasse but a second later she stooped, grasped it up off the dusty floor and was on her way. Her bicycle was propped up against the wall around the corner. She dropped the loaf into the basket, swung herself onto the saddle and pedalled away, her head bent down over the handlebars.

She had not eaten for nearly two days. After Tante Luise's suicide she had returned to the Wilmersdorf area counting on the fact that the shopkeepers there would remember her and take pity on her. Most of them were anti-Nazi and when Hermann and Klara had still lived there, the butchers, bakers and greengrocers had always allowed the little Kessler girl to slip in early to give her first choice of their produce before the Gentiles came to secure the best. Jews always came last and there was never anything worth having left for them, but Christiane only had to smile sweetly and they would fill her arms with vegetables, bread and *Bratwurst*. Klara never asked how she did it.

But that had been over two years ago. Things had changed. It didn't take long for Christiane to realize that her smile was no longer enough. No one cared about Tante Luise's death here. So many people had disappeared, why should they bother about someone who wasn't even Jewish? One day Christiane had seen Kurt's mother in the street and had stopped to beg her for food.

'You don't even ask about my son. After what you did to him . . .' the woman replied, astonished.

'What did I do to him?'

'You let them take him away and you didn't tell them you too were one of us.'

'What would have been the point?' protested Christiane. 'So what did happen to him?'

'As if you care!' the woman spat at her. It was several minutes before Christiane realized she still didn't know where Kurt was, but by then his mother was gone.

It was that afternoon that she first began to steal. She worked it out carefully beforehand. She had found an old skirt with an elasticated waistband in a bombed out ruin. Over it she wore a loose top which hung down away from her body, spread out over her stomach by her large breasts. She would enter a shop when it was full and slip something under her top, securing it in the waistband of her skirt under the guise of scratching her stomach. The problem was that she was running out of shops. She couldn't do it too often in the same shop. She knew some of the shopkeepers were beginning to watch her – now one of them had spotted her.

She rode her bicycle furiously to the shattered building on Budapesterstrasse in which she had made her home since Tante Luise's apartment had been reduced to a pile of rubble. She lived in a corner of the ground floor where she had cleared a space amongst the rubble and hidden it from outside view by placing piles of boxes and bits of metal she had gathered from the sites of nearby ruins in a neat square leaving a narrow gap for an entrance. The upper floors of the building were still inhabited and she made sure she remained out of sight of her neighbours. She did not know what had happened to the family living on the ground floor but it was not hard to guess. It was a pity she had not found the gutted apartment before the Nazis had removed all the previous occupants' furniture. As it was she had salvaged a mattress, and a wooden chair with only three legs. How could she ever have wanted to leave her parents and the comfort of the Zehlendorf apartment? She bit her lip firmly. She must not think of Hermann and Klara. It upset her too much. She restricted her thoughts for her parents to Friday on the eve of the Sabbath when she lit a candle and prayed for them although she knew deep down that her prayers were too late.

She was sitting on the chair poised to sink her teeth into a hunk of the stolen bread when the soldier kicked the chair out from under her.

'No, don't move!' he commanded as she tried to roll over. She had fallen face down in the ever-present dust on the floor. It blew in constantly from the mounds of rubble outside, through the windows whose glass had long since been blasted out. Christiane choked.

He kicked her, the toe of his boot connecting with her shoulder, tipping her over onto her back. She lay there for a second or two with her eyes shut, not wanting to see him. Then she heard movement and suddenly she smelled his foul breath close to her face, a mixture of onions and strong liquor that made her retch despite the fact that her stomach was empty. He was trying to kiss her, licking her cheeks, holding her head down on the floor, pulling her hair. She turned her head from side to side, keeping her eyes closed, determined that if she didn't actually see him he would go away. After a while she felt his weight ease off her. She held her breath. Was that it? Would he leave? She opened her eyes and peered at him through half-closed lids.

The sight of him would haunt her forever. A thickset brute of a man kneeling astride her. He had unbuttoned his jacket and pulled his undershirt out of his trousers. Now he was fumbling with his fly and as Christiane watched, mesmerized, he brought out his fully erect penis. It pointed straight up in the air above her, thick and slimy with a massive purple head. Reaching down, the soldier brought her hands up and placed them on it. When she remained immobile he covered her hands with his own and rubbed them up and down. He began to breathe heavily and sway about on top of her. Suddenly he lifted himself off her and pulled at her clothing.

Christiane came to life. She reached up and bit his hand. He slapped her hard across the face and she fell back in shock. He ripped her clothes from her until her naked body was exposed underneath him, wrenched her legs apart at the knees and fell on her. He must have weighed more than two hundred pounds. Christiane was crushed.

Then she felt the pain. Something was piercing her between the legs. A wet knife was shooting in and out of her. The stench of his stale breath was very close now, nauseating, overpowering. He had placed one of his hands over her mouth to stop her crying out. She was completely trapped. On and on he went, thrusting in and out of her, grunting, whispering in her ear the most disgusting things she had ever heard.

She felt something inside herself tear. Her panic made her move beneath him despite his weight. It only excited him and he pushed himself deeper inside her, lifting his great bulk up in the air and crashing down into her. Just as she felt as if her insides were being splintered into a mass of tiny pieces, Christiane passed out.

When she came to, the smell was still there but he wasn't moving any more. He was slumped across her, moaning. She could feel his penis sliding out of her. She was raw and even though it was limp, it hurt her and she winced. He started as if suddenly aware of her existence once again.

'Pretty tight, you were.' He grunted in pleasure. 'I like it like that.' He moved off her then rolled away quickly as he saw the blood all over her legs. '*Scheisse*, you were a virgin. No wonder you were tight.'

Christiane didn't look. She turned on her side and hugged her legs together, drawing what remained of her skirt around her and tucking it into her crotch to soak up the blood.

'You know something?' He had crouched down beside her and was patting her on her haunches. 'You're the best little Jew girl I've had so far. What d'you think of that? Oh yes, I know you're a little Jew girl. Don't look like one, I'll grant you that, but they told me at the shop where you stole

164

the bread. Didn't you see me coming after you? I thought you knew what I wanted, leading me here like this. Here, want to give him a little squeeze before I put him away, say goodbye, like? I must say he liked ripping you apart like that. Shame we won't be able to do that again. Wait till I tell the others about you . . . I'll be back, you know, so don't do anything stupid like move. I'll be looking for you. Long as you give me what I want, long as you give the others what they want too, you'll be all right. But if you won't you're just another little Jew girl ready to be sent away . . .'

When he'd gone she didn't move for nearly an hour. She rocked herself to and fro to ease the pain. Then holding her torn clothes around her she hobbled outside and round to the back of the building to the rain barrel where she gently washed herself, letting the cool water run down the inside of her thighs.

Christiane did not run away. She did not even consider it. She lay down on her mattress – how ironic that it should have happened to her on the dusty floor when she had a mattress right there – and waited. For on her return from the rain butt she had found he had left her fifty marks lying casually on the three-legged chair.

He did not return for a week by which time she had replaced her torn clothing and built up a small larder of food. Out of some desperate longing to be saved from what she knew she would be unable to resist, she visited the synagogue and prayed. She bought a candle and stared into its flame. She tried to ride her bicycle but found she was still too sore to rest easily on the saddle. She wondered if perhaps she should seek out a doctor to see if any lasting damage had been done but what would she tell them? She did not want to give away her hiding place. She had deliberately not made friends. Gone were the days when she could roam the derelict city safe in the knowledge that no one took her for a Jew. Now, in order to survive, she must remain underground. Whatever it took to survive she would do it and if being raped turned out to be the only way then so be it.

He brought seven of them.

'There she is: *meine kleine Sonnenblume*.' My little sunflower. 'I call her that because of her yellow hair. But don't be fooled, she's a Jew. Treat her accordingly.'

The first soldier turned her over on her front and rammed his penis up her arse. Christiane screamed as the pain seared through her. Three other soldiers immediately dropped to their knees and held her face down in the mattress. The next one wanted her to suck him as he sat astride her and as she tried to do so another wiped her buttocks. She had voided herself in her terror. The third and fourth raped her quickly, climaxing almost as soon as they entered her. The fifth bent over and bit her breasts and nipples while sticking his finger inside her and masturbating himself at the same time. The sixth asked her to stroke herself while he watched. He became exasperated when she couldn't bring herself to orgasm and plunged his head between her legs, licking her until she was so wet with his saliva he convinced himself she must have climaxed.

The seventh soldier brought out a whip.

Afterwards Christiane waited until it was dark and then crept outside to immerse her ravaged body in the rain barrel.

Five hundred marks and three packets of cigarettes.

That night, huddled in her corner, two weeks after her seventeenth birthday, Christiane celebrated her complete independence in the world by smoking her first cigarette.

They came every two or three days – sometimes the same soldiers, sometimes others, all of them with different demands. They asked her what she did for protection but it seemed they were less worried as to whether she would conceive a child as to whether she would give them a dose. They showed her how to put on their contraceptive sheaths. After a while they began to bring her flowers and other presents. The Little Sunflower had become a kind of mascot for them.

By now Christiane was numb. She never thought about what she was doing. She knew that she had to keep going. She was alive, she was eating well and she began to regain her confidence about moving freely about Berlin. It was a chance encounter with her Onkel Otto that brought home to her the enormity of her betrayal to her fellow Jews.

She was cycling down the Unter den Linden one afternoon when she saw him walking down the street. She watched him approach a girl and talk to her for a few minutes. Then he walked with the girl to Kranzler's Café. Christiane was intrigued. She knew what her uncle had been after when she had sheltered with him during the air raid. Now here he was, picking up a young girl right off the street. Well, she wasn't much better. She could tell he hadn't seen her as she slipped between the tables at Kranzler's so she sat down behind him and listened. She noticed that Onkel Otto wasn't wearing his Star of David; nor had he been when she'd seen him in Onkel Wolfie's shop. Well, she didn't wear one either but Onkel Otto really did look Jewish. How did he get away with it?

She heard him ask the girl: 'How long have you been living underground?'

Christiane saw the girl start and look round nervously. 'It's all right,' Onkel Otto told her, reaching out to stroke her arm. 'I'm living underground too. It's hell, isn't it?'

The girl relaxed visibly. 'I'm with my parents. We lost everything. We knew it was only a matter of time before they came for us. We're getting used to it. You know, it's good to meet someone in the same boat, to be able to talk about it. I wander the streets day after day not daring to talk to anyone.'

Christiane watched, bored. Onkel Otto was surely just trying to get this girl into bed. But when they left Kranzler's, Otto merely shook hands with the girl and left her to go off in the opposite direction. Then, just as Christiane was going to call out to him, he stopped, turned and discreetly followed the girl until she disappeared through a hole in a wall.

By now Onkel Otto was but a stone's throw from Onkel Wolfie's shop. He drove off in a van Christiane recognized as Onkel Wolfie's and she followed him on her bicycle.

He drove to the Gestapo Headquarters and walked inside. Christiane nearly fell off her bicycle in horror but after a few minutes she saw him re-emerge with several men. Onkel Otto led the way, the Gestapo followed in another van, and with a sinking feeling Christiane knew exactly where he was taking them.

Onkel Otto was a Jew-catcher. Christiane had heard about them. Indeed, she lived in fear of falling into their hands. They were notorious yet no one knew who they were. They operated in a simple but lethal procedure. They approached people they believed to be underground Jews on the street and struck up a conversation with them, maintaining that they too were in the same state. Then they denounced them to the Gestapo. Usually they were Jews who had been arrested by the Gestapo themselves and who had been 'turned'. In the eyes of Jews they were worse than the Gestapo themselves.

As she saw him point to the place where the girl had disappeared through the hole in the wall, as she watched the girl and her aged parents being brought out minutes later and thrown into the back of the Gestapo van, Christiane knew without a doubt that it had been Onkel Otto who had denounced her own parents. She remembered how he had listened as Hermann had proudly announced he was never going to wear his yellow star and how he had left soon afterwards. If she had only known the danger she had been in when she had sheltered with him at Onkel Wolfie's shop . . . Up to then he must have thought she was dead for she had never been in touch with him while she had been living with Tante Luise.

The next time the Nazis came to visit her she refused payment and they stared at her as if she had lost her senses.

'Oh, it's only just this once. There's something I want

you to do for me which is worth far more to me than money. There's a Jew-catcher. His name is Otto Kessler. You think he's working for you but he's a spy. You let him into the Gestapo Detention Centre in the Grosse Hamburger Strasse and it's true, he's throwing you the odd Jewish family living underground . . . but do you know what he's doing while he's at the Gestapo HQ? He's freeing people and you don't even notice. He finds out who you've got in there for those outside and he arranges their escape for large sums of money. He's fooling you all . . . Don't let him get away with it any longer. Arrest him. Deport him. Make sure he never returns . . .'

They believed her.

Every day she cycled to the end of the street by Onkel Wolfie's shop and on the fourth day she was rewarded by the sight of Onkel Otto being dragged into the same Gestapo van she had seen before. As he tried to resist she saw one of the Gestapo officers take out his pistol and hit her uncle over the back of the head. Otto slumped to the ground. As the van drove away the doors were not quite closed. Otto Kessler was hanging out head first and each time the van struck a piece of rubble, his head was banged onto the road. If he wasn't unconscious when they threw him in the van he must have been almost dead by the time they reached the Unter den Linden, noticed the open doors and hauled his body inside.

That night Christiane almost had an orgasm while two Nazi soldiers entered her at once. Not that it had anything to do with sex. Her eyes were tight shut as usual and she had almost persuaded herself that she had exacted retribution for what they had done to her parents. Then she opened her eyes and looked into their faces and screamed, for she knew that she would never be able to atone for what they had done to her . . . or rather what she had done to herself.

'*Luftgefahr 15!*' warned her last client on the afternoon of Tuesday, 23 November 1943. Air raid danger 15 – massive enemy formations were approaching.

Christiane wasn't really listening. She was concentrating on the hundred marks he was in the process of laying down on the table. As soon as he had gone she would embark upon her favourite occupation: counting her earnings. She had amassed quite a bit, stashed away in envelopes under her mattress, and she was beginning to think about diversifying. Word had obviously got round about her and she had a never-ending stream of clients, but the day before someone else had strayed into her hidden corner in the Budapesterstrasse: a civilian. He said he had been watching the soldiers come and go and had put two and two together. Well, why not, thought Christiane as she reached out and ran her hands down his chest, sliding them round his back and pulling him to her, just so long as the Nazis didn't find out. They had never exactly stated that they had a monopoly on her services but she imagined it was better to let them think they did. Meanwhile it wouldn't hurt to investigate other areas.

So it was that when the first violent flak of what would become known by the Allies as The Battle of Berlin opened up, Christiane was cycling along the Kurfürstenstrasse intending to make her way to the Embassy district. She wasn't quite sure what she would do when she got there but she had a vague notion at the back of her mind that she might run into a better class of client. It was a ludicrous notion for a Jewish girl with no papers to entertain and in the event it was perhaps just as well that she never arrived.

The sound of exploding bombs was almost directly above her as she entered the Lützowplatz and seconds later broken glass showered out of the windows all around her. The sound of falling masonry crashing down was earsplitting and flames began to spread through the buildings. People ran outside clasping wet towels to their faces in order to breathe through the smoke. A sliver of glass punctured the rear tyre of her bicycle and she swerved into a mound of smoking rubble. As she fell to the ground a wall collapsed and she was crushed beneath it.

As she lost consciousness, Christiane's last memory was

of a woman's extraordinarily elegant ankle above a high-heeled crocodile shoe, a hand reaching down to her, a ring glinting through the smoke, and a low, clear voice saying: 'Friedrich, please, Friedrich. Help me get her to the car. We can't just leave her here. I don't care who she is, this one I have to save, Friedrich.'

Sixteen

Christiane opened her eyes and screamed in terror.

A beast was towering over her, a giant animal with huge teeth and a long pink tongue. It lowered its head until all she could see was the inside of its mouth. Any moment now it would devour her.

But it didn't. It just stood, silently, above her. She waited for the nightmare to retreat and the relief that always came with returning consciousness that it had been just that: a nightmare, nothing to do with reality.

But it was real and she screamed again.

'Benz, get down at once. Down! Benz! Come on, you heard me. Down! Come on, you ridiculous animal, that's it, off the bed, go on, out!'

The woman had blown into the room like a miniature hurricane, a tiny creature moving very fast, clapping her hands, shooing the beast away from Christiane.

'I'm so sorry. I don't know how he got in. It's just that he does love this room so and he's got this passion for sleeping on beds. I expect he just wanted to see who was in it. He must have given you a terrible fright. Now up there to your right, just there, above you – there's the bell. I'll leave you to wake up properly. Just ring down to the kitchen when you're ready for your breakfast. Friedrich's there now. I'll tell him to wait until you ring, then he can bring you something. He's all I've got left, dear old Friedrich . . . I'll be back later. Take your time.'

Christiane hadn't said a word. She sat up once the woman

had left the room, heaving open the heavy brocade curtains before she did so and letting the sunlight flood the room. Christiane blinked. The top of the bed (one of the widest she'd ever seen) was empty. Benz, whatever he was, had gone. She ran her hand tentatively over the crisp linen covering the *Federbett*. She reached out and patted the bank of plump pillows beside her and felt the gossamer lace edging of the pillowcases. She noticed the embroidered family crest and wondered whose it was.

She slipped out of bed and found that she was very stiff. She hobbled over to a window, opened it and leaned out. Below her a forest stretched for as far as she could see. She looked to right and left, and to her amazement saw turrets projecting from the roof.

Where was she?

The chest of drawers and the *armoire à glace* were turn-of-the-century, hand-painted pale green with clusters of roses either side of the mirror and in the centre of each drawer. The fact that they had been brought from England was lost on Christiane. Nor did she realize that the bed was Louis Quinze. The furniture in the Zehlendorf apartment where she had been brought up had been light and functional. A few pieces of Bauhaus had crept in at the end but nothing more adventurous than that.

She explored further and found a tiny round bathroom leading off the bedroom. She realized she must be in one of the turrets. The round ceiling curved up to a point in the middle. She turned the brass and porcelain taps above the marble-topped sink and bent her head in wonder, almost expecting rose-scented water to come out.

On her way back to bed she looked again out the window. She must be high up to be able to see so much land below her, and the building she was in stretched away to the left.

She was in a castle.

She rang the bell once, quickly and lay nervously waiting.

173

Friedrich – she supposed it was he – arrived five minutes later bearing a silver tray.

'Where would you like it, madam?'

Madam!

Christiane couldn't speak. Helplessly, she gestured in front of her.

'There, madam.' Friedrich placed the tray on her knees. At the door he paused. 'Shall I send *die Gräfin* to see you now?'

So the woman was a countess. Christiane nodded. Then she fell on the food. Rolls, croissants, plenty of butter, ham, smoked meats, a hard-boiled egg. Honey, a selection of preserves and a jug of strong, piping hot coffee. She had almost emptied the tray and was in the process of stuffing a roll into her mouth when the woman returned.

She was quite beautiful. Exceptionally thin but clearly not because she did not have enough to eat. Corn-coloured hair, scraped away from her face into a knot at the nape of her neck, emphasized her fine facial bones. Deep-set, turquoise eyes slanted above high cheekbones. Her nose was rather long but straight with a slight tilt at the end. She was not tall but perfectly formed, with slim wrists and elegant hands with long slender fingers. Christiane might not have appreciated the provenance of the furniture but she knew immediately that she was in the presence of an aristocrat of the old school.

'I've brought Benz back to be properly introduced. Come on, Benz. We call him that because my husband found him in a Mercedes when he was still a puppy. No, Benz, *not* on the bed. Lie down! There!'

Benz was a Great Dane.

Christiane felt ill at ease. She was uncomfortably aware that the outline of her large, spreading breasts was visible through the thin lawn of the nightgown in which she had been dressed. She felt decidedly clumsy beside this fawnlike creature. She crossed her arms across her chest but the woman chose that moment to hold out her hand.

'I'm Nina. That's all I can tell you, I'm afraid. It's too risky otherwise. What's your name?'

174

'Christiane.' She spoke for the first time. 'Christiane Kes
. . .' She stopped. Would Kessler make her sound Jewish?
Was it safe to be Jewish in this castle?

'Christiane. Don't tell me any more.'

'Where am I?' asked Christiane.

'Outside Berlin. In the country. That's all you need to
know. Don't be frightened, you're quite safe. We thought
we'd lost you for a second. How you survived is a miracle.
You must have been born to survive, literally.'

'Why do you say that?'

'Darling, half a building falls on top of you and you
emerge with barely a scratch . . .'

'That's what happened?'

'It was quite incredible. We whisked you back here and I
called a friend who's a doctor, but you're fine. You've had a
knock on the head and you need to rest but other than that . . .'

As Nina talked Christiane noticed an exquisite little
black pearl ring on a thin band of gold. It was the only
jewellery Nina wore.

'Now, I'm going to run you a bath and then I'm going to
bring you some clothes – my sister's, don't worry, mine
would be much too small for you, I know – and then you can
come downstairs and sit by the fire so we can get to know
each other. But today you must rest. Dear Christiane, I am
so glad I found you . . .'

They did not venture outside for four days. Later that day
Christiane collapsed with delayed shock and returned to
bed where Nina insisted she stayed in order to get complete
rest. The enforced rest was a mixed blessing. For the first
time in months she was experiencing comfort, warmth,
plenty of food and above all peace. Peace in the quiet of the
countryside but more important, peace of mind. No
soldiers would appear to thrust themselves down on their
'Little Sunflower', no enemy planes would bring hours of
ear-splitting chaos as bombs exploded and people's screams
rent the air. She had forgotten all about normal life.

But as she began to relax she began also to recall life as it had been when her family had been alive, for it was clear what had happened to Onkel Wolfie and her parents. Tante Luise had ended her own life and Christiane herself had been responsible for Onkel Otto's demise. It was the first time she had been able to pause and reflect on the enormity of her situation. Nina was right. She had been incredibly lucky to survive but Christiane was not thinking about the escape from the Lützowplatz. Nina did not even know that she was Jewish. She was lucky in that she was the only member of her family to have survived in Berlin.

As Christiane wept she was not sure whether she was crying for her lost family, for herself or with sheer physical relief at having come through alive, but not once did she think of Saskia. For some time now Christiane had blocked her out of her mind, so bitter was she that Hermann and Klara had chosen to send Saskia away to safety while she, Christiane, had been left to face the horror of war-torn Berlin on her own. Deep down she knew that of course her parents had not planned to leave her on her own, but still the resentment festered inside her.

What surprised her more than anything was that she eventually told Nina all of this. Once Christiane had fully recovered the two women developed a daily routine: breakfast in their rooms followed by an hour's bicycle ride along the wide clearings between the endless lines of looming pines. This was Christiane's idea and Nina laughingly insisted they wear proper riding breeches and boots. Benz loped after them occasionally disappearing into the forest after rabbits. On their return they lunched, served by Friedrich, in the old white-tiled kitchen.

Christiane had walked through room after room, hall after hall, filled with furniture covered by dust sheets. Nina explained to her that they lived in what had originally been the nursery wing.

'I grew up here as a child as I expect you've already realized. My husband's family comes from the East but we

176

decided to live here at Mittenwald so as to be close to Berlin. So these are the children's rooms.'

'Your children?'

Nina was silent for a second. Christiane feared she had said something wrong.

'No. I don't have children,' Nina said eventually.

They spent the afternoons in the library curled up on a sofa in front of a roaring fire and it was here that Christiane began to slowly open up to Nina. It was the Countess's beauty that disarmed her. Christiane couldn't help staring at her all the time.

Late one night Nina gently asked the question Christiane had been dreading: 'Christl, you're Jewish, aren't you?'

'How did you guess? I don't look Jewish, do I?'

'Not really. You are blonde and buxom and earthy and feminine, but none of these things are peculiarly Aryan. You could be anything. You don't fit the stereotype picture of the dusky Jewess, I'll grant you, but your nose is Jewish if you compare it to, say, mine which is equal in length but . . . different.'

Christiane leapt up to look at herself in the heavy oakframed mirror hanging above the fireplace. Nina rose quietly behind her and moved to stand beside her. Christiane could see what she meant. Nina's head only reached her shoulder. Suddenly Christiane felt a rush of gratitude for this extraordinarily brave woman. She slipped an arm around Nina's shoulders and drew her to her. Nina's arms encircled Christiane's waist and they stood together in silence for several seconds. Then Christiane thought she felt Nina's lips gently brush the side of her neck and she was shaken by the excitement the sensation sent through her body.

When they returned to the sofa Christiane told her everything: about Hermann and Klara's arrest, about Tante Luise, about Onkel Otto and finally about her role as the 'Little Sunflower'.

Finally she turned to Nina and whispered: 'Why . . . why did you bring me here?'

'I bring people here, people I find on the streets of Berlin. I've been doing it for a year now. It's all I can do. I felt so terrible – I hadn't been into Berlin since the war started and I was driving through with my husband to dine at the Hotel Eden, I forget why exactly, and I just couldn't believe what I saw. My husband, I won't tell you his name, well, he works for the Nazis. No, not exactly for the Nazi Party but his work is being used by them and I can't stand it.'

'Why are you telling me all this?'

'I'm trying to explain . . . the reason why you're here, why I bring people here. You could call it guilt.'

'Why? Are you Jewish?' Christiane sat up and hugged her knees.

'Me? Heavens no! But through my husband I know what's happening to them, I know why I must help them if I can . . .'

'What *is* happening?' Christiane couldn't look at her, could barely breathe.

'When they say they're "resettling" them it means they're sending them to the slaughterhouse. They put them on trains, herd them in, and send them to camps.'

'How do you know?'

'Through my husband . . . because he's . . . no, I'd better not tell you what he does. He's still my husband, after all. So when he's away, when he's in Frankfurt, Friedrich drives me into Berlin and I rescue anyone I can find on the streets – anyone who is hurt – and I bring them back here to Mittenwald. I feed them up, nurse them back to health and then I return them to the world like opening a window and letting a bird whose broken wing has healed fly out. I like to think that while they are here the Gestapo can't find them. Of course, when I have to send them back, who knows? But at least while they're here they're safe. I so admire the Berliners, how they dig themselves out of the rubble every morning and go about their chores. They say that the Berliners are the least Hitlerized of all the German people. Friedrich thinks I'm mad, I can tell, but he's known me since I was a little girl, he worked for my parents and he would not let them down by denying me my wish.'

'And if your husband comes back?'

'Oh, I let the birds fly away before he returns. He knows nothing. I prefer not to think what he might do if he knew there were Jews in his castle. Once he came home unexpectedly and Friedrich had to smuggle out four small children while I entertained him . . .'

'So he might return at any moment?'

'No, not for another two weeks. We're quite safe. And what's more, we're on our own. Friedrich wouldn't let me stay and pick up any others after we found you so, darling, we'll be girls together. Such fun!'

'And Benz?' Christiane was beginning to relax a little. The Countess was clearly a little mad but Christiane didn't think she had ever seen anyone so beautiful.

'Oh, Benz is a real old woman,' she said, stroking his head.

Later, as Christiane lay in bed awaiting sleep, she felt a deep sense of release. Nina might think that by taking her in and feeding her for a while that she had helped Christiane, but it was in allowing the girl to confide in her that she had really saved her. For Christiane knew now that she really was a survivor in every sense of the word. Nina had given her back her strength and her faith in herself; now she could go back and face whatever the future held for her in Berlin.

She barely heard the door open and it was only as Nina approached that Christiane saw her outlined in the moonlight. Nina slipped into bed beside her.

'Do you hate men for what they have done to you?' she whispered in the darkness. Christiane didn't answer. 'It doesn't matter,' continued Nina. 'What you must know is that they have never given you love. You need love so badly and if I only show you just a little it has to be better than nothing. I want you to be able to love your body after all the abuse it has received at the hands of those pigs, I want to show you what happens when you receive love instead. Lie still . . .'

Christiane felt the soft, fine hands begin to stroke her shoulder and massage her upper arm and she experienced the same thrilling sensation she had had in the library. Nina's hands moved across her chest and down to her large breasts. Christiane moved to protest, not because she didn't like what was happening but because she was embarrassed about their size. Nina ignored her and proceeded to knead them gently and rub the nipples between thumb and forefinger till they hardened. Then she moved the palm of her hand over Christiane's stomach and stroked slowly before arriving at the mound of her pubic hair.

It was all done so tenderly that Christiane succumbed willingly. Her vagina was so wet she barely felt Nina's finger enter her. When she climaxed she shuddered and Nina held her tightly.

'That's what happens. You've never known that before, have you? You're beautiful, Christiane, and . . . and I love you.' As she fell asleep in Nina's arms, Christiane's last thought was that up till that moment no one, including her family, had ever told her that they loved her.

The next morning she awoke to find that Nina had already rung for breakfast and when Friedrich entered with the now familiar silver tray and placed it before them without so much as a flicker of an eye, Christiane realized that it was by no means the first time he had found his mistress in bed with someone other than her husband, let alone another woman.

Returning to Berlin was far more of an ordeal than Christiane had anticipated. One minute she was riding in style in the back of the Mercedes with Nina by her side, clasping her tightly by the hand as she stared resolutely at the back of Friedrich's head. The next minute she was stepping out into the bombarded ruins of the Budapesterstrasse and turning to catch a last glimpse of Nina's gloved hand waving through the rear window as Friedrich drove her away. Nina's husband was returning that night from Frankfurt. Would Nina have to share his bed? Nina had sworn that they had separate bedrooms, that she could not bear him to touch her, that he understood and went his own way, allowing her to go hers. The fact that they had no children after ten years of marriage seemed proof of this.

A further shock awaited Christiane. Her building had been bombed almost beyond recognition. What was so extraordinary was that a bomb appeared to have fallen on it dead centre, slicing it in two. One half was still standing while the other lay in rubble, sprawled all over the ground. The house was like an architect's model, the kind you can look into from one side and see all the rooms.

It was also empty.

Christiane checked her meagre belongings, and since she owned nothing of value almost everything was still there. Mercifully her side of the house was the half still standing. Only her clothes, such as they had been, had gone but she would have thrown them out anyway since Nina had given her a suitcase full from her sister's elegant wardrobe. Christiane decided she would be better off on the first floor so she lugged her mattress up the exposed staircase that now ran up the side of the house instead of the middle as before. The place she would now inhabit must once been have been a fine reception room. The remains of a chandelier hung miraculously from the centre of the ceiling. It didn't work, of course, but it looked impressive. Christiane heaved the mattress over to lie underneath it in the centre of the room. Then, to her delight, she found an old clothes rail on which she hung her new wardrobe.

She had two days' peace before the word got round that she was back and a party of soldiers arrived to be serviced, but somehow, despite the dingy surroundings, the sight of her in such fine new clothes unnerved them. She sensed this immediately and played on it.

'Well, have you brought something to drink at least?' she asked and when they shook their heads in confusion, she shrugged as if to say, 'Well, what are you here for then?' To save face they took her out for a drink at the Kempinski where she attached herself to one of them, making it look as if she was his regular girl and not the one he had hired for the night. She let him walk her home afterwards where, to her amazement, he produced a pair of silk stockings. She let him put them on her, sliding them carefully up her legs, then she made him take them off again in case he ruined them in what was to come. As he prepared to mount her she pushed him gently away and proceeded to show him, as Nina had shown her, how she wanted him to handle her. His clumsy, rushed attempts at foreplay could not compare with Nina's tender touch but at least it was better than the usual evil-smelling, drink-sodden naked body forcing its way into her.

He left considerably more money than she had ever been left before. Christiane recalled that when she had been hit while cycling through the Lützowplatz she had been on her way to the Embassy district to seek a better class of client. It seemed that in future she need not bother: they would come to her.

As her life slipped back into its old routine, albeit a more exalted version, at the back of her mind was always the worry that she should be doing something to get her away from Berlin, to obtain proper papers – dare she admit it? – non-Jewish papers.

When the man approached her on the Ku'damm at first she thought he was a potential client. Then, when he revealed swiftly that he knew she was Jewish she feared he was a Jew-catcher and tried to push him away with the palms of her hands. It was only when he whispered, 'Nina, *die Gräfin* Nina sent me,' that she understood. This man had been sent to help her. She took him back to the Budapesterstrasse house and told him to act like a client for his own safety, forcing him to put his arm around her waist and slip his hand over her buttocks, which clearly embarrassed him. Once inside, he stepped away from her and followed her up the staircase not realizing that he was still exposed to the street.

'I can arrange black market papers for you. *Die Gräfin* Nina will pay 5,000 marks. I'll do it through Hamburg.

Their records have all been destroyed in the blitz so you give me a false name, place and date of birth and I tell them in Hamburg that you lived in a part of the city that was destroyed but that you wish to visit elsewhere for a while but never mentioning Berlin. They give me new departure papers for you to go from Hamburg to some other place that has not been bombed. The Gestapo suspect any papers originating from Hamburg because they know there is no way of checking the original records. But if your papers from Hamburg to this place in between are converted into papers from the place in between to Berlin, they won't suspect a thing. You'll have a false identity from some little place you've probably never even heard of. What do you say?'

'How is Nina?' whispered Christiane.

'*Na* . . . don't even ask. When her husband's around we have to wait for her to contact us. You'll see her again. Don't worry, *Schatzi*, she'll be back . . .'

Several weeks later the black marketeer accosted her again and presented her with her papers.

Christiane stared at them. She could leave. She had a brand new name, a new passport, a non-Jewish passport. She could leave whenever she wanted – but she stayed on because she knew she could not leave without seeing Nina again.

One afternoon following a particularly heavy raid the night before, as she was walking down the Kurfürstenstrasse, Friedrich pulled up beside her in the Mercedes. He put a hand out to stop her and opened the rear door, motioning to her to get in.

She was so overjoyed at the prospect of seeing Nina again that she did not notice Friedrich's morose silence during the drive out to Mittenwald. On arrival, without even offering to take her coat, he showed her into the library where Nina had first kissed her neck.

The figure standing in front of the fire was not Nina.

Christiane stopped short when she saw him. He turned and she knew at once that this was Nina's husband. Like his wife he had the fine bone structure of aristocratic breeding. He was dressed for riding in breeches, jacket and an open-necked shirt. In his hand was a large brandy. Benz lay sprawled sat his feet, mournfully licking his boots. 'Please forgive me for not changing, Fräulein. I have had a shock. Please sit down.' He gestured to the sofa where Christiane had sat every evening with Nina.

'I ride every morning at dawn. On my return this morning I was told some distressing news. My wife . . . Nina . . . was killed last night, crushed under some falling masonry. She had made Friedrich drive her into Berlin. It seemed, as far as I can gather, that she wanted to see you. Apparently she feared that you might be leaving Berlin in the near future. Friedrich was with her when she died. She asked him to make sure you received this . . . I gather you were rather close,' and he dropped something into Christiane's lap before turning once again to face the fire.

It was Nina's tiny black pearl ring.

As Christiane slipped it onto her finger she knew she would not need it to remember Nina. For the first time she realized that old saying would turn out to be true: you never forget your first love.

Seventeen

The day they saw Saskia for the last time they awoke to a chilling frost. It was a Sunday. No one wanted to get up. Saskia huddled under the bedclothes while Barney ran into the room and gathered Klara up to take her downstairs.

'I'll bring her back to you after I've given her her bottle. You can keep her with you while we go to church.'

'I admire your devotion going to church in this weather,' mumbled Saskia into her pillow, 'You must be mad.'

'It's not my idea as you well know. Bloody Selwyn! Any more remarks like that, Sassy, and I'll let you get up and feed Klara . . .'

By the time he brought Klara upstairs, Saskia had fallen asleep again. Barney laid Klara beside her and sat down on the bed. He couldn't believe how beautiful Saskia looked, her dark hair spread out all over the pillow, her breath escaping softly from her slightly parted lips in little puffs. Barney gently lifted the bedclothes away from her and saw that her nightdress had slipped off her shoulder exposing her breast. He bent his head and planted a kiss, pulling slightly on her nipple. At the same time Klara made a cheerful gurgling sound and Saskia opened her eyes.

She smiled sleepily at them both.

'My family,' she said and no two words could have made Barney happier. He buried his face in the warmth of her neck and her hair and half climbed into bed alongside her.

'Wait,' said Saskia, 'let me put a couple of pillows on the

185

other side of Klara in case she falls off the bed. Now she's all right. I can give you my full attention.'

They had started to snatch moments together like this. Not only did Selwyn's presence inhibit them but they had single beds, and in the hours that Klara let them they needed all the sleep they could get. But every now and then they slipped naturally into each other's arms and if Selwyn was out they made love. The bond between them was strengthening every day and they both knew that soon they would have to tell him.

Barney lifted his head and saw that the tweed of his jacket had rubbed against Saskia's soft white skin, causing it to redden in a rash. He planted kisses everywhere trying to erase the redness.

'Barney! Where are you? Come on, we'll be late.'

'You'd better go before he comes up here looking for you,' whispered Saskia. 'Kiss me first.'

She sat up in bed, her long hair falling down her back, her now naked breasts pressed against the wool of his jersey as he wrapped her inside his jacket. Their lips met and parted and their tongues stroked each other. Saskia raised both hands and clasped Barney's shock of blond hair.

Suddenly she pulled herself away and flopped back down on the bed.

'Go!' she commanded, 'go now before I am no longer responsible for my actions.'

'What do you mean, you're no longer responsible? How do you think I'm coping with you lying there in a state of undress?'

'I know how you feel,' said Saskia, looking serious for a moment, 'and I love you too.'

Barney stood up and slipped out of the room blowing her a kiss as he went. On his way downstairs he knew he couldn't wait any longer. That night – after supper, after Selwyn had retired for the night, after Klara had gone to sleep – he would ask her to marry him.

★

Selwyn had resigned himself to being back at Laurel Bank. It was his home, after all, and he tried in as much as he was able to restore something of the former atmosphere he had enjoyed with Saskia and Barney. He wondered what had become of poor Smudger – presumably Saskia had found a way of ending the short-lived engagement.

Saskia had been aware of a slight tension in the air following Selwyn's return and was relieved when it evaporated. As time slipped by, she became less preoccupied with Selwyn and more enchanted by little Klara.

The one time she was alone with her daughter was on Sunday mornings. Selwyn insisted Barney accompany him to church but Saskia could not bring herself to return to the place where she had first met Klara's father.

Left behind, her old fears overcome, Saskia had begun secretly to discover motherhood. She found herself able to concentrate on her baby, to wonder at her, to take pride in the fact that she had created this perfect little creature. She saw her own dark hair and brown eyes and knew that this was truly her child, the one person in the world who belonged to her and who genuinely needed her. And slowly she had begun to love her. She didn't actually say as much to Barney but she knew he was aware of it. She continued to leave the night time routine to Barney but on Sunday mornings the love affair between Saskia and her daughter had blossomed and as Klara's first birthday approached Saskia had found herself regretting more and more that she had not begun to appreciate her child until so late.

If only Mutti and Vati could have seen how well her life had turned out. Not for the first time, the fleeting picture in her mind of her parents' faces caused her to hug Klara closer to her. She would never allow herself to be parted from Klara. Ever.

Nancy Sanders, up from London for some reason, left church before the sermon ended and as she came down the aisle, Barney felt the full force of her particularly triumphant smile and wondered why. He and Selwyn returned to Laurel Bank to find that Saskia had made an exceptionally tasty onion and potato pie. After lunch Selwyn insisted on going for a walk.

'Schnutzi and Putzi! Utterly ridiculous names for Labradors. They sound like two stupid little lap dogs and if we don't give them some solid exercise that's exactly what they'll become. Come on, Barney, on with the wellingtons.'

Barney groaned. 'Saskia's turn to go out,' he mumbled. 'I've got some drawing to finish.'

'Not on the Sabbath, you haven't. Saskia can bring Klara to the end of the drive in the pram and after that we're on our own. Come along, don't dawdle.'

Later, as Saskia manoeuvred the huge pram into the hall of the Bell House, she didn't hear the police car coming up the drive behind her. As she turned to close the front door the policeman standing there took her by surprise.

'Here, let me give you a hand with that,' he said as he lifted the back wheels of the pram over the threshold.

'Thank you, officer,' said Saskia. 'Now, what can I do for you? I'm afraid Mr Reilly's out at the moment.'

'Well, it's you I'd like a word with actually, miss. Or should I say missus,' he added with a glance at the pram, 'if your name is Saskia Kessler, that is?'

Saskia didn't answer the question. Instead she said: 'Would you like a cup of tea?'

'Well, that's very nice, Don't mind if I do.'

Saskia peeped inside the pram. Klara was fast asleep. Saskia motioned to the policeman to go down the passage and into the kitchen while she wheeled the pram through the door and into the ground floor weaving room. It would be quiet there. Klara could sleep on in peace. She left the door open. Klara would wake up soon wanting her feed.

She made a pot of tea in silence while the policeman prattled on. Then she nearly dropped the pot when he suddenly asked to see her passport and her national Registration Identity Card.

'And the baby's too, of course. Just routine, you know, routine.'

'Yes, of course,' said Saskia, her heart hammering. 'I shall just go upstairs and get them for you.'

'Oh, have your tea first. Join me in a cup, won't you?'

'No,' said Saskia as if in a trance. 'No, thank you. You drink your tea. I'll be back in a minute.'

As she passed the open door to the mill she thought: *This is it, Klara, my little one, they've found us. What are we going to do?*

She was halfway up the stairs when she suddenly needed to hold Klara in her arms. She tiptoed down again and into the weaving room. Klara was still sleeping. Saskia leaned over and picked her up.

Then she dropped her for the first time as her hands flew to her mouth to stop the scream rising in her throat.

The ground was hard underfoot from the frost and they walked quickly across the fields, their breath clearly visible in the freezing air. Putzi, brave and adventurous, ran ahead, often disappearing altogether in his search for rabbits and other excitements. Schnutzi, more timid and ever her master's pet, loped obediently at Barney's heels, misunderstanding and wagging her tail at him when he entreated her to run off and enjoy herself with Putzi.

'I'll put the kettle on,' yelled Barney when they returned an hour later, rushing into the kitchen. 'Sassy, we're back.'

No reply.

'I simply can't believe that lazy so-and-so's gone back to bed again,' laughed Barney, climbing the stairs to find out. 'No,' he called down, 'she's not up here either. Probably popped down the garden for something.'

'Like what exactly in the middle of winter?' scoffed Selwyn but there was more than a trace of anxiety in his voice.

They searched the Bell House. She simply wasn't there. Then they moved through the entire mill. No sign whatsoever.

189

'Where has she gone? And where's Klara? If Sassy's gone outside she'd have taken her in the pram but it's in the ground-floor weaving room.' Barney's voice was beginning to shake.

An hour later they were frantic and when they heard the sound of a car coming up the drive they both rushed to the window. When they saw the shooting brake Selwyn literally hugged Barney in relief.

'Sarah! Bloody woman! She must have come over and taken Saskia and Klara off somewhere. Why didn't they leave us a note? Women!'

It was indeed Lady Sarah but it wasn't Saskia who was with her. It was a policeman.

'Any sign of her, sir?'

'Any sign of who?' Selwyn glared at him. 'Come along inside, Sarah, Saskia's out.'

'Would that be your German lady, sir?'

'What exactly do you mean "your German lady"?'

'A Miss Saskia Kessler, I believe her name is. That's what the young lady told me anyway. I'd like to come inside and ask you a few questions about her, if you don't mind, sir?'

'Actually I do mind. I mind most awfully.'

'Selwyn!' Lady Sarah's tone of voice was uncommonly stern. 'Do as he says. I fear something terrible may have happened.'

'It was the young lady at the Vicarage, sir,' explained the policeman when he was safely ensconced in the kitchen with a cup of Barney's undrinkable tea.

'Nancy,' prompted Lady Sarah. 'Pray God, Selwyn, one day you'll forgive me for what she's done.'

'What has she done, for heaven's sake? Will somebody please tell me?' Selwyn was barely able to restrain his temper.

'I'm trying to, sir,' said the policeman in infuriatingly polite tones. 'She came to see me. Told me there was an illegal alien living here and I should come and investigate. Of course, I came straight over, met the young German lady just as she was coming back from walking the little one. I even helped her with the pram.' He looked around him as if he was expecting applause. When no one said a word he continued: 'I asked her if she was Miss Kessler and she didn't answer, just said would I have a cup of tea? Just like I'm doing now. Very nice of her but I could tell she was a Jerry the moment she opened her mouth.'

'A Jerry!' yelled Barney, outraged. 'Saskia's not a Jerry!'

'All right, Barney,' Selwyn interrupted. 'You must have seen Miss Kessler before, officer. She's lived here for over five years. I know we're a bit cut off but they all know her in the village.'

'They do indeed, sir. I asked around.'

'So what is all this?'

'Just routine, Mr Reilly. I merely asked if I might see her passport and her national Registration Identity Card for her and her baby.'

'Ah, well, you wouldn't have been able to see the baby's. Bit of a problem there. My fault entirely. We just haven't got around to getting one yet. I keep meaning to do it.'

'Funny, she didn't mention that at all. Said everything was in order and would I wait a minute while she went upstairs to get them? One small problem.'

'What's that?'

'She never came back.'

'What?'

'I waited for half an hour, poured myself another cup of tea, in fact. She makes good tea for a German, I'll say that for her. Better than this if you don't mind my saying.'

'We mind everything you're saying,' said Selwyn rudely. 'Get on with it, man, for heaven's sake.'

'So after half an hour I went to look for her. Called her name up the staircase. No reply. I didn't want to search the house uninvited so I left. Thought it best to come back later and sort it out.'

Selwyn and Barney looked at each other.

'Selwyn, what's happened?' Lady Sarah was becoming suspicious.

'She's not here,' said Selwyn simply. 'We went out for a walk, Barney and me. We were gone for at least two hours and when we got back she had disappeared. She's taken Klara with her, what's more. Barney, where are you going?'

Barney had rushed out of the kitchen. When he returned he was flushed.

'It's gone. It's not there any more. She's taken her passport.'

'I want her found,' Selwyn told the policeman before sending him away. 'I want a search party organized at once and I want to be part of it.'

'Me too,' said Barney.

'And in the meantime, Sarah, I want a word with Nancy.'

'Don't we all?' sighed Lady Sarah. 'The trouble is she seems to have disappeared as well. None of us has seen her since she walked out of church this morning.'

'Well, I'm coming back to the Vicarage with you just in case,' said Selwyn firmly.

They were greeted by the bizarre sight of Angela Appleby almost flying down the Vicarage steps to meet them.

'Angela, is Nancy back yet?' Lady Sarah regarded her warily.

'Oh, she won't be back for quite a while by the looks of things. Here, read this. She left it in my room to give to you.'

Lady Sarah opened the small cream envelope and gingerly removed a sheet of paper. She read it and within seconds she had crumpled it into a ball and stuffed it into the pocket of her cardigan.

'Eloped! That's what she says she's done. I doubt she even knows the meaning of the word.'

'Who with?' asked Selwyn.

'She says he's an American called Irving, part of General Patton's lot. What are they called? The Third Army. He's been stationed over at Peover Hall in Cheshire, but Nancy appears to have met him down in London when she was staying with her father. First Saskia, now Nancy.'

'Saskia?' Angela's ears positively flapped.

'Disappeared. Police went to ask for her passport and she did a bunk . . . something to do with Nancy. You wouldn't happen to be in a position to fill us in, by any chance, Angela? Having been so close to Nancy . . .' Lady Sarah advanced upon Angela, Barney close behind her.

'Well, it's obvious, isn't it?' replied Angela triumphantly.

'Regrettably not to us. Perhaps you'd be so good as to enlighten us.' Selwyn's tone was icily polite.

'That passport of hers – said she could only stay in England a year. I think you'll probably find she never bothered to register with the police when she arrived. Then when she realized she was in the country illegally she opted to keep quiet about it.'

'What I don't quite understand, Angela, is how you know all this?' Selwyn was by now no more than inches from her and she stepped back nervously.

'Oh, you know, Nancy and I were . . .' she stopped realizing she had incriminated herself when she saw Barney's look of horror.

'She thought he'd take her prisoner, send her to an internment camp, I suppose,' said Selwyn bitterly. 'Oh, why didn't I check on her when she first arrived? It's all my fault.'

But the saddest thing of all, thought Lady Sarah, *is that my own daughter has run off and it means nothing to me. But if I never see Saskia again it will break my heart.*

Selwyn and Barney huddled together for three long nights in the freezing February of 1945. When darkness fell the search for Saskia was abandoned each day and Selwyn cursed the fact that it was winter and that there was so little daylight.

'We took her for granted,' he told Barney over and over again. 'I don't mean we ignored her good qualities or treated her badly. It's just we never realized how insecure she must have felt. She was Jewish and we talked in front of her about all the awful things that were happening over there without a thought for her feelings. And the worst of it is that she hardly ever said anything. We just assumed that because she'd been here for a few years that she felt as English as we did and thought nothing of it. But she must have been terrified they would find out about her passport, that they would come and get her. And now they have in a way. She's a refugee all over again except this time she's fleeing from the very people to whom she came for shelter . . .'

They never found Saskia, but a week later the police made a horrific discovery in a ditch about six miles across the fields from Laurel Bank. Thorny bushes growing across the ditch made a natural hiding place. At first they thought an animal of some kind had tried to bury her young but as they uncovered more of the soil from the mound they found that the body was that of a human infant, still clothed in a baby's robe and wrapped in a cot blanket.

It was Klara. Selwyn had to identify the body. Barney begged to do it but Selwyn would not allow him near it. How the child had died was a mystery. It was suggested that an infant exposed for even a minimal amount of time to the freezing temperatures could die of hypothermia but Barney knew Saskia would never have let such a thing happen to little Klara.

He wept at night alone in his room. After a while he took to sleeping in Saskia's room, remembering that last Sunday morning with her. One day at dawn, he took the cradle he had made for Klara outside and burned it. Selwyn watched from his bathroom window and decided not to interfere. It was Barney's business how he coped with his grief.

Out of respect for Saskia, Selwyn and Barney conducted their own funeral for Klara, burying her down by the river at Laurel Bank close to the weir. Selwyn barred the Applebys from the occasion and allowed only Lady Sarah to attend. Together he and Barney went to Manchester to see a Jewish friend of Selwyn's and learned from him the exact words of the Jewish burial service. As they said the unfamiliar words hesitantly over the grave, a grave made all the more poignant because of its pathetic size, both of them added their own silent prayers for Saskia's return.

Eighteen

'Hey, Sal, you know what I was trying to figure out?'

'No, Bobby, I'm driving. Can't you see? Rain's coming down like we was in the ark instead of a Jeep. I can't see beans in front of me . . .'

'I was trying to figure out how many women you've had since we came over here. How many you reckon you've had?'

'Jesus, Bobby, I ain't exactly been counting.'

'You figure you had more'n fifty?'

'Reckon so. Maybe. Hell, I don't know. What's it to you, anyways?'

'We got a reputation. All over England. We got a reputation.'

'Who has?'

'Us. GIs. With women. We got us a reputation. They say English women ain't never seen anything like us.'

Sal shrugged and concentrated on steering the Jeep through the sheet of rain. It was more important that they get back to Burtonwood camp before they were completely soaked. Sure, he'd had a lot of women. Who hadn't? What else was there to do for kicks? It wasn't as if he was off fighting in France. Burtonwood was a giant supply and repair base. He didn't get to go anywhere except Liverpool and Warrington.

'Well, we're going home soon. You gonna marry Sylvia? Take her with you? Broad like her has really got It. Loaded with SA from head to toe. Hey, Sal, you heard what I asked?'

'Hey, take a break, will you, Buddy? I'm trying to get us back to base alive and all you want to talk about is women.'

'Well, she's telling everyone you're gonna marry her. I just thought maybe you oughta know. Sylvia and Salvatore Carlino. Mr and Mrs Carlino. Syl and Sal. Sounds okay to me, sounds like . . .' Suddenly Bobby leaned forward in his seat. 'Hey, speed it up around here, will ya, Sal?'

'I am speeding it up. That's what I've been trying to tell you – '

'No, ya gotta go faster. This is the place.'

'What place?'

'Where they seen her.'

'Bobby, I'm warning you, I'm through with talking about women.'

'Nah, she's a ghost. You must have heard about her.'

'Oh, Jesus, Bobby. You don't believe that crap?'

'I don't know but I don't want to get the chance to find out. They say she haunts this stretch, comes out at you from the woods over there and just when you figure out she's a woman, she's gone. Billy Joe Lee done drove his Jeep right off the road and into a ditch, swear to God. She made him do it. They say if you see her you're never the same again . . .'

Sal shook his head in the darkness of the Jeep. He'd never heard such crazy garbage.

'Cool it, will you, Bobby. Any gum, chum? I need something to chew to keep me awake . . .' Still, when they reached the barbed wire surrounding the camp and saw the hangars looming out of the mist, he did feel a sense of relief and he wasn't sure it was just because he had made it through the rain.

The next night he was by himself. The rain had stopped. The sky was clear. Leaning forward and looking up he could even see stars. He began to hum to himself. Women sometimes told him he looked a little like that new band vocalist everyone was talking about. Probably nothing more than the fact that the guy was Italian just like him. Hell, Sinatra was a little guy and he, Sal, was big. Very big – especially where it mattered.

Sal chuckled. Then his face sobered. What was he going to do about Sylvia? Sylvia was a handful whichever way you looked at her. She was stacked in all the right places and ever since she'd let him take her out to a field, lay a blanket on the ground and have him lift her legs high up on his shoulders while he showed her how big he really was (having bragged about it for weeks), he hadn't looked at another woman.

Only now she wanted to get married and move back to the States with him. She claimed she was Italian way back on her mother's side and he believed her. She was dark enough. And if he went home with a bride it would put an end to his mother lining up the nice Italian girls all around the block for him day in, day out. Sylvia had made it clear she would come with her own small private income. Her father was something to do with the Adelphi Hotel and he had put 'something aside for our Sylvia's wedding day'. He wasn't important enough to get his prospective son-in-law into the Adelphi, which was for officers only. Enlisted men like Sal were shown the door.

But there was something about Sylvia that Sal didn't quite like. She was coarse. It had been she who had asked to be taken to the field rather than the other way around. It wasn't even the first time they'd gone all the way. She'd dragged him out of the pub one night and down an alleyway, pulled his raincoat around her, opened his trousers and thrust herself against him. She was small boned, despite her big breasts, and when he'd grasped her by her skinny hips and lifted her onto him, she'd screamed so loud in his ear that he'd dropped her, thinking he'd done her a terrible injury. It was the way she climbed right back onto him that made him recoil in slight disgust. Sal liked to be in charge. He had to call the shots. He didn't want a lover who would take the initiative and when he married he wanted a wife who wouldn't move without his say so.

And Sylvia was pushy.

Sylvia!

Jesus Christ! He'd just seen her streak across the road in

front of him. What was she doing all the way out here on her own in the middle of nowhere? Had she followed him out of town? How? What was she trying to do? Haunt him?

He swerved off the road in panic as it hit him where he was. He'd arrived at that stretch where Bobby said guys had seen a ghost and Sylvia had run across the road in front of him and disappeared.

Yet it couldn't possibly be Sylvia. He'd left Sylvia back home in Liverpool waving goodbye at her parents' front door, looking as innocent as pie even though she'd taken his dick out her mouth only half an hour earlier.

So had he seen a ghost?

Sal pulled over and leapt out of the Jeep. The ghost – dammit –the woman – had run from left to right and disappeared. He looked across the fields and saw the woods just like Bobby had said. Sal stopped to put a match to a cigarette within his cupped hands and stumbled across the field. It wasn't till he reached the outskirts of the woods that he realized he could hear his own heart hammering in his chest.

He was terrified!

He heard a scuffling somewhere in the woods in front of him. He had no idea what to expect. He was a city boy from New York. He'd never been out in the country in his life except in the safety of his Jeep and certainly never in the pitch black of night.

He had no torch so as he moved deeper into the heart of the wood he struck match after match to light his way. His hands were shaking so much he dropped half of them. Then he saw a glow ahead of him. He stuffed the matchbox back in his pocket and advanced cautiously.

As he drew nearer he could see a small campfire and behind it a little cottage. Sal was so curious to investigate further that he forgot his earlier fear.

He did not sense the presence crouched in the tree above him until an animal landed on his back and tried to scratch his eyes out.

*

When Saskia had found Klara dead in her pram that last day at Laurel Bank she had been propelled into frenzied action. Sweeping up the stiff little body in the cot blanket, she had carried her in her arms, running silently out of the house and away across the fields as fast as she could until exhausted. Then she had sunk down and rocked her tiny lifeless daughter in a state of total numbness.

She had known Klara was dead the moment her hands had touched her in the pram. Later she would force herself to accept that Klara must have died upstairs in her cot while she was down in the kitchen making lunch for Selwyn and Barney. Klara might well already have been dead – although still warm so Saskia hadn't noticed – when she was lifted into her pram for the walk after lunch. But when she had gone into the weaving room and touched her, the little body had emanated an eerie coldness and in one split second Saskia had known there was no way she was going to leave her baby behind, dead or alive. *Leave her baby behind.* It was then that she realized she had decided to make a run for it.

She had dug Klara's grave with her own hands, scrabbling down into the frozen earth like a dog searching for its bone. She had sat shivah for two days before she had forced herself to leave and look for food.

For one fleeting moment she contemplated her own death. All she would have to do would be to remove her clothes and expose herself to the freezing cold of the night air. Her body was small and fragile; she would not last long without food and warmth. She could even lie down in the ditch beside Klara and wait for death to take her. But what would it serve? She was convinced by now that her parents were dead. Now her child was dead surely it was up to her to try to go on living.

As she dragged herself away from the pathetic little mound of earth at the bottom of a ditch, her only comfort was in her certainty that nothing worse could possibly happen to her for the rest of her life. What made it even harder to bear was the knowledge that she had paid so little

199

attention to Klara in the beginning. Then, just as she had begun to love her with a ferocity she did not know existed within her, she had lost her. She had been punished. So be it.

To say something died within Saskia with Klara's death would be an understatement but at the same time a fierce and horrible strength was born. Now Klara was dead Saskia felt a new determination to survive, to live with her memory and to honour it as each new day dawned. The hardest moment came when she had returned to the ditch having stolen some food, creeping into a nearby kitchen through a back door while the household slept, to see Barney and Selwyn climbing down into it. She had wanted to run to Barney, to feel the comfort of his arms, to let him take her back to Laurel Bank and the security she had known for the last six years. But then she had seen the policemen swarming out of the ditch holding Klara's tiny body aloft . . .

She had wanted to cry out to them to honour the dead, to leave her baby buried in peace, but they were police and she could not reveal herself to them. She was a fugitive. Overnight she had developed the natural cunning of someone on the run. She knew they would not return to the ditch having already searched it so she stayed there, breaking the ice and drinking the water from the stream, and moving when it was dark to sleep in a nearby barn for warmth.

Then she began what she would always think of as her trek. She was small and dark and dishevelled and she looked foreign. She could not afford to be seen by anyone. She must only move at night. She walked for four nights and what she did not know was that she was walking in the wrong direction. She wanted to get to Liverpool. There she would hide herself away on board a ship and . . . Her ideas were fantastical but she was operating as if in a dream and what would have happened to her if Joachim hadn't found her on the fifth morning didn't bear thinking about.

She had been so tired and weak that she had fallen asleep

in the hayloft where she had hidden herself for the afternoon. She had awakened with a start and rushed to the ladder to climb down and make her escape. Joachim had watched her descent with interest.

'*Guten Tag,*'

Saskia slipped in shock but it was not the sound of his voice that had shaken her; it was the German greeting, the German she had not heard since she had left Berlin.

Joachim was a prisoner of war who had been let out of a camp to work on a farm. He was a simpleton who did not speak a word of English but to Saskia he represented a lifeline.

'*Kannst nicht hier bleiben,*' he had told her matter-of-factly. '*Muss dich was anders finden*'.

And he had found her somewhere else to live: a derelict cottage on the edge of the estate on which he worked. In different circumstances it would have been idyllic with its tiny dormer windows under the eaves and rambling rose bush round the front door.

Saskia had made it her home – at least for the moment. Simple mind that he might be, Joachim had enough sense to suggest she stay there till the war was over because, who knew, things could change then and they could all go home. He had brought her food every day from the farm. He had brought her books to read and newspapers. And then he had begun to tell her about the film he had been made to watch by British soldiers standing over him and his fellow prisoners, a film about Belsen . . .

'*Was ist Belsen?*'

When he told her she wished she hadn't asked. 'Look what you did to the Jews,' Joachim said they had accused him, but while he wasn't Jewish he knew he would never have done anything like that.

Saskia believed him. He was a comfort to her. She was not ready to talk about her own experiences and he never asked but it was a comfort to be able to talk in her own language, to hear about life on the farm, to listen to his hopes for the future when he went back to Hanover and his family.

Then one day he had arrived with the news that the son of the family at the farm had come home to announce his engagement. Now he was back Joachim would no longer be needed on the farm. He was to be sent away, back to his camp.

Joachim would not be able to bring her food so he told her to run across the road at night where she would find the milk churns in the farmyard and the eggs in the henhouse. He left a long list of instructions along with an assortment of household goods he had been able to salvage. Finally, he looked up at the sky and told her to make good use of a poacher's moon when there was one as it would light her way across the countryside late at night to seek provisions at the farm.

Then he had left her to return to his camp and she had realized she would never see him again.

Thus, unknown to her as she streaked across the main road and the fields in the moonlight, she became the GI's ghost. Now for the first time since she had taken up residence in the cottage someone had come trespassing on her territory in the woods off the road. Someone in uniform. She had been watching him approach from her lookout in the tree. As he passed underneath her she leapt off the branch onto his back and clawed her nails across his face.

In one seamless movement he clasped her by the arm, pulled her over his shoulder, flung her on the ground and instantly placed a hefty boot on her chest.

Saskia had prepared herself for this moment time and time again. She braced herself for the beating she was convinced would follow, the interminable questions, the end of freedom. Not once did she imagine she would hear the words: 'Gee, little lady, did anyone ever tell you you look a lot like Sylvia?'

'Listen, honey, all I want you to do is say something to me so I know you're real. Aw, no, that sounds dumb but you

202

wouldn't believe the stories they're telling back at camp. They think you're a ghost. Ain't that something? So tell me, is this where you live or what? Just kidding! You can't live here. I know that. This place is filthy. But why do you come here? You meet someone here? Is that it? I see you got a mattress in there, you got your clothes strung up about the place, you even got a toothbrush . . . Say, what's with you? Do you really live here? And what's this little cross over here in the corner? You buried a little animal here or something . . .?'

She sprang at him and he was knocked sideways for a second in his surprise.

'Leave it,' she hissed. 'Leave it alone.'

'Okay. Okay. Look, no can touch.' He held his hands up, palms out. 'You buried your little puppy there or something?'

'There's no one buried there. It's in memory of my daughter.'

'Aw, gee, I'm sorry. Hey, how old was she?'

'A year.'

'A year when she died. Say, that's too bad. Your husband, he . . . he passed away too?'

'I'm not married.'

'Hey, look, I'm sorry. I know we got a bad reputation. My buddy, Bobby, he was just telling me . . . Boy, if I ever got one of you English girls pregnant, believe me, I'd stand by her, I'd –'

'The father was English. I am not.'

'Hell, ma'am, I give up. I don't know what to say next. You don't sound English, tell you the truth. I hate to say this but you sound –'

'I'm German.'

Sal sat down heavily on a log and pulled out a pack of Lucky Strikes from his breast pocket. It was so dark he couldn't see the expression on her face. All he knew was that it was breathtakingly beautiful, a beautiful version of Sylvia's coarse dark features.

'Smoke?' He proffered the Luckys. He sensed her shake her head.

'So are you going to arrest me?'

'What in hell for?'

'For being German in England. For not having the right papers?'

'That's limey business. They take care of that stuff. Far as I'm concerned, you're in England, you're English. What's your name anyway?'

She hesitated.

'C'mon! My name is Salvatore. They call me Sal for short. I'm Italian, well, Italian-American. See, I ain't English either. You heard of Frank Sinatra? No? Where you been? Well, he's this band singer, see, over in America. He's huge. All the girls, they swoon all over him. And they say I look just like him. Course, I'm bigger'n him. Taller and my nose is longer, I got a squarer jaw and I'll bet my eyelashes are longer. Fact is, I don't think I look much like him but if the girls can kid themselves I am it gets me further down the line, *capisce?* That's Italian for "understand?". How d'ya say that in German?'

'*Verstehen Sie?*' Saskia answered automatically, 'if you don't know the person very well, but when you get to know them better you use the word *du* like *tu* in French – so it becomes *verstehst du?*'

'Honey, you speak French as well. You've had an education. Maybe you even speak Italian? No? Well, I'm going to teach you because we're going to become big buddies, you and I, *verstehst du?* You're going to trust me, you'll see. But first you have to tell me your name.'

'Saskia.'

'That's so pretty. So, Saskia, who's this little cross down here for?'

'Klara.'

'There! That wasn't so hard, was it? Another pretty name and you gotta keep saying it. You gotta remember the dead and respect them. I'll bet you pray for her, don't you?' Saskia nodded. 'That's terrific. So where's her English poppa?'

'*Tot.*'

'What's that? *Morto*? Dead?'

'*Ja.*'

'*Mi dispiace. Come?*'

'He was shot down . . .'

'See, you understand Italian already.'

'. . . by Germans.'

'So how did the kid die? Okay, okay, you don't want to tell me any more. You don't have to but you have to do one thing, promise me?'

She looked at him in silence. She wasn't about to promise anybody anything. She had already said too much. What if he came back with the police?

'Okay, so you don't trust me yet but I'm going to help you. I'm going to raid the PX and come back with a whole load of stuff that's going to make your life much more comfortable. You want to live out here like you're queen of the jungle, you go right ahead, but at least let me help you. Winter's coming on and you're going to be mighty cold living in this place in the middle of the woods. If me Tarzan, you gonna be Jane in style . . . Oh, never mind, it's just a movie . . .'

He came back two days later and helped her uproot Klara's little cross and move it to a special clearing he made behind the cottage. He brought her candles. He brought her Lifesavers. He brought her Camp Coffee and showed her how to paint her legs with it to make it look as if she was wearing stockings and then he brought her nylons anyway. He even brought her sanitary towels without being asked (he confessed he was one boy among several sisters). He brought her pillows for her mattress and a kettle which she could fill with water from the stream at the far end of the wood where she washed every day. He built her a makeshift steel frame, which he placed above a fire so that she could cook on-it, and he brought her the kind of food she hadn't eaten in months including fruit – and most luxurious of all he brought her perfume.

'But what would you really like? More than anything else?' he always asked her and finally she told him.

'A sewing machine? Are you crazy? Where in hell am I going to find a sewing machine? And I suppose you want cloth to go with it?'

When he arrived with it she cried and he was so embarrassed, he dumped it on the ground and went away again. When he returned the next day an unfamiliar whirring sound greeted him as he made his way through the woods. She had set it up on the trestle table he had made for her and she was hard at work making herself a skirt. He watched her for quite some time before she noticed him and when she turned her head, Sal was rewarded with Saskia's radiant smile for the first time. He walked up to stand behind her and tentatively laid his hand on her shoulder. She didn't flinch so he patted her once or twice and ran his finger up and down the back of her neck but before he could think of going any further, she had begun to turn the handle again and her head moved away from his touch, bent over the rise and fall of the needle.

This is what it'll be like when I'm married, thought Sal. *I'll be coming home from work and my wife'll be sitting there doing something domestic. Only thing different, she won't be doing it in the middle of some goddamn wood.*

He walked slowly back to the Jeep, unaware of the tears falling down Saskia's face. Sal's touch had penetrated deep into her flesh, warming her, moving her for the first time since she had held Klara in her arms before placing her in her grave. She rose from the sewing machine and went to Klara's cross to say a prayer and as she did so, it hit her that in all the time he had been coming to visit her she had not told him she was Jewish.

As Sal steered the Jeep back to Burtonwood with one hand, the other flicking a cigarette nervously in and out of his mouth, he realized that not once had he mentioned Sylvia's name to Saskia and sooner or later he was going to have to deal with the reason why.

Nineteen

'I'm pregnant,' said Sylvia. 'Well, what are you going to do about it!' she screamed when Sal didn't answer. Sal winced. She was always screeching at him, nagging him, asking him what he was going to do about things, never waiting to let him think things through in his mind and tell her.

Her parents were out for the evening and they had the house to themselves. She'd begun unbuttoning his trousers in the kitchen whilst the sound of her parents' footsteps could still be heard echoing down the tiled hallway to the front door. By the time he heard the click of the garden gate she had lifted her dress over her head and was standing in her slip, about to ease the straps over her shoulders.

'Upstairs, fer Chrissakes,' he'd muttered but she'd wanted it right there in the kitchen, up against the range. Then she'd pulled him up the stairs to her room, dragged him into bed with her and expected him to be ready to do it all over again. It was when he had requested a moment's rest that she had decided to drop her bombshell.

'Well, since you obviously don't seem to know what you're going to do about it, my lad, I'll tell you. You're going to marry me and you're going to do it sooner rather than later. Sylvia Carlino . . .' she muttered to herself. 'It actually sounds Italian, doesn't it? Sal! I said, it sounds Italian, doesn't it? Right then, we'll tell me parents, then we'll tell your commanding officer. We've got to get his permission, don't we? Sal? Are you listening? Are you going to ask me to marry you or do I have to ask meself?'

Sal held Saskia in his arms, softly crooning in her ear. They were dancing in the pool of light thrown out by the headlamps of Sal's Jeep. He had driven it as far as he could into the woods, left the headlamps on and leaped out yelling, 'Let's cut a rug, baby, let's cut a rug right here!' He had not been able to persuade her to leave her hiding place and come with him to a dance at the camp so he had had to bring the dance to her. They had no music so he had to sing:

> '. . . *my stardust melody,*
> *the memory of love . . .*'

At the end of the song they stopped moving and she rested her head against his chest. She was too small to reach his shoulder. He stroked her long, dark hair till it fell in an even sheet down the centre of her back. She had washed it in the stream with the shampoo he had brought her.

'My mother was musical,' she whispered. 'She could sing and she could play the piano and the violin. Sing me something else. I want to go on dancing.'

Sal could not know that she was reliving the times when she had danced with Barney round the kitchen table at Laurel Bank. 'One, two, three; one, two, three . . .' she giggled and Sal held her tight and whirled her round the clearing till she was breathless. She was light and sweet and gentle and so very, very different to Sylvia.

That night before he left he held her face between his hands and lifted her lips to his.

'May I kiss you?' he asked. 'May I?'

In answer she opened her lips a little and brought the tip of her tongue to touch his upper lip. He hardly dared to breathe while she ran it softly from side to side. Then she brought it down to do the same on his lower lip. Finally she brought it to the centre to meet his. Slowly, they explored each other's mouth. Then, as if they both knew exactly the right moment, they each began to retreat until their closed lips were pressed together. Sal raised his face slightly and kissed her on the forehead.

I trust him, thought Saskia as the Jeep's headlamps swung an arc of light around her while she stood waving goodbye. Finally I trust him. Finally I have found someone to trust again.

'I'm beginning to wonder if it's worth it,' grumbled Sylvia. 'I mean, you should have seen your commanding officer's face when I had my interview with him. You'd have thought I were a bloody tart or something. And the questions he asked me: was I married already, by any chance?'

'Did he ask you if you were pregnant?'

'He flipping well did.'

'And?'

'I told him no. I'm a decent girl and I'm not about to let him think otherwise.'

'So he gave his permission then?'

'Well, of course he did and you might look a bit more cheerful about it. Now I've got all these flipping papers to deal with. I've got to get meself a visa, whatever that is, a British passport, two copies of me birth certificate, two copies of me police record if I possess one – that's a laugh – me marriage certificate, three photographs, and money to buy a railway ticket in case you're not there to meet me.'

'Not there to meet you where? And why do they want your marriage certificate if you're not married.'

'Oh, you're dead stupid sometimes, you are, Sal. This is what I'm going to need after we're married so as to be able to come with you back to America.'

They made love for the first time by candlelight in the cottage. It was a cold February night in 1946 but the small paraffin stove Sal had brought over before Christmas gave out enough heat for them to be able to take off all their clothes without shivering.

Sal was amazed by Saskia's passion. Even though she had had a baby he had somehow fixed her in his mind as a virgin who would have to be initiated with care, but it was as if he had struck a match and the flame had ignited within her. Yet she waited for him. She was not like Sylvia. She let him lead her and coax her and bring her to her climax, but when she came she was wild. She arched her back and ran her hands frantically through her long black hair spread out on the pillow. Sal felt his penis swell inside her. She was so tiny he thought he would bust her apart but although she admitted it was sore to begin with, whispering quietly in his ear that it had been a long time since anyone had entered her, she soon began to move with him. Very soon she was so wet he knew he could not be hurting her any more.

When he lowered his head to suck on her nipples, first one and then the other, she stroked the top of his head tenderly and he felt her to be almost maternal but then when she climaxed she was anything but.

Afterwards she lay in his arms and he could feel her trembling.

'I'm trapped,' she told him suddenly. 'I have no papers. My passport is out of date. I cannot get back to Germany. I can't move. Soon you will go back to America and then what will I do?'

'I love you,' he told her in reply, 'and you mustn't worry. The war's over now. You're going to be okay. I'll take care of you.'

Sal married Sylvia the next day in style. His parents sent a telegram from New York saying they were sorry they couldn't be there but they were looking forward to meeting their new Italian daughter-in-law even if she had been born in England. Sylvia's father organized the catering through the Adelphi Hotel. They had a three-tier wedding cake and Sal recalled an Italian recipe for making ice cream and had a gallon made, which was distributed all over Sylvia's street. Sylvia's dress was made from damaged parachute silk and when they were alone in the honeymoon suite at the Adelphi she ripped it to shreds in her eagerness to get it off and thrust her naked body at Sal.

'What about the baby? I'm not hurting my baby.' Sal pointed at her by now slightly distended stomach and rolled over on his side. Sylvia promptly crouched over him and tried to suck his penis.

'Stop that,' he told her. 'You heard what I said. I'm your husband now. You do what I tell you.'

Sylvia ignored him.

Sal's fist slammed into the side of her head, caught her on her ear and sent her flying across the room.

She sat up, put her hand between her legs and began to rub. 'I loved that,' she told him, 'but if anything'll hurt the baby that will, but you can come and finish me off if you like.'

A month later her passport arrived with its visa for America. 'Look at this.' She showed Sal. 'It says, "British by birth, wife of an American serviceman." '

'Better give it to me for safekeeping,' said Sal, and slipped it into the inside pocket of his jacket.

'When I'm gone look under your pillow,' Sal told her as he kissed her goodbye. Saskia struggled to go and see what he had left her. 'Sshhhhh . . . stay here and kiss me,' he ordered and was pleased when she obeyed meekly, clinging to him. Through his uniform she felt him harden against her and rubbed herself against him till they both climaxed, shuddering in each other's arms. It was the only way. There was no time to undress.

Then he was gone, the Jeep bouncing him away through the woods on the first leg of his journey home to America.

Saskia rushed to look under her pillow. The narrow gold band fitted perfectly onto her finger but it was the other item, so vital to her, so totally unexpected, that filled her with the utmost joy.

★

211

'*The bastard's only bloody gone and left me behind!*' screamed Sylvia at the top of her voice when her parents broke the news to her that Sal had left without saying goodbye.

'No, he hasn't, love,' her mother reassured her without much conviction. After all, it was a familiar story, Yanks going off and leaving girls in the lurch. 'You'll be able to join him later, when he's settled, like.'

'Oh, yeah, I suppose you're right.'

'That's it. I expect he had to go sudden, like. You'll be getting a telegram. After all, his parents are expecting you and everything.'

'There you are then, lass,' said her father. 'Nothing to worry about.'

'Nothing to worry about,' repeated Sylvia.

Three hours later she remembered she'd given her passport to Sal for safekeeping.

Saskia was surprised how sorry she was to say goodbye to her woodland home. As she looked forward each day to Sal's visits, she had been almost happy for the first time since she had left Laurel Bank. She had fretted about the future but now that a solution had presented itself, she was apprehensive. Sal had instructed her to travel light and the real pain had been in leaving behind the sewing machine. She could hear Sal's voice saying what he would undoubtedly have said had he still been there: 'What are you, nuts? We got sewing machines in America, honey. We got every damn thing in America!' Well, now she'd find out for herself and as she packed the battered little suitcase she had taken when fleeing from Laurel Bank, she comforted herself with the thought that at least she had been able to make herself some clothes on the sewing machine to take with her.

Saskia arrived at Waterloo Station in London on 14 March. She was put on a special army train which took her to an army camp at Tidworth on Salisbury Plain. She finally arrived at Tidworth by bus in the middle of the night and was fast asleep. As she awoke she heard German voices below her and she froze.

The GI brides' camp at Tidworth was serviced entirely by German prisoners of war. They cooked and served the food into basic tin trays. Every now and then the loudspeakers would warn the brides not to fraternize with them. For Saskia it was very hard not to engage them in conversation, but that was the last thing she must do. She was supposed to be English. She saw that in the passport Sal had given her he had even changed her name to an English one: Sylvia. The photograph did not look much like her but it did not look unlike her. Whatever its conditions, along with a wedding ring which she wore with pride, Sal had left her her passport to America.

Once she had been vaccinated and given a thorough medical inspection, Saskia left the camp early one morning to travel by train to Southampton where she boarded a small boat called the SS *James Parker*. She shared a cabin for two with three other women, two of whom were nursing small babies.

For the entire ten days' crossing to New York Saskia suffered the most unbearable seasickness, but that was as nothing compared with the pain she felt being at such close quarters to two small babies. Memories of Klara flooded back. Memories of her train journey from Berlin to London all those years ago returned to haunt her. As she tossed and turned in her narrow bunk she had to face the fact that she had left the country where, for a while, she had found both security and the beginnings of an identity. Now she was on her way to a strange new world where she would have to begin all over again.

Would Sal be there to meet her when she arrived?

Why had he suddenly given her the name Sylvia? If she had a passport calling her Sylvia Carlino, did it mean that Saskia Kessler had gone forever?

And most important of all, now that she was leaving England, would she ever see Barney again?

Twenty

Barney Lambert was in love.

He turned on his side and looked across at the girl's face resting on the pillow beside him. He watched while she slept. He'd been awake for nearly an hour and he marvelled that she could sleep so soundly, that nothing whatsoever stirred deep in her unconscious alerting her to the fact that someone was watching her so intently. Sooner or later her eyes would open and she would see him. She would remember what had happened the night before.

He would start to feel guilty soon. He always did when he slept with someone. He felt he was betraying Saskia in some way yet two years ago, in the summer of 1945, six months after she had left Laurel Bank, Barney had known she would not be coming back. Selwyn could not be persuaded that she was gone for ever. He had tried to get a full-scale national search under way. He had implored the police to cast their net wider, alert their colleagues all over the country but, with the war on, missing persons were the norm. Selwyn had no legal hold over Saskia, he was neither her official guardian nor her husband. Furthermore she had left of her own accord. Selwyn had begun a systematic correspondence of enquiries to all the internment camps to see if she had turned up in one, and had drawn a blank every time. And so it was that he had started to assume that once the war was over she would come back to Laurel Bank as if nothing had happened and Barney had suddenly understood for the first time that he had not been the only person in love with Saskia.

Barney knew Selwyn was disappointed that his interest in design had waned and he was especially grateful to Selwyn for his help in getting him into Liverpool College of Art. Ostensibly he had got in on the strength of his portfolio – he wanted to be a portrait painter and had amassed a collection of paintings and sketches he had done during the time Selwyn had been away, many of them of Saskia – but Barney knew that Selwyn's influence at the college had swayed the decision.

He had worried about leaving Selwyn on his own. It was ridiculous to worry about a man still in his forties but Barney knew Lady Sarah was concerned about him too. Selwyn had not been the same since his return from France and he seemed to be deteriorating infinitesimally every day. He looked as striking as ever with his mane of silver hair framing his head, but his voice no longer had the same resonance and there was now a listless air about him.

Barney went home from Liverpool as often as he could but the lure of the city, the docks, the trams, the bustle and excitement, was often too tempting. Each time he walked up the steep hill with the cathedral on the right at the top and the art college on the left, Barney remembered Vera's words to Joe when they'd visited the cathedral one Easter Sunday.

'Keep yer eyes down, Joe.'

'Why's that, Vera?'

'Tarts down there beyond the cathedral, you know as well as I do. Prostitutes. Don't want our Barney seeing them. Into the cathedral, quickly now!'

Barney was always tempted to go and look for the legendary 'tarts' but by the time he reached the top of the hill he always turned left and made for the Philharmonic pub by the college. There were plenty of tarts at college anyway, some of them posing in his life class. One fascinated him with her long and unwieldy appendix scar which seemed to be sucking into it all the extraneous fat of her sagging stomach.

He could not have arrived in Liverpool at a worse time for

the jubilation which prevailed following the Allies' victory had been somewhat dissipated and the country now faced a period of miserable austerity which in many ways was even harder to bear now that there was no longer a war and with it a reason to tighten belts. Rationing not only continued but worsened, but the most frustrating thing of all for hungry, excited students was that there was simply nothing to do and nowhere to go other than the Philharmonic pub. There was no money and nothing to spend it on but for Barney, having been closeted away at Laurel Bank for so long, it was paradise.

He thought about Saskia every day but admittedly less and less as time went by and he became aware that he was extremely desirable in the eyes of the female students, with his shock of blond hair, contrasting dark brown eyes and olive skin. In short, within a year, he was having the time of his life and it was something of a blow when his call-up to National Service came. There was no convenient accident to get him out of it this time. His ankle had healed, he passed the medical and he was off.

Yet he could not have been more lucky with his posting.

He had wanted more than anything to go to Berlin to find out what had happened to Saskia's parents, to her sister – maybe even by some miracle what had happened to her. It was ironic that it was Saskia's German lessons that had enabled him to do so.

Now here he was, Bombadier Barney Lambert, posted to Berlin as an army interpreter with the British occupation authorities and to his utter amazement he found that he could actually understand what the people were saying to him. It was the fact that Saskia herself had been a Berliner that had been crucial. She had unconsciously familiarized him with the dialect and he found that he was able to slip comfortably into the colloquialisms of the natives.

He had arrived on a British military train early on a spring morning of 1947 at Charlottenburg Station, the rail terminal in the British sector of Berlin, and when he had stepped down from the train, his greatcoat buttoned up to his neck, his Lee-Enfield Mark IV clasped firmly in his right hand, a small boy had slipped up behind him. The child looked Barney up and down and proceeded to march along beside him.

'*Bist du ein Tommy?*' the boy asked and Barney replied proudly: '*Ja ich bin ein Tommy.*' I'm a Tommy.

'*Was für ein Tommy?*' persisted the boy who, by now, had been joined by several others. What kind of Tommy?

'*Ein Ubersetzer.*' A translator.

The children looked at him suspiciously for a moment and ran off.

The sight of war-ravaged Berlin filled him with horror and shame. Barely a building stood intact. Great piles of rubble filled the streets. Windows devoid of glass hinted ominously at gloomy interior wreckage. Collapsed roofs, gaping holes in walls, exposed rafters, all served to instil in Barney the all-pervasive mood of destruction. The Berliners themselves seemed to go about their business in a trance as if they could not bear to look to the right or to the left of them and see what had been done to their city. But more than anything Barney was struck by the near silence of the place. It did not reverberate with sound as most cities did. True, after Liverpool and London, this was only the third city he had ever visited but still he felt it was unnatural.

Yet he loved it. The jagged skyline formed by the broken buildings thrilled him. It was surreal, exciting. Out of it, he sensed would come a whole new world to replace the old. He watched the industrious *Trümmerfrauen* – the rubble-women – at work, who went around hacking bits of mortar off still useable bricks and stacking them, and he knew that here was a city where progress would be made. Their city had been devastated but the mood of the Berliners seemed less austere than that of their British counterparts, if that were possible. And there were children everywhere. Orphans. Barney shuddered, remembering Saskia.

He was billeted right in the centre in the Tiergarten district, and as soon as he was able to get a pass he made his way to the Zehlendorf. He didn't quite know what he expected to happen when he got there, if anything, and as it was, when he finally reached the apartment building where the Kesslers had lived, still identifiable from Saskia's fond descriptions of it and, more important, still standing, he drew a blank.

'The Kesslers?' You say they lived here before the war?' the woman on the second floor asked him when he knocked on her door. Saskia had said that her family lived on the second floor. '*Ist möglich. Ist möglich*,' she repeated irritatingly implying that anything was possible. It was the same with everyone he asked. They were clearly wary of strangers, particularly Tommies in military vehicles. They wanted to live and let live. When, in desperation, he cried out that they had been '*Juden – eine Judische Familie*', he received a collective look of pity, almost contempt, as much as to say, 'And you thought they'd still be here?' He could read in their eyes what they were thinking: *Are you mad*?

Still he stayed for the rest of the afternoon, walking around the suburb, absorbing the place where Saskia had grown up.

Above him the woman on the second floor watched him as she picked up the phone to make a call.

'There's been a man here – English, a Tommy. Asking questions. About the Kesslers. I thought you'd want to know.'

'So,' said the husky voice at the other end of the line, 'do me a favour, Renate, get your little Hans-Georg to follow him on his bicycle when he leaves. Find out where he's stationed. Then tell him to come and find me. I'll be in the Kempinski this evening. I'll take it from there.'

Barney noticed the girl two days after he had made his abortive attempt to find Saskia's parents in the Zehlendorf. By the end of the week he knew she was following him. She seemed quite brazen about it, making no attempt to duck into an alleyway or suddenly bend to do up her shoelaces if he turned and saw her behind him. Sometimes he even caught her eye and she stared straight back at him until, eventually, it was he who looked away.

By now Barney was working at HQ British Military Government, acting as translator for the endless stream of Germans who came in to moan about their ration cards or apply for British licences for this or that. Inevitably all he had to do was refer them to the appropriate German authorities as soon as he'd seen the questionnaire they all had to complete. They invariably went to great lengths to explain how much they hated the Germans and what they had done. Barney could never quite understand this rigmarole they felt they had to go through. They were German too, weren't they? Were they trying to explain that they hated themselves for what they had done or were they attempting to dissociate themselves from the past? Either way it only served to make him feel that much more uncomfortable. He didn't need to be reminded that he was sometimes dealing with people who must have been former members of the Nazi party, former *SS* and Gestapo, even though this was never acknowledged.

In a way he was not surprised when he passed her one morning in the long queue of people waiting to see him at HQ Mil. Gov. She was ushered in to see him a couple of hours later.

'You've had a long wait,' he said as he went on writing. He deliberately didn't look up to meet what he knew would be her penetrating gaze. Her ensuing silence unnerved him as he knew it was meant to. When he finally raised his head she was smiling down at him.

'Sit, please.' He gestured to a chair. Still she said nothing but moved to the chair. She sat elegantly, straight back, ankles crossed, hands resting palm upwards in her lap. Her face was looking down demurely but as he watched her he saw that she was in fact still smiling.

'What's so funny?'

Suddenly her whole position changed. First her legs (encased in nylons he noticed) slithered apart, one stretched out to one side, the other arched in front of her over her highheeled shoe. She thrust her shoulders forward, put her hands on her hips, threw back her head, stretched her neck and laughed out loud.

He asked again: 'What's so funny?'

'You are, you sweet little Tommy.'

Barney bristled. This girl was about his own age. There was no way he was going to let her get away with such insolence.

'What is the purpose of your visit?' he asked as formally as he could.

'I want a licence, a British licence so I can act in British movies. I have to come to you to get that, *Ja?*'

'You're an actress?'

'Sort of.'

He ignored that. 'May I see your questionnaire? You did complete one while you were waiting?'

'*Natürlich.*' She handed it across the desk.

'It says here your name is Marlene Dietrich and you give your address as Hotel Esplanade, Potsdamer Platz. Are you aware, madam, that the Esplanade was severely bombed? I understand the ballroom is still standing. Are you living in that?'

He knew this would get a laugh and he was right. She rocked back and forth, then swayed from side to side in her chair and her large hands gripped her haunches as if she was trying to hold herself in.

'So what's it all about then?' he asked, smiling himself now. 'How did you get them to let you in downstairs? What do you really want?'

'You,' she said simply, looking straight at him, no longer smiling.

That night she took him to her apartment. She had two rooms in an empty shell of a building on Budapesterstrasse. Only one half of the building remained intact. The bomb had sliced the house right down the middle leaving the central staircase exposed to the sky above as if it were built onto the outside. Her rooms were on the first floor and as they climbed the staircase Barney tried not to notice the sheer drop to the ground on the left-hand side.

There was no glass in her windows. She had tagged up old blankets for curtains. The floorboards were bare. A tap jutting out of the wall had nothing beneath it but a bucket. There was no indication she had anything to cook on. An old sofa had been pushed up to stand in front of the windows. Beside it on the floor stood a gramophone and a small pile of records. There were ashtrays everywhere, brimming over with cigarette stubs. She saw him looking at them.

'*Ja*, I know, but what shall I do with them? I used to throw them out of the window but there were complaints.'

'I should think so. It's disgusting.'

'Okay, fine. You take them downstairs five times a day.'

'Where do you get so many cigarettes?'

She shrugged. 'Where do you think? You want a drink? Some schnapps?' She brandished a bottle at him, dangled two liqueur glasses by their stems between the fingers of her other hand.

He took a gulp and spluttered.

'*Vorsicht!*' she cautioned. 'Never had schnapps before? What a little innocent.'

Barney grinned, trying to laugh it off, but inside he felt awkward. Maybe he should leave. Why had he come anyway? It was all extremely irregular. She'd asked him and he'd agreed to come but beyond that he had no other reason for being there.

Except to have sex.

He'd had an erection the minute he'd stepped into her dingy rooms and had understood at once that there would be nothing else for them to do there. Then she took him by the hand and led him into the second room. He had never seen such a huge bed. It was big enough for four people let alone two. It dominated the room. There was no other furniture except for a full-length cracked mirror propped

221

up against one wall and a rag trade clothesrack on wheels on which hung a line of dresses, so many they were all crammed together. A row of shoes, at least eleven pairs, stood underneath.

'*Komm. Setzt dich, Süsser.*' she said patting the bed beside her.

Barney turned round and jumped slightly when he saw her. She was already naked. She lay back on the bed and put her arms behind her head. Her large spreading breasts flattened out like two upturned soup plates. Slowly she raised the heel of one foot up the inside of her other leg until it came to rest against her vulva. Gently, she massaged herself with her heel and brought her hands out from behind her head to stroke her own nipples. They hardened to points, like meringues.

Barney stumbled over to the bed and collapsed onto it beside her. As he brought his feet up he saw he still had his great Army boots on. She had to help him undress. He was trembling with so much excitement he could never have done it by himself. First the boots, then his socks, his thick worsted battledress (there was an Army saying: if it fits, you must be deformed), his rough woollen khaki shirt. For a fleeting second he contemplated asking her if he might put his trousers between the mattress and bedstead in order to maintain the crease in them. Then he too was naked as she pulled off his underwear.

Suddenly, before he could stop her, she had grasped his penis and begun to stroke it firmly up and down, up and down. He exploded into her hand before he was even aware of what was happening.

'I did that on purpose,' she explained. 'You were going to climax the minute you entered me anyway. I thought we might as well get it over with so that we could both have some fun next time. Now, come, lie against me, that's right. See, he's up again. What did I tell you? Now, let him rest against my stomach. There. Now we'll just hold each other for a while, hmmm?'

222

After a few seconds she pushed his head away and looked him in the eye.

'Relax, for heaven's sake. You're stiff as a board. It's okay to move a little. Go to sleep if you want.'

Barney had never felt so wide awake in his life.

'I just know it's going to happen again, if I move, I mean . . .'

'So what if it does? I'll have a sticky mess on my stomach and you can dry me off. Perhaps we should help it along again.'

She leaned down to take his penis in her mouth. She sucked slightly and once again he ejaculated. This time he couldn't help himself: he cried out, an unintelligible roar of a kind he had never heard before, least of all from himself.

Suddenly, almost roughly, he pushed her back down on the bed and climbed on top of her. He reached down with his hand between her legs, searching for the opening. It was slippery and wet. He pressed tentatively against the insides of her thighs until she moved her legs apart. Then he lowered himself onto her and very tenderly she guided him in with her hand.

'Now we must lie very still for a while,' she whispered in his ear. 'Because if we move you'll come again and then it will be all over. So let's talk. Think about something else. It feels good, doesn't it?'

'Very,' he agreed.

'Okay, so now you are Bombadier Barney Lambert and you have come to Berlin as an interpreter. Where do you come from in England?'

This was absurd. She wanted him to make small talk when he'd just got inside. He shifted a bit and almost exploded again. She was right. Best to calm down while he was still inside her then they could have a go a bit later on.

'Liverpool.'

'And do you have brothers and sisters?'

'Hey, wait a minute. I don't even know your name.'

'Guess.'

'Don't be daft. How could I possibly . . .'

'No. Go on. It'll help pass the time. What's my name?'

'Well, of course, I know it, don't I?' said Barney entering into the spirit of things. 'The one you put down on your questionnaire today: Marlene.'

'Okay. Marlene. That's who I'll be.'

'No, come on. What's your real name?'

'Marlene. Just Marlene. It's enough.'

'Barney and Marlene.'

'Marlene and Barney. Already we're a couple.'

'Not until we . . .'

'You're ready now?'

'Can't you feel me? I've been ready for the last . . .'

She raised her hips to him in answer and he plunged down into her.

This time it was she who came quickly. Barney lost control. He thrust himself into her over and over again, banging himself hard against her long after he had climaxed. He shuddered. It seemed as if everything were moving and he couldn't stop it. Dimly he recalled that the building was in a precarious state. Was it safe to perform with such energy? Had they rocked the foundations? Would the house come roaring down around their ears?

In the night he awoke with an urgent need to urinate. He groped his way half-asleep through the pitch black until he came to an open door and a blast of fresh air hit him. He was outside. It was the middle of the night. He would piss outside. No one would see him. He took a step forward and suddenly there was nothing there.

He came awake instantly, suddenly realizing that he was on the outside staircase and that he had almost stepped out to his death. He urinated into the darkness involuntarily now, in fright. When he made his way back to the bed Marlene was awake and reached for him. She cradled him in her arms for a while then lighted a candle. For an hour she let him explore her body, presenting every part of it to him for close inspection. She demanded that he kiss each part before she showed him another. They made love once more, gently, slowly and fell asleep in each other's arms.

He awoke before her and looked across at her still sleeping. He propped himself up on one elbow and watched her for nearly twenty minutes. When she awoke she reached up and stroked his tousled blond hair.

'See, *mein Tommy*, we have the same colour hair. Did you fall asleep at last?'

'I fell asleep,' he answered quietly, 'and I also fell in love.'

Later, after he had gone, she opened the cupboard and took out the telephone she kept hidden there. She dialled the number in the Zehlendorf.

'Renate, is that you? *Ja, ja*, I've seen him. But I need your little Hans-Georg's help again. Tell him to find out if Werner Mahrenhertz has left for his trip yet. *Mahrenhertz*. Werner Mahrenhertz. He was due to go to Frankfurt this morning. I need to know. No, I cannot ring there myself. He asked me not to. You know this. But Hans-Georg can do it for me, *ja*? There's a pair of nylons in it for you.'

When she had hung up she saw that Barney had left his beret behind in his haste to get back to barracks.

'So now I'm Tommy Marlene,' she sang lustily as she paraded, naked, in front of the cracked mirror, the beret perched on top of her flowing blonde curls.

Twenty-One

Barney was besotted. He did not know he was confusing lust with love. All he knew was that he could not get enough of her. Her breasts were large and spreading but firm. They began under her arms and rose to form a plateau beneath her collarbones. Her shoulders, while broad, were by contrast fine boned and elegant as were her long thin arms.

But it was her backview which had the strongest draw on Barney. Particularly her rump. It was high and rounded and she often favoured an unusual stance that accentuated it. She would stand with her legs wide apart, her feet turned slightly out and her large hands placed squarely behind her on her buttocks, her long tapering fingers pointing downwards. Then she would begin to walk and this was when Barney could barely control himself. She walked with the slow, rolling gait of a large black mammy, swaying her hips from side to side, sashaying almost. In the cold winter misery of war-torn Berlin she gave the impression of having been out in the sun all day and, frankly, it was too darn hot. Her smile echoed this – lazy, mocking, her eyes always teasing him so that he worried constantly that she did not take him seriously.

He worried that she would not tell him her real name. She assured him that there was no reason for this other than that it amused her to have him call her Marlene. It worried him that he did not know any of her friends. She claimed not to have any. It worried him that she was often unavailable for long periods of time. He would bound up the crumbling steps to her rooms only to find them empty day after day. Then suddenly she would be there again, arms outstretched to receive him, fingers stroking his blond hair, her low husky voice reassuring him that she would never go away again. But she did.

'Well I'm damned,' he exclaimed during one of the spells when she had been around for nearly six weeks, 'they're showing the film of the Royal Wedding.' They were strolling down the Kurfürstendamm on a crisp January morning in 1948 and came to the Astor cinema at the corner of Fasanenstrasse.

'*Die Königliche Hochzeit*,' read Marlene, staring up at the giant cardboard figures of Princess Elizabeth in her wedding dress with Prince Philip beside her. 'But look at those queues. Will we get in?'

'I'd like a wedding like that,' she breathed afterwards as they strolled back to Budapesterstrasse.

'I could give you one,' said Barney quietly.

'Oh, don't be silly.' Her laugh was mocking.

'I don't mean we'd be married in Westminster Abbey but you'd have a fine dress like that and I'd be in uniform and . . .'

'And I'd be a princess? Oh, Barney, such a romantic!' She stroked his cheek. 'Don't you have a little princess waiting for you back home?'

He frowned.

'Come on, Barney, tell me,' she persisted, 'Haven't you ever been in love?'

He shook his head.

'Never?' She hung on his arm and looked up into his eyes.

'Well, maybe just a little.'

'What was her name?'

'Saskia.'

Christiane let go of him abruptly. 'That's not an English name.'

'She wasn't an English girl. Matter of fact she was German like you.'

227

'Go on. Don't stop now. Whereabouts in Germany did she come from?'

'Berlin. I've been trying to find her family but I've drawn a complete blank.' Christiane had gone white but he didn't notice. 'This man who took me in when my parents were killed, he already had a German girl living with him, a Jewish refugee from Berlin. I never really got the whole story but it seems my guardian, Selwyn, had a friend in London and she was going to adopt this girl but she died before the girl arrived so my guardian just whisked her up to his home. He gave us both a home and then he went off to war leaving us alone together.'

'And you fell in love. How sweet.' Christiane's tone was bitter.

'Don't call it sweet!' said Barney angrily. 'It wasn't sweet. Don't be so patronizing. We were friends. She was probably the best friend I'll ever have,'

'So if she was such a good friend, is she waiting for you back home?'

'I may never see her again . . .' said Barney, and leading Christiane into a café he settled her into a corner. He told her about the horror of the last Sunday they had seen Saskia, and of her disappearance, but somehow he could not bring himself to talk about little Klara.

'Was she beautiful?' Christiane asked suddenly.

'Unbelievably,' said Barney, 'Oh, not at all like you,' he reassured her hastily, 'a different kind of beauty entirely. Saskia was dark and tiny whereas you are . . . well, you're you.'

'And she came from Berlin . . . Maybe I knew her?'

'Maybe you did. It'd be a hell of a coincidence, highly unlikely but who knows? She was about your age, a bit older maybe.'

Christiane leaned further back into the dark corner so her face was in shadow when she asked: 'What was her other name? Saskia who?'

And Barney could not see her face as she silently mouthed the name she had been expecting ever since she

228

had heard from Renate that he had been asking questions at the Zehlendorf apartment.

'Saskia Kessler. Did you know her?'

'Name rings a bell,' said Christiane, 'but it's a common name, Kessler.'

'I suppose so,' said Barney sadly. 'Listen,' he said, changing the subject, 'I'd like to take you to a dinner party tomorrow night. Will you come?'

'Friends of yours?'

'Not exactly. Colonel Arlington – well, he's an officer for a start and I'm other ranks – Colonel Arlington's part of the Military Police but he also happens to be an acquaintance of my guardian back in England, Selwyn Reilly. It's a sort of duty invitation. Be much more fun if I could take you along.'

'We'll see,' she replied enigmatically.

Barney hadn't actually asked the Colonel if he could bring anyone but as it turned out there wasn't a problem.

'Permission to bring someone with me, sir, tomorrow night, if that's all right?'

'Aha! A lady friend?'

'Sir.' Barney nodded.

'Jolly good show! Bit of a dark horse, aren't you? A Fräulein, is she?'

'Yes, sir, if you're sure . . .'

'Fine, fine. Not much else about, is there? Not too serious, hmmm? Mustn't let these things get out of hand.'

'Of course not, sir. Thank you very much.'

They were the first to arrive. Colonel Arlington's wife, Molly, was a fussy little woman with grey hair slipping down out of an untidy bun.

'We don't have a butler, I'm afraid,' she apologized before they'd even had a chance to be introduced. 'He left last week. Terribly sorry. Giles will help you to a drink. Giles?'

She blinked repeatedly at Marlene as if mesmerized.

Marlene's tight black dress outlined her every curve. To Barney's horror she took out her cigarette case and coolly lighted herself a cigarette.

'Oh, I say, let me . . .' Giles Arlington rushed forward. 'Now what'll you drink, eh . . . ?'

'This is Marlene,' said Barney quickly.

'Marlene . . . ?' Giles looked enquiringly at her.

'Dietrich,' she replied with a ravishing smile and Giles and Molly roared with laughter. 'Oh, I say, jolly good, jolly good.'

The other guests arrived: another Army couple as dowdy as the Arlingtons; an American Air Force colonel and his wife who hailed originally from Saratoga and made sure everyone knew about it. With them came their plain and awkward daughter who had clearly been asked for Barney.

The Arlingtons evidently loved to flog a joke to death and insisted on introducing Marlene as Marlene Dietrich over and over again. Barney was rather relieved that what promised to be a rather heavy evening was being momentarily enlivened by something so feeble. He wished he had not invited Marlene. Standing behind her, he itched to rub his hands over her ample buttocks, to reach up and take the two slides out of her golden hair so that it would cascade down her back, something he always did when they were alone. Then the final guest arrived.

'Bill's on his own tonight. Margie's making a quick trip back to London, lucky girl, so we thought we'd invite him along to cheer him up.' Giles Arlington threw a skinny arm around the stocky shoulders of a smaller man with a florid face. 'You all know Bill? Bill Warner, from the Press Corps,' he added as Barney clearly didn't.

Bill Warner shook Barney's hand and his palm was warm and damp. Barney took an instant dislike to his lascivious smile. Then Bill Warner turned away to be introduced to Marlene. And he froze.

Barney glanced at Marlene. She had gone white. She allowed Warner to take her hand for an instant then withdrew it, almost rudely as if she were afraid of catching something.

'You two know each other?' Even the dozy Molly sensed something in the air.

'We've met,' said Bill Warner quietly.

'Have you, by George, lucky you. Not everyone knows Marlene,' chuckled Giles.

'Marlene?' Warner looked nonplussed.

'Dietrich. Ha-ha!' Giles slapped him on the back.

'Of course,' said Warner without smiling and turned away.

The food was excellent and no shortage of it. Giles and Molly must have good black market contacts whatever else they lacked, thought Barney. Marlene was making a big effort with the American Air Force Colonel, rather too much effort judging by the look on his wife's face. Barney smiled to himself. The American could enjoy her while he had the chance. He, Barney, was the one who would be taking her home.

But she wouldn't let him come up to her apartment in The Shell as they had dubbed the still-ruined building where she lived.

'Not tonight, *Barneychen*.'

'Don't call me that.' It made him think of Saskia.

'I want to get my beauty sleep.'

'Marlene Dietrich needs beauty sleep? Come on!' He pushed her against the wall of her building underneath the outside staircase and plunged his tongue into her mouth. He felt his penis stiffen inside his uniform and rubbed himself against her. Already his hand had gone round to roam up inside her skirt to squeeze her bottom.

'I want you. You know I do,' he whispered urgently.

She moved her legs apart and let him rub himself against her fiercely till he came. He rested his head on her shoulder for a moment and then looked up into her eyes. To his horror she was staring blankly straight ahead.

'You didn't . . .? For you, nothing happened?'

'Of course, of course,' she said immediately, looking down at him and blowing softly in his ear. 'With you something always happens.'

231

But as she climbed the exposed staircase, stepping carefully amongst the weeds growing on the steps, she did not look back at him and he walked back to the Tiergarten feeling strangely unsettled.

The next morning he had a phone call.

'A Mr Bill Warner. From the Press Corps. Said you met last night.'

'Put him through.'

Bill Warner came straight to the point. 'Good to meet you last night. Look here, I won't mess about. There's something I think you ought to be aware of. I was a bit surprised to see that woman with you last night. Not really the sort of person one takes to people like the Arlingtons, if you get my meaning?'

'To be honest I'm not sure I do,' said Barney.

'Well you must know about her . . . what she used to do . . . maybe still does for all I know?'

'Know about her? What is there to know about her?'

'Good God, you don't know anything, do you? Well, brace yerself, I'd better tell you. She's a prostitute, more a high-class call girl, really. Been at it for a while. Very discreet and all that. Completely fooled Molly and old Giles so don't worry about them. Bit of all right, as I'm sure you've already discovered. Had her myself once, but she wasn't too keen on the rough stuff, you know? Well, never mind, it's just I do think you ought to watch it. I mean, she's been around a bit, you just don't know what you might catch, know what I'm on about? Course, bound to be a thing of the past now she's seeing that IG Farben fellow but better to be safe than sorry.'

'IG Farben fellow,' repeated Barney numbly.

'Yes, name of Mahrenhertz. Think he might even be a von. Von Mahrenhertz. Word is he's getting quite keen on her, tying up quite a bit of her time. One of the reasons I was a bit surprised to see her with you. Thing is, he's a bit of a problem area.'

232

'You don't have to tell me,' muttered Barney.

'No, no, don't misunderstand me. What I'm trying to say is there's a bit of a stink about IG Farben and their involvement with the SS over the last few years. Mahrenhertz's name doesn't smell too good at the moment, if you get my meaning. Something to do with the camps.'

'I suppose so.' Barney could barely speak. He didn't know what Bill Warner was talking about.

'Leave them to it is what I say. You're well out of it. Christiane can take care of herself.'

'Christiane?'

'You mean you call her Marlene too? I thought that was all just for that duffer Giles' benefit. Pretty name, Christiane.'

'And her other name?' Barney held his breath. He'd only ever heard the name Christiane once before.

'Oh, come on. This is ludicrous! Christiane Kessler. Glad to have been of help.'

Barney's head collapsed into his hands.

Saskia's sister. A prostitute!

'I think you had better start by telling me your real name,' said Barney as they sat across a table at the Kempinski.

'That man, what's his name, Bill? He told you.'

'Bill Warner. But of course you would know him as Bill.' She looked at him sharply. 'What did he tell you?'

'No, Christiane, I think you'd better tell me what you think he told me and anything more you'd care to add while we're about it.'

She reached for her constant crutch, the cigarette case, and her hands were shaking as she struggled to light one. He didn't help her. 'Okay, so my name is Christiane.'

'Christiane who?'

'Kessler.'

'And you're Jewish.'

'Shhh! Bill told you that?'

'No, but if you're the Christiane Kessler I think you are then you're Jewish.'

'Why should that worry you?'

'It doesn't worry me a bit, Marlene, I mean Christiane, but obviously it bothers you if you go "Shhh!" when I mention it. Come on, tell me, I want to know. Are you that Christiane? Is Saskia your sister? Did you live in the Zehlendorf?'

She nodded, wouldn't look at him.

'But why didn't you tell me? I've talked to you about Saskia. I've told you all about what happened to us during the war. You must have realized I was talking about your own sister. Didn't you even care enough to ask?'

'Of course I cared. I found you, didn't I?'

'You found me. What do you mean?'

'I came after you. Don't you realize, Tommy! You came to the Zehlendorf to look for me, for my parents. You met Renate Ascher.'

'Renate who?'

'She lives in our old apartment now. She was one of our neighbours before the war.'

'But she said she had no idea where you were.'

'Of course she did. To protect me. She didn't know who you were or why you were looking for the Kesslers. I had told her if anyone came asking for us she was to contact me. Maybe that way I could find out what had happened to Saskia. She rang me and I had her little boy follow you on his bicycle. He told me where to find you.'

'And you followed me. Don't think I didn't notice you. I thought it was because you'd taken a fancy to me.'

'Barney, it was. I had. But I needed to get to know you, to understand why you wanted to find out about my family.'

'So that first night, it was just part of your job.'

'What are you saying?'

'Your job. Bill Warner told me all about you. I imagine I must owe you quite a lot of money by now.'

She slapped him hard across the face. The bartender came over as people turned to look at them.

'Christl?' He looked questioningly at her.

'No problem,' she told him quickly, 'no problem at all. *Wirklich.*'

234

'I warned you,' he said leaning over and removing the overflowing ashtray, 'you can use this place but no trouble.'

'Sure, sure,' she growled. 'Anyway we're leaving. Barney, *komm*, we'll go to my place.'

'No,' he said fiercely. He was consumed with rage. He didn't feel hurt but that would undoubtedly come later. At the moment all he felt was blind rage that she was acknowledging everything as if it were quite normal. '*No*,' he spat at her again, 'we'll stay here until you've told me a bit more, quite a bit more, if you would be so kind.'

'That's why I want to go to my place, *Barneychen*. So I can tell you everything. About my family. About my sister. About my aunt and uncle. About what happened . . . during the war . . .' she stumbled, 'and afterwards.'

'Just tell me one thing, Christiane.' This time he had no problem saying her name.

'Yes?'

'Were you . . . are you . . . a prostitute?'

'Of course I was. Don't you understand anything? I knew you would find out one day. That's why I couldn't tell you I was Saskia's sister.'

'Christiane!' He reached out to take her hand but she got up and left. There was nothing for him to do but throw a few coins down on the table and follow her.

They had begun to rebuild The Shell inside. Her two rooms had been replastered and painted. There was now glass in the windows. She had proper curtains, a basin under the tap in the wall. On the floor below, the stinking old lavatory had been replaced with a new one. But she still had the old battered sofa in front of the window, the only piece of furniture in the first room. She motioned to him to sit down.

'Shut up!' she said firmly as he began to speak. 'You wanted to know things. I will tell you. I shall begin at the beginning. Pour me a drink first. Help yourself.'

Barney poured her a shot of Scotch but nothing for himself.

'Saskia left. She was a good kid, Saskia, what I remember of her.'

'A good kid. Is that all you can say? Your own sister!'

'Oh, for Christ's sake, Barney, stop all this "your own sister" rubbish. I haven't seen her in nearly ten years. I was a little girl when she left.'

'You talk about her as if she were your baby sister. You were the younger one. Have you forgotten?'

'I know, I know. I was a spoiled brat, but don't you understand? Now it's like I'm a woman who's been an adult all her life. When I think of Saskia, I think of this little creature. She was so small, like an elf, smaller than I was even though she was older than me. She was fragile. I'm tough, Barney. I can take care of myself in ways that Saskia couldn't begin to understand.'

'Oh, that's where you're quite wrong, Christiane. Saskia took care of herself – and me – perfectly well throughout the war. You take care of yourself in your way and she takes care of herself in hers, but don't you ever tell me that you're better at it than she is . . .'

'Oh *mein Gott*, don't be so saintly, Barney. You and Saskia were right out in the country, safe and sound. I was here, here in Berlin and I was Jewish. Don't you understand what that means?'

'But I thought you went to be with your aunt because neither of you looked Jewish and would be safe together?'

'Nobody was safe in Berlin in the war.'

She did not look at him once while she told him what had happened to her during the war, nor did she spare him any of the gruesome details, but she stopped short when she arrived at the point where she had been hit by falling masonry while cycling through the Lützowplatz. She did not tell Barney about her visit to Mittenwald.

He was silent for a while.

'I know, Barney, you feel I have betrayed you but you have betrayed yourself. You are so young. I never asked you to fall in love with me, I never encouraged you. You are going to fall in love many times, *Barneychen*. That's how you are and it isn't my fault. I don't want to hurt you . . .'

236

'Werner Mahrenhertz!' said Barney suddenly, remembering what Bill Warner had said.

'What about him?' said Christiane defensively.

'Who is he?'

'My fiancé.'

'What?'

'He's a very important man. He has a lot of responsibility. He is going to take good care of me. I'm very lucky to have found him.' She was speaking automatically as if they were sentences she had said to herself over and over again to try and make herself believe them. 'We wanted to wait for a while before we got married. There are people who know about me and what I did during the war. Like that man Bill Warner. Poor Bill. He couldn't do it, you know? I had to help him quite a bit. No wonder he remembers me. And he was cruel. He blamed it on me and he wanted to beat me for it but I –'

Barney interrupted her, gripping both her arms. 'You say you are going to marry Werner Mahrenhertz?'

'Oh yes, and we'll go and live in Frankfurt. That's where IG Farben is. Werner's there all the time. That's why I've recently had so much time to see you, *Barneychen*. We were going to wait but now I think I am going to have to ask him if we can be married very soon.'

'Why?'

'Can't you guess?'

'You're pregnant.'

'Yes.'

'And you weren't going to tell me. You were just going to go away and marry Werner, have his baby and forget all about me.'

'Oh no, I was going to tell you, *Barneychen*. We're going to tell Werner about the baby together.'

'Bit scared of how he'll react, are you? That doesn't sound like the tough Christiane you make out you are. Can't you do your dirty work on your own?'

'Of course, I can. But this is your dirty work too. Werner's been away for nearly two months. His work often

237

takes him away, as I said. Work it out, Barney. This baby's yours.'

A week later Barney was summoned to meet Werner and Christiane for lunch at the Hotel Adlon. Barney hated Werner on sight. The older man was utterly in control. He barely lifted a finger and a waiter sprang forward to take Barney's drink order. Werner launched straight into a description of his work – something to do with chemicals that Barney could not make head or tail of. Werner went on and on about *Forschung* – research – and it was only when Christiane gently reminded him of the reason for Barney's presence that he came down to earth.

'You must excuse me. It is such an important time for us. We have to rebuild completely here in Germany, we have to be very ingenious.' Barney didn't know how to react to this information given that it was undoubtedly due to the British that they had to rebuild at all. So he said nothing. Christiane nudged him. Werner waited politely for a few seconds and then continued. 'Christiane has told me all about the baby. I am delighted.'

This time Barney regarded him in utter astonishment. If it came as a shock to him that Christiane had already talked to Werner about the baby, he was even more surprised by Werner's reaction to the news.

'You are?'

'Delighted? *Ja, sicher*. We are to be married, Christiane and I, and we want children.'

'But it's my –'

'No matter. We will raise him as our own.'

'Him?'

'Oh, he will be a boy. I know these things,' said Werner with confidence.

You bloody well know everything, don't you? thought Barney miserably.

'He – I mean it – will be our baby,' he said fiercely. 'I am the father. I want to take him – or her – home to England. I want to take Christiane too.'

'Barney – may I call you Barney?' Werner had slipped his arm around Barney's shoulders. Christiane had excused herself to go to the lavatory. 'Barney, my friend, I think maybe she has not told you why we want to keep him here. Christiane and I are to be married. You must accept this. Oh, I know about her – how can I describe them? – little adventures and, of course, you were more than an adventure. She really cared for you and she always will. She has told me. But her place is here with me. She has a life to rebuild. She cannot run away and I am here to help her. I can give her so much yet there is one thing I am unable to give her.'

Barney looked at him, already knowing what it was.

'I have never hidden from her the fact that I am unable to give her a child. You see, I . . . I . . .' Whatever it was Werner was trying to say, Barney realized it was causing the overconfident German severe embarrassment. '. . . I have a problem. I am not properly . . . *formed*.' This last word was whispered, his face turned away. 'And yet Christiane has said she will stand by me and when she told me she had become pregnant by you and what should she do, I was able to tell her straight away: have the baby, it will be ours, it is the answer to our prayers.'

Barney looked back at Christiane who had returned. He had begun to imagine how he must appear to her beside this ambitious, professional man some ten years his senior: nothing but a callow Tommy who'd given her a good time between the sheets. He knew he ought to feel relieved he'd been let off the hook. He'd gone and got a Fräulein in the club and no one was going to make him pay for it. Now Werner had come up with a load of rhubarb which implied that he was unable to make love, let alone father children. Should he believe it? And what about Christiane? Would someone with a sexual appetite as hungry as hers be faithful for long with such a cripple? Barney decided he did believe Werner's story. Suddenly it was Christiane's behaviour that was suspect. When he thought about it he realized she had consistently lied to him ever since he had met her. He was becoming weary with confusion. He had thought he loved her but the only emotion he felt at the moment towards her was anger, anger at her betrayal, and suddenly he wanted to be as far away from her as possible.

'I want you to promise me something,' he said, looking directly at her.

She glanced nervously at Werner. Barney had noticed that her whole attitude had changed in Werner's presence. Gone was the brassy prostitute with the flirtatious manner and in its place she became an almost demure young woman, ready to defer, not to him, but to Werner Mahrenhertz. Barney hated this new subservience, sensed it was all some kind of ploy. He hated Werner's oily arrogance, his naked delight in his power over Christiane. He may have confided in Barney about his weakness but only in order to gain his sympathy. To make up for it, it was quite clear to Barney that Werner would not lose any opportunity to wield authority over others. Barney shivered. This man was going to be the father of his child and there was nothing he could do about it – for the moment.

'Well?' He looked over to Christiane.

She shook her head, changed her mind, shrugged helplessly, asked: 'Well, what is it? How can I promise you anything if I don't know what you want?'

'I want you to promise me that one day you will tell our child who his real father is. As soon as he, or she, is able to understand, you will explain that Werner is not the real father, you will tell my child about me. *Verstehst du*?'

Christiane glanced again at Werner, opened her mouth to answer but Werner cut in: '*Ja!* She can do that but only if you promise something in return.' Barney stared at him. 'You have met me now,' continued Werner. 'You see that I am a good man, that I have a good job, I can take care of your son and Christiane. So now you can go home with no worries. But from this day on you do not see Christiane

240

again. Ever. Understood? *Verstehen Sie?*' Werner almost barked this last question.

Barney didn't answer. He reached out his arms and drew Christiane to him. He buried his head in her neck, in her long blonde curls. Then he grabbed hold of her hair and jerked her head back, looking straight into her face.

'Tell my child or I'll find it and tell it myself,' and with that he kissed her hard on the mouth, pushed her roughly aside and began to leave the restaurant. Before he reached the door he flung a last taunt at Christiane: 'It's good to know you give your important clients such good service . . .' he began.

'Oh, I wasn't a client as you call them,' Werner interjected smoothly. 'I met Christiane at my house. She was a close friend of my beloved late wife, Nina. Didn't you know?'

But Barney had gone, slamming the door behind him.

Twenty-Two

'What have I done?'

Over and over again Saskia asked herself the same question.

When the boat docked at New York there was no one to meet her. It was Liverpool Street Station 1939 all over again, yet there was no use hoping that Selwyn would come striding across the docks in his long coat and sweep her away to Laurel Bank, USA.

Sal had left her a passport in the name of his wife and a band of gold. Didn't that mean he felt he'd as good as married her and wanted her to join him in America? She'd cabled him with her arrival date and the name of the boat. Was it crazy to expect him to meet her at the docks? Maybe it was. Maybe he was working, but wouldn't he have sent someone? But how would they know what she looked like? She searched the crowds for someone who seemed to be looking for someone until she realized just about everybody fell into that category and sooner or later they found them just like they had at Liverpool Street.

'What have I done?'

What she had done was to turn her back on everything she had known or loved in search of freedom and survival and the comfort of a man's arms, a man who could conceivably have forgotten all about her.

Saskia tensed. Her eyes began to prick with tears. She knew the signals. She was beginning to panic. Tall alien buildings towering in the background and raucous, hustling crowds all around did not help. There was no one here who wanted her. Why had she ever come here?

'You got an address, lady?'

Saskia jumped. 'I'm sorry?'

'You got an address? You don't got an address, ain't nothing I can do.'

'And if I have one?'

'I'll take you there. In the cab. See? Over there.' He pointed proudly to a taxi parked across the street.

'Taxi,' said Saskia numbly.

'Sure, taxi. International word. Now, where you wanna go?'

Saskia fumbled in her bag and handed to him the slip of paper Sal had given her.

'Lady, you sure you wanna go here?' The driver looked her up and down. 'This is a rough neighbourhood you're talking about.' He tapped the piece of paper with his finger. 'Italian neighbourhood. Real rough.'

Then Saskia surprised herself. 'I'm Italian.' She tried to stand very tall and proud but she still had to look up to him. He took off his cap and scratched the top of his head.

'Sure you are, baby. C'mon.'

Saskia had no luggage but her little suitcase full of her precious clothes and she hugged it to her as she bounced about in the back of the cab bumping its way over the cobbled streets.

'That there's the Hudson River. Over on the other side we got the East River but it ain't as wide as the Hudson. I heard tell there are women who throw themselves in there when they hear their menfolk ain't here to meet them. They got no money, they got no address, no place to go. All they got is the name of some guy who married them over there and took off.'

Saskia didn't answer.

'They don't get many taxis down here in the West Thirties,' explained the driver as he slowed down to avoid the crowd of children who were beginning to run alongside the cab, jumping on and off the running board, peering in at

her through the window. Saskia stared past them at the
bleak tenement buildings with the fire escapes zig-zagging
down them. Here and there people were sitting out on
them, their legs hanging down over the street. A couple
waved to her.

When the taxi finally drew to a halt there were so many
people surrounding it Saskia could barely open the door.
The driver cleared a path for her and helped her out and
then she realized she didn't have any American money.

'No dollars.' She looked at him, imploring him not to
make a scene.

'The lady ain't got no money. So who's going to pay me?'

'Who is she?' someone shouted.

The driver looked at her and raised his eyebrows in
question.

'Carlino,' said Saskia. 'Sa – no, Sylvia Carlino.'

'Anna Filomena, Salvatore's woman is here . . . She's
here, Anna Filomena, she's . . .'

Four storeys up, a window was thrown open and a head
looked out.

'Help my son's woman, she's carrying my grandchild.
Enzo, give the driver some bread, Carlo, give him some
fruit. What is the matter with you? You stand there like
statues in a square back in Napoli. My Sal's woman arrives
and you don't help her up the stairs? What I gotta do? Come
down and cracka your heads together? Fine, fine. I'm on
my way . . .'

The window slammed shut. It was as if a Hollywood
director had cried 'Action!' Everyone sprang to life. The
driver was loaded up with fruit, vegetables, bread, ham,
cheese. He stood there hardly daring to move in case it fell
out of his arms. Eventually he turned around very slowly
and let it all topple out into the back seat of the cab.

Saskia felt herself propelled forward by several pairs of
hands pressing into her back and as they half lifted her up
the dark staircase, it dawned on her for the first time that
Sal's mother was expecting another person altogether.

*

Anna Filomena Carlino was a proud woman and a shrewd one. As she watched her neighbours bringing Saskia towards her she knew at once that this was neither an Italian woman nor a pregnant one.

She herself had been pregnant eight times. With her first-born, Salvatore, she had nearly lost her life. Her next baby, another boy, had been born stone cold, dead before he even entered the world. The next two sons had died before they saw their first birthdays. But her three daughters, born in quick succession, were strong healthy girls: Angelina, headstrong but lazy; Patrizia, vivacious and *cattiva*; and little Milena, shy and mouselike. Anna Filomena knew she should think herself lucky to have three beautiful daughters to help her in the house but she also knew they were not true Italian daughters. They showed no respect. Angelina and Patrizia were all day out on the street instead of going to school or staying home in the kitchen with their mamma, and while Milena stayed home when she wasn't at school, she buried her nose in a book all day.

But at least Milena helped her look after the *bambino*. When she was forty-four the unthinkable had happened. Anna Filomena had found herself pregnant again. In her mind it was the immaculate conception. Occasionally on Sundays when even Milena strayed outside, Anna Filomena and Marco – the man she had travelled thousands of miles from her native Napoli to marry, whose picture she had clutched in her hands all the way across the ocean, because she could not remember the face of the boy her parents told her had lived next door to them for the first ten years of her life till he went to America, the man who was so poor when she finally reached him that she had to stop him begging in the streets as her pride would not permit it – Anna Filomena and Marco took a siesta after lunch on their bed. Sometimes when Marco had drunk enough red wine he would push her black dress up until he could stroke her spreading thighs on the inside where the skin was still as soft as it had been when she had arrived and given herself to him as a teenage bride. Usually he would fall asleep with his

245

head resting heavy on her bosom but sometimes he would stay awake long enough to fumble with his fly, bring out his flaccid penis and rub it between her thighs until it was hard enough to penetrate her. She only put up with it because, almost as a matter of routine, he always mumbled that he loved her as he climaxed and she liked to hear the words. She no longer believed them but it did her good to hear them like a drug coursing through her veins, giving her a hit of energy.

He also gave her Guido. From behind the walls of her fourth-floor apartment on the top storey of the tenement building she could sense the gossip rippling up and down Tenth Avenue. Anna Filomena, forty-four years old and with child. Salvatore had taken it badly. *Disgraziata*! She could feel his disapproval all the way through her pregnancy and then he had gone away to war before she had the child. The fact that it was a boy must have made him all the more angry. His role as the only son was gone. Up to the time he had left for Europe he had still been her only male *bambino*. When he returned it was to find her with a new infant son demanding all her attention.

Salvatore had dropped his bags and left without so much as a kiss for his mamma. He returned occasionally, sneaking in during the night, raiding the icebox, drinking the wine his father kept for Sundays. He never ventured beyond the kitchen for that would mean he would have to creep through his parents' bedroom. The Carlinos lived in a railroad apartment where there was no corridor and all the rooms led off each other. Anna Filomena kept little Guido in a cot beside her bed but she also kept the door open to the next room where Patrizia and Milena shared a bed. Until recently Angelina had slept there too and often Anna Filomena would get up in the night and slip silently next door to gaze upon her three little girls lying there, dark hair spread out on the pillows, arms around each other belying the competitive sparks that flew between them when they were awake. Anna Filomena knew how her daughters suffered for lack of privacy. She would hear them weeping out on the fire escape and long to go and comfort them but she knew they had gone there to be alone and so she left them in peace. Sal's room at the end beyond the girls' she insisted on keeping empty, maintaining the illusion that he still came home to sleep there every night.

Sometimes she heard Sal talking softly with his sister Angelina, who had recently taken the box room off the kitchen for a bedroom now that she had begun to menstruate and needed her privacy in a different way. It was Angelina who had told Anna Filomena about Sal's forthcoming baby. Milena had been asked to write the letter to Sylvia welcoming her to the Carlino family and later she had read out Sylvia's reply but something had made her leave out the bit about the baby. Sal had talked to Angelina about it when he returned but he had never mentioned it to his mother. Anna Filomena knew what he was thinking: *You gotta baby, Mamma. You don't need mine.*

He was wrong. Anna Filomena had swelled with pride at the thought of her first grandchild. She had taken delivery of Saskia's cable herself and had Milena read it to her at the first opportunity. (If Milena was confused by the name Saskia at the end of the message, instead of Sylvia she didn't say anything. Who knew, maybe in England that was another way of saying Sylvia.) Now Anna Filomena was prepared for her daughter-in-law, she was prepared for the birth of her grandchild.

So who was this stranger walking through her door?

Anna Filomena was nervous that her son had probably learned a great deal that was outside her experience while he had been away from her in Europe. She was wary of the fact that he had taken up with a foreign girl. She had boasted to the neighbourhood that her Salvatore's woman would be arriving soon to bring her her first grandchild. Appearances had to be kept up. Whoever this girl was she was going to have to play a role and play it well.

Anna Filomena surveyed her prospective daughter-in-law and liked what she saw. The girl had not said a word. She was standing her ground and waiting to see what would

247

happen just as Anna Filomena would have done in her position. The girl was tiny but she stood tall. And she was pretty. Long dark hair, dark-lashed soft brown eyes, a long nose, a rosebud mouth but with a line of determination to it. With luck she would pass for Italian. Anna Filomena opened her arms and beckoned to the girl to come to her. As she gave her a peremptory embrace she felt the fragile bones within her grasp. Over the girl's shoulder she dismissed the waiting crowd.

'What are you waiting for? For months I wait for my new daughter-in-law and now I have to share her with the whole neighbourhood. Out! Out! Give us some peace.'

'Why isn't Salvatore here to greet her?' asked someone slyly.

'Because he's a working like you shoulda be too.' No one got the better of Anna Filomena. 'Now out with the lotta you,' and she slammed the door behind them.

'Sit,' she commanded, 'Now you wanta eat? You wanta sleep?'

'Sleep,' was Saskia's first word to her mother-in-law.

'*Stanca*,' Anna Filomena nodded wisely, 'you're pregnant. It's natural.' She looked hard at Saskia.

'I'm not –' began Saskia.

'The crossing was rough. I hear the crossing was very rough,' said Anna Filomena, who had heard nothing of the sort. Saskia nodded. 'So you were sick and you lost the baby? Am I right?' Saskia looked at her, bewildered. 'You don't have the baby any more. I tell everyone my Sal, he gonna have a baby, but you don't have the baby any more so we tell everyone the crossing was very rough . . .'

Saskia nodded. Whatever game this large woman in the black dress, with grey hair and liquid black eyes set in the depths of her wrinkled face was playing, she was prepared to go along with it.

'Sal?' she whispered.

'First you gotta sleep. Then you see Salvatore,' and picking up the laundry bag, Anna Filomena grasped Saskia by the wrist and led her through to the far bedroom.

'Salvatore's room, now yours too.'

Saskia took in the narrow bed with the worn sheets and the iron bedstead. She looked at the jug of water sitting in a big round china bowl and the tarnished mirror. She saw the cell-like window with the light obscured by the fire escape outside and the naked light bulb dangling from the middle of the ceiling.

'It's clean,' said Anna Filomena. 'Every day I clean and wait for you. You rest.' She turned and left the room.

I came three thousand miles for this, thought Saskia, as she undressed to her slip and lay down. *This is America. What have I done?*

Within seconds she was asleep.

A door slammed in the distance as Anna Filomena began her descent to the street. As she weaved her way in and out of the street vendors picking up prosciutto, bread, tomatoes, olive oil, *frutta* – everything she needed for her daughter-in-law's welcome dinner – she sought out her daughters.

'Angelina, whatta you do? Over here, now. Help your mamma. Patrizia, you too. Where is Milena?'

'In the library, Mamma, as always.'

'Whatta she do there? Every day in the library. Now listen to your mamma. I want you to find Salvatore and bring him home for dinner tonight.'

'But Mamma, where –'

'I don't care where. I don't care if he gone to Long Island. You find him and you tell him she has arrived and is waiting for him.'

'Whaaa . . . at? Mamma, what's she like? Is she pretty? When did she get here? Let's go see . . .'

'Leave her be. She's a sleeping. You will see her tonight at dinner. You find Salvatore, you bring him home.'

'But he won't come . . .' whined Angelina. 'He's with that Lucia behind the bakery, he –'

'Hush!'

'Wait a second. Mamma, is she big with Salvatore's baby?'

Anna Filomena's face clouded over. She bent her head and crossed herself.

'The crossing over the sea, it was very bad. The poor girl was sick the whole time. She no keepa the *bambino*. Eh, *bambino* . . .' Anna Filomena came to with a jerk of her head. 'What have you done with your little brother? I give him to you to take for a walk and where is he? Have you sold him for a new dress? Angelina, what have you done?'

'Old Signora Paolozzi is sitting with him.' Angelina pointed to an old crone in black sitting on her steps with Guido on her knee.

'So go fetch him and give him to me. Then you go, Angelina and Patrizia, and you find your big brother and tell him his mother wants him home for dinner.'

The sisters sensed the anxiety behind the command. More than wanting their brother home for dinner, Anna Filomena wanted to test her errant son's respect for his mother.

Saskia awoke to a cacophony. A baby was crying. Pots were being clattered. Anna Filomena's voice could be heard shouting at her daughters.

'Patrizia, take this water to your Pappa. Angelina, hold Guido, give him a crust of bread for his little teeth. How can I stir the tomato sauce as well as everything else. Milena, closa that book. *Adesso*! Guido, donta cry. No, Milena, donta sit there, it's for your new sister, Sylvia. You think she like meatballs?'

'All Italians like meatballs, Mamma.'

'Sure, sure,' said Anna Filomena.

Saskia poured some ice-cold water into the china bowl and slapped it under her arms. Where was Sal? Did she have to meet his entire family without him? She looked at her reflection in the few remaining pieces of clear glass in the mirror and combed her long hair. She pinched her cheeks to give herself some colour and realized she needed to use the toilet fast. She had heard no male voices and without thinking she opened the door to the next room, strode past the bed shared by Patrizia and Milena and opened the next door into their parents' bedroom.

The sight of the muscular little man sitting buck naked in a tin bathtub in the middle of the room gave her such a shock that she stood there for some twenty seconds before she realized he was trying to cover his shrivelled penis under the water with his hands. Then she began to laugh. He presented such a ludicrous picture, she couldn't help it. The man began to laugh too. After a moment Saskia knew she could hold out no longer.

'The lavatory. Where is it?'

Marco Carlino didn't speak much English. He shrugged and raised his palms in the air. He had no idea what she was talking about but, *mamma-mia*, she was beautiful! Saskia was driven to desperate lengths. Moving her legs apart she made as if to squat and mimed water passing out from between her legs.

'Ah, *il gabinetto*,' he cried, clapping his hands in laughter, 'we no have.' Then, to Saskia's utter amazement, he pointed under the bed. Saskia stared at him, then back to the bed. Did he mean her to go under there? Marco continued to gesticulate wildly until she ventured to look – and found a huge china potty. Understanding at last she spirited it away to her room. When she next knocked tentatively on the Carlino parents' bedroom door, Marco opened it fully dressed.

'*Sono Marco Carlino. Salvatore e il figlio mio,*' and he bowed proudly and offered her his arm. Saskia took it and they marched through to the kitchen for dinner.

The two teenage girls giggling together were suddenly silent. The younger sister slowly laid down the book she had been reading and rose to her feet. Standing in a line down one side of the kitchen table, the three Carlino sisters stared open-mouthed at their new sister-in-law.

Marco left Saskia's side and drew back a chair on the other side of the table. Like a waiter in a restaurant, he flipped a napkin over his arm, bowed over the chair and gestured to Saskia to be seated.

As she sat down the infant Guido suddenly reached out from his high chair next to her and grabbed a handful of her hair.

'Help!' squealed Saskia and the three girls opposite her laughed.

'Angelina, Patrizia, Milena, introduce yourselves,' yelled Mamma from the stove. 'Take care of Guido, see he doesn't throw his plate at Sylvia. *Marco, dove la bottiglia di vino rosso?*'

'*Si, si, aspetta.*' Marco was already brandishing a corkscrew, 'Is a good wine. Froma Napoli. You like?'

Saskia nodded resisting the impulse to wink at him. His black hair was parted in the middle and flattened down wet against his scalp after his bath and, as she brought a steaming pot over to the table and banged it down in front of him, Anna Filomena reached over and fastened the top button of his shirt and straightened his collar.

'*Vino, vino, vino!* My, my! Why we have vino tonight?' asked the eldest girl, picking up her glass and blowing into it. 'I'm Angelina, by the way. I'm sixteen.'

'We have the *vino* to welcome Sylvia to our family,' Mamma told her firmly. 'Pappa, pour her a glass.'

'*Un bicchiere di vino per Lei,*' said Marco handing it to Saskia. 'We no waita for Salvatore?'

'Why should we wait for my brother? He hasn't been here in two weeks.'

'*Basta, Patrizia!* Shhhhh!' Anna Filomena lightly tapped her middle daughter's head as she whisked another bowl of food onto the table.

But Saskia had heard. 'Where is he?' she asked.

'Oh, he's around. He spends most of his time over at the bakery,' Patrizia told her.

'Does he work there?' Saskia had been wondering if Sal had found a job.

'No, course not,' retorted Patrizia before her mother could stop her, 'unless you want to say he's working on the baker's daughter. She's not Italian. She's Dutch. Big and blonde. Sal's crazy about her. At least she's not German.'

Saskia started and hoped they hadn't noticed. Mamma looked crossly at Patrizia. Saskia turned to the youngest daughter. 'You haven't told me your name.' She smiled at the little girl.

'Mi . . . Mi . . . Mi . . .' The child's eyes began to fill. She was clearly terrified.

'She's called Mi –' began Patrizia.

'*Silenzio!* Let her say it!' cut in Anna Filomena. She bent and put her arm around her youngest daughter's shoulders. 'Sylvia is your new sister,' she told her softly. 'She will love you as one of the *famiglia*. You can tell her who you are.'

The little girl's mouth worked furiously but nothing came out.

'I know a game,' said Saskia gently. 'Tell me what letter your name begins with and I'll guess it. See, my name is Sylvia and that begins with an S but it could be Sonia or Saskia or . . .'

'Saskia, that's a lovely name. I never heard that before.' Angelina looked across the table.

Saskia didn't wait a beat. 'It is pretty, isn't it? In fact, you know something, it's what Sal often called me as a nickname so why don't you all call me Saskia? That way I'll start a new life in a new country with a new name.'

She caught Anna Filomena looking at her thoughtfully and she silently beseeched the older woman with her eyes to agree to what she was suggesting. Anna Filomena nodded almost imperceptibly. She clapped her hands. '*Bene, bene*,' she said, 'now you are Saskia.' And it was clear to Saskia that once Mamma had spoken the rest of the family obeyed.

'So what does your name begin with? Are you an S too?' Milena shook her head. 'Ma . . . ma . . .'

'M?' asked Saskia. Milena nodded. 'So,' continued Saskia, 'Margharita? No? Maria? No? Mirella? Close?'

'Milena,' said the little girl suddenly with a beaming smile.

'Ah, Milena, another pretty name,' said Saskia. 'See, you can say it perfectly well. Now, say mine.'

'Saskia,' said Milena simply. 'Saskia Carlino. Wife of Salvatore Carlino. Sister of . . .'

253

'Oh, that's enough! So, you've said a complete sentence for a change. There's no need to send us to sleep.' Saskia recognized Patrizia's harsh tongue without even looking up. She noticed the tears returning to Milena's eyes and was about to say something when Patrizia looked directly at her and said: 'You know, you don't sound Italian.'

'That's because I'm English,' explained Saskia.

'I don't think you are.' Patrizia was still looking at her and for a second she reminded Saskia of Nancy Sanders. It was that same 'you don't fool me' look all over again.

'So you know so many *Inglese*? Be quiet, Patrizia. Saskia is now an Italian with us. Angelina, give her some pasta.'

Anna Filomena pushed the giant round bowl across the table. Out of it Angelina fished what looked to Saskia like a mass of long slimy white worms which she dumped onto Saskia's plate.

'Now you take my meatballs in da tomato sauce.' Anna Filomena pushed another bowl towards her. 'Here, I helpa you,' and she spooned a dollop of the sauce onto the top of the worms.

'Was Salvatore very brave in the war? Did he kill lots of ugly Germans?' asked Milena earnestly, suddenly finding her power of speech.

'I expect so,' said Saskia sadly, not wanting to disillusion Milena about the brother she clearly idolized. Obviously Sal had kept quiet that he was never anywhere near the front.

'Pappa, wake up. *Mangia, mangia.*' Marco came to with a start. He had quietly polished off half the bottle of wine and had fallen asleep.

Little Guido suddenly burst into howls. Without thinking Saskia stood up and lifted him out of his chair. She cradled him in her arms and smoothed his soft, wispy hair off his hot little forehead. She lifted him, sniffed between his legs and nodded to Anna Filomena.

'I'll change him,' said Saskia. 'Where do you keep his nappies.'

'Diapers,' said Anna Filomena automatically. 'In a box under his cot. You can change him on my bed.'

As Saskia left the room, Anna Filomena stared after her.

How does she know what to do with a bambino? she wondered. *First we hear she's part-Italian, then we hear she's pregnant, then she turns out to be neither, yet she looks more Italian than my own children and she behaves like she's already a mamma.*

By the time Saskia returned the family were halfway through their meal. Anna Filomena took Guido from her and urged her to eat. Saskia looked around the table. Everyone was deftly twirling the worms around their forks and shovelling them into their mouths. Saskia picked up her fork and dipped it into her plate. She raised the fork. The worms fell off. She tried again but just as the fork reached her mouth, they slithered away.

'Call yourself an Italian wife and you can't even eat spaghetti,' commented Patrizia slyly.

'Spaghetti?' Saskia looked puzzled.

'Mamma, see, she doesn't even know what it is.' Patrizia was triumphant. 'How you gonna cook my brother his dinner? How you gonna make meatballs and tomato sauce?' she jeered. 'No wonder he prefer Lucia. At least she bake a him bread and pastries.'

Milena had crept around the table to Saskia's side.

'Like this,' she said shyly, and took Saskia's fork from her and showed her how to wind the slimy worms round and round until they were fastened securely. Moving her fork very slowly, Saskia lunged at the pasta and managed to pull a few strands into her mouth. She was amazed. She had expected something disgusting but the taste was delicious. She smiled at Anna Filomena who smiled back.

'*Brava*!' she said. '*Brava*, Saskia.'

At around 9.30 Saskia suddenly slipped from her chair to the floor in sheer exhaustion. Marco and Angelina helped her to the little room at the far end of the apartment and Marco left while Angelina undressed her and laid her between the sheets.

She was awakened by screams.

It was Milena. The nightmares had been occurring every night since she had borrowed *Moby Dick* from the library. At first she had sensed Patrizia asleep beside her in bed and in her dreams taken her to be Queequeg, the tatooed savage harpooner with whom Captain Ahab shares a bed near the beginning of the book. As time went on Patrizia became the great white whale rising up out of the sea to devour Milena. Anna Filomena had confiscated the book, not a word of which could she understand, but the nightmares had persisted. Saskia, now fully awake, could hear Anna Filomena calming her youngest daughter. Then she heard her address Patrizia.

'So, Salvatore, why didn't you find him like I asked?'

'We did, Mamma, but he wouldn't come.'

'I won't ask you where he was but didn't you tell him his bride had arrived?'

'*Si, Mamma.*'

'So what he say?'

'He say he'll come. When he's ready.'

Next door Saskia pressed her head into the pillow. When he's ready. When would that be? Should she stay here with these friendly (save Patrizia) poverty-stricken strangers, taking their food and their kindness? Or should she move out and find a hotel? And then what?

Anna Filomena had left her daughters now and Saskia could hear them whispering to each other.

'She's p . . . p . . . pretty.'

'*Si.*'

'You think she l . . . l . . . loves Salvatore?'

'Of course, but does Salvatore love her?'

'B . . . b . . . but he m . . . m . . . m . . .'

'Married her? Is that what you're trying to say, Milly?'

'Don't c . . . call m . . . m . . . me Milly?'

'Why not?'

'Not Italian.'

'Oh, you're the good Italian daughter, the Italian who's going to succeed in the world. Silly Milly! You know why? First you're an Italian and second you're a woman. Passport to nowhere. Go to sleep, silly Milly, and don't you dare have another nightmare and wake me up. *Buona notte.*'

'*Buona notte, P . . . P . . . P . . .*'

Saskia heard the creaking bed before the girls did because she had not gone back to sleep. Then the moans began and suddenly she realised what was happening.

'Anna Filomena, quicker, quicker . . . oh, hurry . . . let me . . . Aaaah, Anna Filomena, I love you, Aaaaaa!'

The long drawn out sigh was all too familiar. Saskia lay staring up into the darkness. If she could hear them two rooms away then little Milena must be able to hear her parents making love that much louder. No wonder she had nightmares.

Sal came home at two in the morning.

He tiptoed through the apartment but when he found Saskia he ripped the sheet away from her and flung himself on her naked body with a whoop.

'Welcome to America, baby,' he mumbled as he rubbed his already erect penis against her. 'Land of milk and golden honey and I want it dripping out of you. C'mon, c'mon, baby. Whatsa matter with you? You were a little tiger back in England, back in that jungle hut of yours.' He forced his lips down on hers and she could smell the drink. He was undoing his shirt buttons with one hand and stroking her hair with the other. He pressed his chest down on her breasts and began to move his pelvis from side to side. His erection nudged at her and, tired and exhausted though she was, Saskia moved her legs apart until he was able to reach down and stroke her. He inserted a finger into her vagina. She reacted in spite of herself. He withdrew his finger and moved his penis into her.

Then he lost control. He bucked against her, hard, and as he came deeper and deeper inside her he cried out. As he collapsed heavily onto her in one final spasm, all Saskia could think of was that through the paper-thin walls of the tenement, Anna Filomena and Marco would undoubtedly have been able to hear every single vibration, verbal or otherwise, of their son's reunion with his bride. And as Sal's drunken snoring reverberated through the apartment, Saskia asked herself yet again the question that was becoming synonymous with her arrival in America: *What have I done?*

Twenty-Three

It was an older and very much wiser Barney Lambert who arrived back in England and made his way north. He had to wait four hours for a train and as he sat in the packed compartment he told himself that if he could survive the hurt and humiliation inflicted upon him by Christiane, he could survive anything.

It was inconceivable that Laurel Bank should ever appear small to him, but somehow that was the case as the taxi advanced slowly up the long drive, past the weir, through the rhododendron tunnel, past the laurel bushes, to deposit him at the front door of the Bell House. The world, of course, was now a considerably larger place in his newly awakened eye, but even so he was shaken to find himself comparing the mill – which he had once thought a palace – with the ruined magnificence of Berlin. It saddened him too because he knew that he had expected to find solace in his return to his childhood home and already he was disappointed.

Selwyn's Brough Superior was nowhere to be seen. It was a Sunday so maybe he had gone to Evensong and stayed on for dinner with someone. After all, Barney *was* four hours late. He paid off the taxi and found to his relief that the front door was open. He dumped his bags in the hall and moved instinctively towards the kitchen. As he opened the door there was a small commotion in the corner by the Aga. Schnutzi and Putzi struggled to their feet and stumbled out of their basket towards him. Barney looked at the basket and all he could see was the tiny bundle lying between them. *Klara*! He blinked and it was gone, and he had to wrestle with the lump that rose in his throat as the dogs jumped all over him.

'Down, down there, good dogs. Missed me, have you? Or are you just asking for your dinner? Where's master, hmmm?'

Further exploration of the Bell House bewildered Barney. It appeared that Selwyn might not even be living there. Dust sheets covered the furniture in all the rooms except for the kitchen and Selwyn's bedroom. A stale, unpleasant smell hung about the house and it wasn't until Barney went in search of food in the larder that he discovered what it was.

There was no food. There was no room for any. The larder was crammed full of old bottles. Empties. Mostly wine but some whisky, gin and the odd beer bottle. Beer! Selwyn never touched the stuff. What was going on?

Barney had a pretty good idea when, a couple of hours later, after he had removed the dust sheets from his room and unpacked his things, Selwyn returned. Barney heard the Brough Superior hurtling up the drive and skidding to a halt outside the Bell House, but by the time he came downstairs Selwyn had already passed out. He lay spreadeagled, half in, half out of the dog basket and not even the gentle licking of Schnutzi and Putzi could rouse him. There was nothing for Barney to do but take himself off to his room and go to bed.

Somehow, during the night, Selwyn must have got himself upstairs since when Barney came down the next morning there was no sign of him in the kitchen. Barney let the dogs out and could not believe the sight that met his sleepy eyes. Half the village appeared to be coming up the drive.

'Good morning,' he called out when they were within hearing distance.

'Morning yourself, Barney lad. Back from the Army then, are you?'

'Good to have you back. You'll be dead useful. Mr Selwyn told us you were coming.'

'Were you in Germany like I was?' shouted a young man not much older than Barney. One by one they greeted him as he stared at them, dumbfounded. There were about twenty-five in all.

'Going to join us then? Our Patrick said you would.'

'Join you?' repeated Barney, holding his dressing gown tightly around him, 'What do you mean, join you?'

'Give the lad a chance to settle in, have his breakfast . . .'

They moved on round the corner. Barney rushed into the hall and peered through the window beside the front door to watch them. He saw them disappearing, one by one, into the mill.

The mill!

Had Selwyn restarted it? Surely not.

Barney had come home to a Labour government flexing its muscles for all its worth. A quarter of the nation's buildings had been destroyed during the war, there had been no new building for six years and still the politicians were promising a home for every family. But housing the homeless quickly was out of the question –bricks and timber were scarce – and temporary solutions had to be found. One of these was to place homeless families in the now abandoned Army camps until new accomodation could be built, often in the form of ugly prefabs.

Selwyn had been put on the spot. There he was, sitting pretty in the midst of acres of empty space, much of it now owned by the council – the perfect site for rows and rows of new prefabs. Naturally he had baulked at the thought of the beautiful countryside surrounding the mill being marred by such construction and he had begun to panic until he had hit on the idea of offering the mill itself as alternative accommodation.

Barney listened in sheer admiration as Selwyn waxed lyrical about the conversion of the Laurel Bank flats.

'They'll be the finest flats in the country. The weaving rooms are being converted into three, sometimes four flats each. They'll be small but big enough to house young married couples and those with not more than two children. And the best part about it is that we're doing it all ourselves. Oh, how I wish Father were alive to see it. All the men from the village, the sons of the ones he had to sack when the mill closed down, if they're fit and able they're working here for the council, building my flats. And the best part – I keep saying that, don't I? – but you see, Barney, there are so many best parts and this one is that they are doing it for their sons, their lads who have come back from the war and want a place in which to settle down with their new families. They get first pick.'

'And the rest?' asked Barney.

'All from Liverpool. Merseyside really suffered, as you well know. We might even see some of your old school-friends at Laurel Bank. Now, are you with us?'

Barney didn't know what to say. It was wonderful to see Selwyn so full of optimism. Of course, the night-time drinking told a completely different story but while he had this going for him during the day, Barney understood there was hope for Selwyn. And if he, Barney, stayed to support him, so much the better.

Except Barney knew he couldn't. If he had never gone away in the first place, or even if he'd just gone as far as Liverpool and returned, it might have been different. But Berlin had opened up a new world to him in so many different ways. He might feel bitter towards Christiane but she had given him a taste of the kind of excitement he knew he would never find if he stayed at Laurel Bank. He had to get away.

Selwyn had gone silent as if he had suddenly guessed what Barney would say. *I owe this man so much*, thought Barney. *He took me off the streets of Liverpool and took me in as if I were his own son. Now, when I have the chance to repay him for everything he has ever done for me, all I want to do is walk away.*

'It doesn't work like that,' said Selwyn simply after a while.

Barney jumped. Had Selwyn been reading his mind? 'What do you mean?'

'You can't spend your life only helping those who help you. It would be nice if you could but you can't. When you didn't answer immediately I realized what was on your mind. It's all right, Barney. This is my project and it's my responsibility. Right now, you don't want anything to do with it. No!' Selwyn raised his hand in protest, 'Don't pretend you do, that would be worse than anything. If you want to go, go – and you do so with my blessing. You can always come back at a later stage.'

Barney was overcome with gratitude for Selwyn's understanding. He'd make it up to Selwyn somehow.

'How's Lady Sarah?' he asked to change the subject.

'Good lord, you wouldn't know, would you? She's in America.'

'She isn't!' Barney was amazed.

'Oh yes, she's gone to visit Nancy. You remember, Nancy married some frightfully wealthy American chap. She ran off with him. Well, now he's something unbelievably important on Wall Street and they have a vast mansion in a place called Westchester outside New York. But at least it's near enough for Nancy to take Sarah into Manhattan on a regular basis. They're having a whale of a time. I had this interminable letter from Sarah, took me days to decipher her scrawl.'

'How long has she been gone?'

'Months. At least two.'

'And when will she be back?'

'Who can say? Anyone with eyes could see that it was Sarah's chance to spread her wings of freedom.'

'What do you mean? What freedom?'

'She's divorced. Didn't I write and tell you? She divorced Geoffrey Sanders, sent him packing and about time too! Poor fellow's in a terrible pickle now. Seems he took a bit of a tumble when clothes rationing ended, which only goes to

262

prove he must have been a black market spiv like we all suspected. Good old Sarah! I do miss her.'

'Why did Lady Sarah marry Geoffrey Sanders in the first place, Selwyn?'

'Who knows? He was working as an odd-jobman for her family over near Ripon. She's a Yorkshire girl, you know, originally, but her people moved here just when she was due to go up to Oxford. They were all for seeing Geoffrey off the premises, but Sarah said she was going to marry him come what may. And married they were. In the end her father bought them The Hall. Of course, Geoffrey thought it was the height of county living, that he was made for life. It was only when he found out he'd have to find a way of supporting her, and the girls when they came along, that he began to diversify into rather odd occupations. The jam pot lids, for example, although I have to hand it to him, he made a small fortune out of that. Sarah hung on to her own money. Only smart thing she did. She's got plenty to see her through now and the girls will have a penny or two I shouldn't wonder. The saddest thing of all, though, is that in her first year at Oxford she met the perfect person for her.'

'Who was that?'

'Anthony Fakenham. Nice chap, went into the Foreign Service. To get over Sarah, some said. Next best thing to joining the Foreign Legion. They should have married. Better suited, same class and all that, but now he's married to someone else . . .'

'What about the class thing, Selwyn? What am I? Working class?'

'Well, you're a bit tricky, as a matter of fact. Of course, you were born working class, you can't escape from that . . .'

'Selwyn, I'm not talking about escaping from anything.'

'Barney, sorry, old chap, you know I didn't mean it like that. As I say, you were born working class but you were raised as a middle-class child after I got hold of you.'

'But my roots . . .?'

'It's no good thinking you can go back to being a

working-class man now. You've left all that behind. You've got different tastes, different interests. I'll grant you we're in a much more democratic society now. Everyone had to muck in during the war and the boys who came home expected a new England. They'd done their bit and they wanted a breaking down of the class barriers, felt they'd deserved it. It'll never happen, but whatever muddle we're in at the moment, Barney, you are no longer working class, take my word for it. Now, let's have a drink on that.'

'Selwyn, why have you begun drinking like this?' They were far enough gone for Barney to be able to slip in a question like that without causing offence.

'Like what?'

'You know, before lunch, during lunch, after lunch, all afternoon, every night . . .?'

'How do you know it's every night? You've only been back two days.'

'I found the empties. And the men, they're one hundred per cent behind you but I've heard them mention it. They joke about how you are the one "weaving in and out of rooms". What brought it on, Selwyn?'

'Loneliness. What else?'

'You're lonely?'

'Well, of course I am. I'm not sure whether I did the right thing for you and Saskia. Nothing very conventional about it but it was the best I could do. Now you've both gone, or almost gone, and I'm lonely. Simple as that. That's one of the reasons I've got the men in the village in to help out on the conversions. Keeps me company. But come five o'clock they're away to their families and I'm all alone again. Schnutzi and Putzi do their best but you know what they're like when they've had their dinner. Into their basket and out for the count. Sometimes I drink so much I join them. No harm in it, old chap, no harm . . .'

He looked away sadly and Barney didn't have the heart to reprimand him any further.

*

Barney couldn't help but be impressed by the flats. Deep down he felt guilty that he had never imagined Selwyn capable of designing more than a chair. There were fourteen flats in all, with a central laundry down in the basement of the mill. The kitchens had their own fitted units with proper draining boards and gas stoves. Small refrigerators were built in. Every thought had been given to designing the small areas with space-saving fixtures and fittings. Tables, and even beds, disappeared into the walls when not in use. Some of the flats were furnished with government-issue utility furniture, but some had furniture specially designed by Selwyn.

When Barney finally left, families were already beginning to move in. The mill would never be the same again. Saskia's sewing room had disappeared forever as had Selwyn's studio on the ground floor. In a simple ceremony over the tiny grave down by the weir, Selwyn and Barney secretly dedicated the council flats to little Klara's memory and named them Klara Court. A plaque was commissioned and placed on the wall next to the main entrance. No one could understand why they had chosen the name Klara Court but they didn't enlighten anybody.

As he turned to look out of the rear window of the taxi as it bore him away to the station, Barney felt sadness at the sight of the great bear of a man with his long white hair standing all alone in front of the Bell House. As Barney watched, Selwyn reached down to stroke the ears of Schnutzi and Putzi, who had joined him on the steps, before he turned slowly to retreat into the house. Next door, at Klara Court, lights blazed on all floors signalling warmth and activity and family life. But at the Bell House a single lamp shone in Selwyn's bedroom telling Barney that there was nothing else for Selwyn to do but take himself up to bed at seven o'clock in the evening and drink himself to sleep.

Barney almost wept.

To take his mind off it he rummaged in his pocket for the letter that had arrived for him that morning. It was from

Germany and he had been putting off opening it all day. Now he extracted the single page from the envelope. It might just as well have been a telegram, so short was the message:

MATTHIAS. AM 16 SEPTEMBER GEBOREN. BLAUE AUGEN.

Matthias. Born on September 16. Blue eyes.

Barney's first stop when he reached London was his Auntie Beattie's. He hadn't seen her since she had married a Londoner and moved down south when he was a small boy. It was Selwyn who had reminded Barney of her existence. When Barney's parents had been killed Selwyn had tried to trace other members of the family but Beatrice Richardson had been the only one he'd found. She'd offered to take Barney off Selwyn's hands then and there but after a conversation on the telephone they had both agreed it would be madness to send Barney into the midst of the London blitz when he'd just escaped the Liverpool one. Beattie had kept in touch with Selwyn by post, assuring him that if there was ever anything she could do, Barney only had to ask.

Now, realizing he would arrive in London broke and knowing no one, Barney asked his Auntie Beattie for a bed. It turned out she took in lodgers. When he saw the woman who opened the door to him he wondered what he'd let himself in for.

'There you are, Barney lad. I'd have known you anywhere. Just like our Joe, you are. The image. Heard it all your life, I expect.'

'Who from?' asked Barney without thinking.

'What d'you mean, who from? Oh, never mind. Come in, lad, don't stand all day on the doorstep. You'll make it mucky. I mean, look at the state of hers next door. She's not cleaned it since I don't know when. So, Barney lad, what do you want for your tea? I've got a nice bit of ham off a bloke I know. That'd be dead tasty in between your bread and butter, wouldn't it? Or would you like a meat pie. I've made one. I have, you know. My Fred always said I made the best meat pie he'd ever . . .'

'Uncle Fred?' asked Barney nervously. He couldn't remember Uncle Fred at all. He couldn't even remember how long ago he had died.

'It was his chest finally got him in the end. Mind you, I always thought it'd be his bowels,' said Beattie darkly. 'Would he empty them? Never! He said it was because he'd had to grow up with an outside lav but we all did, didn't we? I mean, he should have been grateful he didn't have to go across the yard in the pouring rain any more. He could just fall out of bed and into the en suite. I told him time and time again, I said, Fred, if you don't keep your bowels regular you'll come to a sorry end. Well, he did but they said his bowels were all right. I did ask.' She looked fiercely at Barney as if he might be accusing her of having forgotten.

'I'm so sorry he's, er, gone.' said Barney.

'Fifty-five's a young age to pass on and we'd only been married ten years. Oh yes, we were married eventually. I know what your mam thought. Thought he was me fancy man who wouldn't stick by me. Well, he did. Hear that, Vera, you daft old bitch?' Beattie raised her head to shout at the ceiling. 'He married me in the end. He made an honest woman of me. Mrs Frederick Richardson, that's who I am now. And, Barney lad, there you are standing there waiting for your tea. We'll go through to the kitchen.'

The house in Fulham was not unlike the one Barney had grown up in during the early part of his life. He glanced into the front room as they passed and knew he'd seen the same flowered wallpaper everywhere he went as a child. The kitchen was painted a kind of murky brown with lino on the floor and the scullery leading off it was pale green. Beattie filled a kettle at the sink, chattering all the while.

'Fred left me well provided for – there's no need for me to open the door to the Man from the Pru. Now, what's it to be, Barney lad? Ham or meat pie?'

When he chose the ham he realized he'd offended her. He

should have opted for her home-made meat pie but it was too late. She insisted he sit down at the kitchen table while she padded about in her wedge-heeled shoes setting a plate before him, a knife, a fork and a cup and saucer.

'Are you not eating, Auntie Beattie?' he asked her. The 'Auntie Beattie' sounded strange considering he'd only just met her but he could tell she was pleased.

'Let you into a little secret, Barney lad. I went down the chip shop half an hour before you arrived. I just couldn't wait for me tea and I knew if I sat down with me food in front of me you'd walk through the door and catch me at it. Truth is I'm trying to lose weight, me figure's not what it once was . . .' She patted her stomach protruding under her sleeveless flowered pinny. Barney knew he was supposed to tell her she looked fine but he couldn't bring himself to. She sighed and said, 'Well, I'll just sit down with you and have a ciggie with me cup of tea. So, we're back in then, what d'you think about that?'

Barney was busy spreading marge on his bread.

'Back in what?'

'Back in power, of course. Labour. We're in. We won the election. All those lads back from the war ready to start a new life, they'll not put up with what we had before. There was Churchill sitting pretty and safe as houses while they were all out there at the front facing it all, stands to reason they wouldn't vote for him. Too flipping old anyway. Mind you, Barney lad, our lot are no spring chickens either. My Fred said . . .'

Barney just let her ramble on. She'd accepted him as if she'd known him all her life. She took it for granted that he would vote Labour. He was her Joe's boy and that was good enough for her. Every other sentence began with 'My Fred said . . .' and it was clear she was lonely.

'How many lodgers do you have at the moment, Auntie Beattie?'

'Oh, I've only got the one. There's only three rooms upstairs. Shall I take you up?'

He glanced into her room and pulled his head out quickly as he encountered an overpowering smell of stale face powder.

'This is your room.' It was clear he didn't have any say in the matter. He was going to be her new lodger whether he liked it or not. He stood for a while and looked about him. He could do a lot worse. A single bed, a table and chair, a wardrobe and an armchair by the gas fire.

As he came out onto the landing again he didn't see another door so he asked, 'Where's the other lodger's room?'

'Round the corner. That other door, that's the bathroom built over the wash house and the other room's just beyond it. Don't go in. He's asleep.'

The box room. She'd squashed a truckle bed or something equally small into the box room. She was charging some poor bugger for it and pretending her Fred had left her well provided for at the same time.

Downstairs she proudly showed him the front room where a giant aspidistra had been given pride of place in front of the lace curtains. Starched white antimacassars had been placed over the backs of the best chairs to protect the upholstery from the late Fred Richardson's Brilliantine. Barney saw a framed photograph on the mantelpiece underneath a mirror with scalloped edges. He moved closer to study it. A thin, meek-looking man was standing in the sea in his shirtsleeves and braces with his trousers rolled up. He was smiling shyly at the photographer.

'That's him. That's my Frederick. That was at Morecambe where we met. I was on holiday with your father, Barney. And your mother, come to think of it. My Frederick was there with his mother and she struck up a conversation with Vera on the sands. By the end of the first week we were a party. We went everywhere together. Well, my Frederick, he looked after his mother very well just like he looked after me all those years, but once he'd put her to bed he'd naught to do so we let him come around with us, ballroom dancing and that. Oh, he was a one. Up from

London, you know? He taught me all the dances. Do you know "Balling the Jack", Barney lad? My Frederick, he used to do that with all the bits and pieces with his hands. Oh, he was a card that one.'

Barney looked again at the photograph taken on Morecambe Sands. He didn't look like much of a card.

'He was an undertaker, see? And quite a few people kicked the bucket one way or another over the last few years. I always say it's a shame my Frederick missed out on all those killed at the front. He'd have been a millionaire by now if he'd been able to bury all them lot but as I say, mustn't grumble . . . This posh gent you lived with . . .'

'Selwyn?'

'Mr Reilly. What does he do for a living, like?'

'He's a designer, Auntie Beattie.'

'Well, what's that when it's at home? Sounds dead airy-fairy to me. Don't know how Joe and Vera allowed him to look after you all these years.'

'They didn't, Auntie Beattie, they were dead. Selwyn's been like a father to me.'

'Our Joe was your father and don't you ever forget it, my lad. You're not one of the likes of him up there in that mill whatever ideas he may have been putting in your head.'

'I know, Auntie Beattie, I know.' And Barney found he did know what she meant. Here with Auntie Beattie he was back among his own kind. He felt at home already despite her vulgarity and the less luxurious surroundings. She was a drop of Liverpool in the middle of London and a decidedly welcome one at that.

'You're a good lad, Barney.' She kissed the top of his head and for the first time he realized she was taller than he was. He dreaded to think how much she must weigh.

Abigail Wasserman was New England old money stock but right from the start her parents had known she would be a problem. She was so restless, always flitting from one thing to another, so easily distracted. They knew she'd never

270

stick it out in college but the last thing they were prepared for was her marriage to Harold Wasserman.

'A Jew!' Abigail could still hear her mother's voice. Not: 'How did you meet him?' or 'We're so happy for you, dear' or 'How old is he?' or even 'What does he do?' Just the flat pronouncement: 'A Jew! With a name like that he has to be. My daughter will be Abigail Wasserman.'

'How could I do such a thing to you?' Abigail had quipped but there was no lightening the mood of her parents. They moved stoically through the wedding with their noses in the air and had not extended an invitation to their daughter and her husband to visit them since.

Abigail remained unmoved. After all, Harry had gone on to become phenomenally successful. He had begun with one clothing store in Queens and now he owned a dozen as well as the jewel in his crown: Wasserman's on Fifth Avenue. Okay, so it wasn't Bergdorf's or Bloomingdale's or even Macy's but it had a uniqueness to it and now, two years later, it was one of the most popular department stores in Manhattan. Abigail was a living monument to her husband's store. She wore its furs, its jewellery, its shoes, its daywear, its evening wear. She never shopped anywhere else. She never had to. Harry had everything sent round to the apartment every season and all she had to do was pick out what she wanted.

Abigail liked being Mrs Harold Wasserman and she remained eternally grateful that someone up there had been looking out for her that rainy night when her roommate had suggested they double date with the boy with whom she was going steady who was bringing along his roommate. Enter Harold Wasserman. And now here was Harry setting up the first London branch of Wasserman's.

Harry might have made a fortune with his Wasserman's store but Abigail never touched it. She had her own money and her own personal enterprise. She sponsored struggling young artists. Before marrying Harry she had studied history of art and on arrival in England she had wasted no time in following up several introductions to the London art

271

world. She bought a gallery and began to search around for people to exhibit. It was Harry who had suggested to her that she might want to visit art colleges in Britain in order to discover raw talent before anyone else saw it and it was at Liverpool that she had first seen Barney's work.

Barney liked her immediately. She had an outgoing, almost brash personality he had not encountered in a woman before and he found it refreshing. So after he had settled himself in at Auntie Beattie's, the Wassermans' house in Old Church Street, Chelsea was his next port of call.

Abigail Wasserman astounded him. He had come to see her because she had wanted to buy one of his paintings of Saskia when she had seen his work at college before he left for Berlin. He had explained that his pictures of Saskia were not for sale. Now he knew he must change his mind if he was to survive. Besides, Abigail Wasserman might prove to be a valuable contact.

He could never have guessed how valuable.

'Do sit down . . .' He collapsed into a spacious chintz-covered armchair while she took the small portrait of Saskia's head lying on a pillow and placed it on the mantelpiece above the fireplace. 'I'm afraid I'm not going to offer you any money for this painting,' Abigail told him, offering him a cigarette from a silver box.

'In that case –' began Barney trying to clamber out of the armchair.

'No, wait. You don't know what I'm going to say. I want you to paint my portrait too.'

'Will you pay me for that?'

'Nope!' Abigail grinned. She was enjoying herself.

'Now look here –'

'I won't pay you a fig but here's the thing: you're going to have to paint it over in Edith Grove. Wanna go see?'

They walked. Abigail twittered on about what a fabulous day it was and didn't the river look like heaven and oh, by the way, she was pregnant so she wanted her portrait painted as quickly as possible before she started to show. She'd exhibit it in her gallery, of course.

272

Finally she led him round the back of a house in Edith Grove and handed him a set of keys to a separate building with a vast window covering almost the whole of one wall.

'Here's why I'm not paying any money for my portrait or that picture on my mantelpiece. I thought I'd give you a studio instead. Now what do you say?'

But Barney was speechless.

Twenty-Four

The woman was sitting on a chair placed on a round table draped with a white cloth. Behind her a grey blanket had been hung over a looking glass. She sat with her hands in her lap, one foot crossed behind the other. Her auburn hair hung loose over one shoulder down to her left breast.

She was naked.

She stared at Barney and he stared back at her. Then he slipped his paintbrush in amongst the mass of others crowded into a tall china jug, laid down his palette and turned the easel away from her so she could not see the work in progress.

'All right, that's it for today.'

With one bound the woman leapt down from the table and flung herself at him. She wound her arms around his neck and pressed her lips to his, giving him little nips. She undid the buttons on his shirt and pulled it up out of his corduroy trousers. She began to slide down his body until she was kneeling at his feet, resting her head against his bare stomach.

'Come on. Come on, Barney.' Her sense of urgency was unavoidable.

Barney looked down at her, by now lying prostrate at his feet. She drew her knees up and apart and he could see the bud of her clitoris, pink and exposed. He shrugged. The sitting had taken just over two hours. He was exhausted and he needed a drink. He left her lying there as he went to open a bottle of wine. He took a sip and then without warning he dropped to his knees and bent over her to lay his tongue on her clitoris.

The former Lady Poppy Anscombe, now a marchioness whose pictures were scattered throughout the society pages, squealed in delight. She rolled over, pretending to be trying to get away from him, and landed on an open tube of vermilion, squeezing the contents onto her naked skin. She began to smear the red paint over her breasts.

'Oh, look at you,' said Barney, and he tried to rub off the paint with a cloth which only served to arouse her even more. She pulled him down into her but he held her hands at arm's-length on the bare wooden floor as he drove his penis in and out. He knew she always liked to run her hands through his hair while he made love to her and he didn't want it covered in paint. At the back of his mind was the lunch at Lady Bridgewood's and the fact that they were due there within the hour.

'There!' he told her, giving her a gentle slap on her behind. 'Go and get yourself cleaned up,' She tried to cling to him, pressing her large paint-smeared breasts against his chest, reaching down to take him in her hand again. 'Now!' he roared. He knew they liked him to be forceful. He knew it accentuated his working-class image to them. He'd had a young countess of somewhere or other who had even asked him to black himself up a bit so she could pretend she was being serviced by a miner.

Barney Lambert. Young society portrait painter, darling of the social set. At first he had painted them fully clothed, serious commissions by their husbands for that coveted spot above the fireplace in the drawing room. At first he had enjoyed the endless rounds of cocktail parties to which he had escorted Abigail in Harold Wasserman's absence and where he had met the people who were to become his bread and butter. For Barney had very soon learned that while he might be lucky enough to have a studio of his own, if he were to make a success of his chosen profession he could not afford to turn anyone down. And he soon became popular for more than just his painting. Many of his subjects might

275

be socially confident young hostesses but when it came to sitting for him they were often struck by attacks of nerves. Barney had a natural gift for putting people at their ease; it was almost a doctor's bedside manner at its best. He calmed them, chatted to them, poured them glasses of wine, made them cups of tea and above all listened as gradually they thawed, relaxed and opened out to him. They told him about their vacuous lives, their dinner parties, their children . . . and finally their husbands. These husbands, it seemed to Barney, never listened to them, never had time for them, were always away in the City or at their club. And as he listened he studied their faces and watched the real characters emerging, the women inside the chic exterior presented to their husbands' world.

It had seemed a natural extension of this for him to begin to paint nude portraits although it had not come about until Abigail had mounted an exhibition of his work. Abigail was nothing if not shrewd. The minute she mentioned that she might be thinking of such a thing as an exhibition, women competed with each other to have their portrait painted by Barney in time to be included. Still Saskia's portraits stole the show. Her dark haunting beauty stood out amidst the English roses all around her, that and the fact that she was nude in every painting. But perhaps the biggest attraction was that Barney refused to sell a single painting of Saskia. Who was she? Everyone wanted to know but not even Abigail knew the answer. Indeed, details about Barney were vague. He came from the North, that was clear from his accent, but beyond that no one knew much about him. It only added to the intrigue.

Then the Hon. Georgiana Kendrick had taken the unprecedented step of commissioning him to paint her in the nude as, she claimed, a surprise birthday present for her husband. But Jakey Kendrick's birthday came and went and he clearly knew absolutely nothing about a portrait of his wife in her birthday suit. Nor did he know anything of the Hon. Georgiana's weekly tumbles on the bed behind the curtain in Barney's studio.

Abigail Wasserman must have been aware what was going on but she never said a word, nor did she ever try and seduce Barney herself, for which he was extremely grateful. The truth was that having enjoyed an active sex life in Berlin with Christiane, Barney had returned to find the nice young English girls whom he was expected to court were shocked if he even so much as allowed his hand to stray too far down over their shoulder. Older women in their mid to late twenties, married with a certain amount of experience, were much more his style yet he found he didn't really care for any of them. In his own way he was becoming as much a whore as Christiane had been.

'Hurry up,' he said brusquely to Poppy Anscombe who was getting dressed behind the curtain, 'we'll be late. Who'll be there, do you know?'

'Oh, everyone,' said Poppy and Barney sighed. He was getting rather tired of everyone: fifteen to twenty gossiping women, half of whom he'd already painted (and all that that entailed!) and the other half eager to be the next.

When they arrived at Lady Bridgewood's Belgrave Square mansion, which obviously remained impervious to the austerity that prevailed throughout the rest of the country, Poppy sailed in ahead of him and Barney excused himself to the butler and disappeared into the downstairs cloakroom. When he emerged a few minutes later a group of women were gathered together in the marble hall.

Barney slipped behind a pillar, out of sight. He wasn't quite ready to face the onslaught.

'I do adore darling Poppy, but she's had him for quite long enough.'

'Ah, but has she? Do we know for sure?'

'Oh, my dear, Poppy says it's this long, seriously. And apparently he grunts as he climaxes.'

'Does he hit her?'

'No, I don't think so, not yet anyway, but Annabel Warrington swears he beat her black and blue. She couldn't get undressed in front of Toby for weeks. Though I doubt Toby'd notice if she did.'

'How marvellous! What a brute!'

'Does he paint in the nude?'

'Does he have them before or after?'

'Charlotte Forsyth was hopelessly in love with him . . .'

'My dear, she still is.'

'Well, you know what they say . . .'

'What?'

'That dark girl, the one in all those paintings at the exhibition . . .'

'What about her?'

'She's the one. The only woman he loves.'

'Well, where is she?'

'Oh, I expect he keeps her hidden somewhere . . . Dark secret, though; even Abigail hasn't a clue . . .'

Behind the pillar Barney straightened his cravat and watched them troop away. He waited a few minutes then followed them. Old Lady Bridgewood greeted him with a 'So glad you could come' and he was offered a glass of sherry. Suddenly he was tired of endless gentility.

'I'd like a beer, please.'

'Beer, sir?' said the maid, completely nonplussed. She looked to Lady Bridgewood for guidance.

'Beer, Chivers. There'll be some in the pantry. Run along now.'

They took their seats for lunch in the dining room and Barney eyed the steak and kidney pudding as it was served to him.

'Me mam never got the hang of this,' he said rather too loudly, 'She used to give me dad a roast on Sundays, then he'd have to have it cold with lettuce and salad cream for the rest of the week. Not that he minded, like. But he did like his mustard. Where's the Colman's?' He looked up and down the table. Several silver mustard dishes with little silver spoons were in evidence. 'Shame,' muttered Barney, 'I like to mix me own mustard.'

There were titters up and down the table. 'So artistic.' 'Northern, of course.' 'So exciting.'

'Have you seen *Sunset Boulevard*?' a woman next to him

278

asked. She was one of the women who had been gossiping about him in the hall. Barney studied her with interest. She was about ten years older than he, probably in her mid to late thirties. He nodded. 'Isn't it absolutely marvellous?'

'Oh, it's true enough,' said Barney mischievously. 'Plenty of women could wind up like Norma Desmond, relying on young and talented men to keep their dreams alive. But that young man in the film, the one played by William Holden, he's weak. He should have left her in the beginning, not allowed himself to be kept like that.'

'Quite,' said the woman and turned away abruptly.

'They've opened a Trousseaux Room at Harrods . . .' said a woman opposite him.

'Darling, who do we know who's getting married?'

'Well, our daughters will be soon . . .'

'Speak for yourself, mine's only just started at Lady Eden's . . .' drawled a blonde on Barney's other side, lighting up a du Maurier. 'We're not all Norma Desmonds, you know.' She fluttered her eyelashes at Barney.

'Aren't you?' he said.

'Bit quiet today, Barney,' commented Poppy nervously.

'Korea,' replied Barney simply.

'What's that?' asked the blonde.

'Oh, for heaven's sake!' snapped Barney, rounding on her. 'It's a country in the Far East, south of China. If you know where that is?' he added sarcastically.

'Well, now I know. But why should I care a fig about Korea if it's so far away?'

'Because the North Korean forces have invaded South Korea and the United Nations have condemned North Korea's act of aggression.'

'So what?'

'Well, it could mean war with British troops involved as well as Americans and . . .'

'Oh, don't be silly, the war's over . . . I say, Poppy, did you hear that Lucy Fitzsimmons is getting married?'

'Yes, I think I did hear something. She's sort of dropped out of things a bit . . .'

'I should think so. Do you know she's marrying someone called Sidney Greenberg.'

'No!'

'It's true. Her brother told me. Well, that's one wedding we won't be going to.'

'Why not?' asked Barney.

'Well, because he's a Jew, of course.'

Barney had had enough.

'Excuse me, Lady Bridgewood.' He rose to his feet. 'I have a sitting at 2.30. I completely forgot about it till just now. I'm afraid I shall have to leave. Immediately.'

As he left he heard someone say: 'Oh, we are silly. We should have thought: Abigail Wasserman is married to a Jew.'

But Barney hadn't been thinking of Abigail. He'd been thinking of the beautiful elfin face he conjured up in his mind at some point every day since it had disappeared out of his life that cold, winter afternoon at Laurel Bank five years earlier.

Barney had been telling the truth. He did indeed have a sitting that afternoon and he had forgotten about it. He arrived back at Edith Grove seconds before an overweight woman in a fur stole and a crescent-shaped hat with a veil over her florid face arrived. *Christ!* thought Barney. *I can't paint this one, not after that dreadful lunch*. But it turned out he didn't have to. Mrs Barnsley had her daughter in tow.

It was one of the first sittings in quite a while where he hadn't actually met his subject socially and as he led them through to the studio he realized he was quite excited at the prospect of a new face. And what a face! Eliza Barnsley bore no resemblance to her mother whatsoever. She was petite, exquisite even, with tiny hands and feet, yet her neck was long and fine and the head on top of it was such a perfect shape, Barney wanted to reach out and clasp it in two cupped hands.

Mrs Barnsley sank into an old leather armchair without

being invited and moved her bulky weight around in it till she was comfortable like a dog settling in its basket.

'Do you suppose you might offer me a cup of tea?' she asked hopefully.

Barney obligingly put the kettle on.

'Only we've come down from Leeds today and I'm quite exhausted, though at least I can sit down for an hour or so now I'm here. We've to agree money, Mr Barnsley tells me. Fifty pounds?'

'No, that's not possible, I'm afraid.' Barney told her, pouring hot water into the pot to warm it.

'But I understood you painted some people for as little as twenty pounds . . .'

'Fifty pounds is fine but you can't stay here while I work, I'm afraid, Mrs Barnsley.'

'Why ever not?'

'House rules. I want complete intimacy with my subject.'

'I beg your pardon. Eliza's a decent girl, I'll have you know.'

'Of course she is and I'll paint a decent portrait of her if you leave me to get on with it.'

It took him a good twenty minutes to persuade her to leave. Then he turned to the quaking girl.

'What's the matter?' he asked kindly.

This only made matters worse. Eliza dissolved into tears.

'Now, now, my love. What's to fret about? Drink your tea, take your coat off and go and sit over there on that stool. I just want to do a quick pencil sketch of you for me to keep and refer to when you're not here, like. Got any brothers and sisters, have you?'

She sniffed and rubbed her nose. 'Two. Two brothers. They tease me.'

'What beasts.' He took the cup from her, helped her off with her coat, slipped an arm round her shoulders and led her over to the stool. As he sat her down he began to stroke the back of her neck without realizing what he was doing. She gazed at him adoringly, big puppy-dog eyes.

'Feeling better now?' She nodded. 'Good, want to look

over there for me, pretend you can see something nice out the window and I'll sketch your profile.'

The dark hair, the fragile features, those limpid eyes, the vulnerability, it all reminded him so much of Saskia he began to feel a lump in his own throat. He studied Eliza Barnsley sitting bolt upright on the stool. She was rigid with nerves and it wouldn't do at all. He was going to have to get her to relax.

'So what you doing in London then? Don't tell me you've come down just to see me?'

'Oh no. Mummy wants me to do the season. Be presented at Court. Be a deb. Parties and things.'

'Sounds fun.'

'Oh, no, it's positively awful!'

'How do you know? You haven't done it yet.'

'I just know it will be. I just know it.' And her shoulders began to heave again.

'Come on, come over here . . .'

She looked up in surprise, a startled little fawn.

'Over where?'

'Over here . . . to me. Come on.' He was holding his arms open to her. She slipped off the stool and almost tiptoed over to him. He took her by her slender shoulders and brought her into his arms. He stroked the back of her head over and over again and rubbed her back up and down. He could feel her quivering against him like a bird poised for flight. He knew exactly what he was doing. He might pretend to himself that he was calming her down for her sitting but he knew that if he could get her to relax in his arms, he could look down on her sleek, dark head and pretend to himself that he was holding Saskia.

Slowly she began to calm down and he felt her body become quiescent. She lifted her head very slightly and whispered in his ear: 'No one's ever held me like this before.'

'Like what?' He played with her, drawing her in even closer to him, stroking the back of her neck, playing with her ears. Her upturned face was very close to his, the soft

282

downy skin of her cheekbone rubbing his chin. Very gently he moved his face around until his lips were touching hers.

'Open your mouth,' he breathed and when she did so he blew little gusts of air into it and finally slipped his tongue inside.

'Put your arms up around my neck,' he commanded. In a trance, she obeyed. 'Keep them there,' he continued, knowing she would do anything he asked. He began to undo the buttons on her blouse. She was bare underneath and he glanced down to see little buds instead of breasts. In this respect she differed drastically from Saskia. He covered her up again quickly.

He had an erection. She must be able to feel it although it occurred to him she might not even know what it was. Gently, he moved her from side to side against him and felt a thrill of unbelievable pleasure surge through him. He felt her tighten her hands behind his neck and looking at her face, he was amazed to see a dreamy smile had spread across her features. Her eyes were closed and her mouth was slightly open and as he slipped his tongue back inside to meet hers, he felt her move against him of her own accord. They were both fully clothed but any moment now they were both going to climax. She could clearly feel his hardness through his trousers and even though she might not understand what it was, she wanted it.

'You can put your hand there,' he whispered, 'and you'll feel it . . .' but as soon as she touched him he called out Saskia's name in one long, blissful cry.

And at the same time he felt her melt into his arms and whimper: 'James.'

So poor, shy little Eliza Barnsley had a hearthrob somewhere back home in Leeds although he'd obviously never done anything about awakening her adolescent passion.

'You know, love,' whispered Barney, 'that was something special.'

'Was it really?' she breathed, eyes glowing now.

'Well, it happened to you too, didn't it?'

'I think so . . .'

'Even though you were thinking of James.'

She blushed scarlet.

'Tell you what,' said Barney, 'how would you like to take home a present for him that'll make him realize how beautiful you are . . .?'

She stripped quickly behind the curtain. Her sexual awakening had given her confidence and she ran out to perch on the stool with no hesitation whatsoever.

'A charcoal sketch of you in all your glory and he won't look at anyone else, believe me.'

She smiled at him and he couldn't resist walking over and dropping a kiss on each little rosebud nipple while she giggled.

He had almost finished the sketch and was trying to decide whether or not he'd do her more damage than good if he completed her sexual education when there was a loud banging on the door.

'Mummy!' squealed Eliza, rooted to the stool in fear. Barney recalled, too late, that the door was unlocked and soon heard it open and footsteps coming down the hall.

'What the bloody hell's going on, my lad?' demanded a strong Northern accent – but it wasn't Mrs Barnsley's faux refined version, it was the no-nonsense, direct approach from . . .

'Auntie Beattie!' cried Barney and rushed to greet her.

'Aye, but who's she?' Beattie Richardson looked at Eliza and back to Barney.

'My subject. I'm painting her.'

'Disgusting! Put your clothes on, dearie, you'll catch cold . . .' But Eliza had already scuttled away behind the curtain.

'Where's my daughter?' boomed a voice behind them.

'Getting dressed, I hope.' Auntie Beattie turned round to confront Mrs Barnsley. 'Some mother you are leaving her here to run around naked as the day she was born . . .'

'That's disgraceful! I leave my daughter in your care, Mr

Lambert and . . . I'll speak to my husband. She's not of age. We'll sue . . .'

'Oh, don't be so bloody daft, woman.' Auntie Beattie silenced her for only a moment.

'Well, who are you anyway?'

'Mrs Frederick Richardson, Mr Lambert's aunt,' Beattie told her, enunciating every word with agonizing clarity, 'from Liverpool,' she added unnecessarily. 'And I'll thank you to take your leave as soon as you can. I've something to tell my nephew.'

Barney rolled up the sketch and slipped it to Eliza as she left with her mother. She tried to reach up and kiss him on the way out but he evaded her just in time. Even so the look in her soft, expressive eyes gave everything away.

'Go back to James,' he whispered to her, 'he'll be waiting for you.' And he shut the door firmly, locking it behind them. 'Somehow Auntie Beattie, I think you've lost me a sitting.'

'It's you who'll be sitting when you hear what I've come to tell you. I thought I should come in person, like. It's about Mr Reilly.'

'Selwyn? What's he been up to?'

'He climbed up on a chair to put in a new electric light bulb for his tenants in one of the landings at that mill. There were something wrong with the light bulb, either that or they think his hands must have been wet. He got an electric shock and toppled over. It wouldn't have been so bad but the chair was right at the top of the stairs. He fell right down the stairs and broke his neck. He's dead, Barney, lad. Your Mr Reilly's dead.'

Schnutzi and Putzi took up their positions as sentinels on either side of the church door as their master's funeral began. Barney sat in the front pew on his own. He would not look behind him. He could not face anybody. He knew Lady Sarah would be there somewhere and he would see her afterwards but the only person he could think of was Saskia.

285

Now, more than any other time, he wanted to reach out to her for comfort. Selwyn had died, was about to be buried and he had no way of letting her know.

He had gone through Selwyn's things at Laurel Bank and among them he had found a *Songs of Praise*, well thumbed and flagged with pieces of paper. Barney recalled that Selwyn had always liked singing hymns in his bath, sometimes so loudly he could be heard throughout the Bell House. Barney had made the selection to be sung at the service from the marked pages and if people thought it odd that his funeral should begin with 'For Those in Peril on the Sea', too bad. It had been one of Selwyn's particular bath-time favourites, always accompanied by much splashing. William Blake's 'Jerusalem' and Bunyan's 'Pilgrim Song' evoked Selwyn's more flamboyant nature, while 'Lord of all Hopefulness', and the heartrending 'Dear Lord and Father of Mankind, Forgive our Foolish Ways' paid tribute to the more introspective Selwyn whose gruff leonine appearance was in many ways misleading.

Barney bent over and laid his head in his hands. He could almost feel Saskia walking up the aisle behind him wearing a new outfit she had made specially for the occasion. She would have sat up far into the night to make something outstanding for Selwyn's funeral, Barney was sure of it. He could picture her in the kitchen, parading up and down in front of the range for his approval while Stella – no, Schnutzi and Putzi – thumped their tails in appreciation from their basket. What would he do with them now? Could he take them down to London or would they be miserable down there? And too painful a reminder of their beloved master?

Stella, may she rest in peace, had first introduced him to Selwyn. He thought back to the day in 1939 when his life had been changed forever. He had met both Selwyn and Saskia in the space of a few hours and for those precious years at Laurel Bank they had come to mean everything to him.

Yet now they were both lost to him.

Outside at the grave David Appleby's voice intoned the doom-laden words that Selwyn would have hated: 'Man that is born of a woman hath but a short time to live, and is full of misery . . .'

Had Selwyn been full of misery? Surely not all of his life? Barney felt a hand at his elbow and turned to see Lady Sarah, her hair now snow white but her skin still clear and glowing in the morning air. He noticed that she in turn was being supported by a distinguished-looking man Barney had never seen before. He concentrated on the man for he knew that to look at Lady Sarah would bring back even more memories of Saskia.

Later, back at the Bell House, Lady Sarah intercepted him as she passed from the kitchen to Selwyn's old studio where everyone had gathered for drinks.

'Take a breath of air, Barney darling. I can't tell you how pleased I am to see you but we can talk later. I can cope with everyone for a while. Take yourself out for a walk, clear your head. Everyone will understand . . .'

Good old Sarah! Barney could hear Selwyn saying it. She had obviously sensed immediately that he was close to breaking point. She was quite right. A walk down to the weir was just what he needed. He stood for a while on the bridge looking down on the rushing waters below him before he felt himself drawn to a pathetic little mound of earth nearby: little Klara's tiny resting place where he and Selwyn had attempted the Jewish burial service they knew Saskia would have wanted. Would he ever be able to replace Selwyn and Saskia? Was he destined to be surrounded by the inane socialites well-meaning Abigail Wasserman had brought into his life? Or would he have another chance to establish once more what he had now lost twice: once when Selwyn – Selwyn again! – had led him away from the glaring crater in Liverpool the night his parents had died; and the second time when Saskia had walked out of his and Selwyn's lives? For what Barney yearned for more than anything was a family he could call his own. Joe and Vera had been his first family; Saskia and Selwyn his next. Would he ever find a third?

He became conscious of a figure standing opposite him across the tiny grave. He looked up to see a face partially obscured by a beautiful black lace veil. As slender fingers reached up to lift the veil from the glowing face beneath it, Barney found himself staring. Whoever this girl was she was utterly enchanting. Her skin had a faint honey tint to it and her upturned nose and cheeks sported a light sprinkling of freckles. She looked young and fresh and unspoiled.

'We always seem to meet over gravestones, don't we?' She smiled at him.

Barney looked blank.

'You don't recognize me, do you? Although there's no reason why you should, it's been simply ages since we last saw each other. The thing is, I've never forgotten you. I'm Serena. Serena Sanders. Lady Sarah's younger daughter. Nancy's little sister. Don't say you don't remember me?'

Twenty-Five

It was Friday and Saskia had developed a routine on Fridays. She wandered up Tenth Avenue until she came to a broad cross-street when she turned and looked west. At the end of the wide street she could see the river and she watched the sun go down between the tall dark buildings on either side of the street, a fierce red ball disappearing into the water. She needed to be reminded at regular intervals of the river's existence; it comforted her to know that she was living on the edge of an island, that she could still see the place where she had landed. Somewhere beyond that setting sun lay the way back home to Europe – whether to England or to Germany, she was no longer sure.

Once the sun had gone down she made her way slowly back to the Carlino building, jostled by the street vendors and the children running in and out of the stalls clutching bottles of Pepsi and hero sandwiches, past the groups of elderly women, all dressed in black, who sat together, trying to bring back memories of the old country by telling each other stories. Sometimes Anna Filomena joined them and because she was much respected in the neighbourhood, the old women always paused in their gossip to nod and smile in respect at Saskia as she passed, thin mouths opening in wizened faces to reveal toothless grins.

Back home, Saskia slipped through the railroad apartment, going directly to her room, avoiding the kitchen and Mamma's chatter. Once there she closed the door behind her. She could count on being alone. Sal was always out.

She crawled under the bed and brought out the package hidden on the floor in the far corner. She unwrapped the layers of newspaper and brought out two candles, then reached under the bed again and pulled out a wooden box. She took the box over to the far wall and turned it upside down. Next she pinned up a blanket over the window to keep out the light, placed the candles on the upturned wooden box and knelt down before it.

It was Friday night, time to bring in the Sabbath. She covered her head with a kerchief and lit the candles, then circled the candles three times with her hands and began the blessing:

> Baruch Atah Adonai
> Eloheynu Melech Haolam
> Asher Kidishanu Bimitzvotav
> Vitzivanu Lihadlik Ner Shel Shabat

Blessed, art thou, our God, Lord of the Universe, who has sanctified us with His commandments and commanded us to light the Sabbath candles . . .

'Fuck you think you're doing?'

She hadn't even heard him come into the room. He must have crept through the apartment.

The blow hit her on the side of the head and sent her reeling.

'Come on, I'm waiting to hear. What is all this?' He kicked over the tiny makeshift altar and she lunged for the falling candles. He put a foot on her wrist pinning her down while the flames set the threadbare rug on fire. He stamped out the flames and dropped to his knees, bending over her, pinning her down.

'You gonna tell me or what?' He slapped her face.

'I was praying, Sal.'

'You was praying? I never heard no prayers like that. I never heard you say no Bless me Father for I have sinned. Now you get up and make yourself pretty for dinner. I'm going to throw this junk away.'

'*No, Sal!* It's mine.'

But he had gone.

He had taken to hitting her about six months after she had arrived – suddenly, and for no apparent reason. She never knew when he would turn violent. He was still, for the most part, the easy-going charmer who had helped her survive her time in the woods. He even told her regularly that he loved her – or as regularly as he could, given that he was hardly ever there. She had no idea where he went and it was when she had begun to ask that he had first hit her.

'Don't ask questions, baby. Don't ever ask me no questions, see? It's causa me you over here in the first place. You wanna stay, you button up with the questions.'

'But I only want to see more of . . .'

And he had hit her hard across the mouth. Her lips had been swollen for days. Nor did it make matters any easier when he came home in the middle of the night and tried to assuage his guilt by making loud, passionate love to her which she was quite sure could be heard by the entire family.

Now, left to herself, she once again placed her kerchief on her head and quietly intoned the blessing once more: '*Baruch Atah Adonai* . . .' Nothing and no one would stop her from being a Jew, wherever she was.

Sal had left again when she went through to help Anna Filomena with the evening meal, tiptoeing past Marco snoring on his bed in his BVDs. As she entered the kitchen her heart sank as she saw Patrizia laying the table.

'Your husband left,' she said without looking up, emphasizing the word 'husband' and making Saskia think she must surely know she and Sal weren't really married. 'Why donta he stay with his pretty bride? Don't you please him like you should?'

'Patrizia!' cautioned Anna Filomena automatically, but there was weariness in her tone. As far as she was concerned, her middle daughter was beyond help.

'You know what I think?' Saskia didn't say anything. She knew she had no choice. She would hear what Patrizia

291

thought whether she wanted to or not. 'I think he's ashamed of having a DP for a bride. All the other guys got good Italian girls. Poor Salvatore, all he got is a DP. The kids in the street, they laugh at him and shout: "He, he, he, where's your DP?" '

Saskia was bewildered. She didn't know what Patrizia was talking about. What was a DP? She looked to Milena for an explanation but Milena looked away.

'Milly?' It was not like Milena not to come to her aid. 'Milly?' she said again, a little more firmly. Milena got up and came round the long table. She crept up close and whispered in Saskia's ear. 'It stands for displaced person. That's what they call them, displaced persons. Stateless. No country. Foreigners. Refugees from the war. But you don't have to worry, Saskia. You're part of our family now so that makes you Italian.'

Except Saskia knew that she wasn't and it didn't and it never would.

Anna Filomena saw the bruises the next morning. She didn't say anything at breakfast; she decided to wait until she and Saskia settled down to do the mending later in the morning. She didn't know what she had done before Saskia arrived. How could she have managed everything on her own? It was as if Saskia was her true daughter rather than her Sal's woman. She helped Anna Filomena with the housework, with the washing and the mending – her sewing was exquisite – and with little Guido. But best of all she encouraged Milena. Shy, tongue-tied Milly had blossomed since Saskia had arrived. Now that she knew she had Saskia's support, she was able to stand up to the taunts of her elder sisters. Angelina wasn't so bad but Patrizia's sharp tongue had eroded much of Milena's confidence. There had been a time when Anna Filomena thought she was being punished from on high with her two elder daughters who never helped her in the house and showed no interest whatsoever in learning how to behave like decent Italian girls. Now she believed that she had been sent Saskia by way of compensation for her suffering, that her daughter-in-law was a sign. And she would do anything to keep her in the Carlino household.

'*Livido*,' she said conversationally as she threaded her darning needle and plunged it into the worn fabric of Patrizia's blouse. '*Ancora*,' she added.

Saskia looked up. Anna Filomena often spoke Italian as they worked together in the kitchen and she was glad of it for she had learned much of the language. She understood *ancora* – again – but *livido*? She saw Anna Filomena was looking at her bruises. She blushed. Anna Filomena laid down her mending.

'Letta me tella you,' she said, leaning forward across the kitchen table. 'My Sal, he is a good boy but he has a hot temper. Ever since he was a tiny boy, when he don't get what he want he cry, he stamp his little foot, he look like he going to explode. And, as you see, sometimes he does explode. You look at him then, you think *animale*! I know even though I am his mamma. He does not get it from Marco. My Marco is a gentle man, too gentle maybe but I don't care. He is kind and with a husband that is rare. But my Sal, deep down in the bottom of him, he is kind also. You, Saskia, you must calm him. You are a good Italian daughter, now you must become a good Italian wife. I tella you how.'

I'm not Italian. I'm German. And above all I'm Jewish, thought Saskia as Mamma got up to make some coffee. *Where will it all end?* But she said nothing for Anna Filomena had given her a home and Saskia had a feeling that what she was about to hear would be good advice for the only thing she cared about: her survival.

'First,' said Anna Filomena, 'you must do everything for an Italian husband. Let him think he is God and that way you will always have control. Then, occasionally, very occasionally, you say something to him, you – how you say? – cause a scene, make a fuss, you are the one who stamps your foot just for once and then you surprise them. They will submit to you, they will be pussycats for an hour. But only for an hour, maybe two, then they must be God again. So only when you want something very, very badly, you stand up to him. Once a year, maybe twice. No more. The rest of the time you show them respect and that way you have control.'

'But why can't he show respect for me?'

'He has. Mamma-mia! What do you want? He brought you here, didn't he? He brought you into his family so he must respect you, believe me.'

Saskia shook her head. Anna Filomena understood many things but she would never be able to see why Saskia was wrong for her Sal. Indeed, it had taken Saskia herself over a year of hoping and praying that she would grow closer to Sal rather than further and further away, to accept that she had nothing but a sham for a marriage. Yet what could she do about it? She loved Anna Filomena, she loved Milly, she was fond of Marco and in some peculiar way she still cared for Sal.

'Mamma . . .' Saskia had taken to calling Anna Filomena Mamma when they were on their own. She knew it secretly pleased the older woman. 'Mamma, I must get out more. Sal is always out. Angelina is out with her boyfriends. Patrizia is out with her schoolfriends. Milly is out – in her dreams, her imagination, her books – but I am always here.'

'So am I.' Anna Filomena spoke so softly Saskia barely heard her.

'Oh, I know, Mamma, I know you are, and it's not that I want to leave you but I am used to the open countryside, I want to breathe, I can't stand another minute being cooped up in this apartment all day. I want to go ho—'

She was on the point of saying 'I want to go home' but stopped herself. This was her home.

'I did not know you lived in the country.' Anna Filomena spoke slowly, thoughtfully. 'You tell us nothing about your life before here. How can we know? I too, I come from the country, back in *Italia*, outside Napoli. I was a simple girl, my father was a shepherd and a farmer. He sell his sheep to

Marco's father. Marco's father rich, go to America. Marco's father say: send your daughter to America. Marco need a wife. So I come here and I marry Marco.'

'But you knew him back in Italy?'

Anna Filomena shook her head. 'Maybe when I am a tiny child I meet him but I can't remember him. So you see when I first lived here I too was lonely. I wanted to go out but then Salvatore was born. And there were other young girls like me, we were all friends together with our *bambini* growing up in the streets. Now everyone live on Long Island, the husbands of all my friends they make money and they leave the old neighbourhood and we are left behind because my Marco, he is not like his father, he does not know how to get rich.'

'Mamma, I'm not going to leave you behind, but I must get out. I must find work, something to do.'

Anna Filomena looked shocked.

'*Si*, Mamma, help me find work. I can sew, I can help at the dressmaker's shop, I can –'

'*Puttana!*' Anna Filomena spat out the word. The local dressmaker was new and young and had replaced an old favourite. Her ideas were modern and the clothes she made were far too daring for her Italian clientele steeped in years of tradition. But Anna Filomena looked at Saskia out of the corner of her eye and she knew that if she did not help her find something, she would lose her and that would be intolerable.

A month later Anna Filomena found work for Saskia but it was the very last kind of work Saskia could have envisaged doing. In her heart she felt it was demeaning beyond belief and she tried not to think what Klara would have said. Saskia took care not to think too often of her parents and what might have become of them since it invariably brought on a depression that lasted for days. Yet now she could not banish the picture in her mind of Klara, her proudly raised profile, her violin at her chin, her hand holding the bow –

every pore exuding *Kultur* – and the hopes that she and Hermann had had for their daughters. How they would have protested at Saskia's new-found position.

For Anna Filomena had found Saskia a job as a maid.

She worked in a Park Avenue apartment, the home of a young couple – patrician white Anglo-Saxon Protestants. He was called Winthrop Peabody III and he had married the daughter of Porter somebody IV – and between them they had a bundle of carefully nurtured old, old money.

Another young Italian girl in the neighbourhood, the daughter of one of Anna Filomena's cronies, had a job as a maid in the same building and she was roped in to recommend Saskia for the job. When Saskia went for her interview she walked nervously up to the front entrance of the apartment building in the East Sixties only to have her way barred by the doorman.

'Round the back. Maid's entrance, honey,' he told her smartly when she revealed why she was there.

She took the back elevator to the fifth floor where she was received through the back door straight into the kitchen by the outgoing maid.

Mrs 'Cissy' Peabody, who was about Saskia's age, did not address a single word to her directly throughout the entire interview. She drew languidly on a cigarette in a long holder and purred questions at the maid who was leaving.

'Does she speak English? Can she iron? You'll show her how to iron Mr Winthrop's shirts how he likes them? Is she any good at flower arranging? No references? She's worked for Mrs Carlino? I don't think we know the Carlinos . . .'

In the end Saskia was trained for a month by the maid herself before she left, and by the end of the year she had mastered everything – and although she would rather die than admit it to herself, she rather enjoyed her work. She could, she found, take pride in it and she was ashamed that she had ever thought it would be demeaning. A job was what you made of it and Saskia made working at the Peabodys as bearable as possible.

She walked to work: thirty blocks up and across town and

the joy of this was that she could walk up Fifth Avenue and look in the shop windows. If Wasserman's had a particularly exciting display she would leave half an hour earlier the next morning to study the fashion at length. Anna Filomena had an old sewing machine and once she found somewhere where she could lay her hands on some cut-price fabric, Saskia was able to reproduce bargain versions of the outfits she saw in Wasserman's for Angelina, Patrizia and sometimes even for little Milly.

When she arrived at the Peabody's building at eight each morning she took the freight elevator to the fifth floor, let herself in at the kitchen door, put on her white short-sleeved maid's uniform and her white tennis shoes with their silent rubber soles and began to prepare Mr Winthrop's breakfast. He worked down on Wall Street and she served him each morning in the little breakfast room off the kitchen where he read the *New York Times* from cover to cover and, apart from a brusque 'Good Morning' ignored her.

Once he had left for the office, Saskia set about cleaning the kitchen. It was as far removed from the Carlino kitchen as it could be. There was no wet laundry hanging around, no pungent garlic smells as the tomato sauce simmered on the stove, no long strips of fresh home-made pasta draped over the backs of chairs all round the room to dry. Indeed, the Peabodys' kitchen looked as if food was never cooked in it. It was pristine, sterile almost, but with every single gadget imaginable. Saskia learned how to use Frigidaire's new Robot washer. It washed clothes thoroughly, rinsed them twice, spun them damp dry and cleaned itself at the same time – all in half an hour. All she had to do was set a single control dial. How Mamma would have loved one of those, but then of course there was the slight problem of how to find the $300 to buy one.

The gas cooker was a four burner with a divided top, a chromium lined oven, concealed oven venting and a smokeless broiler with drip trays. There was a brand-new table-height Eskimo Freeze which could hold 200 lb of food.

There was a Hoover De Luxe, the old Bendix washing machine, which she used just for the towels, and a Tru-Heat Iron with a fabric selector button. The Peabodys were a tall couple and their kitchen was made for tall people, even though it was clear they never came near it themselves. Poor Saskia couldn't reach the surfaces and had to stand on a little stool which she moved round and round the kitchen as she worked.

But apart from the electric juicer she used to make Mr Peabody's orange juice, the automatic brewer in which she made his coffee and the Westinghouse toaster in which she made his toast, Saskia's hausfrau's instinct told her that nothing else in the kitchen was ever touched. The Peabodys seemed to go out to eat every single night, whether it was to a benefit, a dinner-dance at the Plaza, a private dinner party or just dinner in a restaurant. They just never ate in.

Once she'd finished the kitchen, Saskia took her little housemaid's tray with all its dusters and polishers and began to work her way slowly through the vast apartment, keeping an ear open for the bell that would ring in the kitchen when Mrs Peabody awoke and wanted her breakfast, although this rarely happened before 10.30, or even eleven o'clock. She emptied all the wastepaper baskets, the ashtrays and the ice bucket and then removed the used glasses from the night before to the kitchen. Her employers might not eat at home but they entertained people to cocktails virtually every night. There were three reception rooms filled with mirrors and lamps and Chinese screens with all the walls painted banana yellow, which Mrs Peabody had read was *the* colour in *House and Garden* the year before. All these rooms led off the hall and were quite separate from the sleeping area but even so Saskia never switched on the Hoover until Mrs Peabody had gone out to lunch.

In the morning she did all the chores that made no noise. She cleaned out the hearth in the marble fireplaces and polished the brass on the handcast andirons. She threw out the dead flowers and called the florist to deliver new ones, which she then arranged. She checked the silver cigarette boxes scattered around the tables and filled them with fresh cigarettes if necessary. She plumped up the cushions on the chintz-covered sofas, and ran her feather duster lightly over the wing chairs. She checked the drinks on the butler tray stand to see what was running low. She even checked the ink in Mr Peabody's inkwell on the partner's desk in his study and she made sure there were always little notepads from Tiffany's with freshly sharpened pencils beside each telephone. She polished the sheets of mirror all over the apartment until they glistened.

Finally she returned to the kitchen to make herself a cup of coffee and prepare the Pepperidge Farm Vienna Rolls – 'just brown and serve' – Mrs Peabody liked for her breakfast. Then there was the silver to be cleaned – not every day, but at least once a week. There were platters and trays, all engraved and some American Revolutionary silver which had been in Mr Winthrop's family for years. Mr Winthrop had passed instructions via Mrs Peabody that the silver was to be cleaned regularly and Saskia didn't mind since she loved doing it; it gave her a real sense of fulfilment to see it shining – yet she couldn't help asking herself: when was it ever used?

Her afternoon work, once Mrs Peabody had gone out to lunch, she found more mundane. Each bedroom had a Thermos jug to be filled with ice water and placed on a metal tray beside each bed with two tumblers. Mr Winthrop's shoes had to be polished. In the three bathrooms, cleaning tissues had to be replaced, flagons refilled with bath oil, and fresh towels laid out. Perhaps the only part Saskia really did enjoy was hanging up Mrs Peabody's clothes on their padded coat hangers in her closet. That way she got to look at her entire wardrobe without feeling she was snooping: cloche hats, turbans, lynx muffs, a loose ocelot coat, a beige beret, shoulder bags, Mainbocher suits, a white feather toque, marten jackets, chiffon evening dresses . . . Then she had to remember to summon the doorman to pick up the dry cleaning.

299

Saskia realized she was taking a big chance allowing Milly to visit her at the Peabody apartment but she knew it might be Milly's only chance of actually seeing the kind of place she only read about in books.

'You must come in the afternoon. Wait until at least half-past one and remember to come to the back entrance. Bring a box of some kind so that if anybody stops you you can say you're making a delivery to the kitchen in 5B. Remember to say the kitchen otherwise the doorman might want to bring it up to the apartment himself. And take care with your appearance, Milly. I'll do your braids in the morning before I go to work so try to keep them in place all day. Give this letter to your teacher, no, wait, first you have to get your Mamma to sign it.'

'She can't. You'll have to, Saskia. Or I'll do it myself.'

'What do you mean?'

'Mamma can't write. She never learned. She can't read either. I do it all for her.'

Saskia marvelled yet again at the phenomenal fortitude of Anna Filomena. How could she, Saskia, worry about survival when she was living in the presence of one who had clearly mastered the art automatically.

'Okay, okay. I'll sign it for her.'

The next afternoon the kitchen doorbell rang at 2.30 and there she stood, gangling and awkward, wearing a gingham dress with puff sleeves that Saskia had made for her six months earlier and which was already too childlike for the precocious pre-adolescent Milly had become. Cissy Peabody had gone out to lunch as usual and Saskia led Milly through the empty apartment. For the first time since Saskia had known her, Milena reverted to Italian.

'*Che bellezza! Che bellezza!*' she said over and over again. 'Saskia, can't you just imagine it? Daisy Buchanan and Tom and the Divers would all come here and they'd sweep in like this . . .' Milly ran across the hall and pretended to step out of the elevator through the main entrance, flinging off her coat and running towards Saskia with arms out-stretched. 'Daaaaaarling,' she cried, echoing Cissy with unnerving accuracy given that she'd never met her, 'I'm simply parched. Do give me a drink or I'll die,' and with that Milly picked up one of Cissy Peabody's cigarette holders, selected a cigarette from one of the silver boxes and proceeded to mince up and down the centre of the nearest reception room, waving the cigarette holder in the air.

'Oh, Milly, do stop.' Saskia couldn't help laughing. 'Now how about if I serve you tea, madam? Where would you like to take it? In here? Or in the Yellow Room?'

'They're all yellow rooms,' said Milly, giggling. 'I'd like it in the library. You do have a library, young lady?' Milly adopted a snooty pose, jumping on a chair to look down her nose at Saskia.

'Milly, get down. That chair is Louis something and terribly valuable. It's one of a pair given to them as a wedding present by old Mrs . . .'

'Oh, fiddle-de-dee, Saskia, where's the library, pray?'

'Right here in the hall. Only books in the entire apartment, I'm afraid.'

Milena looked disparagingly at the fourteen-foot wall of books and sighed. 'Oh, well, it'll have to do. I'll sit here. Best silver, mind, got any Paul Revere?'

'As a matter of fact, we have,' said Saskia. 'You mean to say you learn all this stuff in books? I should have had you with me on my first month to tell me what to do. Who are Daisy and Tom, by the way? Friends of yours?'

'Oh, Saskia,' said Milly wearily, 'even Mamma's heard of Scott Fitzgerald'

Milena arranged herself on the sofa and sat as still as she could as Saskia emerged through the swing door leading to the kitchen area bearing a large silver tray. She set it down on a low table in front of Milly who watched while Saskia poured.

Then, just as Milena flicked her long plait over one shoulder out of the way and raised the bone china teacup to her lips, they heard the muffled sound of the elevator coming up the shaft. Saskia froze and listened, holding a finger to her lips. Would the elevator go on past them or would it stop at the fifth floor?

It stopped at the fifth.

'Quick, Milly, into the kitchen . . .'

But it was too late.

Cissy Peabody was suddenly standing in her hall, surrounded by a sea of shopping bags and reaching up to tear her turban from her head so that her long fair hair fell to her shoulders.

Saskia and Milly stood rigid in front of her. Saskia couldn't think of what to say and then she realized Cissy Peabody hadn't said a word either. Saskia had been looking at the ground, not daring to face her employer. Now she slowly brought her head up and snatched a quick glance.

Tears were running down Cissy Peabody's beautiful patrician face.

'Mrs Peabody?' Saskia moved towards her, hand outstretched. 'Can I get you something?'

Cissy Peabody stared at Saskia as if she'd never seen her before and didn't answer. She walked past the trembling Milly without comment and collapsed into the nearest armchair, crossing her long, elegant legs and kicking off her crocodile shoes. Milly immediately ran to pick them up and stand them neatly together to the side of the chair. She stood with her hands behind her back as if awaiting Cissy Peabody's next move.

'Mrs Peabody, can I get you anything?' Saskia repeated.

'I'm so bored, I could die!' exclaimed Cissy unexpectedly.

'Why?' asked Milly immediately with a child's logic.

'I'm bored with shopping. I'm bored with lunching with Claire van Reuten and Mary Kennedy and Caroline Porter and all my other silly girlfriends every day, sitting around waiting for Win to come home and then he doesn't talk to me. He's so tired he has to have his Scotch and soda and his bath and then we have to get dressed and Claire and Mary and Caroline and everyone turn up for drinks only this time

302

there's Chips van Reuten and Perry Kennedy and Harvey Porter as well as all the other boring husbands and Win's so busy telling them all about his day down on the Street and they're all so busy telling him about theirs that I'm left talking to the very same people I had lunch with and then we all go out to dinner and by the time we get home Win's always so tired he has to go straight to sleep. I mean, how am I supposed to have a baby let alone any fun?'

'I don't know,' said Milly.

'Well, who in God's name are you?' Cissy noticed Milly for the first time.

Saskia stepped forward to explain but Milly said simply: 'I'm Milena Carlino, ma'am, but do call me Milly.'

'Milly. That's a cute name. Millicent Peabody, Milly for short. Milly Peabody. Not bad. But you're Milena, are you?'

'Milena Carlino.'

'Carlino. Saskia used to work for them, didn't she? We don't know the Carlinos. Matter of fact I don't know anybody who does. I asked around for references. But it doesn't matter now. I'd give Saskia a reference tomorrow if she needed one. She's perfect. And you're the Carlino's little girl come to visit with your old maid? Well, that's a reference if ever there was one, although I think the Carlinos should have telephoned me first.'

'We don't have a phone,' said Milly before Saskia could stop her.

'Well, your mother should have written me a note.'

'She can't write.'

'Don't be absurd. Saskia, I'm exhausted. Perhaps Milena –Milly – could help you take away the tea things. I'm going to have something a little stronger . . .'

Saskia understood that Cissy Peabody had been indulging in something a little stronger for some time hence the tearful revelation about her life. When the time came for Milly to go home, Saskia had to drag her out the back door to the sounds of Cissy's sobbing.

'We can't leave her like that,' said Milly. 'We have to go back and see what's wrong.'

'Milly, she told us what's wrong and beyond that it's none of our business. Ordinarily she shouldn't have told us as much about herself as she did. I'm only the maid.'

The next day Cissy didn't go out to lunch but moped around the apartment all day clutching a tall-stemmed wine glass. Saskia, going about her work, tried not to look at her as she stood staring out at the sheeting rain, her hair immaculately coiffed in a French roll, a cashmere cardigan slung loosely over her shoulders.

The telephone rang incessantly. Saskia caught snippets of conversation.

'Darling, what am I supposed to do? . . . What? . . . You know, I simply can't remember what we talked about before we were married. There must have been something, I suppose . . . Mother, I'm perfectly all right. I just wanted to know if there'd been anyone in our family who'd ever been divorced, that's all. I just wanted to gossip, if you will . . . Oh, you won't . . . Well, all right, Mother . . . Fine. We'll be there on Saturday. Who else will be there, by the way? . . . Oh, the van Reutens, well, of course, who else? . . . And the Porters. How divine. I haven't seen them in years . . .'

'Saskia,' she said suddenly, finally hanging up, 'I wonder if you wouldn't mind staying late tonight and serving cocktails for me and Mr Winthrop when he returns from the office?'

Saskia wondered what Cissy had in mind. When Winthrop Peabody III returned home from a hard day at the office, she found out.

'Honey, Caroline Porter says you cancelled lunch and my mother called to say you simply didn't show up for tea at the Plaza. What's up, are you sick?'

'Not at all. Just didn't feel like it. Come and have a martini.'

'I'm so tired, I'm going to have a nap and then a bath. Mix me one and I'll take it to my dressing room . . .'

'No, we're going to have cocktails right here. Saskia's going to serve them . . . Here she is.'

'Who? Oh. Listen, I said I'll take mine –'

'Right here, Win. Sit down. Talk to me.'

Saskia stood stupidly, holding the tray with the ice bucket, the cocktail shaker, the olives, the sharp little triangular martini glasses. Without even looking at her, Winthrop Peabody stood and mixed himself a martini right off the tray, picked up the glass and marched off down the long corridor away from the reception area to his dressing room. Halfway there, he stopped and looked back at his wife.

'Knew I had something to tell you. Time we gave a party again. Month's time. Check with Mother, your mother and everyone for a good date then fix it. Get Finkelsteins to cater it, they're the best. Make sure I see the guest list before you send out the invitations. And get yourself something good to wear, Cissy. I want you looking the tops so everyone'll know why I married you. And believe me it will be everyone, because anyone who is anyone will be at our party. See to it.'

Cissy took the tray from Saskia and hurled it at his departing figure only to see it hit the door full on as he closed it behind him.

Win's head came back around the door. Saskia held her breath. He ignored the fallen tray and the mess on the floor.

'Cissy, wear the Cartier tonight. I want Chips to see how a man really ought to treat his wife . . .'

Cissy turned to her and said quietly, tears coursing down her face, 'As you heard Mr Winthrop say, we'll be giving a party soon. I'll discuss the details with you in the morning. Goodnight, Saskia, and thank you.'

Who'd be a society wife, thought Saskia over and over as she made her way home to the misery of the Lower West Side. *Who on earth would want to be a society wife?*

Twenty-Six

In the run-up to the party, Cissy Peabody was a changed woman. Not only did she have something to occupy her mind with the frantic preparations, but Winthrop Peabody's obsession for detail meant that he listened intently to her whenever she consulted him about the party. The Peabodys had had other parties but they had been earlier on in his career, more relaxed, often given for them by her parents or his. The success of this one was of paramount importance: it was the Winthrop Peabodys At Home in their own right, showing the world who they were and where they'd arrived at.

It was Saskia who hit on the idea of having an Italian theme to the party. Since the afternoon of Milly's visit things had changed considerably. Now, instead of ringing for her breakfast, Cissy Peabody came running into the kitchen as soon as her husband had left for the office. Now she sat in her robe at the little round table and ignored the ringing telephone, preferring instead to drink coffee with Saskia and discuss the forthcoming party. And her marriage.

'I shouldn't have said all I said in front of that little girl,' she confessed to Saskia, 'but in fact there's more. I think he's having an affair. I've no proof but they say a wife can always tell. That's why this party is so important for me too. If I can make it a success it will mean so much to Win. I pretend to myself I don't believe this but I know that all he cares about is his precious image. He's Winthrop Peabody

III and he's destined for the presidency of his father's bank and I'm just a beautiful accessory along the way. I guess I knew it when I married him but I thought he would grow out of taking it all so seriously, that I would come to mean more to him. Yet it's come to this: if I make this party a success I will mean that little bit more to him. The only thing that makes me wonder whether the rumours about his affair are true is that the scandal of a mistress – if I were to even breathe the word divorce to him –would cause a serious setback in his career and he wouldn't gamble on that, now would he?' Yet even as she spoke Saskia knew she was seeking reassurance so she gave it to her. And it was during their morning talks that the idea for having Italian food came about.

'You're Italian, aren't you?' Cissy asked one morning out of the blue. Saskia hesitated. Could she trust Cissy enough to tell her the truth? Then the ever-present voice of caution whispered the word 'survival' in her ear and before she could speak, Cissy went on: 'I adore Italian food.'

'Why don't we have it at the party then?' asked Saskia without thinking.

'Well, it would be wonderfully original. Everyone always uses Finkelsteins but I don't know any Italian caterers.'

'I do,' said Saskia. 'The best.'

'Who, for heaven's sake.'

'Carlinos. They're wonderful. So I've heard.'

'No relation to the people you used to work for, I suppose?'

'Well, yes, as a matter of fact.'

'I'm not going to ask any more. Just bring me a sample of their hors d'oeuvres and their canape´s.'

That night Saskia outlined her plan to Mamma. Who made the best meatballs in Manhattan? Anna Filomena, of course, and she could make them tiny, small enough to pop into the mouth on the end of a cocktail stick. Wouldn't everyone provide Mamma with prosciutto, salami, baby pizzas, olives, anything she wanted at cost if she asked them? Of course they would. All Anna Filomena had to do was to prepare a veritable feast for seventy people but in miniature. Sal would be roped in to deliver everything to Park Avenue on the day. Angelina, Patrizia and even little Milly would be given proper maids' uniforms and instructed by Saskia how to serve the food and drinks. Mamma would remain in the Peabody kitchen to supervise the food on its way.

They had several trial runs. If Cissy Peabody wondered why it was necessary for Italian caterers to wander round her apartment and stare open-mouthed at everything several weeks before the party, she kept quiet about it. All she said to Saskia was:

'The young man. I've never seen anyone so breathtakingly handsome. The way he looked at me, I realized I'd quite forgotten what it was like to feel like a woman. Is he going to serve the food? If so, we might have a riot on our hands.'

'No,' said Saskia, 'he's just the delivery boy.' *And my husband*, she thought sadly. Cissy Peabody wasn't the only one whose husband didn't appreciate her. 'Anyway, he has a girlfriend. She works at a bakery, the one that's providing the dough for the baby pizzas for the party.'

Saskia made the maids' uniforms herself and Angelina, Patrizia and Milly were beside themselves in excitement when the day came. Saskia had schooled them well. Saskia herself would stand by the door taking coats which she would then hand to Milly who would run down the corridor to lay them on the bed in the nearest guest room. Angelina would step forward with a tray of champagne. Patrizia would circulate with a tray of hors d'oeuvres, and once everyone had arrived Milly would ferry trays of food and drink to Angelina, Patrizia and Saskia for the rest of the evening till the guests left for dinner.

Only Anna Filomena was uncomfortable. The Peabody kitchen felt like a hospital to her and after she had made one last check of the food and satisfied herself everything was in order she grabbed her son's arm as he was about to leave.

'Salvatore, takea me witha you. I can't stay here. You

come back for your sisters later.' And Sal knew he had to show his Mamma the proper respect. He ushered her through the kitchen door to the freight elevator, then nipped back through the kitchen, grabbing a salami as he went. Slowly he pushed open the swing door leading to the hall. Saskia had her back to him. Opposite her, facing Sal, stood Cissy in a scooped-necked tight-fitting Dior gown with a calf-length pencil skirt. She looked every inch the elegant banker's wife. Sal made quite sure she could see him then he held the salami so it was sticking up in front of him, crotch level, like a huge erection. He ran his hands up and down it, pointed at Cissy, pointed back at himself, blew her a kiss and ran back through the kitchen to take his Mamma home.

Salvatore Carlino had begun taking risks in his life, but his lewd gesture to Cissy Peabody was harmless compared to the trouble he was getting into elsewhere.

Cissy averted her eyes and her hand went to shield her face in her confusion. It was then that she discovered she'd lost an earring. Rushing back down the long passage to her bedroom to select another pair, she tripped and fell heavily on the newly polished parquet floors. She was not hurt but the Dior gown was ripped from under her left arm to the top of her thigh.

'*Saskia, la signora . . . subito!*' Milly squealed and Saskia raced down the passage to help Cissy to her feet. Cissy was fighting off her tears. All this preparation and now she couldn't wear her Dior.

'Wait,' said Saskia, 'there's a sewing machine in a pantry cupboard.'

'There is?' Cissy stared at her, amazed.

'Give me your dress. I'll only be a second.'

She was. They were lucky. The dress had ripped at the seam and it was a simple job for Saskia to repair it.

As the elevator doors parted to admit the first guests, Cissy was walking back down the passage to greet them.

The Italian food had been a surprise to Winthrop Peabody but he could not deny its success. Everyone had complimented him and every now and then he had remembered to refer them to Cissy. Everything had been praised: the flowers (Saskia's arrangements had taken her all morning), the drink, the food, the people. Angelina and Patrizia had moved swiftly to and from the kitchen under Saskia's guidance while Milly checked the overflowing ashtrays and replaced them with clean ones. Cissy had looked – quite simply – radiant.

When Saskia arrived for work the next morning to her surprise she found Cissy already up and waiting for her at the breakfast table.

'I just couldn't wait another minute for a post mortem. Win's sleeping late. He's taken the morning off. Oh, Saskia, last night, you should have seen him. He was so proud of me. When we got into bed he held me in his arms and we . . . you know . . . I think everything will be fine now.'

'I'm so pleased.' Saskia couldn't stop herself putting her arm around Cissy's shoulders and again Cissy surprised her by suddenly clinging to her.

'I owe it all to you, Saskia. You've been such a . . . such a friend.'

'Mrs Peabody –'

'Call me Cissy. Those dumb women I lunch with every day, they're not my friends. They'll probably all be cold as ice to me now because they'll be jealous my party was such a success. They're like that. We're all so competitive. We pretend we support each other but we don't care about anyone except ourselves. But you've helped me . . . genuinely.'

'You paid me to, Cissy.' Cissy looked up at her, startled, but Saskia went on, 'But you know I'd do it anyway. Oh, I don't mean the cleaning and the polishing and the ironing . . . you know what I mean.'

'I can't thank you enough for fixing my dress for me.'

'I've never worked on a Dior before.' It slipped out.

'What do you mean? Did you repair clothes in your last job?'

'I design them.'

'You *do*?'

And that was how it started.

They spent two days going through Cissy's wardrobe. Saskia made numerous suggestions as to how she could streamline certain outfits by altering them. Then she sat Cissy down and quizzed her on what for her would be the perfect wardrobe. Cissy was like a teenager in her excitement. Saskia brought in sketches and together they pored over them. Then they went shopping together for materials. Cissy, who had only ever had her clothes presented to her at couture houses or at fittings by her mother's rather jaded and extremely old-fashioned dressmaker, was fascinated by Saskia's expertise. But her greatest thrill of all was her husband's growing appreciation of the change in his wife. Over the following months, Saskia made as many as fourteen new outfits for Cissy. Cissy had secretly hired a new maid who arrived as soon as Winthrop had left for the office and was duly overseen in her duties by Saskia while Saskia set up her sewing table in Cissy's dressing room. The result was a new Cissy – sexy, alluring, chic in a style all her own. She was no longer a clone of all her Park Avenue friends, and people began to notice. She was mentioned in magazines. Her photograph appeared everywhere. And Winthrop basked happily in his wife's success, proud that she now stood out above the wives of his business associates.

Claire van Reuten, Mary Kennedy and Caroline Porter were not so happy.

'But where, Cissy, where do you get them from? Who is your dressmaker? Oh, do tell. What are friends for?'

Cissy approached Saskia one morning.

'How about it, Saskia? You'd be a huge success. All my friends would take you on immediately and the word would

311

soon spread. You could set up on your own – dressmaker to the rich and famous, providing you let me have first call on your services, of course.'

'It's not what I want.'

'Are you sure? I mean I adore having you all to myself but it seems terribly selfish of me –'

'I don't just want to be a dressmaker. You *can* help me, Cissy, if you want to.'

'You know I do – and will – but how?'

'I want to design. I want to design clothes to be sold in a store. Your friends can go and buy them and so can thousands of other people. I want to create the designs and let *other* people be the dressmakers.'

Cissy laughed. 'I couldn't be more delighted. I never would have guessed you were so ambitious, but why on earth not? Name your store!'

'Wasserman's,' said Saskia immediately. 'Wasserman's on Fifth Avenue.'

'Perfect!' Cissy clapped her hands. 'I'll call Harry Wasserman in the morning. He and Abigail just got back from London. He's been opening Wasserman's over in London, would you believe? Better still, we'll have them to dinner and then I'll be able to show him some of your work. Leave it to me, Saskia, leave it to me.'

' "No Italian who has a family is ever alone." ' announced Milly one night at supper.

'Why, Milena, thatsa beautiful,' cried Mamma and puckering up her lips she planted a big kiss on her youngest daughter's forehead. 'Now helpa me with the clams.'

Saskia smiled to herself, knowing perfectly well that Milena had got the phrase out of a book by Luigi Barzini she'd been reading. The difference was that now she too believed such a statement to be the truth. She could admit it to herself: she was taken for an Italian, she had a family albeit an adopted one, and she was happier than she could

312

remember being in a very long time. At last she was beginning to feel secure in America.

'Angelina, go to the window, call your Pappa. Tell him his birthday dinner is ready.'

The aroma of Mamma's kitchen was mouthwatering. She had gone to a lot of trouble for her Marco's birthday, his fiftieth. She'd made baked clams, stuffed artichokes, fried zucchini, fried calamari as well as lasagne and Italian sausage with peppers. There was *ricotta tutta crema* and *ricotta fina*, (30 cents a pound), which Mamma had fetched all the way from a special shop on Bleecker Street because she knew it was her husband's favourite and to follow there would be cannoli.

'Whatta he do?' Anna Filomena was getting impatient.

'Mamma, he's playing bowls. It takes time . . .'

'*Bocce! Bocce!* Always he play *bocce* when his dinner is ready. Salvatore, go fetch your Pappa, *per piacere*!'

Salvatore was always home for dinner now. He still went out a great deal without saying where he was going but somehow he managed to be home for the evening meal and Anna Filomena was in heaven. Her whole family around her every night.

'Leave him, Mamma, it's his birthday. Let's see what's on the radio. Maybe there's some music. Maybe we can dance.' Sal had brought home a crystal radio set for Marco's birthday and all day the girls had been crowded round it. Anna Filomena was so happy to have her daughters home for once she restrained from asking where Sal had found the money to buy such an expensive gift. They found a music station and Sal whisked the steaming pot of clams away from his mother and clasped her in his arms, sweeping her round and round the kitchen table.

'Salvatore, let go of me. What you do? Are you crazy? Let me go at once,' Anna Filomena protested but everyone could see she was thrilled. Finally Sal let her go abruptly and she pirouetted out of his arms and across the kitchen, landing against the stove with a gentle thud.

313

'Okay, Angelina, Patrizia, Milena, who's gonna play *morra* with me.'

'Me!' shouted Milly. *Morra* was one of the few things that could be guaranteed to draw Milly away from her books. It was a game where two players extended their right hands closed in a fist and as they opened one or more fingers, each of the other players had to guess the total number of extended fingers. Marco Carlino arrived home for his birthday dinner to find all the Carlino women, including Saskia, sitting round the table yelling numbers at Sal. He ate his dinner with relish, kissed his wife and slapped Sal on the back, inviting him to sit down with him in a game of *pochero*. Because it was his birthday, Sal let his father win and Marco beamed with pleasure.

'I know what it takes to make a fulla-housa, a straighto, a flosho,' he told Saskia proudly, 'but one day your Salvatore will beat me, you'll see. Oh, what a beautiful thing it is to be Italian. The *Americani*, they are *superbi*. They are – how you say? – snobs. They look down on us. And they are influencing the Italian children. Mamma and I, we look around, we see our old neighbours all gone to Long Island the minute they are okay in America. Their children, they become *dottori*, lawyers, they marry American girls with yellow hair and blue eyes and sometimes they even become like that pretty boy son of Vincenzo Fanucci. He no likea the women, not even the blue-eyed American girls so he doesn't have *bambini*, he has little white poodles instead and he walka them round the block. Pah! But my Sal,' he flung his arm around his son's shoulders, 'my Sal is a real Italian man. He worka hard, he bring home money to his Mamma and he has a beautiful wife. So, *Saskia mia*, when you give us *bambini*, huh?'

The question caught Saskia off guard and she flushed. Anna Filomena, despite the fact that she was desperate for an answer to the same question, deflected the issue.

'Marco,' she said, purring his name seductively. 'I have one more treat for you. Come.'

The little man stood up to be clasped to the impressive

bosom of his wife before allowing her to take him by the hand and lead him away to their bedroom.

'Angelina, Patrizia, Milena, you wash the dishes and then you go out. Yes, you too, Milena, tonight you go out. Salvatore, take Saskia for a stroll in the moonlight . . .'

Everyone got the message. Saskia and Sal strolled arm in arm up Tenth Avenue to the wide cross-street Saskia loved so much. They stood for a while, their arms around each other, and watched the light of the full moon playing on the waters of the Hudson.

Ever since Sal had gone to the Peabodys' almost a year earlier, he had appeared to turn over a new leaf. It was as if that glimpse of Saskia's other world where, despite the fact that she was only the maid she obviously felt at home, had instilled in Sal a new respect for her.

'I adore your father,' Saskia told Sal. 'I think we made him really happy tonight.'

'He adores you. Mamma too. I couldn't have brought her home a better bride if you had been born in Napoli. The day the old crones came to tell her that it had been decided to get rid of the new dressmaker and put you in her place, I thought she would burst open like a melon with pride.'

Saskia smiled up at him. It was true. Anna Filomena adored the endless coming and going every evening in the tenement apartment as women from all over the neighbourhood trailed up and down the stairs for fittings. Yet Saskia knew that if Cissy Peabody was as good as her word and secured her a position as designer for Wasserman's then she would no longer have the time to be the local dressmaker as well. It would be a bitter blow to Anna Filomena's pride but Saskia decided she would deal with that as and when she had to.

'Sal?'

'Hmmmm?'

'Do you have to go out later tonight?'

'Saskia, you know I don't like you to ask . . .'

'I know, but do you?'

315

'No, as it happens. It's my Pappa's birthday. I get to stay home.'

'Where were you last night?' She felt his fingers digging into her upper arm as his grip tightened with tension. 'Okay, okay. Don't tell me. I don't want to spoil this evening. Let's go back now.'

They crept through Sal's parents' bedroom to their own as Marco and Anna Filomena lay contentedly, softly snoring in each other's arms.

Sal lay for a while with his dark head on Saskia's breasts and she stroked his hair tenderly in an almost maternal gesture as she wondered not for the first time why it was that she did not get pregnant. Sal raised his head and began to suck on her nipples. He heard her sharp intake of breath, her little moan and he knew she was beginning to lose control. He had fallen on top of her before taking off his trousers and now he sat up and began to undo his belt with one hand, playing with her clitoris with the other. She reached down and helped him, urging him to move his hand faster. Her eyes were closed. He watched her climax as she lay there, her dark hair falling around her face as she arched her back and shook her head from side to side on the pillow.

Naked, Sal lay beside her for a while and blew softly in her ear. Now and then he tickled her where he knew she was vulnerable and then clasped a hand over her mouth as she started to laugh for fear she would wake the whole household. Finally he hefted himself up and on top of her, his penis fully extended, and plunged into her and as he did so he stayed hard that much longer for in his mind was the fantasy of his own naked buttocks pumping up and down over the creamy white body of Cissy Peabody. It was a dream that for him would never come true, but as long as he had it in his mind while he was making love to Saskia, he could perform. Cissy Peabody represented for Sal the very American dream his father had deplored earlier in the evening.

Saskia's dark neo-Italian beauty had ceased to interest him months ago.

Harold Wasserman had a particular morning routine. Once he'd arrived at the store, looked through his mail, given his secretary enough dictation to keep her busy for an hour and made the phone calls that couldn't wait, he always went down to the ground floor of Wasserman's to watch the mid-morning action for half an hour. He loved to see the public buying over the counter, to observe their habits, eavesdrop on their requests. Ever since he had come back to New York from London, he had felt a little out of touch with these new postwar customers and their modern ideas. Sometimes he even persuaded Abigail to accompany him, but Abigail was more preoccupied with their newly born baby daughter.

He saw the woman enter by the 47th Street entrance, carrying a large portfolio. He watched her make straight for the floor manager's office and he hurried over to move into the room right behind her. He could hear her pleading with the man inside.

'Please, tell him I have an appointment. It was arranged by Mrs Peabody. Mrs Winthrop Peabody III,' she added for emphasis.

'I'm sorry, miss, I can't just let anybody in to see Mr Wasserman.'

'But she's not just anybody as she's just explained to you,' said Harold, entering the room and overhearing the floor manager's words. 'What is your name?'

'Mrs Carlino. Saskia Carlino.'

'And I've been expecting you. Cissy – Mrs Peabody – called yesterday. Now what I'm going to do is to ask you to come with me to meet our Chief Buyer and if she likes your designs as much as Mrs Peabody does, then I can see no reason why we shouldn't introduce you to a manufacturer of our choice who can make up your designs for us . . . Vision, Mr Epstein,' he said to the floor manager, 'vision at all times.'

'But, Mr Wasserman, we are not a clothing

manufacturers, Wasserman's is . . . But, of course, yes, Mr Wasserman, vision at all times. I know.' The manager looked decidedly weary as if this was something he had had thrust down his throat once too often.

'However, I have a better idea,' said Harold Wasserman. 'Give me the portfolio, my dear, and I shall take it home this evening to show Mrs Wasserman without whose opinion on the subject of ladies' clothing I do not move. Would you mind? . . . No? Swell! Now, give me your name and address . . .'

'Abigail, I swear it was the same girl.'

'What same girl? Oh, Harry, do look. I swear she smiled. I swear it was not wind. I must go and call my mother . . .'

'Abigail, will you listen to me. Please! This woman came into the store this morning with a portfolio of designs which, incidentally, I want you to take a look at and forget about swearing that our daughter just smiled for the first time, I'll swear this woman was the same person as that girl in that painting of Barney Lambert's you bought. I'm prepared to swear on our daughter's life that they're one and the same.'

'Harry, that's a terrible thing to say – on our daughter's life!'

'My darling, I'm sorry. But listen, d'you suppose Barney knows she's here?'

'Oh, for Christ's sake, Harry, how should I know? Why on earth don't you write and ask him. I want to send him some pictures of the baby; you can send them for me and ask him about this mysterious dame at the same time. And don't forget to give him a whole load of my love.'

'I'll do just that. I'll write him tonight. What d'you mean, Abigail, whole load of your love?. He never painted *you* in the nude, did he?'

'Why don't you ask him that too, Harry dearest . . .'

*

Saskia arrived home to find the apartment empty. The person she really wanted to share her excitement with was Milly but Milly was in school. On the way home she had also been thinking of Sal. Sal had no idea that she had been doing anything other than cleaning work all this time at the Peabodys. Like his Mamma he was proud of the fact that she had become the neighbourhood dressmaker but how would he feel about her becoming a designer for a fancy store like Wasserman's? Was that any kind of work for a good Italian wife? Sal would need careful handling over this matter and the sooner she broached it with him the better.

Saskia ran downstairs and into the street.

'*Dove Salvatore?*' she asked everyone. '*Dove il marito mio?*'

'Angelina will know. Ask Angelina,' suggested someone slyly but Saskia did not notice the tone of voice.

Angelina had left school and was now working behind the counter at the *panetteria*. She had taken the place at the bakery of Sal's former girlfriend. When Saskia arrived she was in the process of pulling down the blind and turning the sign to closed.

'They told me you would know where Sal was,' said Saskia.

'Sure I know. He's here. He just arrived. He's in the back.'

Saskia made to go through to the room behind the shop.

'Hey, wait a second, you can't go through there.' Angelina pulled her back.

'Why not?'

'Right now you can't disturb him.'

'But why not?'

'He's doing business with Carlo.'

'The baker?'

Angelina nodded.

'But I know Carlo,' said Saskia, 'He won't mind if I –'

'Saskia, stay out of there. I promised Salvatore. He trusts me. I can't let you go in there.'

'He trusts you? But I'm his wife. Why doesn't he trust me?'

'Saskia, please, you know why. You're not Italian. You're part of our family but you're not Italian. Plus you are so close to Mamma and Salvatore is frightened you will tell her. One day she will have to know but not yet.'

'He has his girl back there? It's not true he finished with her? It's still going on . . .?' Saskia was incensed.

Angelina shook her head.

'Nothing like that.'

'Well then, I'm going to sit here and wait for him.'

Angelina shrugged and left.

As soon as she'd gone, Saskia slipped inside and went through to the back. There was a curtain separating her from the baker's office. She could hear Sal's voice.

'Listen, Carlo, when they get here it's going to get worse. No way can it get better.'

'Salvatore, I've known you all my life, since you were so high. Can't you tell Don Vittorio I don't mean no disrespect but I can't pay this week? I had to have the oven replaced. The old one died on me. I had no insurance, you was my insurance. If anything he should give me the money for my new oven –'

'Hey, hey, hey! You say you don't mean no disrespect and you start talking 'bout Don Vittorio paying you. You got protection from Don Vittorio, you gotta pay him for it. *Adesso. Subito!* You gotta pay tribute, you understand? Before I have to get heavy with you, you understand? Hey, too late, here they are.'

Saskia parted the curtain a fraction so she could see the thickset, swarthy man who entered, a cigar in his mouth, a silk handkerchief in the breast pocket of his expensive double-breasted suit. He lifted the fedora from his head.

'Salvatore, how ya doin'?' The man slapped Sal's cheek.

'Good, good. Don Vittorio, how you doing?'

'Good, good.'

'So whatsa the problem? Carlo got a beef or what?'

'It's just a misunderstanding, Don Vittorio.'

Two henchmen had followed their don and were standing either side of him. Don Vittorio held up a Lucky between forefinger and thumb and stabbed the air with it in Sal's direction.

'Misunderstandings I don't like. This is the second so-called misunderstandin'. Once I can forgive. Twice I cannot. *Capisce?*'

Sal nodded.

'The job you did last week, your first time, am I right?'

Sal nodded again. Saskia could see his hands were shaking as he held them behind his back.

'Well, you did a good job. Now you can take care of this one. I wait in the car. Giuliano and Gianni will help you if necessary.'

To Saskia's horror, she saw the two henchmen take out guns and point them at Carlo's head. Carlo had sunk to his knees and was looking beseechingly at Salvatore. Saskia saw Sal reach into his jacket . . . Suddenly she noticed the old don was looking straight at the curtain. *He saw me!* thought Saskia, and she turned and ran. As she left the shop a shot rang out. Then another.

Saskia ran back to the Carlino apartment. She was numb. Did Sal kill the old baker? Or was it one of the other men? Did it really even matter now that she knew what Sal's 'business' was?

So much for the American dream: she was a gangster's wife.

After the horrific revelation at the bakery that night, Saskia had one ray of hope in her life. The Chief Buyer at Wasserman's had liked her designs and put her in touch with a manufacturer on Seventh Avenue. She couldn't wait for the day when she was due to have her first meeting with the manufacturer.

Yet that day never came.

Saskia was in her room putting the finishing touches to the designs she was going to take to the manufacturer the next day. She had rigged up a makeshift drawing board in the corner and providing she put it away each evening, Sal

321

appeared to have no objection to it. She realized he probably didn't even recognize what it was. She didn't tell him that she still converted it into an altar on Fridays if he wasn't around.

The banging on the door in the kitchen resounded all the way through the apartment. It had to be a stranger. Everyone else just walked in.

'I'll go,' called Patrizia from the next room. 'Mamma's out.'

Saskia was concentrating so hard on her drawing, she didn't answer.

'Saskia, are you there?' *Maybe she went out*, Patrizia said to herself as she went to answer the door.

'No, I'm here . . .' Saskia said, realizing too late that Patrizia could no longer hear her. Saskia was halfway across the girls' room when she heard the voice of a woman.

An English voice.

It was such a long time since she had heard an English accent that for several seconds Saskia stood, listening, without taking in what the woman was saying. It wasn't just an English accent. It was a Liverpool one.

'Are you listening to me? Have you heard a word I said? My name is Sylvia Carlino. I'm Mrs Salvatore Carlino and I want to see my husband. I'm told this is where he lives. What are you looking at me like that for, girl? Aren't you going to let me in? Who are you, then? One of his sisters?'

Saskia heard Patrizia's voice.

'Yes. I'm Patrizia. Salvatore Carlino does live here. Not for much longer though. He makes so much money, my brother, that soon he'll be able to buy his own apartment . . .'

'Well, that's very nice. We'll need space when I bring his son over.'

'His son?'

'Yes. I've told you. I'm his wife and he has a son back home in England. He left me, did your brother, when I was pregnant and he took me passport and he never gave me his address. I was such a right dozy mare all the time before he left that I never asked him for his address in New York. I was that mad when he left, I thought sod it, I'll stop here and find meself a decent bloke. But it's hard with a child on yer own and me mam won't help any more and no man would look at me with a brat on me hands. So last year I thought, right, that's it, I'll get meself a new passport and I'll track him down. Well, here I am.'

Saskia had to wait and hear Patrizia say: 'This is going to sound a little strange but he's got a wife from England already.'

'Well, I don't care if he's got fifty wives. I'm the only one that's real and I've got the papers to prove it.'

Saskia rushed back to her drawing board. Frantically she scribbled a goodbye note to Milly and pushed it under her pillow. If this woman was telling the truth then she had to have a passport saying she was the real Mrs Salvatore Carlino as well. Saskia's most treasured possession in the world was her passport and now it had been declared a fake.

Yet she could still use it.

She had to get away. She crammed as many things as she could into a small suitcase, including her candles and a couple of her recently completed designs. She opened the top drawer of the chest and rummaged around in her underwear till she found the passport Sal had given her four years before: Sylvia Carlino's passport. If she left now she could get back to England on it before the authorities realized she was a different woman from the one who had travelled out under the same name. She had her dress-making money saved over the last six months, enough to buy a boat ticket back to London.

There was no time for goodbyes. Her getaway was crucial. Her identity as Saskia Carlino no longer existed. She was a DP once again and the panic she had felt when she had opened the door to the policeman at Laurel Bank began to flood over her again.

It was astonishing how quickly she was able to wipe Sal out of her life. He had helped her when she was desperate and she owed him for that, but now that suddenly she could no longer pose as his wife, he had served his purpose and she realized he meant nothing to her.

She knew Anna Filomena would understand once she learned the true story of Sal's real wife. Saskia would miss her. If there was one reason that she would want to stay it would be for Anna Filomena. Like Lady Sarah before her, she had been a rock in Saskia's life.

Saskia climbed out of the window and onto the fire escape. By the time she reached the bottom of it she would be Saskia Kessler once more – a refugee forced by her own instinct yet again to flee from the warmth of a family.

Biting her lip to stop the tears coming she began her descent to the street.

Patrizia found the note under the pillow in their bed and tore it up before Milly came home. She was glad Saskia had gone. Saskia had never liked her. Now Patrizia could go to work on Sylvia . . .

Milly came home and saw something blue fluttering from the fire escape. She forced herself in spite of her fear of heights to climb down and retrieve Saskia's scarf as a memento of the only person she had encountered so far in her life she felt had truly understood her.

The next day a letter arrived for Saskia and Milly carried it carefully upstairs, realizing she had no idea where Saskia had gone so she could not forward it. It was from England. Milly turned the envelope over and even though the letter would never reach Saskia, it comforted Milly to see the name of the sender and his address:

Barney Lambert
Selwyn House
Holland Park
London W11

Twenty-Seven

Serena sat up in bed and hugged herself. Barney had brought her up the mail before he left for his studio and there were no less than four invitations to parties. She could not believe that life could be so much fun.

There was a light tap on the door and her breakfast was brought in by the woman who came in to clean.

'Here we are, madam. Orange juice, a lightly boiled egg, toast and coffee and Mr Lambert's rose, of course.'

She opened out the low legs of the wooden tray and stood it over Serena's knees. Every day Barney insisted on placing a fresh rose in a stem vase on her breakfast tray. He had promised to do so every day they were married and so far he had kept his promise.

Serena drank her orange juice and wolfed down her egg. Then she lay back on her pillows and sipped her coffee. All around her in her pink and white bedroom were photographs in silver frames of various sizes. Each photograph reflected some part of her life and every morning she looked at them and thought how lucky she was. There was her engagement photo three-quarter profile with pearls by Lenare – which had appeared in *Country Life*, and beside it her favourite wedding photo of her and Barney just outside St Margaret's, Westminster, arm in arm and smiling into each other's eyes.

Serena loved going over the wedding in her mind. It was quite true what they said about it being the best day of your life. From the minute Daddy had begun to lead her up the aisle she had known it would be a day she would never forget. Dear Daddy! How easy it had been to call him that even though someone else had called himself her father for the first twenty years of her life. Thank goodness Mummy had divorced horrid Mr Sanders (as Serena now referred to Geoffrey) and found him again after all these years. Now Mummy was Lady Fakenham. Sir Anthony and Lady Fakenham. If Serena hadn't married Barney she could have changed her name from Serena Sanders to Serena Fakenham. But now she was Mrs Barney Lambert. Forever.

There was a photo of them in the new *Queen* magazine. 'Mr and Mrs Barney Lambert at the ball held at the Hyde Park Hotel . . .' It was rather a good one of her. Maybe she could ask them to send her a print so she could add it to her framed collection. She frowned as her eyes travelled on. Barney had left the door to his dressing room open and through it she could see the photographs on his tallboy. He had one of Mummy, that was fine, and one of Selwyn Reilly which was understandable. And a beautiful one of her, of course, taken on their honeymoon in Venice. Serena knew she was looking exactly as he most adored her: fresh faced, no make-up, fair hair brushed back in an Alice band and a look of almost childlike happiness on her face. But right next to her he had placed a photograph of that dreadful Auntie Beattie woman who had made such a noise at the wedding, singing the hymns at the top of her voice, crying so loudly, blowing her nose and trumpeting into her handkerchief. It had been rather embarrassing at the wedding when her side of the church turned out to be jam-packed full and poor Barney's side had only this Beattie woman and some rather disreputable-looking artistic types. Serena had nearly died when her mother had suddenly taken it into her head to move across the aisle and sit with her. Suddenly everyone was switching from one side of the church to the other just as she and Daddy were trying to move up the aisle.

Serena's gaze finally came to rest on the picture on

display in Barney's room that somehow always managed to upset her. It wasn't even a photograph; it was a sketch of a nude girl done by Selwyn Reilly and Serena knew the girl was called Saskia. She dimly remembered her from her childhood. The girl had grown up with Barney so maybe he had looked upon her as a sister but why he should want a picture of her in the nude was beyond Serena's understanding.

Abruptly, Serena slipped out of bed and closed the door to Barney's dressing room. She had her compensation after all. The reason that she had spent half an hour hugging herself in glee before her breakfast arrived was that soon there would be another face to go into a silver frame – a tiny silver frame.

Serena was expecting a baby.

They had asked Mummy and Daddy to come up for drinks that evening and would tell them then. It was so lovely having Mummy and Daddy living downstairs. It had been Mummy's idea that she and Daddy should buy the enormous stately house set back from the road on Holland Park where they occupied the ground floor and the basement and leased the first, second and attic floors to her and Barney. There had been a rather awkward period when Barney had been against the idea. For some ludicrous reason he wanted to go back to Lancashire and live at Laurel Bank, that mill miles away from nowhere that Selwyn Reilly had left him. Barney had seemed to think he could paint there but who on earth would go all that way to sit for him? No, it had been out of the question and she had told him that if he insisted on going to live up there it would be without her. He had come round, of course, but he had agreed to live in Holland Park on one condition: that Sir Anthony Fakenham's new residence be renamed Selwyn House. To Serena's eternal amazement Daddy had agreed at once.

There were many things about her husband that could be described as odd and Serena knew she was just going to have to live with it. He was an artist for a start, when most of her friends' husbands worked in the City. The thought of Barney in a pin-striped suit made her giggle. It was a bit awkward that he was only a portrait painter which was looked on as being a bit 'commercial', and there were all those stories about what he got up to in his Chelsea studio, but Serena knew none of that could possibly go on any more now that he was married to her.

She had married him without a moment's hesitation. She knew he brought out the best in her and he was the only man she had ever met who made her feel she had confidence in herself. He listened to her, really listened, not just out of politeness, and he remembered everything she said. He seemed to want her opinion on things which no one had ever demanded before. For years and years she had lived in Nancy's shadow and now suddenly she had come into her own. She was Mrs Barney Lambert, the wife of the portrait painter, somebody in her own right, not just Nancy's little sister.

It never occurred to her that she had just exchanged one appendage for another.

She was still in bed when the parcel post arrived at noon. There was a food parcel from Nancy in America accompanied by a long letter.

It was funny how Nancy had never – ever – referred to Barney in any of her letters since Serena had married him . . .

Serena's days had an identical routine of which she never tired. She rose, had her bath and, three times a week, she went to the hairdresser. Then she lunched with a girlfriend and spent the afternoon shopping – a nice frock from Mr Hardy Amies or a browse through Harvey Nichols – or she went to the pictures to see her favourite matinée idol.

But she was always back home in time to change for cocktails at six with darling Barney, followed by dinner.

Barney always walked to and from his studio, down Holland Road, Warwick Road and Finborough Road and then along the Fulham Road, turning right into Edith Grove. He needed the exercise after a day of concentration at his easel and it also gave him time to think. The offer of his father-in-law's car and driver was always there but Barney only took Sir Anthony up on it when it was pouring with rain and even then he sat up front with Farley, the driver. He couldn't bring himself to sit in the back like a toff.

Barney liked Sir Anthony well enough, despite the fact he had nothing in common with him, but he couldn't help comparing the older man with Selwyn and finding him wanting. Sir Anthony might play the charming diplomat at social occasions but within the confines of his own home he was an ascetic, academic man, conservatively dressed and not very forthcoming when Barney was around. Yet he clearly adored Lady Sarah and for that reason alone Barney made an effort to get along with him, while secretly yearning for Selwyn's flamboyance. Why couldn't Lady Sarah have married Selwyn? Yet it was clear that she, in turn, adored Sir Anthony and they complemented each other with their different personalities.

Perhaps, thought Barney, as he strode through the cold evening air, that's why Serena and I are a couple. He wondered, not for the first time, what Joe and Vera would have made of his marriage. Auntie Beattie had already told him she thought Serena had too many 'flippin' airs and graces, has that one!'. But, he reasoned, Serena had led a very different life to the kind of Liverpool Judy Auntie Beattie knew. In many ways she was still a child and with a shock Barney realized that he thought of her as his little girl. He adored her gaiety, her enthusiasm, her laughter. He thought himself amazingly lucky to have won her as his wife. The thought of her glowing, all pink and white, fresh from her bath, waiting for him in front of a blazing fire always spurred him on as he veered off Holland Road on the final leg of his walk. She always smelled so delicious, wafting scent everywhere.

He didn't care much for her friends but he very rarely

had to see them. He could always plead a late sitting if he wanted to get out of something and she seemed quite happy to go off to the theatre or to dinner on her own with a group of people in her set. But tonight was different; tonight she would be there waiting to spend the evening with him. First they would tell her parents their news and then, when they'd left, he would take her in his arms and carry her to their bedroom. His little girl – could he still call her that now she was going to have their child? Did he feel ready to be a father? Could they afford it? It would mean having to accept more lucrative boardroom commissions. Barney cursed. Painting the chairman of a company bored him rigid. Money, money, money, always there, never enough. He wasn't entirely happy about the fact that they lived with her parents. Of course they had their own flat, quite separate from the Fakenhams, but he still felt awkward about it all.

Now he had to walk through the Fakenhams' hall to get to his own quarters and as he did so, Serena called out to him from her parents' drawing room.

'In here, darling. I couldn't resist telling Mummy at lunch and she and Daddy have invited us for champagne.'

Barney was livid. This was his news, his and Serena's, and he had wanted to be the one to break it to Sir Anthony with Serena by his side. He sauntered into the room deliberately slowly, still in his battered old tweed coat, holding his cloth cap between hands and stood before them, saying nothing.

Lady Sarah took one look at him and saw the young Lancashire boy she had first seen in the churchyard during the war.

'Give me your coat, Barney. Don't blame Serena. She was so tremendously excited and I did sort of drag it out of her.'

'Well done, old chap, well done.' Sir Anthony clasped his shoulder. 'Jolly well done.'

Barney flinched. 'Well done what?' he asked perversely. 'What exactly have I done well?'

330

'Oh, Barney,' Serena ran to fling her arms round his neck. 'It's just something we say on these kind of occasions.' She was wearing the little diamond and sapphire studs in her ears that her father had given her as an engagement present. He, Barney, had barely been able to afford a ring. He wished he could control these attacks of resentment about his background but they seemed to creep up on him at all the wrong moments. He was always doing the wrong thing. Only last weekend Serena had dragged him all the way to Wiltshire to stay with some of her friends, only to chastise him going home on the train because he hadn't left anything for the butler and the other servants. How was he meant to know anything about tipping? Selwyn hadn't had any servants. Then there had been that time when he'd heaped his salad onto his plate along with the rest of his meal. And he'd asked where the toilet was instead of the lavatory. The list of his crimes was endless and what on earth did it matter?

'A glass of champagne, dear boy?'

Dear boy! That was the last straw.

'I'll have a pint of Guinness.'

'Good for you. Have to hang on a mo while I see if we've . . .' Sir Anthony was never thrown.

Barney felt a twang of remorse. It wasn't the old man's fault that Serena had married him. Sir Anthony would probably have preferred a Coldstream Guards officer or a young buck working at Lloyds.

'Sorry, sir, wasn't thinking. Champagne will be fine.'

'Well done.'

'Barney, darling, we dined at the Askews' last night. They've hung your portrait of Catherine above the fireplace in the dining room and I must say it does look splendid . . .'

'Lady S, if anyone says "Well done" once more . . . I'm warning you . . .'

Barney broke the ice as usual. In his own way he was a better diplomat than Sir Anthony. Within minutes he had them all laughing as he recounted the details of his day spent painting Lady 'Pwimwose' somebody or other who prattled on for hours about her pekinese called 'Wupert' and her husband called 'Wobert'.

'The only trouble was,' said Barney, drawing Serena close, 'she made them sound absolutely identical!'

'Stay to dinner, Barney, you're on such marvellous form, we can't let you go just yet.' Lady Sarah was adamant. As he followed his wife and her parents into the dining room, Barney reflected sadly that he had been done out of an evening alone with Serena yet again.

He pulled out Lady Sarah's chair and waited for her to be seated and then did the same for Serena who had taught him to do this. Sir Anthony was busy with the wine. Lady Sarah rang for the soup.

Serena drank rather a lot and began to giggle.

'Tomorrow,' she announced, 'I shall spend the whole day in bed. I must start taking care of myself now.'

'Oh, nonsense,' said Lady Sarah. 'You'll be fine for ages yet. A little early morning sickness perhaps. Don't you worry. If you have any problems at all we'll just call Doctor . . .'

As Barney listened to her he remembered how she had reassured Saskia in much the same way when they had learned she was expecting little Klara. Barney looked up sharply. He didn't want to start thinking about Saskia now of all times. She was far away in America if Harold Wasserman was to be believed and she had never even answered his letter. Maybe she was married like him, maybe she had even had another child – or several – to replace Klara.

'Bar-neeee!' Serena was looking at him.

'What? Oh, sorry, I was miles away.'

'Mummy was just saying how Nanny is going to be over the moon to be called back to work again.'

'Nanny?' said Barney blankly.

'Nanny. My nanny. The one I had when I was a little girl. She looked after Nancy too. She's part of the family. Of course she'll have to come back and look after the baby when it's born. Barney, where are you going?'

332

Barney was on his feet and halfway across the room.

'I'll not have anyone looking after my child except its mother. I'll not! Flippin' nanny indeed!'

'You married an artist, Serena,' her stepfather told her quietly, 'and you'll have to put up with artistic temperament.'

'Oh, pooh to artistic temperament, he's just being Barney. Mummy, can I be excused please so I can go and see what's wrong with him?'

'Darling, you're twenty-one years old. You really don't need to ask to be excused any more,' Lady Sarah told her wearily, 'but since you were sweet enough to ask, do run along.'

'Nanny's going to find more than one baby to look after,' said Sir Anthony once Serena had gone.

Lady Sarah called Nanny the next day.

'I know, Nanny dear, it's wonderful news especially as Nancy doesn't seem to show the remotest interest in having babies, but there is a slight problem. Nothing you can't handle but let me just put you in the picture. You weren't able to come to the wedding, were you? Well, she's married this rather extraordinary young man. Now don't misunderstand me, I've known him since he was a boy and I adore him. Now, remind me, you come from Lancashire, don't you? Well then, there'll be no problem at all. Come and have tea on Wednesday and I'll tell you all about him . . . You see, there's this woman called Beattie Richardson, Barney's Auntie Beattie. I think it might be a good idea if you two had a little talk . . .'

For the first eight years of Serena's life, before war broke out, Mabel Violet West was 'Nanny Sanders'. During the war Mabel West had to go and look after her mother and by the time she returned Serena had been sent away to school and didn't need her any more.

Nanny Sanders – she was never Nanny West, she always preferred to take the name of the family she was working for, it made her feel more like one of the family – was not a smart Norlands nanny. As a girl she had grown up in Lady Sarah's parents' house, the child of the cook. That cook had come from Liverpool originally and Mabel West had spent many a happy holiday with her cousins in Lancashire. When she turned seventeen she became Lady Sarah's maid and her confidante. Mabel West had known all about Sarah's early love for Anthony Fakenham just as she had seen that Geoffrey Sanders was a bad lot, but there was nothing she could do.

Now she was going to be Nanny Lambert and she was overjoyed – a new job and a new baby and with people she loved. Furthermore, after all these years she had kept her figure trim enough to still be able to get into her St Christopher's uniform: pink gingham dresses with aprons, stiff collars and cuffs, grey overcoat, round hat with grey and pink ribbon, grey stockings and black brogues for walks in Hyde Park.

As for Barney Lambert, she'd soon sort him out.

Barney held the piece of paper up to the light in the vain hope he might be able to decipher Lady Sarah's scrawl. He had come home to an empty house and found a note from his mother-in-law on the hall table.

> *Darling Barney, Serena received a last-minute invitation to go to the ballet and you know how she adores it. She simply had to go. Anthony and I are out for the evening. I've asked someone to pop up and see to your dinner. You'll probably find her in your kitchen when you get in.*

Most odd, thought Barney, most odd indeed. And so typical of Serena to let her mother organize his needs instead of attending to it herself. Now that he thought about it he could indeed hear sounds from the kitchen.

The woman standing at the stove had her back to him when he entered. As she turned, wiped her hands on her

334

apron and came towards him smiling, Barney thought he had never seen such a kind face.

She was elderly – in her late sixties, maybe early seventies. Her hair was completely white and drawn back into a large bun. Barney had seen the size of it before she turned round and knew that loose her hair must cascade to her waist. Her face was lined and her nose large but her smile was so wide and welcoming and her eyes so very much alive and intelligent that she seemed to radiate cheerfulness.

'Mr Lambert?'

Barney nodded. He couldn't help returning her smile.

'You'll be wanting your tea?'

'Me tea?' Barney was incredulous. It was a long time since anyone had offered him his 'tea' at 7.30 in the evening.

'Or perhaps you'd like to take a bath first? Only I'd like to know or else me meat pie will spoil.'

Barney sat down at the kitchen table.

'I wouldn't want to be responsible for spoiling a meat pie. Now's fine.'

'Right you are. There's tatties too and a nice egg custard to follow. Your Auntie Beattie said you liked an egg custard . . .'

'I don't believe it. You know me Auntie Beattie?' Barney had taken off his jacket and rolled up his shirtsleeves.

'In a manner of speaking.'

'Well I never. Nobody tells me anything. How long have you been working for them downstairs?'

'I worked for Lady Sarah for years. How's the pie.'

'Delicious. Dead tasty. So I expect you know my wife, Serena.'

'Like the back of me 'and.'

'She's having a baby.'

'I know.'

'Do you really? Oh, I expect they all know downstairs. So if you know Serena that well, tell me what kind of mother you think she'll make.' Barney sat back in anticipation of all the platitudes he'd been hearing all week: 'What a wonderful mother Serena will make', 'Well done, both of you, jolly good show', 'Patter of tiny feet, eh? Well done' . . .

335

'She'll have problems to begin with but she'll grow into it eventually. Ready for your egg custard now then, are you?'

'Now I'm not, but I'm ready for more of your meat pie if there is any, I've not tasted meat pie since I last stayed at me Auntie Beattie's and that was before I was married. But what do you mean about Serena having problems? At the birth, do you mean? Will it be painful because it's the first?'

'Aye, course it will, but you'll be there to tell her you love her when it's all over and that's the main thing. There's some that don't have a husband to take care of them . . . No, it's after I'm talking about.'

'What do you mean – after?'

'May I sit down with you?'

'Please.' Barney pulled out a chair.

'I've known little Serena since she was tiny. Literally. She lives in people's shadows. First it was her sister Nancy's. Now it's yours. No, let me finish. When this baby arrives she will live in its shadow too. She's still too young and insecure to be having a baby of her own to look after. She's still too much of a baby herself but she is beginning to gain a little confidence recently, so I understand. She's lived behind the mask of her prettiness. She bounces about all over the place and convinces herself and everyone around her that she's terribly happy all the time when inside she's still a frightened little girl. Marrying you has helped, I'll not deny that. The fact that you love her is beginning to have an effect on her and you and she need to build on that as much as you can. If she has to devote all her time to looking after the baby, she won't have much time left for you and she'll get confused. She'll hide behind the baby; she'll become Serena the Mother when she's nowhere near ready.'

'Why are you telling me all this?' Barney knew everything this woman was saying was true. He knew he'd known it himself for some time, that he thought of his wife as his little girl even though she was only six years younger than him. But he loved her bubbling, childlike gaiety; he didn't want one of those sophisticated worldly bitches he painted for a wife. Yet he had always known there would be a time when he would have to let her – to help her – grow up, and now she was going to have a baby herself that time had come.

'I'm telling you all this because I want you to realize it's the best possible thing for Serena for me to be there to help her when the baby comes.'

'But why you?'

'Because I'm Nanny, of course. I was Nanny Sanders and now it's time for me to be Nanny Lambert.'

Barney burst out laughing. He'd been conned in the nicest possible way, set up by Lady Sarah and quite possibly by Serena herself, into agreeing to something he'd been violently against.

'I know it's alien to your way of thinking, lad,' Nanny patted him on the shoulder. 'I know it's the last thing yer mam would have done even if your father had had the money, but your Serena's from a different world and if you love her you'll understand what she needs. I just wanted to have this talk with you to show you I understand your own feelings. I'm from your background not theirs, I'll bridge the gap, you'll see. Trust me.'

'Trust you? I'll worship you. You're going to have to be my Nanny too. After all, you're a friend of me Auntie Beattie's . . .'

'She gave me the recipe for her meat pie. Said it was one of your favourites.'

'Nanny, I'll let you into a secret. Don't you dare tell her but I've always hated Auntie Beattie's meat pies, but yours is quite delicious! I'll be wanting one a week at least from the day you start.'

Lucy Louise Lambert was born at five o'clock on the morning of 12 November 1952. It was not for quite some time that Barney realized the significance of the date. His daughter had entered the world at almost the exact same moment as little Klara was born nine years earlier.

Twenty-Eight

When Saskia stepped off the boat from New York and made her way nervously through immigration at Liverpool Docks they accepted her without question as Sylvia Carlino returning home. Once out of the dockland area she tossed the passport in a rubbish bin. There would be no way she could use it ever again given that the real Sylvia Carlino would be probably returning herself any day now.

She had few belongings with her: a small suitcase crammed with her clothes and her portfolio of drawings. She had very little money left but she knew there was just one place she had to go first.

She caught a train to Preston and from there took a taxi, instructing the driver from memory how to find Laurel Bank. It was a bleak March afternoon and the weir looked as if it was frozen over yet, as they entered the tunnel of rhododendrons leading to the Bell House, Saskia felt warmth flooding through her at the thought of seeing Selwyn – and, she hoped, Barney again.

She had not planned this visit. Indeed she had resisted all temptation to contact them since she had fled Laurel Bank. Yet as soon as she had stepped back on British soil once more she had known she had to come. As the taxi emerged from the tunnel Saskia gasped. The Bell House was still there but the mill beside it was unrecognizable. It appeared to be have been transformed into dwellings. Lights blazed from the windows. People were coming and going.

'This what you want then, love? Klara Court?'

Klara Court. Klara!

Without waiting for an answer the driver went right past the Bell House and deposited her at the entrance to the flats. She paid him and stood uncertainly on the steps looking up at the converted mill. A man accidentally brushed past her and apologized.

'Sorry about that. Who are you looking for? There are no names on the bells but I know all my neighbours.'

'No, thank you. I'm going next door to the Bell House to see Mr Reilly.'

The man stared at her.

'Which Mr Reilly's that then?'

'Mr Selwyn Reilly. Doesn't he still live here?'

The man shook his head. 'You've not seen him in a while then?'

'Not since the war.'

The man reached forward and took her elbow. 'Best come into ours, lass. Me and the missus'll make you a nice cup of tea . . .'

They broke the news about Selwyn's death to her gently, explaining how it had happened, how he had built the flats, how he had never really been the same since young Mr Lambert had left.

'Mr Barney Lambert?' asked Saskia, although she knew it had to be. 'He's gone too?'

'Well, he's not dead as far as we know. He moved down to London. Of course he came back for the funeral but that were a while back.'

'And where is Sel . . . where is Mr Reilly buried?'

'Do y'know, I'm not rightly sure. There's a gravestone down by the bridge over the weir but to tell you the truth I've never been near it. Didn't like to trespass somehow . . .'

They let Saskia make her way through the fog, which had come down suddenly, to the grave beside the weir and because of the fog they lost sight of her. They did not see her stumble over the little burial mound and drop down to read the wording on the gravestone.

Klara's grave.

Saskia collapsed. She remembered instantly the picture of the policemen swarming out of the ditch holding Klara's tiny body aloft. And this was where she had finally been laid to rest.

Saskia sat shivah by her daughter's grave till the cold began to eat into her bones, then she retraced her steps through the fog to the Bell House. Her pathetic possessions were still sitting on the steps. She looked up at the clock set in the face of the brickwork above her. Nearly midnight.

Then she reached into her bag and took out the key she had been carrying with her ever since she left, the front door key to Laurel Bank, and she let herself in.

The place was desolate, like something out of *Great Expectations*. Saskia recalled Barney's love of the book and how he had read parts of it aloud to her when her English was still shaky. Now she expected to find Miss Havisham in every room she entered. There were cobwebs everywhere, dust sheets over all the furniture and a pile of rubbish in the corner of the kitchen. As she gave it a tentative kick the old dog basket that Schnutzi and Putzi had slept in slipped away to the side. With tears streaming down her face, Saskia pulled it over to the light and dusted it down with her overcoat, remembering how they used to lay little Klara down to sleep between the dogs. A basket big enough to house two large Labradors and a baby was big enough for her to sleep in. Laying her coat down inside it, Saskia stepped into the basket, knelt down and curled herself into a ball to sob herself to sleep.

She had come back to Laurel Bank.

Later Saskia would ask herself if everyone experienced a time in their lives when it seemed as if everything had come to a halt. That was how she felt when she awoke the next morning and she could not bring herself to move. After an hour she got up, rummaged in a cupboard till she found a glass. She rinsed the dust off it and drank a glass of water. Then she returned to the dog basket.

340

She stayed there for two days.

She left the basket only to go to the lavatory and then she moved as if in a trance. She slept and when she was awake she forced her mind to go blank.

On the third day she staggered across the kitchen to open the back door. There, on the steps, was a loaf of bread and a pint of milk. A note from the couple she had met at Klara Court told her they had left the provisions for her two days ago. She tore off chunks of bread and stuffed them into her mouth before rinsing out a glass from which to drink the milk. Her energy partly restored, Saskia ventured outside. She knocked on the couple's door to thank them. As she waited for them to answer she looked about her and began to work out exactly which weaving room the flat had once been part of. She paced up and down the corridor, looking this way and that and finally she was certain, so certain that when the couple opened the door she pushed past them and straight into their bedroom and began banging on the wall.

'Look here, what do you think you're doing?'

'Please,' begged Saskia, 'I know it's got to be here. Listen.'

The wall sounded hollow. Saskia was scraping away at the wallpaper and finally the man pushed her firmly to one side but not before there was a click and a concealed panel in the wall clicked open.

Just inside was Saskia's old sewing machine, its pretty stencilled flowers coated in dust.

They helped her carry it back to the Bell House and the man was just setting it down on the kitchen table when they heard the sound of a car coming up the drive.

It wasn't just any car. Selwyn's old Brough Superior was still going strong. Barney brought her smoothly to a halt outside the Bell House and came into the hall through the open front door.

'Someone here?' he called out.

'Only me,' said Saskia appearing from the kitchen and taking two steps towards him before she passed out.

*

341

'Like bloody *Gone With the Wind*,' was the neighbour's parting shot as he watched Barney carry Saskia up the main staircase of the Bell House and disappear from the landing into Selwyn's old bedroom.

As Barney laid her down in the middle of Selwyn's bed she opened her eyes and looked up at him.

They stayed like that for minutes, looking at each other, examining each other's faces as if they each thought they would be able to read there all that had happened over the last seven years.

'Any moment now,' Barney said finally, recovering first from the shock, 'one of us is going to say: "What are you doing here?" Do you want to go first or shall I?'

Saskia pointed dumbly to him.

'Sassy . . .' At the sound of her old nickname she started and brought her hand up in the air. He caught it and held it, stroking her fingers. 'Easy, Sassy, it's all right. Listen to me, maybe you don't know, there's something I must tell you first of all . . . Selwyn . . .'

Saskia spoke for the first time.

'I know. They told me. Poor Selwyn.'

'That's why I'm here. He left me Laurel Bank. I come up here occasionally just to make sure the place is okay and –'

'Klara's here too,' Saskia interrupted.

'Klara what? Oh, you mean her grave? You saw it, down by the weir? We buried her, Selwyn and I. We said the Jewish burial service for you . . . we . . . Saskia, what happened? What on earth happened to you?'

It took nearly four hours. Saskia poured out everything. It was the first time she had been able to tell anyone the truth. She owed it to Barney. It was, she realized, something she had needed to do for years, admit that the life she had been living in America had in many ways been a lie. She wept as she told him about Anna Filomena and Milly and he wrapped her in his arms. By the time she had finished and

342

he in turn had told her about Selwyn's death, it had grown dark and to keep warm they had slipped underneath the blankets of Selwyn's unmade up bed.

Barney went down to the car for the food he had brought with him and came upstairs with a picnic on a tray together with a bottle of Selwyn's claret. Saskia was exhausted with the telling of her story and content to lie in Barney's arms. Eventually she fell asleep and when she awoke the following morning, it was to a feeling of such unadulterated happiness that she dared not move in case she broke the spell.

She had come back to Barney. Laurel Bank was now his. She was home with him where she belonged.

The sound of the phone ringing on Selwyn's bedside table shattered her moment of bliss. Barney reached out automatically for the receiver.

'Hello? . . . Serena . . . Yes, of course I'm here. Surely you didn't expect me to drive up and down to London again in one day? What's the matter, darling? . . . Don't be silly. I'll be back tonight . . . Okay. See you then. Don't fret. 'Bye.'

What's the matter, darling? Saskia lay silent for several seconds. Finally she looked across at the back of the blond head on the pillow beside her.

'Serena?' she asked.

'Don't you remember her? The other one. Not Nancy, her little sister. Lady Sarah's younger daughter.'

'Serena Sanders?'

'Serena Lambert. She's my wife. We were married last year.'

Saskia froze.

They drove in silence all the way to Liverpool, tears streaming down Saskia's face. She would not look at Barney. As he gripped the wheel of the Brough Superior he tried to reason with her.

'Please understand, Sassy. I didn't know where you were. You haven't heard my story. You fell asleep. Please,

343

come down to London with me. Come and meet Serena but most of all come and see Lady Sarah. We live with them now, in their house, she divorced Geoff Sanders, you know, she married . . .'

But Saskia wasn't listening. She made him deposit her at the Adelphi Hotel where he booked her a room for two nights and paid for it in advance.

Then he handed her an address. She was to make an appointment and go to see Selwyn's solicitor the next day. Selwyn had left her £5,000 but because they had not known where she was they had never been able to give it to her.

He tried to kiss her as he left her in the hotel foyer and could hardly bear the look of hurt in her eyes. He gave her his address in London and walked away knowing he must wait for the day when she would forgive him and that that day might be a long way away.

As he drove back down to London he remembered that Serena was not the only person she had not known about. He had not told her about Christiane.

Saskia acted swiftly.

With three of the £5,000 she bought a little shop in Liverpool with two rooms above it for her to live in. She spent six months sewing furiously, making up all the designs she had been going to sell through Wasserman's in New York and at the beginning of the seventh month she opened her dress shop.

At first she spent a great deal of her time shooing out groups of sixteen-year-old 'totties', giggling all over the place and only buying one dress between them. Then gradually word began to spread and the 'better class of customer' started appearing. Saskia devoted her entire life to making the shop a success. She contacted no one, hired no one to help her and steadfastly refused any invitation to socialize, especially from men. The only thing she did was to write to the Carlinos and give them her address and in due course she received a reply.

Milly had written the letter, of course, but Saskia could hear Anna Filomena's voice speaking to her.

Saskia cara,

We have your letter and at last we can stop worrying. Mamma was so happy that you wrote. After you went I cried every night for a long time but I understand. Mamma and me, we know you are not Italian and you have to return to your country. We miss you. Mamma has asked me to send the enclosed recipes for tomato sauce and lasagne. Salvatore make lots of money and now he has taken Sylvia and little Tommy to live in a new apartment. This is very good because now I have your room for myself. Patrizia and Angelina each have a room. We are all very private and we don't need to go out on the fire escape any more. Sylvia makes Salvatore come to dinner with us every Sunday so Mamma is very pleased but sometimes I know she wishes she still had you to talk to. For example we have just had a big family problem. Patrizia was going to have a baby and she did not have a husband. Then she fell down the stairs. It's terrible to say but I know she did it on purpose. She lost the baby. Somehow Sylvia's Tommy is not one of the family. Sylvia does not understand how to be Italian like you did. I am doing okay at school and maybe I can go to college. It's my dream. Everyone in the neighbourhood misses your clothes and like I said we all miss you. I am in love with Johnnie Ray! Write us again soon.

> *Your Italian sister,*
> *Milly*

Saskia made a note to parcel up some dresses from the shop and send them to Milly the very next day.

Saskia's success could be put down to one thing: she was brilliant at costing. Costing a dress was nerve-racking. First she had to find the right quantity of material at the right price, then she had to work out how much all the things were going to cost that would go into the finished dress to make it distinctive as one of hers. Selling her clothes off the peg meant Saskia had to cater to different sizes and naturally large sizes meant more cloth. Would she sell more larger sizes or more smaller ones? Somehow, she always guessed right and her stock cleared instantly.

In her second year she began to make a profit. Within four years she decided to move down to London. She took one look at the individual style of the black-stockinged Chelsea girls and knew that Chelsea was going to be the place to be. She sat in a coffee bar and after seven espressos, just as she was about to take off into the atmosphere she was so speedy, she rushed out and told an estate agent that she would offer for a little corner house in a street that ran between the King's Road and St Leonard's Terrace.

As she had in Liverpool, she turned the ground floor into a shop and called it, quite simply, The Shop. She installed huge Victorian mirrors, hung her clothes on hatstands and placed a cash register on a small bamboo table. Upstairs she slept only on a mattress until she made enough money to have the whole place completely revamped. Those were the limbo days. She knew she was on her way but she was not yet sure where to. All she knew was that she was determined to succeed – for the memory of her parents and of little Klara and finally, though she was too proud to admit it to herself, in the hope that one day Barney would become aware of what she had done . . . without him.

Saskia stood outside on the pavement and wondered for the umpteenth time if she had made a mistake in expanding the shop. The sheer plate of glass stretched from the door to the wall and through it the dummies wearing her clothes stood in the window for all the passers-by to see. They were so exposed to view they seemed almost naked but she had to admit they would be hard to miss.

Of course, she really ought to be right on King's Road

instead of in a side street just off it. Mary Quant's shop, Bazaar, had already proved an enormous success; was there room for another so soon? Well, they'd find out by the end of the year. The window display was just the beginning. The interior of the shop still had to be gutted, redesigned and fitted out. She walked round the corner to look at the window that had not yet been refitted. The square panes of glass already seemed dated, belonging to a bygone era, although only a week ago her little shop had been crammed with customers, scrabbling among the hatstands and stumbling up to the cash register, their faces hidden by the piles of clothing they wanted to buy. Inside, the hatstands on which she had hung clothes, jewellery and accessories for sale, now stood bare, awaiting removal before work started on the streamlined new interior. It was time for a change. She knew she was doing the right thing but she still couldn't suppress the nagging question: would the customers come back to the new shop?

She made her way through to the stockroom behind the shop, past the kitchen and up the narrow staircase to her little sitting room on the first floor. The floor above housed her bedroom and bathroom. Two up, two down and two more on top was how she thought of it but it was still a corner shop.

Barney had grown up in a corner shop. Was that why she had bought it? But she must not think about him. She had almost succeeded. She had come so far yet there was still so far to go.

A new decade was dawning. Maybe everything would happen in the sixties.

'Serena, I don't suppose by any chance you can explain to me why our daughter is walking round and round the garden with her eyes closed. She's bumping into things all over the place and she's dragging poor Bella right along with her.'

Bella was Stella's granddaughter, the prize black

Labrador pup in Schnutzi's only litter. Barney had left Schnutzi and Putzi up at Laurel Bank following Selwyn's death, but when their new owners had telephoned just before his marriage to say that Schnutzi had given birth to a litter of seven, he had not been able to resist taking one to give to Serena as one of her wedding presents. Only to find that Serena didn't like dogs so he had kept the little bitch at his studio and now he was glad he had done so for she was Lulu's pride and joy.

'It's too boring. Nanny's gone and fed her some claptrap about the blind and she thinks she's training Bella to be a guide dog. It's been going on all week.'

'Poor little thing. She's out there trying to do something constructive since she's not allowed a birthday party.'

It was 12 November 1961. Lulu's ninth birthday.

'Well, why on earth should she be? She had that wretched fireworks party last Sunday. I told Nanny to explain to her that that was meant to be her birthday party as well. It's not my fault if Nanny forgot.'

'In that case I'm going to come back from the studio early and take her out to lunch tomorrow. We'll go to the Buttery at the Hyde Park Hotel and have a proper grown-up lunch. I'll let her order anything she likes. She'll love that.'

'No wonder she's so bloody spoiled, Barney. It's all because your sort don't know how to bring up their children properly, letting them run wild all over the place. And to think you expect me to have more little brats like her . . .'

Barney ignored her. He knew she was unhappy but he did not know what he could do about it. These jibes about his background were flung at him in a kind of childish protest. He knew it was Serena's way of getting back at him for the fact that he paid more attention to Lulu than he did to her. Yet since Lulu's arrival she had changed so much. Or had she? Maybe he was being unfair on her. Maybe she hadn't changed. Maybe he just hadn't understood at the outset that underneath her vivacity and frothy personality there really hadn't been anything there. He had married a rather sad little girl and made her happy and now poor

Serena was caught in a trap, not really very mature herself yet envious of her own daughter. The problem was that he wanted more children and she flatly refused to have any. At least that's what he pretended.

The real problem, of course, was that ever since he had seen Saskia again he had realized what a mistake he had made in marrying Serena. Poor Serena. She had sensed something was wrong right from the moment he had returned from Laurel Bank, and over the years he had watched as the youthful gaiety he had thought he loved disintegrated into a bewildered misery. She had needed his love so badly and she had known the minute she had lost it.

Nanny didn't run away when Barney came storming out of the drawing room. She'd been listening but she didn't care if Barney knew it. He put his arm around her shoulders and together they slowly climbed the stairs.

'Do I spoil Lulu, Nanny?'

'A little but no more than any normal father would if he adored his child as much as you do.'

'Why doesn't she see it? Why doesn't she love Lulu as much as I do?'

'You know why,' said Nanny, shaking her head. 'She just sees Lulu as competition. She always has, right from the minute she brought her home from the hospital, handed her over to me and you started spending all your time in the nursery. I'm partly to blame, I admit it. All those years ago I said to you that if we let me take care of the baby, you'd have more time for her. D'you remember? Except you fell in love with your daughter and forgot about your wife.'

'What shall I do? I could go down and talk to Lady S. I suppose. I've always been able to talk things over with her. And with you, Nanny, of course,' he added hurriedly.

'Oh, don't go bothering Lady Sarah with it. She can see how Serena is and she'd do something about it if she wanted to. Serena probably goes down there moaning enough as it is. Always one to run to her mother for comfort. No, what you should do is take her away for a weekend.'

349

'What a wonderful idea. How about Castle Combe? Lulu loves it down there and –'

'Without Lulu. On your own. Just the two of you.'

'Without Lulu?'

'That's just it. Take Serena away on her own and make her feel as if she's important to you again. A romantic weekend as if you didn't have any children. I'll be here with Lulu. Take Serena somewhere and tell her you love her.'

Even if you don't, she thought to herself, *even if you don't*.

A week later Barney drove Selwyn's Brough Superior furiously out of London along the Kent roads towards Dover to catch the ferry to France. He had decided to treat Serena to a weekend in Paris. She sat silently by his side in the passenger seat. She had a silk square tied round her head and knotted in the nape of her neck and she was wearing dark glasses. Barney had a vague feeling of unease. She had barely said a word to him for nearly twenty-four hours whereas he had anticipated that the notion of a trip to Paris would rekindle a little of the former enthusiasm that had first attracted him to her.

He accelerated round a corner and glanced at her to see if his foolhardiness at least would get a reaction but she hardly seemed to notice.

'Serena, you all right?' There was a village coming up. Maybe they should stop and have a drink if there was a pub. They had plenty of time and he wanted her to get rid of whatever it was that was on her mind. 'Don't worry about Lulu, darling. She'll be fine. She always is with Nanny.'

'Nanny! Nanny! Nanny! I wish she'd never come.'

'But it was you and your mother who suggested –'

'I know I did but I'm not always right, am I?'

Barney said nothing.

'It's just I'm such a hopeless mother. Hopeless!'

'It's your first time,' said Barney reasonably. 'You'll get better with practice. You'll be fine with the next one, you'll see.'

'Barney, how many more times do I have to tell you? I DON'T WANT ANY MORE!'

'But, Serena, seriously, you'll feel differently after this holiday, you'll . . .'

He'd gone too far. She swung out at him, grabbing the wheel.

'Stop the car. Stop the car at once. I want to go home. I don't want another baby. I want to go . . .'

She never finished the sentence. Her scream reverberated through Barney's head. When she had grabbed the wheel he had lost control and they were careering straight towards the brick wall of a country pub at seventy miles an hour.

Twenty-Nine

'*Kaffeetrinken!*'

Christiane called out into the garden through the kitchen window.

Kaffeetrinken. Promptly at five o'clock every afternoon, just like she was told the English took tea, she served strong dark coffee and a plate heaped with *Kuchen* – a variety of pastries – all laid out on the low coffee table in the L-shaped living room. In the identical homes on the newly built postwar surburban Frankfurt housing estate, all the other housewives were undoubtedly doing the same thing. The only difference was that most of them would be serving coffee to their husbands as they returned home from work.

In the mornings they often invited Frau Mahrenhertz – Frau *von* Mahrenhertz in fact, they often whispered to each other – to their *Kaffeeklatschs* and allowed her to join in their banal gossip. But they never asked her to their homes in the evenings. She was far too pretty and although there were no apparent signs that she was a particularly merry widow, she was a widow all the same and they didn't want her anywhere near their husbands.

Christiane sat at the coffee table and waited for Matthias and Friedrich to join her. She would try not to have more than one pastry today. She was now thirty-six and the spreading rump that Barney had so much admired had now spread too far, upwards and outwards so that she already had to wear relatively loose garments to hide a thickening waistline. Today she wore a twinset – a short-sleeved,

round-necked sweater with a matching cardigan which she
had slung loosely around her shoulders, leaving the empty
sleeves dangling. A rope of pearls fell between her large
breasts. This was her English look, copied from a picture
she had seen in the magazine Barney had sent her with the
pictures of his wedding in it. Why had he done that? Had it
been to hurt her? What would he make of the picture of
surburban respectability she now presented? What would
her neighbours say if they were to learn of her wartime
career as '*die kleine Sonnenblume*'? Every now and then she
was gripped by an almost uncontrollable desire to shout out
the truth: that the woman they invited into their spotless,
antiseptic, characterless homes was none other than a
Jewish prostitute risen from the dusty rubble of war-torn
Berlin!

She had never been able to decide whether Werner had
married her out of pity or whether it had been the other way
round and it was she who had felt sorry for him. After
Nina's death he had insisted that she stay at Mittenwald for
a while before she returned to her ruined lodgings in the
Budapesterstrasse. She guessed that Friedrich must have
reported back to him the state of her living quarters.
Friedrich was often waiting for her in the Mercedes with
invitations to dinner from Werner and, inevitably, dinner
was often followed by sex. Only she did not take Werner
back with her to Budapesterstrasse; she stayed with him at
the Adlon. So far as she was able to make out, he actually
worked in Frankfurt but he was often away for long
periods. Sex with him was, to put it bluntly, manual. On
the first evening he had asked her over dinner if she would
be prepared to 'service' him, as he put it. Assuming that he
wished to hire her like her other clients, she had quoted her
fee mechanically at which point he had risen in anger and
left the dining room. Christiane had followed him to his
room, running down the long hotel corridors after him,
tripping, hampered by the narrow skirt of the long evening
dress he had bought her. At his door he had paused and
then, without looking behind him, knowing she was there,

he had reached out and grabbed her by the wrist, pulling her into the room.

'Sit!' he commanded as if she were a dog, pointing to the bed. She obeyed and he stood directly in front of her. He unbuttoned his fly and pulled down his underpants.

'So, can you see it?'

She understood at once what he meant. She was, she supposed, in a position to be able to compare him with literally hundreds of other men, but Werner's equipment was practically nonexistent. His testicles reminded her of two tiny purple grapes with his penis a little red cherry in the middle.

'Nina was kind,' he explained. 'She said it made no difference to her. I am never able to become fully erect, I never climax but I do feel something . . . if you would be so kind.'

Christiane had knelt before him. He had spoken the truth. After twenty-five minutes he had gently run his hand over the top of her head and said: 'Nothing will happen. I cannot ask you to go on forever but please believe me when I tell you I was in ecstasy.' He buttoned himself up again. 'Now, shall we go down and finish our dinner?'

He had not asked about *her* wishes, Christiane noted. Had he known of Nina's preferences? Did he assume Christiane was the same? Was he right?

For so many years, long after Werner had been gone, she had asked herself that question. She, who had had so much sex during the war, was now celibate but if the opportunity were to arise which sex would she choose? That which she had enjoyed with Barney – or with Nina? She could hardly go knocking on her neighbours' doors, seducing housewives to find out. Yet since Werner had left her, almost immediately after Matthias' birth, she had become obsessed with keeping her reputation above reproach. Deep inside her lurked the devil and it had enabled her to survive in Berlin. Now she needed to behave like a saint in order to survive. The idea had become engraved upon her mind that if she allowed a man to get close to her he would immediately see her for the whore that she was.

She never knew why Werner left. He had taken her to live in Frankfurt, in a small apartment near the *Bahnhof*. He had shown her with pride the giant, nine-storey, six-winged office block in the north-west of Frankfurt where he used to work. He told her of the corridors lined with marble inside along which he used to stride to meetings.

Used to.

Now the building was surrounded by security fences and patrolled by American guards, occupied by the American Army. Yet Werner went every day just to stand and stare at the vast headquarters. It dawned on Christiane only as she was about to give birth that not only did Werner no longer have a job, but that she had never known much about the job he now appeared to have lost.

Werner left her with enough money so that she did not have to contact Barney for two years. Perhaps he left because he was ashamed of being sexually incapacitated, yet somehow she doubted it; he had lived with it for long enough. She assumed he had gone back to Mittenwald but then Friedrich appeared out of the blue with the news that the place was on the market and there was no trace of Werner. It was then that Friedrich had told her about Nina's last words to him. *Die Gräfin* had asked him, Friedrich, to watch over Christiane. He was to transfer his allegiance from Nina to Christiane. Thus, his continuation as Werner's driver had not been to serve Werner but to enable him to be close to Christiane. Now that Werner had abandoned her, Friedrich's place was to remain with her.

Friedrich found work at a garage despite his age. As Matthias grew into an energetic little boy, Christiane and Friedrich made a plan. They sold the apartment and bought a small house on one of the new housing estates with a garden at the back. Christiane set herself up as a widow, Matthias the child of the marriage, and while it was never actually stated, they let it be assumed that Friedrich was her father and the boy's grandfather. Matthias was told his father was dead. A photograph of Werner was placed in his bedroom but Werner was raven haired and as the boy grew,

355

it was clear that he did not get his blond good looks from him. They came, it was stressed, from his mother's side.

Together, they made an admirable, indeed poignant, picture of a little family struggling to keep together – a forgery whose surface was about to be scratched away to reveal the lies beneath.

'*Kaffeetrinken*,' Christiane cried almost to herself as she sat waiting. Where were they? Had something happened to them? Friedrich always came home from the garage by bus and waited outside Matthias' school to walk the remaining half a mile with the boy. Matthias worshipped Friedrich and for the last eighteen months they had rushed away after *Kaffeetrinken* to the small garage beside the house in which Werner's Mercedes still stood. The old car impressed the neighbours and allowed them to persist in their notion that he had indeed been a 'von'. It had not been the ideal car on which to teach the young Matthias to drive, but Friedrich had succeeded. The empty unfinished outer roads of the housing estate were the perfect place for the boy to practise, and practice had made perfect. Although still a few months shy of his fifteenth birthday, Matthias could drive his mother to the shops.

The doorbell rang. Christiane peeped through the filmy nylon curtain that prevented passers-by seeing in through her plate-glass window. To her amazement, Frau Schinkel, one of her most prestigious neighbours, the leader of the *Kaffeeklatsch* no less, was standing on the doorstep.

'*Bin gleich da*,' called Christiane and paused to pat her hair in the hall mirror.

'Have you seen this?' Frau Schinkel flapped a newspaper at her without even offering a greeting first. 'Page five. Call yourself a widow!' And without further comment she threw the local paper into Christiane's hall and left.

'Can't I invite you in for *Kaffeetrinken*?' Christiane called after her but she was gone.

Christiane sat down again before her coffee-pot,

bewildered. Then she remembered: page five. She turned the pages slowly, noting the weather for the following day, an advertisement for a sale at one of her favourite stores. She assumed that all she would find on page five would be nothing more exciting than a recipe Frau Schinkel recommended. Then why had she said something about Christiane calling herself a widow?

She saw the photograph first, then the headline below it:

IG FARBEN SUICIDE
The body was discovered today of former IG Farben executive Werner Mahrenhertz in a bathtub in a small hotel in . . .

It was Werner. There was no doubt in her mind once she had looked at the picture. It was the same as the one in Matthias' room. All his schoolfriends had seen it. They had all been told that Werner was already dead. So, for that matter, had Matthias.

Matthias was obsessed with James Dean. He had been told he looked like him, the only difference being that his hair was a shock of blond thatch, much fairer than James Dean's had been. He dreamed of owning – or even driving – a Porsche similar to the one in which James Dean had died eight years earlier. He had seen the film *Jenseits von Eden* seven times, he had even waded through the Steinbeck book, much to the excitement of the teacher of his literature class at his *Gymnasium* who was beginning to wonder if he might have a live one amongst all the Philistines. Young Mahrenhertz was due to take his *Abitur* examination the following year after which he might even go on to the *Hochschule*, the *Universität* . . . The teacher recommended Thomas Mann and to escape further attention, Matthias agreed to read *Der Tod in Venedig* if only because it was very short.

It was a disturbing book for a boy on the brink of

manhood to read in that Matthias immediately identified with the character of Tadzio, the beautiful boy spied on at the Lido in Venice by the dying man, von Aschenbach. It also coincided with the appearance of a man who began hanging around the school gates. Matthias only noticed the man because he seemed to take an inordinate amount of interest in him. Sometimes he smiled. Matthias, well brought up, smiled back.

He was there the day someone brought a newspaper to school with the article which was to change his life.

'Thias, thought you said your father was dead.'

'He is.'

'Who's this then?'

'Didn't know your father was responsible for Auschwitz?'

'How does it feel to be the son of a mass murderer?'

'But my father wasn't in the SS. He was a chemist.' Matthias was confused.

'Oh, yeah? Read this then.'

Matthias couldn't understand what it was all about. His father had been dead for years but the paper maintained that he had killed himself only a few days before. It stated that he had been a prominent IG Farben executive who had worked closely with the Third Reich during the war.

At the school gates the man moved to walk alongside Matthias when he saw the boy was crying and put his arm around Matthias' shoulders.

'*Was ist los, junge? Was hast du?*'

For no reason that he could identify, Matthias was suddenly excited by the man's touch. He was also very frightened. He sensed danger and he ran. He was halfway home before Friedrich caught up with him. He too had the paper in his hand.

Christiane met them at the door.

'Friedrich, what do we do?'

'We tell Matthias everything.'

'Tell Matthias! What about me? I don't understand. Why did he kill himself. The *Polizei* have been here. They tried to get here before I saw it in the papers but they have only just been able to trace us. Friedrich, he cut his wrists . . . the blood . . .'

'Shhhh! That he doesn't need to know,' said Friedrich glancing at Matthias. 'Bring a bottle of schnapps. The boy is going to grow up very quickly now and, young as he is, he'll need a drink. We all will.'

Friedrich talked fast and quietly.

'Werner worked for IG Farben, our giant chemicals group. He was based mostly right here in Frankfurt at the nerve centre, that big building he used to go and watch. You remember?'

Christiane nodded.

'IG Farben supported Hitler's preparations for war through its manufacture of synthetic oil and rubber. They built a new plant in the Polish Silesian area on an eminently suitable site – a village called Auschwitz. In fact, in the end, there were four Auschwitzes: the original concentration camp; Auschwitz II – the extermination centre with the gas chambers and the ovens at Birkenau; IG Auschwitz, the plant and IG Monowitz, the concentration camp built by IG Farben – all filled with Jews.'

'Oh, *no!*' Christiane buried her head in her hands. She had begun to guess what was coming.

'Do you know what happened to the Jews at the hands of the Third Reich, Matthias? Have you heard of Hitler's Final Solution? Tell me, do you know?' Friedrich's tone was urgent.

Matthias nodded. He had heard. There had been a Jewish child in his class but he had left with his family to go to America. The boy had spoken of other members of his family and what had happened to them. At the time, four or five years ago, it had been nothing more than a grisly tale greeted with a certain amount of relish by the group of young listeners. In the subsequent years, he had been aware of rumours that so-and-so's father had been in the SS and he had always been relieved that his own father had been nothing more than a chemist – or so he had thought.

'A new asphyxiating agent, an insecticide called Zyklon B, was introduced at Birkenau,' Friedrich went on. 'It was manufactured containing a special smell which would warn humans that it was a poisonous gas. But the SS demanded an immense order without the warning smell and it was supplied by the manufacturers, Degesch.'

'Did IG own Degesch?' asked Matthias.

'You're very quick,' said Friedrich, startled into a smile in spite of his gruesome story.

'So IG Farben supplied the gas which killed the Jews at Auschwitz?'

'More or less,' confirmed Friedrich.

'What are you trying to say, Friedrich?' asked Christiane. 'Why did Werner kill himself?'

'He worked for IG all those years, right through the war. He supervised the building of IG Auschwitz and IG Monowitz. He knew exactly what was going on. He –'

'But how do you know all this?'

'He told *die Gräfin* Nina everything. By confessing to her he absolved himself . . . but he placed the burden on her. That's why she did what she did in Berlin.'

'But he told me too – when we were first married, he told me about the Nuremberg trials, the Allies arrested the IG directors –why didn't they take him too?'

'Werner helped them with their investigations and in return he was granted immunity. But by that time his guilt had caught up with him, he couldn't go back to IG Farben . . .'

'Was that why he married me? He had killed so many and now he had a chance to save one?' Christiane's tone was cynical.

'Mutti, are you Jewish?' Matthias stared at her, astonished.

'*Na, und* . . .?' Christiane shrugged.

'It's possible,' said Friedrich. 'He would do anything for Nina. You were a friend of *die Gräfin* . . . I told him you were Jewish. Forgive me.'

'How did you know?'

'*Die Gräfin* told me everything.'

'So why did he leave me?'

'He knew it would come out one day. Someone would point a finger and say, "But he knew. He was there." He did not want you to be implicated. I suppose someone has caught up with him, someone has pointed the finger and he has broken.'

'Friedrich, had you been keeping in touch with him?'

'I gave him reports of you, of the boy, from time to time, but recently I had lost contact.'

Christiane sighed. She had been keeping Barney informed while all the time Friedrich had been in touch with Werner.

They both looked at Matthias.

'I am going upstairs now,' he said in a curiously calm voice. 'I'm tired. I just want to go to bed and sleep.'

The next day the mysterious man was waiting outside the school gates again but Matthias saw Friedrich waiting for him and ran to the old man.

'How did it go today?' asked Friedrich, 'Did they give you a rough time?'

Matthias remained silent and looked down at his feet. Friedrich rumpled his hair and hugged him close.

'Listen, Thias, I have something else to tell you. No, don't shy away, it may make you feel better. The thing is, Werner Mahrenhertz wasn't your father. Don't look at me like that. It's true.'

'*Die Gräfin* Nina told you that too?'

'No. She never knew about Werner and your mother, don't forget, because she was dead. But I kept my word to *die Gräfin*. I watched out for your mother. I followed her, discreetly of course, but I saw the men she went with –'

'Went with? What does that mean? How many? You make my mother sound like a whore.'

Friedrich ignored that one.

'It's not a thing a mother can tell a boy easily but you would probably have found out one day: Werner couldn't have children. You could never have been his son. But there was one man Christiane was seeing for a few months before she became pregnant. He was an Englishman. A soldier. His name was Barney Lambert. Your mother telephones him about you and he sends her money for you.'

'Why don't we live with him? Is he in England? Will she be able to marry him now Werner is dead?'

'She can't. He's married already.'

'But why hasn't he ever been to see me if he knows about me? Doesn't he care?'

'Your mother thought it would be upsetting for you.'

'How could she think that? What's he like? Do I look like him?'

'Very like him although I haven't seen him for several years.'

'Will we tell Mutti that I know about him?'

'That's up to you.'

'Let's keep it just our secret for the moment. Do you have his address in England?'

'Yes. He lives in London.'

'London,' whispered Matthias. 'London!'

He had always known he was different and now he knew why. He was half-English. And he was Jewish! He checked. If the mother was Jewish then so was the child. He longed to be able to tell the kids at school, to explain to them that Werner Mahrenhertz was nothing to do with him. It also explained the misgivings he had always felt about his mother. He could never quite put his finger on it but it always seemed as if she were playing a role. She took so much time with her appearance and even then she looked all wrong. She was beautiful, he had to admit that. At nearly fifteen he was beginning to appreciate the opposite sex and he could see that Christiane was something special, but she was not like the mothers of his friends. The only time he had ever seen what he imagined his mother truly looked like was when he had wandered into the bathroom by mistake a year or so ago and found her languishing in the tub. The expression on her face was quite new to him and afterwards, thinking about it, he realized that it was the first time he had seen his mother relaxed, being her true self, being Christiane as opposed to the widow Mahrenhertz. Well, she really was the widow Mahrenhertz now, Matthias reflected. Would that change her? Would she agree to his having a birthday party in the cellar with a little beer and dancing to his theme song, 'Walk Like a Man' by The Four Seasons? Or would she just bake a special *Kuche* for *Kaffeetrinken*? Somehow Matthias knew nothing would change unless he did something about it himself.

'You're looking better,' the man at the school gates told him the next day. 'Something good happen?'

Matthias nodded, smiling.

'Want to tell me about it?'

So Matthias told him the whole story. He had to tell someone, better to tell a stranger, someone he would never see again.

But he did see the man again. He was there waiting for him every afternoon. Matthias told Friedrich that he would prefer to stay later at school to study for the important *Abitur* and would come home on his own from now on.

The man's name was Karl and he took Matthias to the movies where he sat beside him and stroked his thigh. Matthias knew it was wrong but in a way it was exciting and Karl never wanted to do anything else. He bought Matthias gifts – clothes which Matthias had to hide from Christiane and Friedrich and only wear when he went out with Karl. He didn't know what Karl had in mind but he knew if he continued seeing him, it would lead to something different happening in his life and he was right.

Gradually Matthias began to withdraw from Christiane's clutches – at least that was how he saw it. He rushed off to school each morning in the middle of breakfast, snatching a *Brötchen* from his plate and stuffing it into his mouth as he ran out the door and he never appeared at *Kaffeetrinken* any more. He was quite open about seeing Karl, described their visits to the cinema, to coffee bars. He merely omitted to mention that Karl was in his thirties, implying that he was another fifteen-year-old like Matthias himself.

'Bring him home so we can meet your new friend,' Christiane implored him, pleased that Werner's suicide didn't seem to have affected him unduly. Of course, she had no idea that he knew about Barney. She was worried about Barney. He had not rung for weeks. She assumed he was away. She dared not ring him herself but if it became necessary she would have to. She had to tell him about Werner.

Matthias was almost sixteen when Karl invited him to go to England with him. It all seemed extraordinarily simple. He had a boat, he explained, and they would sail there from Hamburg. He could organize Matthias' passport but Matthias had to bring him his birth certificate and not a word to Mutti, eh?

Matthias felt bad about it but he had to enlist Friedrich's help in getting hold of his birth certificate. He threw a bit of a teenage tantrum and pretended he didn't believe the old man's story about an Englishman being his father; he wanted proof. Friedrich looked hurt but he came through. He knew where Christiane kept her private documents and he removed the birth certificate.

'It's not exactly as if it's something she wants to take a look at every day, is it? Not something she wants to remind herself about, eh, Pops?' Friedrich didn't like the way Matthias had taken to calling him Pops but he said nothing. The boy was beginning to change in so many ways. Christiane didn't appear to have noticed but he had. They all changed at this age but somehow Friedrich was nervous. Had he done the right thing telling the boy who his real father was?

Matthias thought it was nothing short of a miracle when Karl produced a passport with Matthias' name on it and returned the birth certificate which Friedrich, filled with relief, duly restored to Christiane's desk. But it wasn't just the passport that amazed Matthias; it was his new name staring at him from the long oval window: Matthew Lambert.

It was a British passport. Karl had somehow secured him a British passport. It said so on the front above the emblem of the lion and the unicorn dancing round the crown and the words '*Honi soit qui mal y pense*' and '*Dieu et mon Droit*'. Inside he found a photo of himself and he remembered when it had been taken. He and Karl had been having fun in one of the booths at the station and Karl had stepped outside and let him be photographed on his own.

'But how on earth did you manage it?'

'It's all perfectly legal. Your birth certificate states your father is British so you're entitled to a British passport. The only thing is we can't actually use it till you're sixteen, but not long now.'

'Matthias, I thought we'd do something special for your birthday.' Christiane was trying to sound casual. Matthias seemed to have grown away from her over the past year; she could barely get him to exchange more than a few sentences a week with her.

'Don't bother. I've got plans of my own,' he said, sounding bored with the whole notion of his birthday.

'Oh, that's great. What do you think we should all do?'

'I've got plans for myself, Mutti. Myself and my friends.'

'But Friedrich and I . . .'

'I want to do something on my own for a change, with people my own age, go to a club, take some girls . . . It's not as if we're exactly a close family.'

Christiane bit her lip. In the old days, when she had still been accepted into the homes of the other mothers on the estate, she had been warned of this kind of truculent adolescent behaviour by those women whose children were already going through the troublesome stage.

'I don't know what you mean by that. Friedrich and I are always here for you when you want us. We love you, you know that.'

'You and Friedrich. Always you and Friedrich. What about my father? That's what I'd really like to know about.'

'Friedrich explained. I know I should have told you about him earlier, told you he was alive, about his work. One day I hope you'll understand why I chose not to. He left us, Matthias, it's not as if your father was asking after you or anything . . .'

'I don't mean Werner Mahrenhertz. He wasn't my father. For God's sake, Mutti, I'm going to be sixteen! When are you going to tell the truth about my real father? Barney Lambert.'

'Who told you?'

'Well, it was old Friedrich actually.'

'What else did he tell you?'

'You mean there are other secrets you've been keeping from me? How do you expect me to trust you, Mutti?'

'WHAT DID HE TELL YOU, MATTHIAS?' Christiane was shouting now. Did her own son know about her days of prostitution?

'Tell me about my father – my real father – and I'll tell you what Friedrich told me.'

Christiane began to gabble in panic. 'He was a British soldier. He loved me, truly he did. He told me so many times. It was just after the war. Many people were coming and going. It was not unusual to have an affair like the one I had with him. I became pregnant but he was going home to England.'

'So how come you didn't go with him?'

'I was engaged . . . to your father . . . I mean to Werner.'

'Why? Why were you engaged to another man when you were going to have a baby, when you were expecting me? You know what you sound like? You sound like a whore!'

'Is that what Friedrich told you I was?'

'Mutti, is that what you were?'

Christiane didn't answer. He did not really know what he was asking. He couldn't really know the truth. In any case, by the time she had met Barney she was no longer . . .

'Are you in touch with my real father? Friedrich said you were.'

'Often,' she said, relieved to change the subject.

366

'Do you have a picture of him?'

Christiane rose and went to her desk. Without thinking she showed Matthias the clippings from the magazine of Barney's wedding.

'That's your father,' she said pointing to Barney standing outside St Margaret's, Westminster.

'And who's that?' asked Matthias pointing to the woman in her wedding dress beside Barney.

'He's married.'

'So that's why he doesn't ask to see me. He has children of his own.'

'I think so, yes. A daughter. But he does ask to see you. He has your picture – several I've sent him over the years. He sends me money.'

'What does he do? Is he rich? Is he still in the Army?'

'I don't really know. I don't think so. We don't talk much. Just about you. I don't like to pry.'

'You don't like to pry? About the father of your child? Mutti, are you crazy? I'll never forgive you for not telling me about him. Never!'

And Matthias rushed out and upstairs to his room where minutes later she could hear music being played very loudly.

Christiane's face crumpled and she sat down miserably at her desk. The life she had struggled so hard to build up seemed to be disintegrating around her. She would talk to Matthias, maybe she would even try to find the money for a trip to London, arrange for him to meet Barney. Maybe she should have done that years ago, but she had always been so afraid of dealing with anything to do with her past. She only hoped it was not now too late.

She turned to the papers on her desk. At least she was making headway in one direction, the only area of her past that she had dared to investigate. She had begun to have a response to her months of enquiries. She had never dreamed there could be so many Kesslers in Germany alone. Already many of them had proved to be no relation to her but she would go on searching for the truth about her parents' fate even if – when she found – it turned out to be the news she dreaded hearing more than anything else.

Matthias spent the night of his sixteenth birthday at home with his mother and Friedrich. When Christiane kissed him goodnight she thanked God that his outburst of the day before had obviously been nothing more than a teenage tantrum. She watched as he embraced Friedrich and thanked the old man for his present. Christiane thought she had never seen her son so affectionate.

The next day, a warm September morning in 1964, Matthias took his overnight bag to school and left with Karl for England that afternoon.

Thirty

'Hell and damnation!' Barney cursed the next day as he turned the corner. He had forgotten his gloves. When he had first ventured forth in a wheelchair at Stoke Manderville hospital, a pretty young nurse had stepped forward and whispered: 'Be sure to always wear a pair of thick gloves when you're out and about on the street.' When he'd asked her why, she'd blushed and told him: 'You'll find out, Mr Lambert, you'll find out soon enough.'

Dog muck! Who would have thought of it? Bowling along the pavements, pleased as punch with yourself, turning the wheels faster and faster with your hands and suddenly there they are, covered in dog muck! He couldn't avoid it on the pavements even if he saw it. The wheels always went right through it.

He reached the high stone pillars at the bottom of the steps leading up to Selwyn House and rummaged in his pocket for what Lulu called his clown's hooter. He squeezed the rubber ball, gave two short blasts and waited. This was the worst thing of all: having to wait for someone to attend to his needs all the time. He couldn't go out without pre-arranging it with Jean-François, Sir Anthony's current chauffeur. Jean-François was the only one strong enough to carry him and the wheelchair up the steps.

Luckily Jean-François had seen him coming and was running down the steps.

'Did you have a nice treep, sir? You did not get caught in the rain like yesterday?'

'No, it was fine.' Barney smiled. He liked Jean-François. At least he spoke English. Sir Anthony had an obsession about hiring only foreign drivers in order to converse with them and keep up his languages. Sometimes, however, they didn't speak a word of English, which was a bit rough on the rest of the household. 'Is my daughter back from school yet?'

'Mees Lulu very excited because it is the end of term. Tomorrow you go to your studio in the morning?'

'No, I'm going to take the week off and spend some time with Lulu over the Easter break.'

Jean-François wheeled him through the hall towards his study but Nancy called out from the drawing room.

'No sneaking by, sugar, I can see you. Come in and keep a girl company with a drink.'

Barney tried not to wince. Nancy had arrived from New York for Serena's funeral and she had never left. She had moved into Selwyn House and didn't seem to show any signs of moving on. First she had gone off travelling for eighteen months – the Far East, Australia, India, then back to Europe and Paris, Biarritz, Monte Carlo, Portofino, Rome, Capri – leaving Nanny to cope with the grieving Barney and Lulu.

Serena had been killed. Barney had been lucky. He had suffered a crushed fracture of the lower spinal vertebrae resulting in pressure on the spinal nerves causing paralysis in the lower extremities. At first he had gone into a state of spinal shock, the early stage of the body's responses to the spinal injury. The doctors were unable to give a final prognosis for several weeks. If there had been a complete cutting of the cord at the lower back level, that would have been it: no regeneration. But there wasn't. Barney lost his reflexes and the power of his legs and at the National Spinal Unit of Stoke Manderville Hospital near Aylesbury they worked with him for months on complete rehabilitation: daily exercises using monkeypoles to pull himself in and out of bed, pulling a spring with a handle to full arm extension, starting with a light spring and progressing to a heavier one as his muscles built up. They worked on his toes, his legs, re-educating his gait, and after a year they could find no medical reason why he should not be able to walk again. Yet somehow he couldn't. Or wouldn't.

They talked to Lady Sarah about the 'emotional overlay', the mental shock he had suffered as well as the physical one. It seemed that the reflexes were there and the muscles were waiting to be used, but Barney just didn't have the mental will yet; he had received such a shock to his system that he just couldn't bring himself to move his legs.

The extraordinary thing about this was that Barney was an optimist by nature. A psychiatrist confirmed that there was really no sign of depression and he could see no reason why Barney should not make a full recovery. Meanwhile, it was as if he had confined himself to a wheelchair in order to give himself time to come to terms with Serena's death.

While Nancy was away, Barney amused himself, with Sir Anthony and Lady Sarah's blessing, by completely re-designing the ground floor of Selwyn House to suit his new life in a wheelchair. He put in sliding doors and ramps everywhere and commandeered a small room at the back of the house as his study cum bedroom in which he had special worktops built with wider spaces underneath into which the wheechair could slide. These desks had drawers which could be pulled out from either side to save him going round in his wheelchair. He converted the downstairs cloakroom into his own bathroom and a lavatory with enough space to get his wheelchair alongside it. He had all the deep pile carpets taken up and replaced with smooth fitted carpets and, where possible, plain wooden floorboards with no rugs in which his wheels could become trapped. The electric power points, he found, were often in awkward places, too near to the ground or out of reach behind tables, and rewiring was necessary.

What Barney hated most about being in a wheelchair was having to look up all the time when people were talking and he often acquired a serious crick in his neck. It was amazing how few people were sensitive enough to pull up a chair and talk to him at his level. As a result of this he became rather antisocial and the yearning to shut himself off and paint returned. Sir Anthony promptly devised what he called the 'school run' and he put his driver at Barney's disposal. In the morning they dropped off Sir Anthony at his office, then Lulu at her school, and finally the driver took Barney to his studio, which had been appropriately refitted. Thus every morning Sir Anthony had twenty minutes in the car with Barney and Lulu, and was able to report back to his wife how things were progressing. To their immense relief, Lulu seemed absolutely fine for the simple reason that she had never really liked sharing Barney with her mother.

Then Nancy had come back.

The first thing she tried to do was to fire Nanny.

'Jesus Christ, Barney, who needs the old bag? I mean, she was my Nanny when I was a kid, she has to be as old as a dodo by now. She's probably dangerous. She's completely superfluous. Lulu's wild as hell and the sooner we send her to boarding school the better. Then I'll have you all to myself . . .' There were endless coy references to the time she would have him 'all to herself', followed by a rumpling of his hair or an arm being slipped around his shoulders as she stood proprietorially behind the wheelchair.

But Barney wouldn't listen. Lulu was his daughter, not hers. He would make the decisions about her upbringing and the one thing he did know was that Lulu was devoted to Nanny. If she left then Lulu really would be miserable.

'Nanny stays,' he said firmly.

'And I'm not going to boarding school. Ever!' Lulu told her aunt whenever the subject was raised. 'I know you and Mummy went, but look how strange you turned out.'

'Lulu, don't talk to your aunt like that,' said Barney reprovingly, although secretly he applauded the way she stood up to Nancy.

'Why can't I talk to her like that? We didn't ask her to come here. Why doesn't she go back to New York? What's happened to Uncle Irv or whatever he's called? Why doesn't he come and take her away? Or is he as sick of her as we are?'

372

'Go to your room, young lady. I want to have a serious talk with your father about what to do with you. I don't happen to want to go back to New York. Uncle Irv and I are getting a divorce and I've come home because my family needs me.'

'You've come looking for a new husband, haven't you?' shouted Lulu. 'Well, you can let go of Barney.'

There was a silence.

With the unwitting accuracy of a child, Lulu had put her finger on the very reason Nancy had decided to stay on at Selwyn House. Of course, she had weighed up the pros and cons throughout her Mediterranean trip. It was all over with Irv and once everyone in Westchester and Manhattan had understood this, it had been frightening to witness how they had systematically cut her out of their lives. Without Irv she was nothing over there.

Then Serena had obliged her by being killed.

Nancy hadn't really been overly fond of her younger sister but she had always envied her her marriage. She, Nancy, had been dumb to elope with Irv without noticing Barney Lambert's potential. If she'd stayed behind, little sister wouldn't have stood a chance with him. Nancy had come home for Serena's funeral partly out of boredom and partly to score Brownie points by playing the loving, grieving older sister, but nothing had prepared her for the sight of such a gorgeous hunk of a man being wheeled helpless up the aisle, his blond thatch of hair caught in a shaft of sunlight streaming down through the altar window. When they had lifted him into the pew beside her, she had sat down and held his hand for the rest of the service.

On her return from Capri she had made a few discreet enquiries about his ability to 'function' and on hearing what she wanted to hear, her mind had been made up. The child could be sent away to boarding school and she'd begin her seduction in earnest.

Nanny, however, caught on immediately.

'I know what you're up to, Nancy, and you can put a stop to it right now. Anything Serena wanted when you were little, you always had to make sure you got instead, and you haven't changed a bit'

'Nanny, you always did prefer Serena to me. You're a mean old woman and if you keep this up, you're going to have to go.'

Nanny kept it up with a vengeance safe in the knowledge that Barney had told her she would never have to go as long as he was still at Selwyn House.

Nancy watched Barney like a hawk.

'It's no good sneaking off to your study. I've invited some people over. We've got to get you back in the swing of things, Barney. From what I hear you knew how to have a pretty good time over there in your studio before you turned into a boring saint and married my little sister. I want to see some of that action . . .'

Barney wondered how she could be so insensitive. Nancy's idea of giving him a good time was to sit on the telephone for an hour and invite twenty people over, rush upstairs and don one of her little black petticoat dresses with shoestring straps that were all the rage, open as many bottles of his champagne as she could find and push back the rug in the drawing room.

He never had a clue who any of them were. None of them talked to him. They were all too busy perfecting the twist, the hully-gully, the locomotion or the madison. The women were all years younger than Nancy, who didn't seem to realize they all found her faintly ridiculous.

Occasionally a girl would drape herself over Barney's wheelchair as he watched the dancing he couldn't take part in and say something like: 'You painted Mum back in the fifties, didn't you? It's in the hall but I hear there's another one of her in her birthday suit, that true?'

Inevitably, towards eleven o'clock, they all rushed out to a nightclub, usually Helene Cordet's The Saddle Room in Hamilton Place or the Garrison right opposite. Hours before, Barney would have wheeled himself silently out of the room and across the hall to his study and there, sitting on the stairs, would be Lulu, eating a bag of crisps, waiting for him. Barney would bring his chair to a halt at the foot of the stairs and wait for her to come down and kiss him goodnight. He stayed until she had gone upstairs and into her room before wheeling himself to his own room, the thumping music reverberating behind him. How was a child expected to sleep with that racket going on?

One night, as the autumn of 1964 drew to a close, Nancy followed him, something she had never done before. It was an unspoken law that his study was his domain, to be visited only by invitation. She lounged in the doorway, her little black dress hitched up her thigh, one of the straps falling down her arm. Her blonde hair had half fallen out of its chignon and was hanging dishevelled down one side of her neck. Her make-up was smudged, her eyes blurry. She was very drunk.

'I've been here over a year, Barney darling, and we never speak. S'gotta change. We have to get closer. S'why I've bearded the lion in his den.' To Barney's horror she reached a hand inside her dress and scratched one of her breasts. Then something caught her eye. Before he could stop her she had run over to the tallboy and grabbed Saskia's picture off it.

'You won't be needing this any more.' She was gone before Barney could say anything, taking the picture with her. There were screams and laughter in the hall and then the front door slammed behind them.

'Lulu's alone upstairs,' thought Barney for the umpteenth time. 'I can't get to her if anything happens. What if there's a fire . . .?'

'You call me, of course,' Jean-François told him the next morning. Barney had decided to go to the studio after all since Lulu had gone to a friend's for the day. Jean-François lived in a flat above the garage. Barney sighed. It would have to do. Pray God he never needed him.

'How's her Ladyship this morning?'

'Not good, sir. She's getting worse not better. Sir Anthony is very worried.'

Lady Sarah had cancer. It had been discovered five years earlier, she had been operated on twice and the prognosis had been excellent. Then Serena had been killed and her mother had appeared to go into a decline. It was as if she had simply given up the will to recover. This was so unlike the Lady Sarah he had known as a boy that Barney had found himself unable to know how to comfort her. Yet, in a way, it helped him to go and see her. Tragedy had struck him but he was alive. His innate optimism enabled him to expect a full recovery for himself one day, yet when he looked at Lady Sarah he knew she was dying and it was for this reason that he could not bring himself to tell her of his worries about Nancy – and, more important, for Lulu's future. Lady Sarah had helped him so much in the past. Now it was his turn to be her crutch inasmuch as he was able.

He could hear his telephone ringing as he wheeled himself unaided up the ramp to his studio. He fumbled with the locks and let himself in.

Still thinking about the ever-increasing misery at Selwyn House, it never occurred to him when he picked up the telephone that yet another burden would be added to his load as he heard Christiane say: '*Barneychen*, thank the Lord I've reached you at last. I've been calling and calling and the only person who answered the phone was someone called Nancy who said she'd tell you to call me. It was weird. She asked me if I was Saskia. Saskia! When I explained I was her sister, this Nancy woman hung up on me. Who is she?'

Briefly, sadly, Barney explained about the car crash, about Serena's death. He said nothing about his own injuries. Nor did he mention Saskia. He had never told Christiane about his meeting with Saskia up at Laurel Bank. Pride had prevented him from telling anyone.

'Barney, I am so sorry. I wish I did not have to add to your troubles but I do not know who else to speak to. The

376

most dreadful thing has happened. Matthias has run away from home.'

Lulu did go to boarding school but only because, having discussed it with her at length, Barney decided she would benefit from it. She was leading rather an isolated life at Selwyn House and seemed loath to bring friends back there.

As was the custom she was allocated a 'school mother', a girl who had already been there for a term, to show her the ropes. Margaret Donovan, a bossy little redhead several inches shorter than Lulu and who looked rather like a Cairn terrier, marched Lulu straight into tea. Margaret wore an 'afternoon frock' of green velvet. The girls were allowed to change out of their uniform into their own clothes for tea, prep and supper.

'It's from Harrods,' explained Margaret proudly displaying the label. 'Where are yours from?'

Lulu hadn't a clue. Her first letter home to Barney asked him to send a parcel of clothes labels, not clothes she stressed, just the labels. Barney, mystified, obeyed immediately but Lulu had forgotten to mention that she was going to sew them into her afternoon frocks and was rather worried when she received a selection of labels from well-known men's outfitters. Nor would 'Harris Tweed' be of any use whatsoever. In the end only a Fortnum and Mason label could be used but it had the desired effect. F&M was, apparently, a step up from Harrods.

'New girls,' explained Margaret, 'must never, never ask for anything to be passed to them at meals. You must wait politely until someone passes you something.'

Lulu sat, starving, watching a dozen girls pass each other bread and jam and cakes and biscuits. No one passed her anything. Margaret, who turned out to be a malicious little creature, never spoke to her for the rest of the meal. The same thing happened the next morning at breakfast and again at lunch. Lulu thought she would faint. It was time to take action. She began to drum her fingers on the table beside her plate. Several of the older girls looked at her then turned away. On she went, pressing her fingers harder and harder till they sounded like a galloping horse.

'Are you a new girl?' asked someone eventually.

Lulu nodded furiously, drumming away.

'Well, would you mind stopping that, it's driving us all mad.'

Lulu shook her head.

'Who are you? Who's your school mother?'

'Margaret Donovan.'

'Margaret, for heaven's sake, make her stop.'

'Why are you doing that?' asked Margaret innocently at which point Lulu picked up a bowl of carrots and flung them at Margaret before rushing out of the dining room in floods of tears.

Another function of the school mother was gradually to teach her 'daughter' the name of everyone in the school. Lessons were carried out at mealtimes where Lulu had to memorize the names of the eleven other people sitting at her table. Sometimes Lulu got lucky; the same girl sat on her table three meals in a row and her name became fixed in Lulu's mind, but there were days when Margaret would ask: 'Who's that sitting opposite you?' and Lulu would look at her blankly. 'But, Lulu, you sat next to her at lunch the Friday before last. How can you *possibly* say you don't know who she is?'

Things in the dormitory were no better: sixteen beds, sixteen little chests of drawers, sixteen flea-bitten little bedside rugs and sixteen ratty green bedspreads. Lulu knelt down beside her bed for Bible Time when everyone else did and asked God to please bless Sonny and Cher, Bella's puppies. Matron turned the lights out once they were all in bed and left the room. At least six people immediately leapt out of bed and clustered together. On came the lights.

'Who is out of bed? Stand where you are.'

Matron then ordered the culprits to strip their beds and remake them. When she came in and caught them out of

378

bed a second time, she ordered the entire dormitory to strip and make their beds. This happened virtually every night and dark circles began to appear under Lulu's eyes.

Then there was a brand new language to be learned. The lavatories were known as The Skates. Lacrosse was Lax. Muzapp was Musical Appreciation: how to fall in love with Gluck in twenty-five minutes. Flip-Flap involved dressing up in pale pink, grey, green or blue bits of shiny material tied round the middle with a piece of string and galumping round the hall pretending to be Bunny Rabbits in Spring Time while an old trout tinkled absent-mindedly on the piano. And then there was Ethel.

'Have you had Ethel?' Margaret asked her one night.

'I don't know,' replied Lulu thinking she must be one of the teachers. 'Who is she?'

'Lulu thinks Ethel's a she,' Margaret told the entire dormitory, which was greeted with whoops and giggles.

They wouldn't tell her what Ethel was but Lulu finally managed to deduce it must be some kind of bodily function. Lulu asked Barney in her next letter and received a curiously guarded reply suggesting that she write to Nanny. Nanny wrote back saying she would explain everything when she saw her in the holidays. Curiouser and curiouser.

Button Sunday intrigued her. Margaret was surprisingly sweet and friendly when she explained: 'It's a competition which everyone in the lower school enters and it's judged at the end of term. You have to sew a design in buttons on a pillowcase. The winning design is exhibited on Founder's Day and has been known to earn people scholarships. Most people have already begun their designs. You'd better buck up and get someone to send you some buttons so you can begin . . .'

Nanny sent twenty packets and some Cadbury's Dairy Milk.

They walked to church in a crocodile on Sunday mornings, where they played pass the penny during the sermon. One person held the penny at the start of the sermon until the vicar said a word beginning with A, at which point the penny was passed to the opponent who had to pass it back when she heard a word beginning with B. Back and forth went the penny throughout the entire alphabet. Thus if the unsuspecting vicar spouted out something like: 'And the Lord said, Behold the children of Israel did enter . . .' the coin whizzed back and forth so fast it was inevitably dropped and lost beneath the endless rows of pews. The point of the game was that whoever had the penny when the vicar said a word beginning with Z kept it. Lulu immediately raised the stakes to sixpence, and was promptly branded as *bumptious*.

To be bumptious was a cardinal sin. Lulu had to look up the word in the dictionary and found it meant self-assertive. Then she looked up assertive and learned it had to do with claiming one's rights. On the other hand she was not allowed to be wet – which had nothing to do with the fact that she was allowed only two baths a week and one shampoo a fortnight. It was, however, quite common practice for girls to share each others' baths in an effort to keep clean.

'*Lesbienne!*' shrieked Mademoiselle who taught French and officiated on Lulu's bath nights but that, she discovered, was one of the things that was definitely allowed.

Who was she going to choose as her Pash? That was the big question. Pash, short for passion, the passion that would burn inside her for a girl in the upper part of the school. Lulu didn't get it. There she was, old enough to fall head over heels in love with the Walker Brothers, the Righteous Brothers and all the Beach Boys put together and they expected her to fall in love with a schoolgirl. What was more, if she was invited to someone's birthday party during tea and offered a slice of the delicious birthday cake someone's mother had sent, she was expected to save it for her Pash and coyly stalk her through the corridors and offer it to her as a sign of her unrequited love. All over the school, after birthday parties, little girls huddled themselves in their long woolly capes and tore round and round corridors clutching soggy pieces of fruit cake to their flat little chests. Greedy-piggy Pashes, Lulu noticed, would saunter into tea and immediately look round to see if there was a birthday party and if, more important, their Pashite had been invited. If so, they would lick their lips in anticipation. Sadly, as in the outside world, love caused pain and sorrow as well as joy: ugly, fat plain girls didn't have Pashites and were never given cake.

In order to fend off Margaret, whose job as school mother it was to inform whichever girl Lulu chose of her new role, Lulu picked someone at random. Margaret threw up her hands in horror; the girl in question already had two Pashites and protocol required that they be consulted as they might object to a third vying for their beloved's attention.

'Oh, stuff it then,' said Lulu and turned her attention to Montgomery Clift. She even refused to go to Saturday Night Dancing where the entire school danced with each other round and round the Big Hall, pair after pair of marathon hikers in their afternoon frocks, one going forwards, the other backwards, a hand on a shoulder at arm's length, the other dangling self-consciously while the radiogram belted out 'Wolly Bully', 'King of the Road', 'Hang on Sloopy', 'Stop! in the Name of Love', 'Mr Tambourine Man' and, finally, when the lights went down and the Pashes strode across the hall to ask their little Pashites to dance, 'You've Lost That Lovin' Feeling'. The words weren't very appropriate but 'My Girl' by the Temptations had gone missing.

Towards the end of term, Margaret reminded Lulu about Button Sunday. Lulu thought her design was wonderfully original. She had embroidered a rolling stone in little mother of pearl buttons on her pillow. Everyone gathered round and assured her it was one of the best they had ever seen. On the penultimate Sunday she took it to the Sewing Room at the appointed competition hour, seething with anticipation. As soon as she stepped through the door she was faced with the moment of truth: instead of a panel of

381

judges she was met by the rest of her dormitory who explained to her that it was a trick played on New Girls. 'Button Sunday' didn't exist. It was merely But One Sunday to the end of term and they'd all stood around watching Lulu and her buttons and had a good laugh. Blinded by tears Lulu tore her pillowcase to shreds . . .

Everything changed her second term. She became a school mother herself, she was moved to a tiny dormitory with only four other girls, she joined the Play Reading Society, she was made goalie in the lacrosse team because of her height and she joined The Gang. The Gang consisted, by their own appointment, of the most popular girls in the class. To Lulu's utter delight, Margaret Donovan, was excluded.

She gained further popularity in a manner she was not sure she entirely approved of. Barney had not been allowed to visit her the first term but now he came down once a month to take her out, sometimes driven by Sir Anthony's driver, sometimes by Nancy. Parents were thoroughly scrutinized. Every weekend the girls hung around the car park and observed whose mother was pretty and what kind of car the fathers drove. As soon as they saw Barney in his wheelchair, Lulu was catapulted into the sympathy section, that special status reserved for girls whose parents were dead or who, horror of horrors, were adopted. By unspoken agreement they were never teased and were regarded with almost sycophantic reverence.

Nancy's floor-length mink coat didn't hurt either. Nor did the Brough Superior. Forget lacrosse: social climbing was the natural sport of St Cecilia's!

Towards the end of her second year, Lulu looked out of her dormitory window one afternoon as she was changing for games and saw a dark-haired workman in a donkey jacket on the other side of the school wall watching her intently. Before she ran onto the lacrosse field, she slipped over to the school gates and quickly opened them. He was right there.

She stood in goal and glanced several times in his

direction as he watched her. He looked just like Montgomery Clift, only meaner.

He was there the following week and as she opened the gates she whispered: 'What's your name?'

'Kevin. What's yours?'

'Lulu.'

'Woo-hoo! Wanna come to the pictures with me Friday?'

'Okay,' said Lulu and blew him a kiss.

She was amazed at herself. She'd been to a couple of dances in the holidays in London and found herself bored to tears by the pimply, damp-palmed Etonians and Harrovians who marched her woodenly round the dance floor.

She met him at eight outside the Rialto having shinned down an obliging tree outside the dormitory window. He gave her a giant leather jacket to slip over her afternoon frock and some lipstick and eyeshadow to make her look old enough to get into an X film and took her in to see *The Servant*. Lulu had heard Nancy talking about *The Servant* and how she had met James Fox at a party. It appeared that it took at least a year for London films to make their way down to the sleepy Wiltshire town near St Cecilia's. With luck, and Kevin's help, Lulu could catch up on everything she was missing in London.

Kevin gawped at Sarah Miles for a few minutes and then proceeded to plunge his tongue down Lulu's throat. She let him carry on for a few minutes and then pushed him away to watch the film.

The following Friday he took her to *From Russia with Love* and squeezed her breasts while she looked over his shoulder at the screen and pretended he was Sean Connery. In *Charade* she pretended she was Audrey Hepburn and in *The Carpetbaggers* she decided she didn't fancy George Peppard much and let Kevin stroke her thighs all the way up under her afternoon frock and tickle her *there*.

Suddenly she saw the games mistress in the row in front snogging with a man with a beard. Lulu watched them closely. The games mistress often had a rash on her chin and this explained it and . . . Lulu leapt to her feet and ran out of the cinema as the games mistress looked up and saw her.

The next morning Lulu was summoned in the middle of Algebra to see the Headmistress in her study. What a swizz, she thought, I'm going to be raked over the coals for seeing a man who's never said more than 'Fancy a choc ice?' to me in all the time I've known him.

'Sit down, Lucy. Have a biscuit.'

Lulu was stunned. This was a bit odd, being offered biccies for going to the pictures with an Irish brickie.

'Your father has telephoned with some very sad news. I'm afraid you've lost your grandmother.'

'What do you mean?' Lulu had visions of Lady Sarah wandering around Notting Hill Gate. 'Where's she gone?'

'Oh, to heaven undoubtedly.'

'You mean she's died? Dead? Is that it?'

'Your aunt is on her way to collect you. We'll pray for her Ladyship in chapel tonight.'

Yeah, you do that, thought Lulu as she tossed a note out of her dormitory window over the wall to Kevin:

> *Granny's kicked the bucket. Can we go and see* The Cincinatti Kid *with Steve McQueen when I get back next week? I'll make it worth your while.*
> *Love, Lulu*

The morning of Lady Sarah's funeral, Lulu went shopping. She'd saved up almost £7 from Barney's generous pocket money allowance, which for some time had been stagnating – and increasing – in her underwear drawer, not to mention the added income from pass the penny. Biba had just moved from Abingdon Road to much larger premises in Kensington Church Street where she picked up a couple of boat-necked, drawstring T-shirts. She didn't find anything in Granny Takes a Trip at World's End on the King's Road, although she was rather tempted by a second-hand white satin blouse but at £3 10s it would take too big a bite out of her budget. Hung on You and Bazaar were so packed with

384

people she couldn't get near the clothes and didn't have time to wait. She needed time to take a quick look at a new shop she had heard about called Saskia.

The first thing she noticed about it was the music. Someone had made a groovy compilation tape so that Stevie Wonder's 'Uptight' went straight into Percy Sledge's 'When a Man Loves a Woman'. Lulu began to boogie round the shop, pushing the clothes up and down the rails as she searched for the labels giving the size and, more important, the price. By the time the tape had moved on to 'Summer in the City', she'd got the picture. This was a pretty expensive shop. She simply didn't have the bread to afford anything here; she'd have to bring Barney back in November and get him to buy her something for her birthday. She smiled at the little dark-haired woman sitting behind the glass table at the back of the shop. Good haircut! Vidal Sassoon or maybe Raphael and Leonard. Lulu longed to have her hair bobbed short at the back with a heavy fringe and long pointy bits hanging down below her chin but she knew it wouldn't suit her. Her face was still too chubby and the long straight locks hanging either side of it did make it look a little thinner. She glanced again at the woman who was staring at her, really staring. Lulu felt uncomfortable. It was almost as if she knew her but how could that be? She was about Nancy's age, old enough to be her mother. Why didn't Nancy get herself a groovy haircut like this woman's?

Lulu took a bus to Knightsbridge and rushed to Woollands 21 Shop to take a look at Mary Quant's Ginger Group clothes. She tried on a slippy crêpe dress with long slim sleeves, wavy white cuffs flowing over the hands and a wavy white collar. Then she looked at the price: nine guineas! In the end she had to settle for a blouse version of the dress for only six guineas at Peter Robinson.

And some plum-coloured tights.

Nancy wore a black Persian lamb fitted coat and matching hat for her mother's funeral. She was riding in the first car with Sir Anthony. Sir Anthony asked Lulu to join them as Lady Sarah's only grandchild, but Nancy brushed her aside, staring disapprovingly at Lulu's Mary Quant placmac.

'It's black,' said Lulu defensively, 'and besides, I want to ride with Barney. If I don't he'll be all alone.'

'Sweet of you, darling,' drawled Nancy, 'but someone should have told you – PVC at a funeral. One just doesn't –'

'If anyone should have told her, it should have been you,' retorted Barney. 'Come along, Lulu, you look fine.'

Nancy was in for another shock outside the church. Geoffrey Sanders was waiting for them. He stepped forward and took Nancy's elbow.

'We've lost touch, love, but you knew I'd be here for you, didn't you, at a time like this?'

Nancy glanced quickly at the man with the thin black moustache in the shabby overcoat and cheap trilby and looked away. She was with Sir Anthony and she was going to stay with him – and Barney. Walking up the aisle with this common little man would be embarrassing under the circumstances. She took up her position behind Barney's wheelchair. Just like at Serena's funeral she wanted to make sure she was the one everyone watched pushing Barney up the aisle.

'Geoffrey, there you are. Sorry, I can't get up. Have you met my daughter Lucy? Lulu, this is Mr Sanders, Nancy's father, your grandmother's first husband.' Barney shook Geoffrey's hand warmly, and recalled his talk with Selwyn about Lady Sarah and Geoffrey Sanders and the fact that Lady Sarah had once cared for this man. He had a right to be there and the fact that Nancy seemed intent on disowning her own father was truly galling.

The family party were already seated at the front of the church behind the raised coffin covered in flowers when Saskia slipped in and sat at the back. She couldn't see Barney and in a way she was relieved. She had agonized for hours as to whether or not she should come. She had read of Lady Sarah's death in the paper and she was devastated. It was the first time she had been to a Church of England service since she had sat between Barney and Selwyn on Sunday mornings during the war and Lady Sarah had befriended her in the churchyard.

The funeral service began. Saskia tried to follow it in *The Book of Common Prayer* but when they came to the first psalm and she opened her mouth to sing, she broke down and sobbed on her knees, burying her head in her hands. It was a big church, but while a large crowd had turned out to say goodbye to Lady Sarah, Saskia was alone in the very back pew. She had suddenly realized that she was here for all of them, everyone who had died in her life whose souls she had not properly laid to rest: her parents, little Klara, Selwyn and now Lady Sarah.

And she was here to see Barney.

She couldn't deny that. However much she might want to pay her last respects to Lady Sarah whom she had loved deeply, she had seen it as a heaven-sent opportunity to 'run into' Barney. She had read of the accident, of Serena's death. She knew he was now in a wheelchair. Yet she had not wanted it to seem as if she were going to him out of pity. Besides, she was forty-four, no longer a lovesick girl but a successful designer and businesswoman. Whatever happened in the movies, it was unthinkable for her simply to contact Barney out of the blue. And yet ever since he had deposited her at the Adelphi Hotel following their extraordinary meeting at Laurel Bank, not a week had gone by when she hadn't thought of doing exactly that. She knew that secretly she had lived for the day when their paths would cross naturally but that day had never come.

Then she heard his voice. She craned her head but she could not see him. He was obviously in his wheelchair, low down. He didn't need a microphone. However else he might have suffered, his voice was still strong.

'I have been asked to read a few words by Henry Scott Holland that my mother-in-law first gave to me on the death of my guardian, Selwyn Reilly. They were of great comfort to me then and I have saved them to share with you now:

'Death is nothing at all. I have only slipped away into the next room. I am I and you are you: whatever we were to each other, that we are still. Call me by my old familiar name, speak to me in the easy way which you always used. Put no difference into your tone; wear no forced air of solemnity or sorrow. Laugh with me as we always laughed at the little jokes we enjoyed together. Play, smile, think of me, pray for me. Let my name be ever the household word that it always was. Let it be spoken without effort, without the ghost of a shadow on it. Life means all that it ever meant. It is the same as it ever was; there is absolutely unbroken continuity. What is this death but a negligible accident? I am but waiting for you, for an interval, somewhere very near just around the corner. All is well.'

As Saskia listened to his voice she realized she had to see him again. The service was drawing to a close. Soon he would be coming down the aisle. Saskia moved to the end of the pew. The church was packed. She couldn't see anything. She leaned out and looked up the aisle. The coffin was being slowly carried out by the pallbearers. Behind it she could see wheels – the wheels of Barney's chair – advancing towards her. The coffin passed her and the wheelchair came into sight.

His face shocked her. The face she remembered had been still quite young and unlined, healthy, smooth-cheeked, merry eyes full of hope and laughter. Now it was drawn and sad. The shock of blond hair had thinned and was tinged with grey at the temples. Yet the eyes were still there: alert, intelligent, kind – if only she could see him smile. She stood rigid, unable to move. She wanted him. She wanted to run to him and she had to force herself to stand still.

She looked above him and nearly screamed out loud. She was looking straight into the eyes of Nancy Sanders. Nancy was staring straight at her.

As Saskia stood, mesmerized, she saw Nancy mouth the words: 'He's mine. Go away. Go away. Go away.'

Saskia felt as if she were being hypnotized. Through the

tears that were now streaming down her face she recognized the girl with the long blonde hair who had been in her shop that morning. So she had been right in her guess. The resemblance to Barney was uncanny. This had to be his daughter.

'*Go away!*'

Nancy had said it out loud. The organ was thundering. Nobody could have heard except Saskia.

And Barney.

He had been looking down at his hands resting on the blanket spread over his knees but at the sound of Nancy's harsh voice, he looked up quickly. He caught a glimpse of an elfin face and a small figure dashing out of the last pew, running down the aisle ahead of him, slipping around the coffin and out of sight.

Barney knew who it was. He realized that Nancy had actually stopped the wheelchair and was waiting until Saskia had gone.

'Lulu . . .' He looked round frantically for his daughter. 'Lulu, get me out of here. Fast!' Lulu grabbed the handles of the wheelchair from her aunt. 'That's it, careful of the coffin. Over there, down the ramp, cross the road after that woman. Quick!'

They lost Saskia and Barney sat cursing and beating his useless legs.

'I've seen her before,' Lulu told him.

'Yes, of course you have, in the picture in my dressing room.'

'Yes, but somewhere else too. Why, Barney, why do you want to see her?'

'Because I love her, Lulu darling, and your grandmother did too.'

'But why did she run away?'

'If only I knew,' said Barney. 'If only I knew.'

I am but waiting for you – he whispered to himself the words he had just read out in church – *for an interval, somewhere very near just around the corner . . .*

But until you come back to me, Saskia, all is not well.

389

Thirty-One

Matthias slept for most of the drive through Germany and France until Karl woke him to board the ferry for Dover. It was only when they were on the final leg of their journey, within about an hour of London, that Matthias began to wonder what was in store for him. Karl had been curiously silent. He seemed suddenly rather disinterested in Matthias, giving monosyllabic answers whenever Matthias tried to engage him in conversation.

'Can we go round via the Tower of London and Buckingham Palace?' Matthias asked excitedly as they arrived on the outskirts of London.

'Plenty of time for that later,' snapped Karl. 'We're almost there.'

Almost where, wondered Matthias. Was Karl taking him straight to his father's? Surely he would have told him if he was. Anyway Karl didn't even know where Matthias' father lived, did he? The one thing Matthias was relieved about was that Karl had not once put his hand on Matthias' thigh as he often had during their visits to the cinema.

They drew up outside a block of flats.

'Where are we?' asked Matthias.

'Kennington.' Karl told him. 'South London,' he added, 'south of the river.'

'The river Thames?' asked Matthias.

Karl didn't reply.

Karl led him into a lift stinking of urine. Graffiti was scrawled on the walls all around them. On the top floor they left the lift and walked along a balcony past a line of front doors. At the end Karl stopped and rang the bell. The door was opened by an older man with pink cheeks and smooth skin like a baby. He was slightly bald but what hair he did have was white and fluffy like cotton wool. He was immaculately dressed in a button down denim shirt and rather tight blue jeans, an incongruous outfit for a man who had clearly celebrated his fiftieth birthday if not his sixtieth. The smile on his face was undeniably welcoming.

'Here he is then,' said Karl giving Matthias a little push through the front door. 'I'll be off now. '*Wiedersehen*.'

He was gone before Matthias could say anything. He raced after Karl but he was just in time to see Karl stepping into the lift and disappearing. He turned to find the older man right behind him.

'Come along now. Give us your bag. Back we go now, get to know each other. My name's Ronnie . . .'

It could have been a lot worse.

For the next few weeks that's all Matthias could think about. Brought to London, kidnapped almost, deposited with a total stranger.

'I owe you an explanation,' said Ronnie in very bad German, still smiling. 'No, that's not true, I don't owe you anything, but I want to explain why you're here. You have to understand one thing: I am not, repeat not, going to harm you or molest you in any way. That's a promise. See, you're surprised, aren't you? Thought I wanted you for your body. Well, that's quite true but you can rest assured, I've no intention of doing anything about it. Go on, eat up and I'll tell you a story.'

The first thing Ronnie had done was to cook Matthias a meal: steak and eggs followed by ice cream washed down by Coca-Cola, which Mutti had never allowed him.

Matthias looked at him suspiciously but said nothing. The man pushed back his chair and brought one foot up to rest on his thigh.

'My name's Ronnie and I'm English. I picked up my German here and there. I've got a bit of a gift for languages. Some people are born with it. For the last twenty-five years I've been a cab driver. Straight up! That means: I'm not kidding. Wife was a hairdresser, had her own salon. We've both done all right. No kids. Funny that, but it just didn't happen. So there I am, few years ago, coming up for fifty and I'm working all the time, day and night. We started up this cab service, see, me and some of my mates. CabCall. The customers just have to ring a number and you're on their doorstep. It was going like a dream, all over Central London. And the thing is, you get to know your regulars. Some blokes would have me booked every morning to take them to the office so every day there I am going: "How's the missus, how was that dinner you went to last night, how's your daughter?" – you get talking, you know how it is?'

He looked up at Matthias who was tucking into his steak. Matthias nodded. He hadn't a clue what the man was talking about but his instinct told him he'd better go along with it. Ronnie went on with his story.

'So there I am, I think I'm made for life and what do you think happens? Well, you'll never guess in a million years so I'll tell you. One of my regular blokes snuffs it and it turns out he's a poof, living all on his own, no family – no parents, no wife and kiddies, no brothers and sisters – and it also turns out he wasn't short of a bob or two. Why he took taxis I'll never understand. He had a Porsche and a Mercedes in his garage. I saw them. Well, I didn't get them, much as I'd have liked to. But I got a packet of money. Can you imagine? I often wondered what his solicitors must have thought when he put that in his will, leaving some of his money to a taxi driver.'

Matthias thought he'd better make some contribution to the conversation now he'd finished his food.

'What's a poof?'

'Well, talk about hitting the nail on the proverbial head. Sorry, I used the English slang there. It's a homosexual. A man who likes boys not girls.'

392

'So why did this . . . poof . . . leave you some money?'

'It took me a while to come to terms with it, but basically because underneath it all I'm one too and he must have understood that. I don't know how. I mean, I didn't know it myself at the time. I just thought I'd made a mistake about fancying the wife and was too lazy to look around for a bit on the side. He wrote me this letter, see, this bloke did. His solicitors gave it to me. It told me that I'd be able to live the life I wanted now I had his money. I could leave the wife and leave her well provided for and all. Then I could live the life I wanted. That's all it said. I was well foxed, I can tell you.'

Matthias was becoming intrigued.

'So what about your wife? Did you leave her like he told you to?'

'He didn't tell me to. He suggested it, subtle, like. But the thing is, in the end she left me. She's got the money, bought herself a nice big house and I'm still stuck here courtesy of the council. But he was right, was my benefactor, I have now got the life I wanted. Mind you, the neighbours are none too happy but providing I keep myself to myself they've done with going on about the wife leaving and my new life. To begin with I went abroad . . . to find boys and that. That's where I met your Karl. He was a bright lad, he knew what I wanted all right but he also knew that I was too scared to break the law too flagrantly. He made a suggestion to me. For a suitable fee he'd find me a young boy in Germany, get him a passport and bring him to stay with me in London for a while. I've had six now; you're the seventh. But you know what?'

Matthias was leaning forward right across the table, his face in his hands, mesmerized. Now he had entered the story himself he was slightly apprehensive but he had to know what was in store for him.

'I can't go through with it. I tried with the first lad Karl brought down but it's too late. I realized then that I was fantasizing and that's all I wanted to do. Dream away in my mind of what it would be like but never actually go through with it. I'm sure that's how a lot of men like me feel. We just

393

want to watch. What do they call us? Voyeurs? No, it's not that, I don't need to watch people at it. I just love to look at beautiful young boys and fantasize. No harm done, know what I mean?'

Matthias nodded. 'Like von Aschenbach in *Death in Venice*,' he said.

'Von who, when he's at home?'

'Never mind,' said Matthias, smiling, 'but what about Karl, does he understand what happens?'

'Oh, no. Karl thinks I get up to all sorts of tricks with you young boys. I've got my reputation to think of!' He winked at Matthias.

'Of course,' replied Matthias, entering into the spirit of things. 'Nothing will happen but it'll be our secret, is that it?'

'Precisely. You flaunt yourself all over the flat if Karl ever shows his face again.'

'And then I'll go back to Frankfurt?'

'Now, hold on a minute. Karl told me you wanted to come to England to stay. Said your dad was here or something and I was to help you find him. Providing you keep your mouth shut about me and my little ways . . .'

Matthias was speechless. It was as if someone had handed his dream on a plate and was now asking what he wanted for extras.

'I think,' he began breathlessly, 'to start with, it would be a great help if you could teach me English.'

Ronnie was a brilliant English teacher. Matthias picked up a vocabulary of East End rhyming slang mixed with quaint, subservient old-world English. Within a year he was bilingual.

Matthias liked Ronnie. He was the first person he'd met who was completely comfortable with himself. He had allowed his past to become his present and hang what the neighbours thought. He called Matthias a 'bloody Jerry' four or five times a day and didn't care what Matthias thought about it. Yet when Matthias told him all about his mother and Friedrich and Werner's suicide and how his real father was English, Ronnie listened carefully.

'Barney Lambert?' He screwed up his eyes trying to remember the details. 'I've heard of him. He paints pictures of toffs, women mostly. I think I picked him up once and dropped him off at the house, great big place on Holland Park. But you probably know all this.'

'I didn't know he was a painter,' murmured Matthias. 'Friedrich didn't mention that.'

'So what you going to do, then? March right up to the door and say: Hello, Dad, I'm your long lost son?'

'He wouldn't believe me and even if he did, the first thing he'd do is call up my mother and pack me straight home to Germany. I'm hoping she won't be able to have me traced straight off. They'll be looking for Matthias Mahrenhertz and I'm Matthew Lambert now with a British passport to prove it. No, I want to work in London for a while, find my feet . . . tell me about this taxi driving.'

'No way, my son. First you have to do the knowledge, go round London on a motorbike learning where every single street is, takes quite a while. Can you drive?'

Twenty-four hours later Ronnie realized he'd asked a stupid question. The boy was a natural and Ronnie wasted no time in organizing for him to take his driving test for which he was now old enough. He needed a few lessons to make sure he was used to driving on the correct side of the road and then Matthias passed the first time.

Ronnie had a plan. A bit of research revealed that Barney lived in the house of Sir Anthony Fakenham, his father-in-law, and that Sir Anthony hired his drivers from a particular agency on a regular basis. If Matthias were to join that agency, one day he stood a fair chance of being hired by Sir Anthony and, through him, getting closer to his father.

Eighteen months later Matthias climbed the steps leading up from Holland Park to Selwyn House aware that somewhere inside was the father he had never seen.

*

After Sarah's funeral Barney closeted himself in his study and wouldn't speak to anyone. Lulu was put on the train at Paddington which would take her back to school (and Kevin) by Nanny. Once she had left, Nanny had a blitz on her room at Selwyn House. Posters of The Stones and Simon and Garfunkel had replaced the Kate Greenaway prints and Nanny took them all down. When she saw the make-up scattered all over Lulu's dressing table she collected it into a plastic bag and deposited it in the rubbish bin.

'Whatever are you thinking of, letting a child her age wear make-up?' Nanny demanded of Barney.

'I'd no idea she did.' said Barney, worried.

With Lulu back at school, Nancy was more or less alone in the house with Barney. Nanny and Sir Anthony both retired early and with her mother gone, somehow Nancy felt braver. Barney was hers now to play with as she chose.

And she chose to seduce him.

He didn't actually lock his study door, she observed. He merely closed the door behind him and did not invite her in. Sometimes, as she paused on her way upstairs, she heard him snoring.

She picked a cold night and slipped in earlier to make sure a fire was blazing away, awaiting him after supper. Sir Anthony's cook, Mrs Walker, cooked for him too.

'Why they can't eat together now her Ladyship has gone is beyond me,' she complained frequently. 'I'm forever rushing up and downstairs with half a shepherd's pie for Sir Anthony and the other half for Mr Lambert. It's as well Mr Lambert dines half an hour later otherwise I don't know what I'd do. Will you be dining with your stepfather from now on, Miss Nancy?'

Since Barney wouldn't speak to her she hadn't much choice, reflected Nancy, but give it time. That night after taking a brandy with Sir Anthony she made her way to Barney's quarters. She turned the handle of Barney's study door as slowly as she could and slipped her head inside. He was asleep in front of the fire. Over on the far side of the room, his bed was turned down ready for him to heave himself out of the wheelchair and between the sheets. If he slipped, there was now a bell by the fireplace which rang in the flat above the garage to summon Sir Anthony's chauffeur.

Nancy stood before him, watching him. With his eyes closed his face was softer, younger, the fair eyelashes casting fine shadows on his cheekbones in the light of the leaping flames in the fireplace. She didn't turn on a lamp. She decided the light of the fire was rather romantic and highly appropriate.

She knelt before him between his legs which were splayed out at wide angles from the wheelchair. She ran her long red talons gently up and down the inside of his thighs. He shifted imperceptibly in his wheelchair but did not wake. She reached for the zipper on his crushed velvet trousers. He stirred a little as she pulled it down.

Nancy pulled Barney's penis out of his underpants and studied it. How wonderful that it had not been damaged in the accident. Had little sister Serena enjoyed it, she wondered? Had that Jewish cow Saskia ever . . .? Nancy fell on him and devoured him so that he woke with a start.

Looking down at the top of her sleek blonde head bobbing up and down at his crotch, Barney did something he had been wanting to do since he had first heard her telling the children in the churchyard that Saskia was Jewish: he took hold of a handful of her hair, pulled her head away and hit her hard in the face.

She fell away from him and lay sprawled across the rug for a moment but then she was back up on her knees and crawling towards him again, unbuttoning her blouse as she did so.

'Let me just show you what I can do . . .' she pleaded, her tongue out of her mouth and sliding lasciviously across her lips. 'Serena was just a child. I've been places, I know what you want, I . . .'

Barney had grabbed hold of the wheels and was backing away from her but she caught him and stopped the wheelchair. She climbed on top of him, pulled away the long silk foulard at his throat, pushed aside his brocade waistcoat, began unbuttoning his loose shirt and licking his nipples. To his horror, Barney felt himself becoming aroused. Taking hold of the wheels once again, he turned them as fast as he could so that he was propelled forward at full speed into the wall of books in front of him. Nancy, draped across him, took the full brunt of the collision. She was thrown off him and onto the floor once more. Barney seized his chance and reached out to press the bell by the fireplace. He kept his finger on it until she came at him like a tiger and tried to pull him out of his wheelchair. He fought her off and suddenly, before he knew what was happening, he was on his feet. She let go of him abruptly, expecting him to fall to the ground at her mercy.

For a second she was distracted by the sound of the door opening behind her and she turned. Barney began to walk towards her . . .

He was walking . . . walking . . . one, two, three steps . . . She had shocked him into action.

As Barney realized what had happened his legs collapsed under him and he fell to the ground.

The driver was new, he remembered. He'd only arrived the day after the funeral. They had not yet met. As Nancy fell on him on the floor and dangled her naked breasts a fraction of an inch above his nose, Barney desperately searched for the man's name that Sir Anthony had told him . . . The driver hovered in the doorway, embarrassed.

Barney, pinioned by Nancy, shouted to him: 'Come in, come in at once! Do you understand English? This is not what it looks like. Get this woman off me, or go and fetch Sir Anthony to do it for you.'

At this Nancy raised her head and spat at him. She climbed off him. The driver turned to leave.

'No!' cried Barney. 'Don't go. Help me back into my chair, then I want you to escort this woman off the premises. Get dressed, Nancy, and get out.'

'Well, you can look the other way for a start!' she hissed

at the driver who turned and faced the door.

'Nancy, you are to go upstairs and pack and then you are to leave this house and never return. Never!'

'Listen, you!' She advanced on him, her blouse buttoned, 'Aren't you forgetting something? This isn't your house. It was my mother's and –'

The driver surprised Barney. He came forward without being instructed and took hold of Nancy by the elbow. He marched her to the door without a word.

'No, it's not my house,' agreed Barney, 'I'm well aware of that. But it's not yours either. Now get out!'

The front door slammed behind Nancy for the last time twenty minutes later and the driver returned to wheel Barney's chair over to the bed. He bent forward as if to lift him out of the chair and suddenly Barney remembered his name.

'Don't worry, Matthew, I can manage. Not a word of this to Sir Anthony if you wouldn't mind. Goodnight . . . and thank you!'

As the young man left Barney stared after him. He had recognized him the minute he came in. He was a few years older than the last photograph Christiane had sent him but it was unmistakably Matthias. His own son. Later, as sleep eluded him, Barney wondered if his son had been aware of the miracle he had witnessed on his first meeting with his father.

'I can walk!' Barney said aloud in the darkness. 'I can walk again.'

Matthias climbed the stairs to his little flat above the garage. He didn't go back to bed. He knew he wouldn't be able to go back to sleep now that he had seen his father close to for the first time. He had only been in Sir Anthony's employ for two days and as it was the weekend, he hadn't expected to see Barney Lambert until he drove him to his studio on Monday. To see his own father for the first time grappling with a naked woman on the floor was hardly an auspicious introduction yet Matthias couldn't rid himself of the feeling that he had encountered Barney at a particularly important moment.

Barney Lambert knew who he was. Of that he was sure. Maybe nothing more need be said. Father and son were together and that was all that mattered.

'I gather Nancy's left us,' said Sir Anthony on Monday morning as the Bentley with which the Foreign Office provided him purred its way down the Mall.

Barney grunted. In the driver's seat, Matthias, in his new chauffeur's uniform, stared straight ahead. He dared not look in the rear-view mirror in case he caught Barney's eye.

'Gone back to America, has she?' enquired Sir Anthony.

Barney nodded towards the back of Matthias' head.

'Matthew, close the partition, there's a good lad,' called Sir Anthony. Matthias reached behind him and slid the window into place. 'Be frank with you, Barney, never liked her,' continued Sir Anthony. 'Thing is, I don't believe Sarah did either. Serena was always her favourite. But what I wanted to ask was what are we going to do about you now? With Nancy gone and Lulu away at school . . .'

Barney had worked out the answer to that before he fell asleep the night before.

'I might need the services from time to time of someone . . . someone who could lift things, help me in and out of my chair if need be, I rather thought . . .'

Again he inclined his head towards Matthias.

'Excellent idea. I'll have a word with him this evening.'

'What's his name? Matthew? Matthew who?'

'Well, heavens above, I never thought of it until now but he's called Matthew Lambert. No relation, of course. Ha ha!'

'And what nationality is he?'

'Well, now that you ask it's rather an odd name because he's German. Oh, he's got an English passport but my ear tells me that's a German accent he speaks with, somewhere in the north.'

'Not Frankfurt by any chance?'

'Oh, could easily be.'

'I see.' said Barney.

The next morning after they had dropped off Sir Anthony and were on their way to his studio, Barney reached for his cane and tapped on the partition. Matthias opened it.

'You wanted something, sir?'

'Did Sir Anthony have a word with you last night by any chance?'

'About giving you a hand now the young lady's left? Yes, sir, I'd be delighted, sir.'

'We've got a secret, you and I,' Barney told him and noted with satisfaction the boy's startled expression in the mirror. 'The other night . . . awkward business, best not to mention it.'

'Of course not, sir.'

'But that's not the secret.' Again the startled look. 'No, you saw something no one else knows about. You saw me walk for the first time since my accident over five years ago. That's what I want you to keep quiet about. And I want to ask you – will you help me with my exercises? I've booked a physiotherapist to come while no one else is around and I'd like you to take up where she leaves off so I'm walking properly as soon as possible. In a way I want you to help bring me back to life. What do you say?'

He was rewarded with the boy's broad smile as he touched a finger to his cap.

'Right you are, guv!' he said.

'Thank you, my son,' whispered Barney to himself.

That night he telephoned Frankfurt.

'Christiane, I think it's time you came to London. He's here. Matthias is right here working for me. I suspect he's chosen to work here deliberately. He's a fine boy. A fine young man, I should say. We haven't acknowledged to each other who we are, not yet. I'd like you there when we do. And he's not the only missing person who's turned up. It's going to be quite a family reunion for you. I've seen Saskia . . .'

Thirty-Two

JEWISH REFUGEE MAKES IT BIG IN SWINGING SIXTIES.

Saskia winced. They really had laid it on a bit thick. It was all there: her escape from Berlin, her separation from her parents, her evacuee life in Lancashire during the war, her departure to New York and her return to build a thriving business with her fashionable King's Road shop. It was exactly the kind of success story the press loved. They had compared her to Mary Quant and Barbara Hulanicki. She hadn't meant to talk quite so much about her past, her background, but the girl had sat there smiling, coaxing the story out of her, just as she was paid to do, Saskia reflected.

The photos of her were good. In her habitual black polo neck and mini-kilt, they had snapped her climbing out of her psychedelic Mini, walking into her shop and standing behind the glass table. Would Barney see these? There was no use kidding herself: she had agreed to the profile in a major national newspaper in the hope that Barney would read it and come and find her at the shop.

'What about the love life?' Saskia recalled the girl had asked but there Saskia had drawn the line. After all she hadn't actually been married to Sal. Even so, the girl had managed to dig out a few shots of her with various men about town. As Saskia looked at them she had to stop and think for a minute to try and remember the times she had been out with these men. Their names were often well known and she was definitely the woman in the photographs but these 'dates' had been one-offs, nights out arranged by well-meaning friends. She knew it made them uncomfortable to see an attractive woman in her forties on her own however much she might claim to be preoccupied with her work.

Then Saskia read something which made her want to vomit: *Saskia's parents, deported to a concentration camp, were victims of the Holocaust. Saskia wipes a tear away from her eye as she tells me: 'If only my parents could see me now . . .'*

How could they put something like that? She had never said her parents were in a concentration camp. She had not cried during the interview. They had made it all up for a better story. She pushed the paper aside and climbed down from the high Habitat stool by the cash register. Soon it would be time to close for the day. The music from Natalie's latest tape pounded in her ears. Natalie had been playing the same compilation all day – only it wasn't much of a compilation: just two songs – 'Light my Fire' by The Doors and 'Somebody to Love' by Jefferson Airplane. Natalie was obsessed with The Doors and lately with what she told Saskia was the new West Coast sound that had hit London, acid music. Everybody longed to be in San Francisco with flowers in their hair and the big question was whether or not you had taken your first 'trip'. The shop reeked of joss sticks and incense dabbed on the top of hot electric light bulbs. Natalie had draped Indian silk scarves over every lampshade she could find regardless of whether or not they became singed.

Natalie! Saskia wandered wearily into the stockroom and sniffed the all too familiar smell of Acapulco Gold.

'Natalie, I've told you before. Not at the shop!'

'Oh, c'mon, man. It's fantastic stuff. Have some, Saskia. You gotta hang loose.'

Natalie was sitting on the floor in a long flowing caftan nipped in on her top half by a purple brocade waistcoat worn over it. A long Indian scarf was wound several times round her neck and tied at the side. Bangles jangled and beneath her wiry black hair, which seemed to spring away from her head at all angles, she wore large gypsy earrings. Natalie was into flower power with a vengeance but she was also invaluable to Saskia in that she minded the shop single-handed leaving Saskia free to design upstairs for most of the day.

'I'm hanging loose as anything,' said Saskia squatting on the floor beside Natalie and putting an arm around her shoulders. 'Here, have you seen this? Have you ever read such rubbish?'

Natalie grabbed the paper from her.

'Hey, Saskia, far out. They wrote a piece about you. That's really groovy. Or is it about you? These pictures are all you, but who's the Jewish refugee?'

'Who do you think?'

'You're Jewish? You never told me.'

'Well, why should I? It's not something you go around telling everyone the minute you meet them.'

'Well, Leon's Jewish.' Leon was Natalie's lover of four months.

'It had crossed my mind that he might be with a name like Leon Finkelstein,' laughed Saskia. 'Is it important to you that Leon's Jewish?'

'Yes. No. Oh, not particularly. I couldn't care less either way but it's important to Dad. He's anti-Semitic. He more or less forced me to get engaged to this boy called Archie when I was eighteen: blond hair, blue eyes, Eton, Oxford, the Blues. Dad thought he was perfect and I thought I did too. I mean, here was this perfect Adonis being presented to me as a husband, how could I say no? But it didn't work out. I just felt strange around him all the time, as if I didn't belong with him. So we broke it off. Dad was furious. I've seen a few guys but none of them blew my mind until I met Leon. Yet Dad won't even meet him. I'm going to be twenty-one next month and Mum and Dad are giving me this big party. It's going to be a real bummer if Leon can't come. Saskia, would you come to the party with him? Of course you'll be asked to the party. You're my employer. In their eyes you're respectable. Oh, I don't mean I think you're straight. I think you're really groovy. But if Leon came with you and if they know you're Jewish and he's with you . . . oh, do you see what I'm trying to say?'

'If you really think so. Do you know why your father is so against Jewish people? I'm not sure I want to volunteer to be exposed to an anti-Semite.'

'Oh, he's not that bad, honestly! It's just where I'm concerned and my older brother and sister. Ever since I can remember he's had this fear that we would get involved with Jewish people. We've always been aware of it. We used to tease him about it but it's not a joke any more. Oh, please. Saskia, please say you'll come with Leon.'

'Of course I will, if you really want me to.' Saskia knew she could never refuse Natalie anything. She was young, she was lively and fun and she was someone through whom Saskia was able to relive her life as she might have wanted to live it if she'd had the chance.

'Oh, thanks!' Natalie leapt up and hugged her employer. 'But Saskia, this stuff about your parents – I'm really sorry. I never knew . . .'

'How could you when I don't even know if it's true either?'

'What do you mean?'

'I just don't know what became of my parents. I can't go back to Berlin. I'm completely cut off. They sent me away when I was sixteen.'

'Haven't you, you know, tried to find them, write letters, things like that?'

'I've thought about it. I know there are people, organizations who would help me but the thing is I can't bring myself to start. I'm so terrified of what I might find out. I can't face up to it. I'd rather just go on blindly hoping they'll try and find me if they're alive. I've even stopped trying to find my sister.'

'Your sister! You have a sister?'

Saskia told Natalie about Christiane. 'I did try and find her. I wrote to our old address but my letters were returned. Now I'm just going to wait. What will be will be. Anyway, enough of this gloomy talk about me. What are you going to wear for your party? Have you decided yet?'

A month later Saskia found herself dressing for Natalie's twenty-first, unsure what to wear for the first time in a long while. She knew her figure was still slender enough for her to wear girlish clothes and she kept her skirts as short as those worn by the young girls who were her customers, but this would be a chic affair and she knew she must not let Natalie down. Finally she selected one of her own designs: a black crepe dress that fell away beneath the bust in a wide swirl to end three inches above her knee. But it had long tight sleeves and a soft round neck and was somehow demure. There was no grey yet in her newly bobbed black hair over which she wore a black sequinned cloche. She tossed long black ostrich feathers around her neck and let them trail down her back, selected opaque black tights and little black patent flatties.

The doorbell rang downstairs.

Leon stood there in skin-tight crushed velvet which left very little to the imagination around the crotch area.

'Good evening, Miss Kessler,' he said politely.

'Oh, Saskia, please,' said Saskia. 'Miss Kessler makes me feel like I'm 103!'

He grinned and she noticed his face completely changed. When he smiled colour seemed to flood into his normally pallid skin and she saw why Natalie had fallen for him.

'Okay, Saskia, that's cool. Shall we get a cab in the King's Road or walk?'

In the cab he asked nervously: 'Have you been to their pad before? Her parents' place, I mean . . .'

Saskia shook her head. 'It'll be fine,' she told him.

It wasn't fine. The minute the cab drew up outside a building in Eaton Square Saskia knew they had made a mistake. Through the window they could see men in black tie and women in elegant cocktail dresses.

Saskia hooked her arm through Leon's elbow and together they marched into the room. To Saskia's

406

amazement, Natalie had abandoned her hippy caftan clothes for a little pink chiffon number. Her wiry hair had been scraped into a knot at the back of her head and in her ears and at her throat were pearls.

Pearls! Natalie in pearls. Saskia couldn't believe it.

A tall blonde woman, very thin, with haughty facial bone structure came to greet them.

'I'm Annabel Rivers. You must be . . .?'

'I'm Saskia Kessler and this is Leon Finkelstein.'

The whole room had gone silent. A waiter hovered at Saskia's elbow proffering a silver salver bearing glasses of champagne. Saskia took one, handed it to Leon with a smile but Annabel Rivers ignored him.

'Miss Kessler, we've heard so much about you. Natalie never stops talking about the shop and of course we've read about you in the newspaper. So exciting! Such fun! My husband can't wait to meet you . . .'

She steered Saskia away and it seemed as if she was deliberately leaving Leon standing on his own in the middle of the room. Out of the corner of her eye Saskia saw Natalie rush over to him and fling her arms around his neck. Annabel paused for a split second and raised her eyes to heaven. Saskia looked in amazement at the young people in the room. Here and there she recognized a familiar face as she saw one of Natalie's friends who frequented the shop but, like Natalie, they were disguised in frigid little cocktail dresses and restricting suits and ties instead of the free-flowing Indian and Moroccan clothes they usually wore.

'Has Natalie told you about my husband?' Annabel was saying, 'About how he was injured during the war?'

'No,' said Saskia, puzzled. Annabel didn't seem like a woman prone to imparting confidences so early on.

'You see, he was rather badly burned and they did quite a lot of plastic surgery. The skin is a bit tight in places, shiny. I wouldn't want you to get a shock. Of course, he looks marvellous but people have reacted rather badly occasionally when they meet him for the first time and as we don't really know you . . .'

The way she said it made Saskia cringe. 'We don't really know you' was a euphemism for 'You're not our kind so please don't let the side down by freaking out in an emotional Jewish way when you meet my scarred and tragic husband . . .' Or was she overreacting?

As they reached the man by the fireplace Annabel was called away.

'Darling,' she said as she tapped him on the back before moving away, 'I've got to dash, The Pilkingtons have arrived. This is Miss Kessler, Natalie's employer . . .'

The way she said 'employer', it could have been servant.

Then Saskia almost went into shock.

Natalie's father turned and, ignoring her outstretched hand, he gripped her by the shoulders and drew her to him. He placed his lips tenderly on her cheek, high up and she felt his breath in her ear. She noticed the skin pulled tightly over his bones.

He released her and stepped back.

'Sorry, Saskia,' He looked around quickly, 'I just couldn't help it, it's been so long. I don't think anyone saw us.'

The voice was very familiar yet she couldn't place it.

'Don't you know who I am?' he asked.

'Oh, yes, Natalie's father. Mr Rivers.'

'Not Mr Rivers. Especially not even mister to you. When you last saw me I was a Flight Lieutenant. I'm Jonathan, Saskia, Jonathan Rivers.'

If I didn't know she was my sister, Matthias thought to himself for the umpteenth time as he pushed Barney's leg back and forth, I wouldn't give a toss what she did. If Barney Lambert weren't my father and his daughter weren't my half-sister, I wouldn't give a damn.

He was at Barney's studio helping him go through his daily exercises. Barney had had Matthias sit in on several sessions with the physiotherapist who had then instructed Matthias how he could help Barney in his complete rehabilitation in learning to walk again. Once a week Matthias took Barney to Chelsea Baths and helped him with his hydrotherapy in the swimming pool but every day they went through the same routine at the studio, away from the curious eyes of Mrs Walker and Nanny. Barney wanted his walking to be a surprise to everyone at Selwyn House.

To begin with, Matthias would move his legs passively for him while he lay on his back, picking them up and putting them down, bending his hips, bending his knees, stretching his ankles. Then Barney would resist movement, pushing his foot away, lifting his leg himself and trying to straighten it. There were endless exercises all done at first with gentle resistance since he fatigued very quickly, but gradually he began to build up his muscles.

The great day had come when parallel bars had been installed at the studio and a floor-to-ceiling mirror. With Matthias close at hand, Barney began to walk between the bars, watching himself closely in the mirror, bringing one leg forward, then the other. The next step had been crutches and now he could actually stagger about unaided.

And all the time Lulu was running wild all over London.

She had been expelled from St Cecilia's – not for snogging with Kevin who had in fact tired of her once he realized he wasn't going to get his evil way with her – but for reading *Valley of the Dolls* all through prep three nights running, and for calling Miss Tewksbury a frustrated old cow when she tried to take the book away.

Now the old 'school run' had been reinstated. Matthias drove Sir Anthony to Pall Mall, then doubled back to Queen's Gate to drop Lulu off at the secretarial college at which she'd been installed, before going on to Edith Grove and Barney's studio. Until one morning when Barney had sent him straight back to the secretarial college because Lulu had left her notebooks in the back of the car.

They knew nothing about Lulu's whereabouts at the college. They recalled she had indeed been registered once at the beginning of term but only a week later they had received a letter cancelling her tuition, saying she was going abroad. As they had already received a cheque in advance for the whole term, they had not thought it necessary to contact Mr Lambert.

Matthias decided not to tell Barney but the next morning after he had dropped him off at the studio he returned as fast as he could in the direction of Queen's Gate in time to see Lulu striding down Old Church Street. She turned left into the King's Road, walked along it, past Chelsea Town Hall and stopped for a coffee at the Picasso. Matthias drove around the block a few times and caught her coming out again about fifteen minutes later. He followed her to Shawfield Street and watched her walk into Shawfield House. She did not reappear for the rest of the day.

Matthias embarked upon a bit of research and discovered that Shawfield House was the headquarters of a company called Cammell, Hudson and Brownjohn who made commercials. Lulu, they told him, was a fresh young model who had come by one day without even a portfolio to show them, but a photographer who had been working in the studio across the courtyard that day had been so impressed by her mass of blonde hair and long legs, not to mention her upturned nose and wide apart brown eyes, that he had amused himself by taking a few shots of her. Since then she had worked regularly for them. No, they didn't know her last name, they just booked her as Lulu. She was over in hair and make-up right now if he wanted to see her . . .

Then there were the evenings. Barney asked Matthias if he wouldn't mind ferrying Lulu to parties at the houses of her young friends and picking her up again around eleven. After all she was only just sixteen.

The first time he had held the door open for her to step into the rear of the car but she had brushed it aside.

'Oh, no, let me sit up front with you. Much more fun.'

She was dressed in a skimpy bit of nothing barely covering her behind and great big thick-heeled shoes. She had painted little silver stars all over her cheeks and pointed eyelashes below her lower eyelid. On top she wore two layers of false eyelashes.

410

'You're going to the Hutchinsons, that right, miss? Walton Street.'

'Well, yes, officially. As far as Daddy's concerned I am but if you don't mind I'd like to go to some other friends near Sloane Square. I'm not going to the Hutchinsons' party. It'll be such a drag. I'm meeting my friends and then we're going on to Sibylla's. You needn't wait. Want some?'

She had pulled out a small rectangle of black hash and a packet of red Rizzlas and was expertly rolling a joint. Soon the sweet pungent smell was wafting all over Sir Anthony's car. Matthias wound down the window to let in some air and then wound it up again as they passed a policeman.

She went out every night and she wouldn't tell him where to pick her up. The occupants of Selwyn House retired early but Matthias stayed up each night, watching from the mews flat till he saw her creep in through the kitchen door, often as late as one or two in the morning. She was young enough to be fresh again the next morning – not for shorthand and typing lessons but to face the cameras without bags under her eyes.

One night she wasn't home by three and Matthias began to worry. He slipped on his leather jacket and opened the garage doors. The Bentley glided silently out. He parked at the end of Swallow Street off Piccadilly and walked to Sibylla's. They wouldn't let him in, didn't know him, knew he wasn't a member.

'Lulu!' he cried in desperation. 'Is Lulu still here?'

It said something about Lulu's growing reputation as part of the London scene that they asked: 'Which Lulu? The singer or the model? They was both here tonight.'

'The model.'

'She left an hour ago.'

'Who with?'

'One of the Pink Flamingoes.'

'What's that?'

'Oh, stone the crows. They're a bloody group. Didn't you see them on *Top of the Pops* this week?'

'So where would they have gone?'

411

'Dunno, mate. Think they're staying at The Alderney in Knightsbridge.'

Matthias was gone, leaping into the Bentley and driving back to Cadogan Square as fast as he could. He marched up to reception and demanded to know which suite the Pink Flamingoes were staying in. When they refused to tell him he shouted: 'They've got my sister up there, she's under age and if you don't let me go up there right now I'm going to ring the police and . . .'

'Fifth floor, sir, 524 and 525. Lift's over there. Will you require any assistance . . .?'

Matthias was already on his way across the foyer as the receptionist motioned for the bellhop to follow him, giving him the pass key. 'Make sure there's no trouble. We don't want the press getting hold of this.'

The Pink Flamingoes were into Dexies in a big way. With the help of Dexedrine they only had to go to bed to sleep every three days. There were five of them and that night they were all on Dexies except for Marty, the rhythm guitarist who had dropped a tab of acid and was tripping in the corridor outside the lifts thinking he was in the Sahara. He was stark naked and convinced he was riding a camel. Or maybe he was a camel. He leapt from side to side, reaching behind him searching for his hump as Matthias came out of the lift.

The door to Suite 524 was open and Matthias walked right in. Clothes were strewn all over the sitting room. On the coffee table empty bottles of Scotch lay overturned amidst still-burning roaches. Matthias turned and quickly slipped the bellhop a tenner, sending him on his way. If Lulu was mixed up in this there was no need for anyone else to witness it.

There were eleven people in action on the king-size bed in the master bedroom. Matthias was so taken aback he actually stood and counted them. He found he could also identify three Pink Flamingo dicks plunged into three female orifices, two further male organs disappearing into two sets of Pink Flamingo buttocks while two girls were entwined with each other's naked bodies.

Lulu wasn't there.

Matthias felt nauseated. He made his way into the adjacent bathroom thinking he might throw up and there, crouched shivering on the tiled floor beside the lavatory, was Lulu. She was crying, hugging her knees, rocking back and forth on her haunches.

They couldn't find her clothes. In the end Matthias removed one of the hotel's towelling robes from behind the bathroom door and made her put it on. He got her out of the suite and down in the lift as quickly as he could. The doorman looked away tactfully as he shepherded her into the Bentley. On the way home to Holland Park he quizzed her.

'What happened? How many of them touched you? Did any one . . .? What happened?'

Lulu wouldn't answer.

She never told him what happened but he figured she must have received a hell of a shock since she stopped going out in the evening. Yet every night he saw a light burning in her window till late. He would wake up at four or five in the morning and it would still be on. And he noticed that she was losing weight rapidly. Her eyes were out on stalks every day and she kept bursting into tears. Matthias had been around London long enough to know all the signs.

Lulu was hooked on speed.

Barney had it all planned. He would arrive at Saskia's shop just before lunch, wander in casually, look around and then ask her to lunch.

When he had seen her profile in the newspaper he had still been on crutches. Knowing where he could reach her had spurred him on in his rehabilitation programme. He could now walk easily from a car into a house and back again, up steps and stairs and he could also stand for up to twenty minutes at a time without feeling tired. He planned to surprise Saskia with a triumphant entrance to her shop that would obliterate the humiliating moment when she had witnessed his pathetic progress in a wheelchair down the aisle at Sarah's funeral.

Over lunch – the table was already booked at Mario and Franco's 'trattoo' off Kensington High Street – he would talk about Lulu and gradually get around to telling her about Christiane and his relationship with her – and finally he would let her into the secret about Matthias. It would be the first of many lunches and dinners and when Christiane came over there would be a wonderful family reunion between the two sisters, the mother and her son and Lulu's introduction to him as her half-brother.

He also had a perfectly valid reason for going to Saskia's shop. Lulu had asked for one of Saskia's dresses as a birthday present. She had warned Barney that they were expensive but worth every penny. She had described to him in detail the one she wanted and just to make sure she had pointed it out to Matthias.

'What do you make of my daughter?' Barney asked Matthias unexpectedly as he was being driven to Saskia's shop. Barney had elected to sit up front beside Matthias, which had made Matthias decidedly nervous.

'Very pretty, sir.'

'Oh, I don't mean that. Of course she's pretty but do you think she's all right, since she left school, I mean?'

Matthias glanced at him from under the peak of his cap. It would be risky to tell the truth but the man was his father. It might bring them closer together. He decided it was a risk worth taking.

'She's in a terrible state, sir, to tell you the truth. I've been wondering whether I should say something, didn't know if it was my place . . .'

'Go on, Matthew, spit it out.'

Once he'd heard everything, Barney was silent for a long time. He was appalled at what Matthias had told him. He had been so proud of himself for taking Matthias into the house and drawing him into his life. Slowly but surely they were getting to know each other in a perfectly natural way. Barney was convinced Matthias knew exactly who he was.

In a way it could be regarded as a charade on both sides, but in another way it gave them a chance to adjust to the shock of meeting each other. Barney was conscious of the similarity between his adoption of Matthias and Selwyn's guardianship of himself during the war. But Barney had spent so much time concentrating on Matthias he had lost sight of Lulu. Had Selwyn at one time favoured him and lost sight of Saskia?

'Thank you for telling me all this, Matthew. I can't tell you how much I appreciate what you've done for her. I regard you as part of the family, you know that, don't you? From now things will be different. Even now I'm on my way today to do far more than buy Lulu's birthday present. I'm going to reorganize all our lives. You'll see, yours too. You'll see!'

Oh God, thought Matthias, *what is he up to?*

They drove along the King's Road and turned left into the street that led to Saskia's shop.

'It's on the end here, sir, on the corner.'

There she was!

'Stop, Matthew! Stop the car. Pull over.'

Saskia had come out of the shop and was waiting on the pavement for someone inside to join her. As the man came out, she nestled close to him and put her arm through his elbow. She was so small that even in her high-heeled boots her head barely reached his shoulder. Arm in arm, they set off together along the street towards the Bentley.

Barney stared at the man. He was so familiar. In a flash he remembered where he'd last seen him, how they had been told by Smudger that he was 'missing, believed killed'. As it turned out he had just been missing and now it seemed that Saskia had once again found her wartime lover, Jonathan Rivers.

Barney ducked his head so they wouldn't see him as they went right past him.

'Take me home, Matthew. Take me home at once. I've been a bloody fool!'

415

Thirty-Three

She hadn't seen him for over twenty years, she hadn't even recognized his face at first, but Saskia was amazed at how quickly she remembered his body.

It was fair to say that she had been without a man for so long she would no doubt have welcomed anybody with enough persistence to break down the barriers she had unconsciously erected around her. After Natalie's party she had not expected to hear from him but the next day Natalie had turned up for work at the shop with a large bunch of flowers.

'For you, Saskia, for saying whatever it was you said to Dad.'

Saskia blushed. 'I didn't say anything to him – well, not about you and Leon anyway. It just didn't seem right,' she added guiltily.

'It doesn't matter. Whatever you said has made him fall in love with you.' Natalie was expansive in her innocence of the situation. 'He said to tell you he would be here at a quarter to one to take you to lunch and when I told him I wouldn't be going to the house in the South of France this summer with him and Mum, that I was going away with Leon instead, he barely turned a hair and I've been fretting all this time about telling him. I thought he'd create no end, but he just said, "Oh, are you?" and then he goes on to talk about you. You've worked wonders, Saskia, believe me.'

It had all been so simple. He had arrived at the shop, given Natalie a peck on the cheek, joined Saskia on the pavement outside and slipped his arm through hers as if they met every day. As they had walked off down the street arm in arm she had not noticed Barney sitting silently watching her from his car.

Jonathan Rivers might have implied that he would not be going back to his wife after the war when he and Saskia had met that last afternoon near Laurel Bank but at the time he had not known he would be so badly injured. When they had finally discharged him from Stoke Manderville, he had gone home to Annabel and his two children. Then Natalie had been born soon after the war and he had more or less resigned himself to stay with Annabel. The chief deciding factor had been her money. Annabel had promoted the perfect role for him to play – that of war hero – and if she would no longer allow his scarred body into her bed she was more than happy to play the war hero's wife throughout Belgravia, Chelsea and the grander country houses of the land. In fact, Jonathan's body had not been badly burned at all. It was only his face that required surgery, but Annabel only needed the flimsiest of excuses. Jonathan's main problem was that having been invalided out of the Air Force, he wasn't really trained for anything else so he elected to live off Annabel's money and dabble on the stock market. Women, inevitably, became an almost immediate diversion.

After that first lunch they had driven out of London in Saskia's Mini Cooper to a quiet country inn in Buckinghamshire. More than a little drunk she had wriggled out of her hipsters and fallen spreadeagled on the bed. To begin with she was dry, unused to having sex and his penis hurt her as he entered her. He wasn't gentle and she cried out in pain, which only seemed to spur him on. Then it began to come back to her – the smell of him, the width of his naked shoulders hovering above her, the way his head ducked down as he closed his mouth over her nipple – it was all familiar. She began to respond, to touch him, to run her hands up and down his long back. Only when she touched the smooth tissue of his cheek did he pull away.

417

'It's all right,' she whispered. 'I don't mind.'

'Sure, but I do,' he said gruffly. 'I don't like being reminded.'

They met frequently, mostly at her flat above the shop, which Saskia had now had changed to resemble the semi-Bauhaus designs of Klara and Hermann's Zehlendorf apartment. She had done it partly in memory of her parents and her childhood and partly to impress Barney if he ever came there. She had often spent an evening sitting in her kitchen imagining Barney's admiring reaction when he first saw it, how they would spend the evening discussing what Selwyn would have made of it, laughing and reminiscing about their life at Laurel Bank and then wending their way upstairs to her bedroom to pick up where they had left off . . .

Never for one moment had she dreamed that it would be another person from her past whose memories would be revived and now here she was, the Other Woman, plunged into an affair with a married man. Saskia asked Jonathan to steer clear of the shop during working hours. It wouldn't be fair on Natalie if they involved her in their secret, so Jonathan came round as often as he could in the evenings and Saskia cooked for him before they went to bed. But lately they had become more adventurous and had taken to going out to restaurants, small Chelsea bistros with red-and-white checked tablecloths and candles stuck in empty wine bottles with the hot wax dropping onto the table and the menu scrawled illegibly on a blackboard.

Until Saskia's birthday loomed on the horizon.

'I'm going to take you somewhere special. I'm going to take you to Mr Chow's and if anyone sees us, to hell with it, I can just pretend I'm talking to you about putting money into the shop.'

Nor was he content with a discreet table on the ground floor but insisted they negotiate the spiral staircase and join the celebrities to be found upstairs. Saskia was relieved when the maître d' directed her to a corner table at the side away from the raucous gatherings at the round tables in the centre of the restaurant.

The meal began quietly enough with her favourite dishes of seaweed and squab wrapped in large leaves of crisp cos lettuce. Jonathan ordered a bottle of champagne and toasted her.

'To the woman who introduced me to my own daughter . . .'

For an instant Saskia froze. She had decided some time ago that there would be nothing to be gained by telling him about little Klara. Part of her was repelled by the way he had hidden the fact that he was half-Jewish to Natalie. If he denied such an important part of himself how could he have ever been a good father to little Klara? Yet for all her frustration at his parental restrictions, Natalie loved her father, that much was clear to Saskia. She relaxed. 'My own daughter . . .' He was referring to Natalie.

'I should be toasting you,' she told him, 'for bringing Natalie into the world. If she didn't exist I don't know how I'd manage the shop. And I'm so pleased you've come round to Leon. He's a terrific young man. Even if he is Jewish . . .' she added, teasing him.

A slight frown flickered across Jonathan's face. Saskia ignored the warning.

'I couldn't believe it when Natalie told me you were worried about him being Jewish. You, of all people!'

'What do you mean, me of all people?'

'Well, you're like me of all people, you're Jewish yourself.'

She couldn't believe it. He turned his head quickly from side to side to see if anyone was listening. Saskia didn't know if it was the champagne making her bold but she knew she couldn't let it rest no matter how much it might spoil the evening.

'Why have you never told her, Jonathan?'

'What's to tell?' He picked at his seaweed sullenly. She noticed he was not particularly adept at handling chopsticks and most of the seaweed was landing on the tablecloth.

'It's how we first met. Don't you remember? Nancy Sanders was attacking me for being Jewish and you came to my defence.'

'Did I?'

'You stepped in and said you were Jewish too. I'll never forget it.'

'Well, I wish you would. It's not remotely important except for the fact that I met you. Anyway, you're Italian now if your incredible story of what you've been up to since I last saw you is to be believed.'

'I'm not in the slightest Italian. I only pretended to be in order to stay in America. I had to. I was a displaced person. Have you any idea what it's like to be without a country of your own? Sal's family took me in and I was proud to make every attempt I could to fit in with their way of life but that never stopped me being Jewish. Every Friday night I brought in the Sabbath, I said the blessing . . .'

'What blessing's that? As for the wretched Sabbath, you're happy to work on the Sabbath now, aren't you? Can't stand to think of all that retail business going to waste. Proper little Jewish shopkeeper you've become.'

Saskia stared at him. He was actually smiling.

'You haven't answered my question. Why have you kept it from Natalie that she has a Jewish grandfather, a Jewish father . . .?'

'Half-Jewish.'

'Oh, so you admit it. But why have you been hiding it?'

'You wouldn't understand.'

'Oh, don't be so patronizing, Jonathan. What wouldn't I understand?'

'I'm not a refugee like you. I'm Anglo-Jewish. We keep a lower profile altogether. My family is assimilated into English society —'

'English society? What do you mean, English society? I'm part of English society now, I'm a shopkeeper as you so rightly pointed out and as someone once said, "England is a nation of shopkeepers". You don't by any chance mean English high society, do you? Think of yourself as part of the English upper classes and all that?'

'Well, what if I do? It doesn't actually hurt anyone if they're not aware that I have any Jewish blood. And if they

420

knew, I can't explain, I'd have a terrible sense of inferiority, there'd be clubs I couldn't join. Whatever you might think, Saskia, if they know you're Jewish they feel you're "not one of us", that you lack class and breeding. I saw what they did to a chap at school, called him a "Jew boy" all the time, singled him out for bullying . . .'

'All you're telling me is something I know already: that the English are snobs. Well, do you know what, Jonathan? I rather think you're a snob too. Now I suppose you'll tell me it's because you're so upper class. Well, if you are, what are you doing out with a jumped-up little Jewish shopkeeper like me?'

The waiters were rustling round them, clearing away the seaweed and the squab and setting a large dish of duck before them. Saskia busied herself with filling a flimsy little pancake, piling high the shredded duck, the diced cucumber and other bits and pieces, topping the whole lot with a dollop of plum sauce. Expertly, she rolled the pancake into a long and manageable parcel and took a bite off the end.

'You know what I'm doing with you. We're good together.'

'Good together as what? Lovers? Sexual partners?'

'Of course. You love it with me. You're not going to deny that now, are you? I might as well ask you what you're doing with a failed Jew boy like me?'

'Oh, don't call yourself that. I admit I see you because it's good with you, but I also know that inside you feel Jewish whatever you say. It's easy to *be* Jewish. Anyone can inherit being a member of the Jewish race. But to *feel* it is different. You told me once that you felt Jewish and the Jew in you, Jonathan, responded to my plight in the churchyard all those years ago.'

Now it was his turn to fill his pancake. He took his time. He ate two before he replied.

'Okay, so maybe you're right but I'm not going to change my ways now. The world knows me as a Gentile and that's how I'm going to stay.'

'Bully for you, goy boy!'

'That's enough, Saskia, I'm warning you –'

'Warning me? What about? What will you do if I go on? Denounce me to the rest of the restaurant as a Yiddishe momma who can't behave herself.'

'Why do you say momma? You're not pregnant, are you?'

'Jonathan, I'm forty-five today. Anyway, what would it matter if I were?' she added slyly, glancing up at him from underneath a layer of false eyelashes. 'Couldn't stand by me, could you? Couldn't leave Annabel and all that luxury? Don't worry, I'm not asking you to. You know something, Jonathan? I've just realized that when we're not in bed together you bore me. You're a hundred per cent predictable. I don't think I can even be bothered to reprimand you any more on your shortcomings as a Jewish man, let alone a Jewish father, although I'd like to see Annabel's face if I were to tell her. But I won't. It's funny, I don't get much satisfaction out of that sort of thing. I've behaved childishly enough as it is tonight. But there's one thing I do want you to promise me.'

'Oh, Saskia, for God's sake, what is all this . . .?'

'I want you to make Natalie and Leon feel as comfortable as possible in your home. I never want to hear from Natalie that Leon hasn't been accepted as one of the family and if they do decide to take their relationship further, then I insist you tell Natalie about her own Jewish blood. You're a weak man, Jonathan. Oh, you were brave in the war but then so were a lot of men and women. It's those who faced up to their lives after the war who are the real survivors. Physically, you're as alive as the next man, especially in bed, but as far as I can make out – and believe me, this is not my idea of the perfect birthday – in all other respects you're dead. I don't know what I ever saw in you.'

Saskia stood up abruptly.

'Can I have my coat, please?' she asked the waiter.

'No stay for banana fritters, madam?'

'You can put some in a doggy bag for me. I'll eat them in front of the television. Please could you have them ready for me at the door downstairs when I leave?'

'Saskia, sit down. People are watching.'

'Oh, how terrible. Am I causing a scene? I've always wanted to cause a scene. So un-English. So alien. Is there anyone here who knows you? Come on, Jonathan, get up. Be a gent. You can at least kiss me goodnight on my birthday.'

He stayed in his chair, fists clenched under the table.

Saskia blew him a kiss and left.

At the top of the spiral staircase she felt a hand grab hold of her arm. Jonathan had come after her.

'Saskia, please,' he hissed, 'I think I love you. I want you. Please come back to the table.'

'Why are you whispering?' She wrenched her arm free and ran nimbly down the staircase. As she reached the bottom step and held out her hand to take her carton of banana fritters, she heard the entire restaurant gasp. Jonathan had reached out to grab hold of her again and missed. But he had leaned over too far and now he had slipped and fallen all the way down the staircase, banging his head against the iron railings and slithering to a stop, upside down at her feet.

'Thanks for dinner, Jonathan,' she said and taking a carnation out of the display at the front desk she dropped it onto his inert form. 'Bye everyone.' She waved at the diners – by now they had left their tables and were hanging over the railings upstairs – and swept out into Knightsbridge to hail a taxi.

Barney was being strangely reticent about the person they were driving out to Heathrow to meet. Matthias turned left at the Post House and joined the lanes of traffic moving slowly towards the tunnel that would take them to Terminal 2. Someone arriving from the Continent. But who?

'If you just give me a name I can stand at arrivals with it displayed on a placard. Then you can wait in the car, sir.' Matthias realized he didn't even know whether they were meeting a man or a woman.

'Oh, not to worry. I rather enjoy hanging around watching the people come through. It's not as if you have to wheel me around everywhere any more.'

'Very good, sir. I'll come with you and when he . . . she . . . they come through I'll run and get the car.'

'Good lad.'

Matthias studied the arrivals. There were planes due in from Paris, Madrid, Amsterdam, Frankfurt, Nice, and Lisbon. The first four had actually landed. The passengers would be coming through at any moment.

Barney seemed nervous. Matthias noticed he tensed every time a woman came round the corner. So it was a woman they were meeting. He noticed that Barney looked closely at every fair-haired woman for several seconds. They were waiting for a blonde. And someone he clearly had not seen for some time since he wasn't banking on recognizing her on sight.

Matthias watched idly as passengers went past with Frankfurt labels on their baggage. Maybe there'd be someone he knew.

He felt Barney stiffen beside him. The woman who had just come round the corner was unexceptional. She had a headscarf tied round her head so it was hard to determine whether she was blonde or brunette. She was just an ordinary middle-aged woman with a slow, rather lazy gait. And she was coming straight towards him, Matthias. As she reached the barrier she dropped her bags and her hand went out to touch his face.

'*Kennst du deine Mutter nicht mehr,* '*Thias?*' Then she turned to Barney. '*Barneychen,* it's me, Christiane. I'm not sure I'd have recognized you either if you hadn't been with my son. Our son.'

'Mutti!' said Matthias, bending low over her hand.

'*Na ja,* and this is your Vati.' She pointed to Barney.

But Matthias had the last word.

'I know,' he said as Christiane and Barney stared at each other in amazement. 'I've known all along. Now I'll go and get the car to take you home.'

Barney grasped Christiane's hand and held it to prevent her from going after him. They had both seen the tears in Matthias' eyes but they knew there would be nothing to worry about. The tears they had seen had been tears of joy.

424

Thirty-Four

Saskia would have preferred the reunion with Christiane to be on her territory but she couldn't resist the invitation to go to Selwyn House and encounter the possibility of seeing Barney.

The telephone call from Christiane had come out of the blue. Brief. Abrupt. Just a few short sentences of invitation.

'Saskia? It's Christiane. No, don't say anything, just take down the details of where I am. You will come and see me, won't you? Selwyn House. Holland Park. It's just opposite Ladbroke Grove. Tomorrow afternoon? Five o'clock? *Ja. Bis bald.*' Saskia hadn't even had time to ask Christiane how she knew where to find her.

Saskia parked her Mini in Ladbroke Grove and crossed Holland Park, screwing up her eyes to try to see the numbers by the doors of the big houses. Then she saw the brass plate beside the gates: Selwyn House. She had three lots of steps to climb before she reached the front door. She studied the two discreet bells nestling in the ivy illuminated by a tiny pool of electric light. The name plates read Lambert and Fakenham. Christiane was presumably staying with Barney. Would he open the door? Was she ready for this?

But the door was opened by a young man with dark blond hair and a shy, almost haunted face. He was dressed in a chauffeur's uniform with the top button of his jacket undone.

'Yes? Can I help you?'

'I've come to see Christiane Kessler.'

'Who? Oh, you mean . . . Was that her name before she married? Kessler? I never knew.'

'She's married?'

'She was. She was Frau Mahrenhertz. Frau von Mahrenhertz, in fact. Anyway, come in.' He directed her to a door to the left of the hall, which was littered with overflowing carrier bags and suitcases as if people were on the point of moving out, and called upstairs: 'Mutti!'

Mutti!

'You're Christiane's son?'

'Yes. I'm Matthias. You're German too by the sound of it.'

'I'm . . . you're . . . you're my nephew. I'm Saskia Kessler. Christiane's sister. Your aunt. You're Matthias Mahrenhertz? Sorry, Matthias von Mahrenhertz?'

The boy couldn't say anything for a second or two.

'I didn't even know Mutti had a sister. I know very little about her past. This is terrible. And, no, I'm not really Matthias Mahrenhertz. I was . . . until my father died, that is. At least the man I thought was my father. Oh, you won't understand a word I'm saying unless Mutti's told you everything.' He looked enquiringly at Saskia who shook her head. He went on. 'I'm called Matthew Lambert now.'

'Lambert?'

'Yes. This is my real father's house. Hey, are you all right?' Saskia had sat down suddenly on the nearest chair in the hall. This was Barney's son. Christiane's son . . . and Barney's!

'I'll call my mother. *Mutti!*'

He helped Saskia to her feet and led her into a large reception room. Saskia wanted to leave. She should never have come. What was she doing, hankering after Barney when there was evidence right before her eyes that he'd had what sounded like a serious affair with her sister.

There was a sudden commotion in the hall and a girl came running into the room. Saskia recognized her instantly: Barney's daughter.

426

'Saskia! Sorry, I don't know your other name. Anyway, I have to call you Saskia. You're Saskia's shop, aren't you? Christiane told me you were coming here. I couldn't believe it. I'm your number one fan. I'd buy my entire wardrobe at your shop if I could afford it. Daddy said he was going to buy me something of yours but he never got around to it. Oh, I'm Lulu. Lulu Lambert.'

Saskia smiled at her. She was such an enchanting creature, all legs and eyes and a mane of Barney's blonde hair.

'You've met my brother. Have you heard the story – it's really amazing! All these years and I thought I was an only child and then I find out I have a brother. Well, half-brother or is it stepbrother? Matthew, which are you? Matthew, where've you gone?'

'He's gone to find his mother. I've come to see her.'

'Christiane? Have you? Daddy's a dark horse suddenly telling us about her after all these years. Do you know my father? Or was it Granny you knew? You were at her funeral, weren't you?'

But Saskia didn't have to answer for at that moment Christiane could be heard coming down the stairs.

'I really loved meeting you,' said Lulu holding out her hand and sounding as if she meant it. 'Bye now.'

She's Barney all over again, thought Saskia. *What undiluted charm*! One minute in Lulu's company and she already adored her. But the feeling of relaxed warmth only lasted a second.

The woman who came into the room was a complete stranger. If Saskia had not been told she was her sister, she would never have recognized Christiane. This woman seemed older than Saskia. Unlike Saskia's, which was cut in its usual Vidal Sassoon geometrical bob and still jet black, Christiane's hair had been permed, waved and lacquered into a matronly set and no attempt had been made to hide the greying at the temples. There were fine lines at the corners of her eyes and running down from her nostrils to her mouth. She wore a Pringle shetland cardigan which looked as if it had been newly acquired from the Scotch House and a pleated skirt which emphasized the considerable breadth of her hips and buttocks. On her feet were low-heeled court shoes. A Teutonic hausfrau in an English matron's uniform.

Before Saskia knew what was happening Christiane was embracing her. Saskia tensed. She couldn't help it. '*Na, was ist's?*' she heard Christiane murmuring. 'It's all right, Saskia. It's me. It really is. *Komm, setz dich,*' She led Saskia over to a delicate little sofa on spindly legs and gently pressed her to sit down. To Saskia's amazement, Christiane was crying quietly.

'Forgive me,' Christiane clasped her hand, 'I had no idea it would affect me this way. If you want to know the truth I really haven't thought of you very much. When Barney told me you were here in London I actually thought twice about coming over. In fact, I didn't come to see you, I came to identify my son. You met him. He let you in. Isn't he beautiful, my Matthias?'

'Matthias.' Saskia said the name in German.

'*Ja. Mein Junge.* And Barney's. You know about that, don't you? How I met him in Berlin? It was all because you told him about Mutti and Vati. He went to the apartment and they told me someone was looking for our parents so I went to see who it was. Did he . . . did he tell you about me? What I was doing in Berlin . . .?'

'Christiane, I have not spoken one word to Barney. Until this week I had no idea he'd even met you.'

'You sound bitter, Saskia. What's the matter? Are you going to tell me your story? Are you going to tell me what happened to you since we saw you off on the train at the Hauptbahnhof? Oh, I know about the war. Barney told me . . .'

'Well if Barney told you everything, why are you asking me?'

'He didn't tell me everything, I'm sure he didn't. I realize you two were very close. It stands to reason. Two war orphans growing up together. He must have been like a brother to you . . .'

'Yes,' said Saskia slowly, 'like a brother. That's exactly like it was. You, on the other hand . . .'

'But what happened after you left that place? I hear you went to America.'

Saskia stood up abruptly.

'I can't do this. It's crazy! I can't recap twenty-odd years in five minutes for you. I barely recognize you. I accept that you're my sister because you say you are but you can't have any idea of what I've been through. Yes, I went to America but the story of how I got there would take hours to tell you. I had to leave, Christiane. I was the one our parents sent away to a strange place, a foreign country that turned out to be the enemy, while you stayed in Berlin all nice and cosy with Tante Luise . . . I was the one who had to survive on her own . . .'

I was the one who had to survive on her own! Christiane seethed inside. Typical Saskia! Sent away to safety while she, Christiane, had been forced to become the *Sonnenblume* in the ruins of Berlin. The trouble with Saskia was that she had never grown up. Here she was, dressed like a school kid in a skirt halfway up her thighs and little black patent shoes. All right, so she was successful. Lulu had gone on about the damned shop until Christiane thought she would scream.

It was ridiculous to sit here and contemplate Saskia's appearance, but in a way her sister had a point: they couldn't simply plunge in and tell each other their life stories. The simple truth remained – they had never been close as young girls and they were unlikely to be on this first meeting.

Christiane tried to bury her resentment at what she imagined to be Saskia's good fortune – a safe comfortable life here in England then in America – but she couldn't. While she knew she had always been their parents' favourite because of her blonde good looks, Saskia had always managed to be the one who landed on her feet, the successful one the teachers had praised, the one other children had admired. It seemed as if that was still the case: a success in business, a growing reputation in London.

Still, she was family and that was really what they ought to talk about, what had brought them together.

'Did you ever hear about Mutti or Vati when you came to England?'

Saskia shook her head. 'You were with them. You must have known what happened . . .' She was almost accusing Christiane of having withheld information.

'They were arrested. Vati wouldn't wear his Jewish Star of David and they came and arrested him and Mutti. I escaped and went to live with Tante Luise until she was killed in an air raid.' Christiane didn't know why she omitted to tell Saskia about Tante Luise's suicide. She realized this part of her life in Berlin was intensely private and she didn't want to talk about it to anyone, even her sister. 'Then I was on my own,' she concluded. Short, sharp, direct, no emotion. Let Saskia try and pull anything else out of her if she wanted.

'Poor Tante Luise. So what happened . . . to our parents? I mean, I can imagine but I've never known for sure.'

'Nor did I until recently. As you know, Saskia, we had very little family in Berlin. You remember Onkel Otto?' Saskia nodded. 'Well, he turned out to be traitor, he was turning Jews over to the Gestapo.'

'I never liked him,' said Saskia flatly.

'Do you remember him, do you remember our parents?'

'Of course I do. I was older than you, don't forget. Most of all I remember Onkel Wolfie. He was the only one who seemed to understand me. Mutti loved me but she was a passive woman. She could never stand up to Vati. I know she was against my being sent away but if she had really had strength she would have fought Vati to keep me with you all. I still cannot tolerate those women who never say no to their husbands and there are plenty of them even now . . . and, of course, Vati always preferred you anyway. So, you say you found out what happened to them . . . It's awful how detached I can feel. I buried my parents in my mind so long ago, the only person I really mourn is little Klara . . .'

430

'Who?'

'Never mind.'

'I have someone who died too.' said Christiane, thinking of Nina. 'I know how you feel . . . But our parents: I asked around after the war, I had researchers writing to all the Kesslers in Berlin and believe me there are many. I made a search of the entire country and came up with nothing. None of the Kesslers still living are immediately related to us. Then someone suggested I get them to broadcast on the radio in Israel where many of the Holocaust survivors are now living. It worked but not in the way I had planned.'

'Why, what did you find out? Were they in Israel?'

'No, but when the broadcast went out, that a couple by the name of Hermann and Klara Kessler were being sought by their daughters, Saskia and Christiane – I included you even though I hadn't a clue where you were – someone heard it and remembered that their mother who had been in Auschwitz had talked about a Klara Kessler.'

'Mutti was in Auschwitz?'

'And Vati. This woman contacted me from Israel, wrote to me in Frankfurt – that's where I live now – and gave me the address and telephone number of her mother in New York. New York! This was an old lady, an *Oma*, who had been in the camps with our mother and who was now living in New York.'

'What did you do?'

'I telephoned her. She couldn't even speak any English. She had gone with her daughter to New York but the daughter had come back to live in Israel. She was so delighted to hear a German voice I couldn't get her off the phone. She described Mutti accurately, told me how Mutti had talked about us both. Apparently when they sent you away she knew she would never see you again.'

'What happened to her?'

'She went to the gas chambers.' Christiane did not add, 'to be poisoned by gas supplied by the man I married.' She had suffered enough guilt and it was this remorse that had driven her to search relentlessly for the truth about her parents.

'And Vati?'

'He was in the men's camp. The woman in New York says that Mutti knew he was dead before she herself went to the gas chamber so that's all we have to go on.'

'If only I'd known, I could have gone to see this woman when I was living in New York.'

'You still could. We could go together.'

'Christiane, I don't have a passport . . .' And then, haltingly, omitting as much of her story as Christiane had left out of hers, Saskia told her sister how she had gone to New York and what she had experienced there.

Christiane moved to stand by her sister in front of the floor-to-ceiling sash window.

'Even though I confess I haven't thought of you much I have always wondered why you never came back to Berlin. Now I know. Of course, it's all changed now, Saskia. There's the Wall dividing the city, it's terrible! I am never going back there until that wall comes down. But that's not the point. You must be allowed to travel. Have you applied for a passport here? You're on your way to becoming a national celebrity. Think of all you're doing for the trade and industry in this country. They'd have to give you a passport. Either that or you'll have to marry an Englishman or doesn't a career girl like you want to get married? Shame you've never had any children . . .'

Shame you've never had any children . . . She couldn't be expected to know about little Klara but it was ludicrous of her to take it for granted that Saskia had never had children.

Trust Christiane to make a hurtful assumption like that. When they were children, Saskia recalled, Christiane had always made assumptions.

But maybe Christiane was right. She could probably apply for a passport now after all this time. She knew why she hadn't: there was still that fear lurking inside her, fear that she would be exposed as an alien, as someone who didn't belong. At heart she was still a refugee and she always would be. She could afford to live somewhere much grander than the little flat above the shop but it had become her refuge, her little home away from home. Christiane still lived in Germany; she was still a hundred per cent German – a typical hausfrau by the looks of things. She looked down at her sister's hand and saw a wedding ring.

'You're married, Christiane?'

'He's dead.'

'I'm sorry.'

'Don't be. And you? Were you married at any time?'

'In a way.'

'Sounds very suspect.'

Saskia shrugged. 'Make of it what you will.'

She turned back to look out of the window. Was Barney in the house somewhere, within shouting distance maybe? Would he come up the steps to the house at any moment?

'You don't seem very concerned about what happened to our parents.' Christiane was saying.

Saskia didn't answer. She knew she had absorbed the information and buried it deep inside her, that it would surface at a later date and she would grieve. How she would grieve! But at the moment she felt detached. She wondered, did other refugees feel as she did, that the Holocaust had happened to other families, not to hers. She shuddered. She sounded like Jonathan in her thoughts. Had she become Anglo-Jewish, cocooned away from the harsh treatment of race? No, she could still recall the outrage she had felt at Hitler's propaganda before she had left Berlin. She still felt German. She would never be English but she would always be Jewish. It was just that at a critical moment in her life she had found another family here in England: Selwyn, Lady Sarah and Barney.

Where was Barney? Did he really live in this austere grandeur? Was all this elegant French furniture his? Had he installed the Turkish carpet on the floor? Could she ever fit in with him in a place like this? Why was she even daring to think along these lines?

Christiane's voice interrupted her thoughts as if she had been reading Saskia's mind.

'Shame he's going to lose all this.'

'Who is?'

'Barney. Of course, this is his father-in-law's part of the house. Barney lives upstairs, but not for much longer. Now he can walk again.'

'He can walk?'

'Oh yes, didn't you know? Bit of a miracle, so they say, seemed to just happen overnight but Matthias told me he'd been helping him with exercises for months . . . Anyway, it turns out the father-in-law, Sir Anthony, had been wanting to sell the house ever since his wife died but he couldn't bring himself to uproot Barney while he was still in a wheelchair. Now, of course, everything's changed so the house is being sold and Barney's going to have to move. The lovely thing is that Matthias and Lulu are ecstatic at having found each other and they're going to share a flat. It's so sweet, brother and sister finding each other after all these years.'

'If only we felt the same way . . .' said Saskia drily.

'We don't, we never did and we never shall. It would be pointless to force it. I take it you know how Matthias and Lulu are brother and sister?'

'I was waiting for you to tell me.'

'He came snooping around the Zehlendorf apartment after the war – presumably you told him where to go. Renate – you remember Renate who lived near us? She told me and I arranged to meet him. We took it from there. He did not know I was your sister, not to begin with anyway. I became pregnant by him but I was engaged to Werner by then. Werner and I decided to keep the baby. End of story. Lulu and Matthias are now trying to force things between Barney and me – want us to get married, be their parents. We *are* their parents, we don't have to get married after all these years. I've never heard of anything so stupid in all my life.'

'How does Barney feel? Does he want to marry you?'

'Heavens no. It was just a postwar fling, for God's sake. No, my true love was someone quite different, quite different altogether. Anyway, nothing on earth would induce me to go and live in the wilds of the English countryside. Now I know Matthias is safe and sound – he ran away from home to find his father – I can't wait to get back to my little house outside Frankfurt. You must come and visit me sometime, Saskia, once you've got your passport. You'll find I've become a real surburban hausfrau.'

You don't have to tell me, thought Saskia. As for going to visit her, Saskia was beginning to wonder if she could stand another minute in the same room as her sister. She had only come to see Barney and Barney clearly wasn't going to make an appearance. It was possible he had not even been told she was coming to his house but she couldn't leave without an attempt at seeing him.

'Is Barney here? I'd like to say hello, you know, see how he's changed.'

'Barney? Oh Lord, no. I told you, this place is being sold. He left last week. He's gone back to live in that mill, the place that Selwyn man left him, what's it called? Laurel Bank.'

Thirty-Five

From the minute he began to drive down into the river valley, past the weir and the large mill pool and saw the elegant Georgian building with its bell tower and the tall square chimney to one side rising clear into the sky, Barney knew he had done the right thing in coming back to Laurel Bank.

Coming home, he thought of it, coming back to the one place he had been really happy.

As the Brough Superior followed the curve of the river, rhododendron bushes arching on either side of him, Barney recalled his first journey here with Selwyn. How apprehensive he had been despite the knowledge that he was about to be reunited with Stella. He remembered Selwyn's description: *It's known as the Bell House because of the bell tower on the roof . . . my great-great-grandfather rang that bell to summon everyone in the village to work . . .*

Barney emerged from the rhododendron tunnel and let Selwyn's old car glide gracefully to a halt beside the laurels in front of the house. He sat in the car for a while recalling what had happened next. It had been the first time he had heard her voice: female, guttural, breathlessly young but, as he listened to it now in his mind, unmistakably Saskia's: *Selwyn! Where have you been? All day I have been waiting. The news! Have you heard the news? WE ARE AT WAR!*

The first week was hard to get through. The memory of her was all around him despite the close proximity of the neighbours in the flats at Klara Court. Barney didn't waste time bemoaning the fact that one of the flats had once been Selwyn's studio – and could now have been his. Instead he set about renovating Selwyn's old sitting room on the first floor of the Bell House. What use did Barney have for a sitting room now? Selwyn's bedroom was spacious enough to accommodate a sofa and a writing table. The sitting room with its northern light was easily converted into the perfect studio.

Barney went for long walks in the crisp February air, tramping over the hard frozen soil, his hands plunged into his pockets. He marvelled at the fact that there had been days in his recent past when he had thought he would never be able to go for walks like this.

It was when he returned to soak in a long hot bath that the memories of the secret bath he and Saskia had taken in Selwyn's giant tub with the claw feet came flooding back.

'Dearest *Barneychen*', she had whispered and he had fallen in love with her.

It was worse when he climbed into Selwyn's old bed and recalled their meeting on Saskia's return from America. What would have happened if Serena had not rung up when she did? Would he and Saskia have stayed together? He tormented himself day and night with the same questions going over and over in his mind.

Had he done the right thing coming back to Laurel Bank? It had never occurred to him that he might feel lonely. He missed Lulu but Lulu was young and wild and made to live in a city for quite a while yet. She would hate being forced to live in such a wilderness. It would be nice to get Matthew up to Laurel Bank, though. Barney had a feeling his son would enjoy the place. But Matthew had his work cut out for him for the time being taking care of Lulu. How wonderful it was that they had taken to each other so well.

Still he did have Sonny and Cher to keep him company. Sonny and Cher were Bella's pups, Schnutzi and Putzi's grandpups and the great-grandpuppies of Stella. They belonged here at Laurel Bank. Barney would have liked to have brought Bella with him but Lulu wouldn't let her go.

'But you can't keep a dog in a flat in London, not a black Labrador anyway. They need exercise,' Barney had argued.

'We know that, Dad,' Lulu had explained patiently, 'but Matthew swears he'll take her to the park every morning in the car and we've always got Grandad's garden to let her loose in.'

This, at least, was true, although Barney wondered if Sir Anthony had been informed that a dog would be let loose in his garden every so often. Sir Anthony had moved to a much smaller house in Chelsea, just around the corner from Barney's old studio in Edith Grove, which had now been converted into a flat for two to be shared by Matthias and Lulu.

That night, nursing a whisky and soda as Selwyn had always done, Barney made his way downstairs after his bath and along the dark passage to the kitchen.

There was a whimpering sound in the corner.

There, nestling against each other in their dog basket, were Sonny and Cher just like Schnutzi and Putzi before them. Barney reached down to pat them on the head.

'What do you think, eh, you two? Do you think she'll want to come and live up here with me? Leave her shop and her fame and fortune? Leave that Rivers bloke? Bit of a long shot, isn't it What d'you say?'

Sonny, always the more lively of the two, wagged his tail in reply.

'There's only way I'm going to find out,' Barney told them, reaching across the table for a knife. 'I'm going to have to ask the knife a question.' He sat the dogs, on either side of the table. 'Stay!' he commanded. 'Stay Sonny! Stay Cher! Now the question is: Will Saskia come back to me here at Laurel Bank? Sonny, you're Yes. Cher, you're No. Now, stay!'

Barney spun the knife and closed his eyes. He opened them to the sound of a little yelp as one of the puppies flopped off the table.

Cher had curled herself into a ball to sleep.

The knife was pointing at the empty space where Sonny had been.

438

. . . And so here I am, no longer Hunted, no longer Dispossessed, and I hope I can say the same for poor Christiane. In a way she has fared better than I have, for at least she has a child, but I know that I must make one final effort to curb my old resentment towards her. In any case, Barney and I have begun to talk about adoption. It may sound ludicrous at our age but we are told there are places in America . . .

We were married six months ago in the little church where Selwyn is buried and where he used to take us to morning service all those years ago. Dear Selwyn! When the congregation say together what they call the Lord's Prayer, I'm afraid I never think of God. I always think of Selwyn and hope he is up there in heaven looking down and seeing how happy Barney and I are. After all, it was he who brought us together in the first place.

Two years! I don't know why I waited so long to come back to Barney. Designing clothes is the only thing I am really interested in, and I can do that just as well from Laurel Bank. The shop in London more or less runs itself so long as I provide it with new designs to sell and I am more than confident in Natalie's ability to take care of everything, especially since she has taken on Lulu to help her.

We have been lucky. Barney's paintings – a new departure, he has begun to paint the locals in the village – have suddenly become fashionable following an exhibition mounted just before our wedding. So down in London there is a demand and together we can live up here at Laurel Bank and supply. No one bothers us. It's almost as if we are back in the war years again, waiting for Selwyn to come home or for Lady Sarah to visit, but they are both gone and all we have here are each other.

As I watch him coming up the drive, past the weir, disappearing for a moment into the rhododendron tunnel and emerging beside the laurels, I look down from my window and recall the time when Selwyn first brought him here. I know that despite all I have been through I am far luckier than most people, for he is all I need and I have him – now, and I pray, forever.